A magic unl

Relkin chewed the inside of his lip and hugged himself against his fears. He wasn't who he'd been. Something in his core had shifted on that great and terrible day in Mirchaz. To be the vessel for so much power could unhinge a man's mind, Relkin had no doubt of it. He had stood before the great gates of the city of the Elven Lords. He had raised his hand and fire had blasted the gates asunder, bringing down the dynasty of the Lords Tetraan.

How was he supposed to be the same after that?

He shivered, but not because he was cold. . . . For solace he turned his thoughts to war. Because the dragon was right, there was bound to be fighting in their future once again. . . .

DRAGON ULTIMATE

**Don't miss the other exciting books in Christopher Rowley's
Bazil Broketail series!**

DRAGON ULTIMATE

Christopher Rowley

A ROC BOOK

ROC
Published by the Penguin Group
Penguin Putnam Inc., 375 Hudson Street,
New York, New York 10014, U.S.A.
Penguin Books Ltd, 27 Wrights Lane,
London W8 5TZ, England
Penguin Books Australia Ltd,
Ringwood, Victoria, Australia
Penguin Books Canada Ltd, 10 Alcorn Avenue,
Toronto, Ontario, Canada M4V 3B2
Penguin Books (N.Z.) Ltd, 182–190 Wairau Road,
Auckland 10, New Zealand

Penguin Books Ltd, Registered Offices:
Harmondsworth, Middlesex, England

First published by Roc, an imprint of Dutton NAL, a member of Penguin Putnam Inc.

First Printing, February, 1999
10 9 8 7 6 5 4 3 2 1

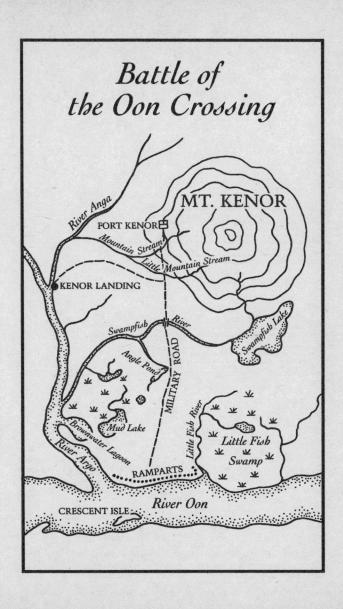

Battle of
the Oon Crossing

MT. KENOR

River Anga

FORT KENOR

Mountain Stream

Little Mountain Stream

KENOR LANDING

Swampfish Lake

Swampfish River

Angle Pond

MILITARY ROAD

Mud Lake

Brownwater Lagoon

Little Fish River

Little Fish Swamp

River Argo

RAMPARTS

CRESCENT ISLE

River Oon

Prologue

On the great slope carved by Eras stood the pyramids of the Sinni. Bathed in the perpetual brilliance of the giant blue sun, they resembled a small city, clustered in concentric rings.

Within the protection of these pyramidal 'structs, the Sinni dwelled in crystal bubbles.

From here they fought the war against chaos and darkness, right across the Sphereboard of Destiny. Thus they had dwelled for aeons. But now an ancient menace had turned its attention to them.

"And I say unto you my brothers and sisters. He was defeated, but not destroyed."

"I hear you, great Yeer," said Vuga, known for his mildness of temperament. "But what can be done? He retired to Haddish, and there he broods."

"We must prepare, for he now knows where we are. For aeons we have kept him from that knowledge, but he has now acquired it."

An anxious silence fell. Then debate welled up, colored by newfound fear.

"If he has learned our location, then it is only a matter of time." So spoke grave Auriga. "He will find a way to attack us."

"How can he approach us? It is not as if he can simply come here. He wouldn't survive a moment on the surface."

"My dear Voolan, you have not thought it through. He will come in some protected form. He is a master of transformations. He will find a way."

"*Then we must destroy him. We must seek him out and put an end to his existence, as should have been done long, long ago.*"

"*But we have never had the strength to do that.*"

"*I fear that he cannot be destroyed. He is beyond the power of the mortals.*"

"*We must make some provision,*" said Yeer. "*For he will come.*"

Chapter One

The bells of the Temple in Marneri rang out with wild exhilaration. Drums thundered in Tower Street and crowds stretched all the way down to the harbor, where the great white ships *Barley* and *Oat* rode at anchor, flying flags at every mast. Their ships' horns blared out a response to the bells of the land, adding to the riotous joy.

The siege of Axoxo was over. The enemy fortress, that matchless barrier of serried walls, mighty towers, and frowning battlements, had fallen. By a brilliant stroke of arms, the most difficult military engagement ever undertaken by the armies of the Empire of the Rose had come to a sudden and complete success.

As a result, the strategic balance of power with the old enemy in Padmasa had shifted toward the Empire of the Rose. Victory in the long war, which had continued for hundreds of years, was now conceivable. Armies of the Argonath cities now held both ends of the Padmasan defense system: Tummuz Orgmeen in the northern Gan had fallen a few years before. Now Axoxo of the White Bones Mountains had succumbed as well.

All over the Argonath bells were ringing as the troops came marching home. The crowds along Tower Street had come from all across Marneri, and even from the other city-states. Together they cheered the men of the Marneri First Legion, the Bea Legion and the Pennar Legion, who had fought alongside the Marneri First in the final assault on the fortress.

There was a manic edge to the joy in the streets. Just a few months before the city had been facing the possibility of a siege at the hands of rebels from the province of Aubinas. Now not only was that threat removed, but the long, draining siege of Axoxo had ended.

Marneri and the other cities had suffered heavy casualties in recent campaigns, particularly the mission to distant Eigo. That cost in lives had a disastrous effect on morale, and the fear of further casualties had inhibited the Argonath army at Axoxo. Now, that mighty fortress was taken, and with the loss of only 130 men and no dragons.

The stunning victory was achieved through a daring surprise assault, performed by meticulously trained troops in the hour before dawn. They had breached the walls and caught the troll guard asleep in quarters.

Trolls that were lying down, groggy with sleep, proved quite killable by men working with spears and axes. They cut the monsters' throats and bashed in their skulls before they could get themselves onto their ponderous feet and seize their weapons.

The slaughter of imps, trolls, and mercenary men had continued fitfully through the day as pockets of resistance were taken, sometimes in fierce fighting. But by then the Argonathi soldiers were assisted by the dragons of the 66th, 59th and 120th Dragon Squadrons, and this kept the casualties down to a minimum.

The city of Marneri was decked out in bunting and flags for the occasion, and the taverns were dispensing free wheat beer, and feasts were being held on every street and every corner.

Folk had flocked in from all the surrounding provinces. Men of Seant, Lucule, and Blue Hills, were there in great numbers. But they also came from places much farther away, like the village of Quosh in Blue Stone, which was a good five days' ride to the south.

There were even folk from Aubinas, the great wheat-growing province in the west. The rebellion there had subsided to a sputtering guerrilla conflict, consisting for the most part of raids by night riders. The towns were pacified, and the chief rebels were either in custody or had fled. The common folk of Aubinas had not been altogether behind the rebellion, except when inflamed by the burning of Redhill a much-misunderstood event during the early fighting. Now the common folk of Aubinas were there in the city to celebrate alongside their fellow citizens.

For once, the 109th Marneri Dragons were not in the ranks of the marching victors. Following their special service in the Aubinan fighting of the previous summer, they had been put on reserve duty. Since then the 109th, the most famous dragon squadron in the Legions, had been cooling its heels up at Dashwood Camp.

During that time there had come a move to disband the unit and disperse its members to other, newer dragon squadrons. Voices high in the army command claimed that the unit was too famous, too well known, and too prone to insubordination. All sorts of rumors abounded about what had happened at the battle of Avery Woods as well as in Aubinas.

The fighting 109th broken up? Never! Roared their supporters. A fierce bureaucratic struggle was joined.

Meanwhile the winter passed, then the spring and the summer. Again and again they received word that they were about to be sent to Axoxo. Again and again the final order never came. Officers relaxed, dragonboys wearily gave back all the extra freecoats and other equipment they'd accumulated for the arctic conditions to be expected in the White Bones Mountains, and dragons cheerfully took up their axes and marched out to the woodlots to cut and haul firewood.

And then there'd come the sudden, groundshaking news that the fortress had fallen to a brilliant surprise stroke. So the 109th Marneri Dragons were standing among the crowds welcoming home the conquering heroes, a change for them, they had noted with some amusement.

"This dragon happy not to have had to march all the way to Axoxo in the first place," said Alsebra, expressing a view held by all.

For the parade they were positioned very well, just where Tower Street opened out onto the wide parade ground in front of the tower. They sang dragon songs and even a round or two of

the Kenor song to welcome the men back, but they really lit up
when the dragon squadrons came marching up the street. The
dragons roared welcomes back and forth.

There was Burthong, the champion Brasshide dragon, who'd
stood beside them at the battle of Sprian's Ridge, and Champa,
the old leatherback veteran from the Teetol Wars.

After the marching and the speeches were over, festivities got
under way in the dragonhouse. Beer and hot vittles were served
up in great quantities, and dragonboys from all the units present
were mixed together in the refectory. It wasn't long before the
question was asked.

"Where's Relkin?"

"Don't ask," came the response from Swane of Seant.

"Poor Relkin," said little Jak.

"What happened?"

"Witches got him. They took him away."

"Where?"

"The Islands. Months back."

"He wrote us a letter once."

"They cut bits out of it before they let us see it."

"He'll never get back."

"Who's looking after his dragon?"

"Curf."

"Curf!"

"Don't ask."

Indeed, dragonboy eyes could instantly see the difference in
the Broketail dragon. His hide hadn't been brushed very well in
a long time. His joboquin was full of loose places. The dragonboys sighed at the waste. The legendary Broketail dragon, which
any one of them would have given an arm to tend for, was in the
care of Curf!

The carousing went on late into the night. The dancing on
the temple forecourt was still going strong as the bells rang for
midnight.

In all the commotion no one noticed the hunched figure stumbling along Dock Street. No one noticed it drop a squirming

sack on the ground behind the run-down warehouses by Bleek Street.

A knife flashed and the sack was cut open to disgorge a dozen or more black rats which streaked away to cover as soon as they were out of the bag.

Chapter Two

Across the Bright Sea from the Argonath lay the Isles of Cunf-shon, the spiritual home of the reborn civilization of the Nine Argonath cities. There, on a bluff overlooking the great harbor of the city of Cunfshon stood the official city of Andiquant, nerve center of the Empire of the Rose.

Within the walls of Andiquant stretched rows of brick build-ings, housing the offices of the bureaucracy that ran the empire. In one of those anonymous buildings lay the Office of Insight, an organization that dealt with diplomatic matters, trade issues, and military strategy.

Buried within the Office of Insight was a hidden suite of of-fices for the shadowy Office of Unusual Insight, the witch-run secret service of the empire.

In a plain little room at the end of a bland corridor of equally plain little rooms, four witches met around a square, wooden table.

On the left side sat a woman of plain and unexpressive fea-tures clad in an old, well-worn, gray smock under a homespun robe. On the right sat a regal figure in black velvet, her face a mask of ancient full-lipped beauty, her eyes alight with a deadly, penetrating intelligence.

Between these two polar opposites—the Gray Lady, Lessis of Valmes, and the Queen of Mice, Ribela of Defwode—sat the minor witches Bell and Selera.

Clad in the robes of their order, the younger witches kept a humble profile while in the presence of these two greatwitches.

It could be very intimidating to be caught in the gaze of those five-hundred-year-old minds. But neither Bell's broad brown face, nor Selera's pale, narrow features betrayed their unease.

"You have worked hard, sisters," said Lessis.

Bell felt her spirits lift. At least that much had been recognized.

"Indeed, as an inquisition it was very thorough," Lessis murmured.

Bell watched for the signs of a spell. Lessis was famous for throwing the most subtle spells in ordinary conversation. She needn't have concerned herself. No spells could be cast under the eyes of the other greatwitch present.

Lessis sighed. "Still, we've learned very little."

This was the embarrassing truth.

"Relkin has no understanding of the processes involved in the magic," said Selera.

"He is an elemental, of a new type," said Bell, boldly.

Both the greatwitches turned their heads at the same moment at these words.

"An elemental? One should not make such claims lightly," said Ribela.

"I know, Lady, but consider the powers involved and the complete lack of the technique required for sorcery on such a scale. Relkin knows not what he does, but still he does it."

Lessis caught Bell's eye.

"The mark of the Sinni, you have seen it?"

Bell hesitated, looked up into Lessis's eyes, and found them peculiarly piercing. The witch peers into my very soul. . . . she thought. But of course Lessis wanted to know if the young witches were sensitive to the mark of the Sinni . . .

"Yes, Lady, I think I have. He is just a child of his time and place on the surface."

"He has virtually no education, Lady," cut in Selera. Lessis ignored her.

"But underneath," continued Bell, "there I sense a difference. He is not just a youth. There are unreadable things there . . ."

"Yes, so we have belatedly come to understand."

Ribela drew back into herself with a slight hiss of dismay.

"They have sent one of themselves. It is an incredible thought."

"But Relkin is a mortal man, doomed to die."

"So an elemental will be lost, voluntarily accepting death." Selera spoke in awe.

"It is an extraordinary thing," said Lessis. "To so love the world that one would accept the pain of life."

Bell's eyes lit up, and she clapped her hands together with sudden excitement.

"It is bound up with the dragon, it must be. But dragons are impervious to magic, they are hard to glimpse in the patterns of the predicted future."

"Beyond this understanding, though, we know nothing." Ribela was still unhappy.

"He cannot describe the mechanics of what he has achieved. How did he project a dream across a distance of many miles and a range of hills so that it was shared by dragons and one dragonboy? He has no idea. And nor do we."

Bell thus adequately described their problem. Relkin had none of the grammar of witchcraft, the knowledge of how sorcery was done. He could not describe his elemental, spasmodic responses to danger and extreme need. And thus he could not answer their questions.

"You have questioned him before, repeatedly. What differences have you seen in him over that time?"

"Little. He is a young man, but one who has seen more than his share of the horror in the world. Then, of course, he is a dragonboy."

Selera spoke hurriedly, as if almost afraid to speak blasphemy.

"He claims to worship the Old Gods. Refuses catechism and all but refuses prayer for the Mother."

Ribela made a silent moue.

"He is particularly keen on Caymo, Lady. The Old God of Luck." Selera's close-set dark eyes sought Ribela's.

"Ah, yes, Old Caymo, the dice thrower," smiled Ribela. "A quaint and rather wonderful deity, I always thought."

"If Caymo still rolls the dice, he has rolled some difficult numbers for Relkin," said Lessis.

"There is a depth in Relkin, but he fears his destiny," said Bell. "He fears that it will strip him from the life he has imagined for himself when he completes his time in the Legions."

"He has completed it," said Lessis. "He just doesn't know it yet. Both he and Bazil are to be retired from active duty very shortly."

"But," said Bell, "he left for Marneri three days ago. He has to stand trial on charges stemming from plunder brought in from Eigo."

"Yes," sighed Lessis. "He remains a dragonboy at heart, no matter what we might suspect about his origins. He must stand trial. Those charges could not be dropped. He has admitted bringing in the gold."

"Could the trial be postponed?"

"It had already been held off for ten months. It has to go forward now."

"We shall return to Marneri ourselves then?" wondered Selera.

"Yes, I'm sorry to have to do this to you, but you have handled this case from the beginning. You know him pretty well by now, I'd say. You will have to continue, at least until the crisis is past."

"Then we shall take a berth aboard *Sorghum,* which sails on the tide."

Lessis noted that Bell had anticipated that they would be sent to Marneri.

"Yes, that would be a good idea." She rubbed her hands together. "You are both to be commended for this work. A difficult task, to be sure."

The younger witches rose with palms pressed together and made deep bows to the greatwitches, the very Queens of Birds and Mice.

When they were gone, Ribela turned back to Lessis.

"I begin to feel that we have achieved the optimum position on this swing of our long struggle. The strategic situation has improved enormously. We might press on to Padmasa itself."

Lessis had to agree. "The gates of Padmasa are open. With both Axoxo and Tummuz Orgmeen in our hands, we can breach the mountains and move onto the inner Hazog. Plus, our alliance with Czardha has borne fruit. The Czardhan alliance is gathering a fresh army to assault Padmasa from the west. And, we have succeeded in tempting the Kassimi back into the ring."

"Ah?" Ribela had not yet heard of this development on the diplomatic front. Lessis continued. "Their defeats had kept them subdued, but now the Great King has heard of the Czardhan successes, and most recently of the fall of Axoxo. He dares to raise his standard once more. Whether he will have the stomach to take an army north to Padmasa is another matter."

"But just having Kassim reenter the fight will increase the pressure on Padmasa."

"And the hidden enemy, the Dominator, what of him?" This was the purview of the Queen of Mice.

"He lies yet in Haddish. Deep within a recuperation chamber."

"And the being that I told you of, the gestalt that arose at the fall of Mirchaz?"

"Can it truly have been gestalt? That chimera they have searched for for so long?"

Lessis shrugged. "I do not claim to understand such things."

"And I do?"

"You understand them, sister. You more than anyone alive."

There was a silence.

"Well, possibly that is true. Anyway, that boy knows more than he has revealed."

"I sense no malice in Relkin. The Sinni have marked him."

"Waakzaam the Great has marked him, too. He sees more deeply in these ways than any mortal. He will have seen their mark. He will know that the Sinni are interfering here, in contravention of their oaths. The malice and hate that seethes within Waakzaam's breast will not let him forgive such wounds.

"The boy can never return to a normal life. I have sent instructions that he is to be housed by the Office and kept under close watch and guard. His dragon, likewise must be protected. The Deceiver will come after them."

"Ah," said Ribela. "Poor lad, his dreams will never come true."

Chapter Three

The tradeship *Lily* plowed her way across the long rolling waves under hurrying clouds. Three days out from the Isles, she was making good time on steady winds out of the south. A square-rigged three-master of three hundred tons, *Lily* carried a cargo of textiles and refined sugar. There were a dozen passengers as well, including a young dragoneer first class, Relkin of Quosh.

As the sun sank in the uttermost west, Relkin leaned against the windward rail and drank in the ocean air. He watched the big seas come toward them, lifting the ship's bow and then running along below the rail before disappearing behind.

He was going home. Back to the dragonhouse in Marneri and his dragon. How he missed that great beast. The dragon was all the family he'd ever known. A constant presence, with that deep, rusty voice that he knew so well. He prayed that Curf hadn't done anything too harebrained or dangerous for the wyvern's health. Of all replacement dragonboys to have it had to be Curf! Curf, the daydreaming musician.

But, he consoled himself, he'd be home soon. Back in the city of white stone overlooking the long sound, with the great Tower of Guard looming above on the hill. Back to the familiar sights and sounds and smells of the dragonhouse. He was longing for it, he had to admit. He really wanted to get his life back.

And yet . . . Another part of him wanted to move on. He was a man now, and he could see clearly to the life that could be his once he was out of the Legions.

In that life there was so much waiting for him.

First, there was Eilsa, long-legged lady of the fells. The heir to the chieftainship of her clan, yet she had held off all the other suitors who had been thrust at her. All for him. He was a very lucky man, he understood. Between them there was a love so strong that he was sure nothing would break it.

Then there was good land waiting in the Bur valley. Land and much hard work until they'd cleared enough land to begin farming. And then more work.

But they'd have that gold, no matter what happened in this trial he faced. Even if they stripped him of the gold he'd banked in Kadein, there was still a cache he'd buried out along the road. There was enough there to buy mules and horses, and to hire a dozen men to help in clearing the land.

Put that together with Bazil, who would happily wield an ax or even a shovel just for the exercise, and after a few years the farm would be a going concern.

And while the farm grew, Eilsa and he would raise a family. And Bazil, too, would fertilize eggs, probably many times, since as the famous Broketail dragon, he would be in high demand among the female dragons.

A glorious future seemed assured. They'd served the Argonath Legions for a full term, and now they would move on to the rest of their lives.

But this dream of the future faced obstacles, any of which might destroy it.

Eilsa was still at the retreat in Widarf. The last letter from her had come the week before he took ship at Cunfshon. She felt stronger. But her experiences under the hand of the Dominator had shaken her, he knew. Waakzaam had assaulted her with his sorcery and tried to break her mind and make her his creature.

He had failed, but she had taken deep hurt. For a long time she was afraid to sleep, so terrible were her dreams. The witches sent her to Widarf, a rustic temple that was renowned for its healing powers, especially for those with troubles of the mind and spirit.

There she had received the best in care. Her days were spent in prayer and working in the weave shop that helped support the sanctuary. Her letters had shown a gradual but steady recovery of her confidence, but it was still not certain that she would ever heal completely. Possibly she would have to remain in Widarf for the rest of her life.

Relkin was devastated by this. He couldn't imagine the future without her beautiful presence, without those piercing blue eyes and corn-colored hair, without that keen mind and ardent spirit. To live without her would be impossible.

Then there was this trial, this stupid trial. They, the mysterious "they" in the High Command of the Legion, wanted to strip his gold and maybe imprison him.

Relkin's anger rose. That gold had damned well been earned. Every pek of every tabi, and the coins and the necklaces, that gold was theirs for pretty damned heroic effort. They'd almost lost their lives a dozen times, but they'd been instrumental in bringing down the foul regime of the Lords Tetraan.

Who ruled in Mirchaz now, he wondered. The Court had sent a message to Mirchaz to inquire about the golden tabis, but when he'd left Mirchaz the place was still in partial chaos. Who knew what had happened there since?

Of the other gold he was more certain. It came from Og Bogon in the form of royal gifts, and King Choulaput of Og Bogon would have vouched for him and the dragon. But that did not take care of the gold tabis that he had taken from the wall of an elf lord's great house. Of course there were elf lords hanging from lampposts all over the city at that point, those that hadn't been thrown onto fires made from the contents of their palaces. The evil reign of the Lords Tetraan was over. Relkin had ended their Great Game, and felt justified in liberating the tabis, those sweet little pillows of lovely gold.

His big mistake had been adhering to the rules and regulations. After banking two-thirds of the gold, he'd reported the transactions and the importation of the gold to the proper authorities. He'd filled out forms in triplicate and answered questions and paid a hefty import tax and thought he'd done everything perfectly legally.

And then his enemies, and the Aubinan interest, had sprung an obscure Legion regulation on him relating to plunder. And so to this trial.

His friend, Lagdalen of the Tarcho, had taken the case, and her reading of the situation had been stark. If they lost the trial, he might be imprisoned. Certainly he would be censured and lose privileges. He would never be promoted to Dragon Leader. He might even be sentenced to five years hard labor on the Guano Isles. And his dreams of a future with Eilsa Ranardaughter would be dust.

It was all such a stupid mess.

And then there was that other thing, that lurking iceberg in his mind that he did his utmost to avoid. The thing he tried the hardest not to think about. That looming, enigma that had sprung forth from Mirchaz.

Awake! it had cried. Awake! As he had called to it, from the Game board of the Lords Tetraan. Awaken the power within you. Become what you must become. He knew what it spoke of. But he dared not open his mind to those dark shadows, to let the magic rise in him, growing active like yeast in a brewer's wort. He remembered the feel of it, bubbling under his skin, skittering on tiny feet up his spine, and shivered at those memories.

Unholy! Abomination! He had seen that power. He had felt it work within him and it terrified him. If he went that way what would he become? A wizard? A sorcerer? Relkin had seen more than his fair share of such creatures, and it was as if evil were baked into their flesh.

He wanted none of that. He wanted his life back, some kind of life, after all these months in Cunfshon undergoing tests and answering questions. He'd seen way too much of Bell and Selera, that was certain.

Now there would be more questions, trial testimony. And if he was convicted? Lessis had already hinted that the witches would take him back to Andiquant and continue to study him. He hated the thought of it, but if it was a choice between that and five years hard labor on the Guano Isles?

The sun was gone, and the air was suddenly chill. Relkin felt cold without a freecoat. He turned and went down the stairs to the lower deck, where he found his way along a dark passage to his tiny cabin. He curled up on the narrow bunk.

* * *

Far away in the west stood the temple of Widarf. On a bluff above the Long Sound it was a graceful collection of towers and stone buildings, with two-hundred-year-old oaks lining the gardens. Eilsa Ranardaughter walked alone on the promenade above the waves. The sea dashed against the rocks below; her hand rested on the cool stone rail.

Out there somewhere in the darkness of the night, far to the east, that was where her Relkin was. Her heart ached.

The young witches were kindly, and they spoke to her with gentle voices and spent much time at her side. But they had no answers for her worst fears.

The Dominator was not dead. He was bound to seek vengeance on Relkin. How could they live a normal life under such a threat? How could they live any life at all?

And in her heart of hearts, Eilsa knew that whatever happened at the trial the witches would take Relkin back to Cunfshon. He was simply too important. They would study him for the rest of his life. He would never escape Andiquant the second time.

And for herself? Where should she go, the heir to Ranard? Should she go back to Wattel and marry some man appointed by the clan to cement the bloodlines? Could she abide such a loveless union after her love for Relkin? She thought not. Widarf seemed the best place, at least for now.

Chapter Four

The city of Marneri basked beneath the sun on a hot summer afternoon. In the harbor the fishing boats were returning on the tide, their sharp little horns audible all the way up Tower Street. The tower by the Watergate responded with its deep blare every so often. Folk moved slowly in the heat, but most were looking forward to the end of the day's work, a time of relative quiet.

Except in the dragonhouse, of course. In that lofty hall the sound of wyverns at play in the plunge pool split the air with many tons of force. Enormous bodies splashed and roared. Blows were exchanged that would have slain almost anything else, but were regarded here as merely play. Fountains of water were hurled into the overflow when another two tons of wyvern dived in with a huge splash.

While dragons cavorted, dragonboys went over joboquins and the rest of the kit. Every day the dragons trained with weapons and armor and the leather parts of the kit always suffered the effects of being worn by two-ton gladiators. The boys of the 109th congregated in a sunny spot near the door to the exercise yard and needles flicked in the afternoon light as they made repairs. Thongs were rethreaded, straps and buckles replaced.

There were a couple of stone benches there, and the boys either sat on them or used them as tables on which to work. All the boys of the 109th were there, except Curf.

"Course Curf ain't here. Curfy's probably off playing his guitar," said Rakama in response to Jak's question.

"The Broketail's joboquin is a shocking mess," said Swane.

"Ah, give him a chance. Curf's heart's in the right place. He's trying." Jak was forced to stick up for the kid since no one else would. Curf was a dreamy youth, while the boys of the 109th were mostly hard-minded types, raised in the school of hard knocks, on their own but for their dragons since they were born.

"Trying ain't good enough. This is the 109th Marneri. We're supposed to be the best," said Ayin, who tended Hurve, the brass who had replaced Churn.

"Listen to the new boy!" groused big Swane.

Ayin was a pugnacious, anvil-shaped boy from Porthouse on the Seant coast. He had a fierce belief in the unit and a desire to prove himself. The older boys found him a bit of a driver on the subject of the 109th Marneri *fighting* dragons.

"Everyone in the Legions thinks so!" Ayin said defensively.

"Yeah sure, Ayin, but let's not hear about it so much, all right?"

"Well, Curf's been acting stranger than normal lately. And the Broketail's joboquin is a mess. It'll fall apart soon."

"Something's biting on Curfy, I can tell . . ." said Jak with a shrug.

In this last remark lay considerable truth.

At the side of the plunge pool, in the shallows, the wyverns would pull out to lie up and rest. While the others threw themselves in the deeper parts of the pool, or wrestled in the water, those in the shallows would bask.

On this sunny day Bazil Broketail was seeking advice from Alsebra.

"Something wrong with boy Curf."

"You have only just now decided this?"

Bazil knew in advance he would get a withering from Alsebra.

"He getting worse, much worse."

"That boy never been anything but lost in a dream. You, on the other hand, have a reputation to consider."

"This dragon confused, don't know what to do. Hate to complain to Cuzo. Boy may be a dolt, but he has good heart. It just that he in the wrong line of work."

"You know when Relkin come back, Curf will leave. Cuzo will never recommend him for dragonboy posting."

Bazil nodded agreement. This was common knowledge. Curf's days in the Legions were soon to be over, unless he reenlisted as infantry.

"But he in some kind of special trouble. I can tell."

Alsebra nodded. Then it had to be true. A dragon could always tell when the dragonboy was anxious and troubled.

"So what can I do about it?"

"Ask your boy. Get him to find out what has happened to Curf."

"I hate to ask boy for favors."

"This could be important. Maybe big trouble for all of us."

"You will owe me big favor after this."

"My sword always be at your side."

"Big. I hate this."

Bazil just stared.

Alsebra floated back into the pool.

That afternoon while Alsebra was being brushed down by Jak she brought up the subject of Curf and his troubles. She even brought herself to ask for Jak's help.

Jak was taken aback.

"Did I hear right?"

She hissed. "You hear this dragon. Broketail needs to know what Curf is upset about."

"Hey, it isn't often you ask this dragonboy for help. Most of the time it's just 'Hey you, fix this!' "

Alsebra hissed again. She did have a tendency to run hard on the boy. Jak was not her original boy, and though she had made the transition, there was still not quite the bond one had with one's first dragonboy. She knew that he did his best, but freemartins were inclined to be snappish, sulky, and short-tempered.

"Sorry," she said at last. By the fiery breath, but she just hated having to apologize to the dragonboy. Dragonboys could be insufferable if they thought they had the upper hand.

Jak knew better than to push it at this point.

"Well, of course I'll help. Just give me a day or two."

After that Jak kept an eye on Curf and caught him the next

time he was slipping out of the dragonhouse. It was right after the evening boil, and the late twilight of summer filled the air with promise. Jak followed him through the postern gate and down Tower Street to the lower part of town. On Fish Hill, above the docks, a few houses were scattered among warehouses. Halfway up, Curf went into an old house with a chipped facade and windows long since boarded up. Warehouses lined the other side. Jak slipped into the shadows of an alley and waited. Another figure came down the street, a tall man in a worn freecoat. He knocked at the door, which opened. As Jak had suspected, there was a guard set on that door. The tall man was ushered in. Jak waited.

At long length the door opened again and two men pushed Curf out into the street. He staggered, stumbled, and went down.

"You better have the money in three days or we break your legs," said one of the men, quite matter-of-factly.

"It ain't wise to try and cheat Felp Bunyard, young un'," said the other. The door closed behind them.

Curf picked himself up and slowly dusted himself off. He grunted every so often as he stumbled along.

Jak slid out of concealment and stepped up beside him.

"What's going on, Curf?"

Curf nearly jumped out of his boots.

"How? What are you doing here, Jak?"

"Never you mind. Just tell me what's going on. This is 109th business now. Nobody beats up one of us without hearing about it."

Curf was in despair, completely trapped. He looked around for help, but none was coming. There was no way out.

"It started with the top clasp for the right leg cuisse. I took the cuisse apart to clean it, but didn't finish it that night. I forgot to reattach the clasp, and I haven't been able to find it since."

"By the Hand, that's the oldest thing in the book, Curf. You always put it back together at the end of the day. Too easy to lose things like that otherwise."

"I know, I know, oh how I know. But back then I didn't, not really."

Curf had clearly been learning one of life's great lessons.

Now he staggered along at Jak's side as they walked back up Tower Street.

"So I borrowed some money from Bunyard to buy a new cuisse."

"Why a whole new cuisse?"

"I was too embarrassed to admit I'd lost a clasp."

"What, it was all right to admit you'd lost a whole cuisse?"

"No, I told the store clerk that it had been wrecked in training."

"Don't let Cuzo know about that, by the Hand, you'd be in real trouble."

"Oh, Jak. I am in real trouble. I have to come up with fifteen gold pieces in three days."

"Why so much? A cuisse costs less than two pieces."

"Yeah. I didn't borrow fifteen from Felp Bunyard either. I borrowed three, and I gambled in the dice game, at the back of Felp Bunyard's tavern, down by the fish market."

"And what happened?" Jak had a sinking feeling in the pit of his stomach.

"I won."

"Oh?"

"Yeah, I had an eleven and seven, and then seven again. Every time I threw the dice they seemed to come up with a score. I had twenty pieces."

"So why are you in debt to Bunyard?"

"I kept gambling. I couldn't leave. I thought I could win even more."

"Ah," said Jak softly.

"I lost everything, and I then I lost gold pieces I didn't even have."

"And whose dice were you using?"

"Felp Bunyard's. We tested them out. They weren't weighted or anything crooked."

"And who else was in the game?"

"Well, when we started there were about five of us. But three of them had left, so there was Felp, me, and these other two men who joined in."

"Who work for Felp Bunyard I'd wager. . . ."

Curf looked stricken.

"Plucked chicken?"

"Oh yes. They switched dice on you whenever they wanted to. Easy to do among three of them. They knew you weren't thinking too straight either, having just won all that gold."

"Well, if I don't get them fifteen pieces in three days, they're going to break my legs."

"Listen Curf, no one's gonna break your legs. Not while the 109th can do anything about it."

"I'll have to hide in the dragonhouse the rest of my days. Bunyard has a bad reputation. I didn't know that when I borrowed from him."

Jak, however, was thinking hard.

"Come on, Curf. We got work to do. Got to put a stop to all this."

Chapter Five

❧

The next day Bazil's joboquin disintegrated during sword exercise. His breastplate fell to the ground with a clang. Dragon Leader Cuzo was forced to whistle the exercise to a halt while the Broketail dragon withdrew from the square. Vlok took his place.

Curf received a reprimand, and the two of them trudged back early to the dragonhouse. Bazil was just a little peeved. Knowing about Curf's problems, however, kept him from complaining.

"I hear boy gambled and lost gold pieces."

"You heard right. I did."

"Gold pieces boy doesn't even have."

Curf was silent for a few seconds.

"Well, yes. I'm afraid so."

"This dragon has gold. We can use some of that."

Curf looked up for a moment in sudden hope. Then he folded back in on himself.

"Thanks, Bazil, but I can't take your gold. I really appreciate your offer, but I've got to find it for myself."

"Not possible in three days. Maybe not possible ever."

"You don't know that."

Bazil cast a sardonic eye upon young Curf.

"One thing this dragon does know. Curf, you not suited to be dragonboy."

There was a long silence. Curf was still favoring his right leg from being thrown out the door the night before.

"I won't be a dragonboy much longer, I know that."

There, Curf thought, he'd said it. His dream was coming to an end and he was ready to admit it to himself.

"I also hear that you were cheated."

"Maybe."

"Then this isn't over. We need to plan. No one gets away with cheating this dragon's dragonboy."

Curf looked up in surprise. This was more than he'd expected. He knew he had let Bazil down. He hadn't done the job he'd wanted to. He'd meant to. He felt he owed Relkin so much that he had to take good care of Bazil. But there were always songs to be written, and tunes to try and pick out on the guitar, and he always took too much time trying to get it right, and that always made him late. Curf wasn't good at keeping to time, and he hated the hours of needlework that you had to put in to keep the joboquin healthy. Since he hadn't done his job, he had naturally thought that the dragon wouldn't care to help him. Of late Bazil had been scarcely polite about his longing for Relkin to come back.

"Plan what? I have to get that money."

"Oh, we have the money. This dragon have all the gold we need. But by the fiery breath of ancestors, we going to do something about cheating." The big head shook angrily.

That afternoon there was a meeting in Alsebra's stall. Jak, Swane, Manuel, and Endi were already there when Curf joined them.

"So we're all in, right?" said an impatient Swane.

"Right."

"Endi's going to do the gambling. The Broketail will bring some gold."

"How will he get gold? Gold is in a bank," said Manuel.

"I asked him that," said Swane. "He sent a message to Captain Hollein Kesepton, right, Curf?"

"Yes. I took it to the tower myself. The Tarcho apartments, no less."

"Right then," said Manuel. "That takes care of that."

The next evening, after the boil, they slipped out of the dragonhouse and went down Tower Street to Fish Hill. Bazil went with them, a huge presence in the street beside them.

There were folk out in numbers, and they stopped to wish him well. They knew perfectly well who he was, for with that kinked tail of his he was unmistakable. Bazil Broketail was a popular person in the city of Marneri. And though it was unusual for a dragon to be out in the city, except on a festival day, no one considered reporting his presence to the watch.

Bazil acknowledged the greetings with nods of his big head and stayed on the right side of the street. Horse traffic backed up, of course, since horses became very uneasy around dragons. He kept moving along, and apart from a fuss from some coachmen there was no trouble.

At Fish Hill they turned and went up past warehouses to a building that looked somewhat the worse for wear. The windows were boarded up. An alley at the side led to an inner courtyard. A low gate that Bazil could easily step over was the only bar to the alley.

Curf knocked at the door with Endi at his shoulder. The others were in the alleyway with two tons and more wyvern battledragon.

The door opened and a tall man looked out.

"What you want?"

"I want to see Felp."

"Squire Bunyard ain't seeing you."

"I have some gold for him."

The tall man drew back.

"Then circumstances are different. Come in. Felp will be notified."

"And tell him we want to throw dice again."

"Both of you?"

"I want to try again," said Curf. "No rule against it, is there?"

"By the Hand, but you are an optimist, ain't you?"

"My friend here wants to throw too, all right?"

The tall man gave Endi a careful scrutiny. He saw only another pigeon waiting to be plucked. Why not? Another twenty gold pieces might be in the offing here.

"Show me the gold."

Endi pulled back his coat to reveal two small pouches.

"All right, come in."

"We want to throw in the same place. Out in the courtyard, right?"

"Fine. Let me get old Felp. He loves it when we throw the dice with fine young gentlemen like yourselves."

Felp soon appeared with an expectant, cheerful air about him.

"Welcome. You have the fifteen pieces?"

Endi handed over a purse. Felp counted carefully.

"This is very good, very good. And I understand you wish to throw again. Please, come in."

They went out into the courtyard. The alley mouth loomed dark at the side. Felp and three of his men gathered around their favorite spot for throwing dice and spread a leather mat to throw on.

Felp let them use plain dice at first, knowing that dragonboys had sharp eyes. The switching had to be carefully done. But his boys were experts at distraction.

Endi was a good dice player. He kept his head, keeping bets low enough never to hurt and ignoring side bets and distractions. Playing the sevens, calling the eights. Endi won steadily, lost less than he won. He took it in silver shillings—five here, twenty there. Five gold pieces' worth after a while.

Felp decided that that was enough. He signaled to Kuvsly to start the distraction.

Kuvsly was a flamboyant player. He always kissed the dice and made elaborate appeals to the Goddess to quit being a witch and a bitch and to bless this throw and reward Kuvsly with gold. This time he went up close to Endi and snarled a long curse. There was elaborate mock hostility in his movements as he stabbed a finger at the dragonboy. Then he threw the dice.

He threw seven and thus kept the dice. He called for eight and six and bet ten shillings. Then, before throwing, he cursed Endi's mother and father as whores. Endi ignored him with a sniff. The dragonboy had his knife in his belt and felt quite capable of handling Kuvsly, but he was determined not to be put off or flustered.

Six came up. Endi paid five shillings. Kuvsly bet again on six and eight. Endi took the bet. Felp signaled impatiently.

Kuvsly was forced to increase his threat posturing by moving too close to Endi to be ignored and waving his hands dangerously close to Endi's face.

Endi drew back a stride and drew his blade.

The sight of steel brought a smile to Kuvsly's face. He dropped two dice, palming the normal ones and put his hand to his own knife hilt.

"What's the matter, dragonboy? You sensitive all of a sudden? Didn't you hear what I called your mother? Oh, I forgot, you don't have mothers. You're all bastards, right?"

Felp suddenly slapped Kuvsly hard.

"Apologies to the dragonboy, but Kuvsly's a bit of an idiot, you know what I mean?" Felp slapped Kuvsly again. "Shut your filthy mouth! Just lay your bet!"

"All right, I will. Forget shillings. How about ten gold pieces on six and eight."

"Ten gold pieces?" said Curf.

"Yeah. You got balls, dragonboy? Or did they castrate you all at birth?"

Curf felt the heat rise above his collar.

"You better not talk like that anymore," he said.

"Yeah? Who's gonna smack my head?"

Curf was about to tell him when Felp slapped him again.

"I am. Now shut up! Throw!"

The dice went down and came up double three.

"Six wins!" crowed Kuvsly. "That's ten gold pieces, from each of you, right?"

"Wrong," said another voice, behind and above them.

They whirled collectively and looked up into the looming face of a certain leatherback wyvern that had slipped down the alley and was looking on from its shadow.

"What's a dragon doing down here?" said old Felp, who was that rarity, a man immune to dragon freeze. His men were less immune, though, and Felp got no answer from them.

The dragon stepped into the yard, immediately seeming to take up the whole corner.

"This dragon comes to keep an eye on dragonboys. Keep them out of mischief."

"Hey, dragons ain't allowed!" said Kuvsly, coming out of the freeze slowly.

"No one tell me this rule," said Bazil gravely.

Kuvsly was a little drunk and became belligerent. "Yeah, well I'm telling you, you overgrown lizard."

Bazil's big eyes got dangerously bright.

"Aw, come on, don't tell me you can't take a joke?" Kuvsly sneered, emboldened by the ale he'd consumed.

"You throw dice again. I want to see something."

"I'll throw. I call six and eight. Ten gold pieces."

"No. You just throw. Throw dice three times. I want to see something."

"Hey, no way, you overgrown—"

There was a slap. The strange tail tip swung back behind the dragon, and Kuvsly was stretched out on the ground. Curf bent and picked up the dice.

"Boy throw dice."

They came up double threes.

"Throw again."

The same. And thus it went, for the dice were weighted and would only come up three and three.

They fixed Felp with inquiring eyes.

"So you were cheating," said Endi. "Just like you cheated Curf."

"Who accused Felp the Bunyard? A dragonboy?"

"Then let's bet while we hold the dice." Endi held them up. "I'll throw for double threes. Five gold pieces on it."

Felp swallowed.

"I'm not betting on weighted dice you introduced to this game . . ."

"You brought the loaded dice. We caught you, and we'll go to the watch. There's laws against cheating."

"Who says? Who's going to take your word against that of Felp Bunyard?"

The dragon shifted in his place and leaned closer. Felp leaned back.

"I says. I watch as that one hide the other dice and drop those dice. He has the other dice in his pocket."

Felp looked uncomfortable. Kuvsly was still lying there like a log.

"I think you're all going to be in a lot of trouble. Coming down here to rob an honest man of his hard-earned gold pieces."

"You're the cheat. By the Hand I'd like to . . ." said Curf.

"Yeah, what? You think you've got me worried by bringing a dragon down here? There's laws against that sort of thing, let me assure you."

"Bazil hasn't threatened anyone," said Endi.

"He knocked poor ol' Kuvsley into next week."

"Man not hurt. He want to call this dragon a lizard, he better do it where this dragon can't hear him."

Endi bent down and searched Kuvsly's pockets. In a moment he stood up with the original dice.

"And look what we have here."

Felp chewed his lip. A couple of dragonboys was one thing, but his men weren't about to tangle with a dragon. Yet fifteen gold pieces was too much to let go without a fight.

"You think you can shake old Felp the Bunyard down like this, you better think again."

"Do you think it'd be cheaper to have the wyvern rip down this house of yours?" said Endi.

Felp saw the logic of that. He did own the building.

Swane and Manuel chose that moment to show themselves, slipping in quietly around the dragon.

"More of you, what, did you bring the whole squadron down here to intimidate poor old Felp Bunyard?"

"Just place your wager. We throw for six, double threes. Five pieces of gold. Rule of three for the double. You pay fifteen for the double threes."

It was the standard rate for betting a double in such games as this. Felp looked around him for a way out, but there was none.

"Come on, Felp. Throw down the money," said Curf.

Unhappily, Felp tossed down the bag of coins just given him by Curf.

Endi threw and up came double three again.

"Six. Isn't that amazing?"

They took up the gold.

"That seems to settle everything. We're quits, I think." Endi looked into Felp's face. "And we're going to take these dice with us. You better not run this kind of rigging anymore or we'll be back."

"We'll tell the Purple Green. He'll probably want you for supper."

The Broketail dragon snorted in mirth.

Chapter Six

From high atop the Tower of Guard, Captain Hollein Kesepton observed the jubilant party returning up Tower Street to the dragonhouse.

He'd suspected that the sudden request for thirty pieces of gold, drawn on Bazil Broketail's account at the Marneri Merchants' Bank, might have to do with gambling down in the lower part of town. The Sergeant of the Guard worked hard to keep gambling under control in the barracks and the tower, but his writ did not run in the rest of the city.

Then word came that the Broketail dragon had left the dragonhouse and gone into the city. This in itself was unusual, though not outlawed by any means. Hollein had finished his dinner and then gone up to the top of the Tower to keep watch. He suspected that any such business involving a dragon would not last that long.

Now as they passed through the gate into the yard beneath the tower, he saw the jaunty strut on the boys and heard their cheerful whoops of victory. Hollein turned away with a smile. He had an idea that this problem had just been solved. Just as long as they hadn't hurt anyone too badly.

He turned back to gaze across the city. Amber lights shone from ten thousand windows. White walls gleamed faintly under the moon. The dark water of the sound lay in the distance, framing Marneri in its embrace. Hollein thought that the city had never looked better. Marneri had come through some hard years lately. Wars and military expeditions had cost the city a great deal in casualties and treasure. The short civil war with Aubinas had cost them, too, in the loss of that complete sense of unity that had always held the city-state together in the past.

But now there was peace. Axoxo had fallen. Padmasa was beaten and on the defensive. Marneri hummed with the expanded commerce to Kenor. Her merchants kept a growing fleet in motion, and the world had brought its rewards and passions to the white city on the Long Sound.

Hollein smiled, recalling his wife informing him that the fire worshipers of Xod had petitioned to build a small temple to the holy fire. Lagdalen said this would be the twenty-fourth temple to an outland divinity to open in Marneri. They were fast becoming a community of all the world's religions. Lagdalen found this idea just a little shocking. Her city was changing, and she felt a little threatened by the changes. Hollein thought it was more amusing that that.

Stretched along the northern wall of the city, close to the tower, shone the green lights favored in the Elf Quarter. From their skilled metalwork had come a great commerce. The making of elf blades, axes, equipment, as well as ornaments had led to other industries spawning employment for skilled and semi-skilled workers. The city was bustling these days, due in large part to the decision a century before to encourage the wood elves of Mount Red Oak to ally themselves with the Argonath. No other city had so completely allied themselves with the elven folk.

Hollein sighed, looking south. For all the good news, challenges remained. The Argonath was increasingly dominated by the power of Kadein, the great city of the south. Four times as populous as Marneri, Kadein had spread widely outside its old walls. Marneri still stood within the walls of stone that had protected it during the dark years of Dugguth and the war with Mach Ingbok, the demon lord.

But now Marneri strained at that restriction. The nearby towns and villages had all grown together into one big suburban ring, the same process that Kadein had undergone a century before. Within the walls there was a considerable sense of equality, even though the fine houses on Foluran Hill were far more substantial than those down on East Harbor. All shared the same security, the walls around them and the spirit of martial Marneri. To keep the same spirit alive in a city that sprawled like Kadein would be very hard.

And Hollein knew that it was in spirit and determined dedication to the great cause of the Argonath that Marneri's true leadership of the Argonath lay. Marneri would never challenge Kadein for primacy in terms of population, no matter how it grew.

Hollein shrugged, clutched himself against the cool of the night, and turned down the stairs into the great tower's interior. The city was changing and nothing would stay the same and there wasn't much he could do about that. He kept going down until he reached the floor of the Tarcho apartments. He entered, nodding to Habu the servant and went down the hall to his wife's rooms.

He found her sitting up in bed sewing by candlelight. His dress shirt had come back from the laundry with a parted seam, and he had to wear it the next day. Dignitaries from the Czardhan Kingdom of Hentilden were coming, and a formal parade of welcome was scheduled in their honor.

"Is all well?" she said.

"They were whooping their heads off when they went into the dragonhouse."

Hollein took off his jacket and sat down to pull off his boots.

"I'm still worried, Hollein."

"For Relkin?"

"Yes. This interest that is set against him has grown powerful of late. This trial stems from the same malice as before. Commander Heiss of the First Regiment, First Legion, filed the original charge, and he refuses to withdraw it."

"Mmm." He knew there were still Aubinan sympathizers throughout the Legions, but he was a little surprised that they would be so open about it so soon after the crushing defeat the rebellion had suffered.

"There are those who favored the Aubinan rebels, and they've allied themselves with the antidragon group in the high command. You know the men I mean. General Sving, Admiral Ledemor, they're mostly cavalry and naval types."

"Oh yes, they're well-known for their views. And there are also those who think that a certain dragonboy has gotten above himself, and been the recipient of too many honors."

"Such jealousies demean their owners." Lagdalen heaved a sigh at the pettiness and meanness brought on by the Aubinan rebellion and its aftermath. "Relkin has given plenty of blood for the Argonath, but on this question of the gold he's vulnerable."

"He never tried to hide it. He registered it on his arrival in the city."

"It was still plunder. We have no word from Mirchaz."

"But we have heard from Og Bogon."

"Indeed, a glowing-commendation from the great King Choulaput himself. He vouches for Relkin and Bazil in no uncertain terms."

"That covers most of the gold, anyway."

"It's the Mirchaz gold that is the problem."

Hollein took up a pot of ale brought in by Habu.

Lagdalen finished the seam on his shirt and started to put away her needle and thread. There was something else bothering her; Hollein could see it. When she looked up at him, the question was in his eyes.

"And then I think that none of it matters," she said. "Because the witches will take him away no matter what the verdict. He will never be allowed a normal life."

Hollein frowned. "You're sure of this?"

"What else would you expect? They must find out what he knows. How he has done the things he has."

"Relkin would live at Andiquant?"

"I expect so. Under constant supervision and inspection."

"He would hate that."

"He won't get a choice, really."

Down in the alleys, behind Fish Hill, in the older parts of town, the rats were sick. They became listless. Their eyes dimmed. Sores opened on their bodies and soon after they died. As their bodies grew cold, their fleas abandoned them and sought warmer ones.

Chapter Seven

Just after dawn, the brig *Lily* entered Marneri harbor under lowering skies with a stiff, pitching sea. Inside the breakwater the water was calmer, but the winds were still sharp and awkward. Other ships were riding at anchor in the outer harbor, offering the chance of collisions galore. But the *Lily* crew were old hands at this. They reefed the sails in no time and she passed serenely behind the enormous bulk of the white ship *Oat* and on into the inner harbor to tie up at the Watergate Wharf.

Relkin stepped ashore into the familiar bustle of Marneri. The alehouses on Fish Street were going full blast, and the flower sellers at the corner with Tower Street were singing of their wares. He shouldered his pack and set off through the throngs, overjoyed at being back in the city that felt closest to home. Up Tower Street he went, past markets jammed with customers, through Foluran Hill with its fine buildings and on to the parade ground before the tower gates.

He was recognized by the guards and greeted with an extremely sharp salute. He might have his troubles with the law, but Dragoneer Relkin of the 109th Marneri was still a respected figure in the Legion.

Relkin returned the salutes as well as he might, but he had a grin on his face. It wasn't often that a dragonboy got this kind of treatment.

Inside the dragonhouse a crowd of boys soon developed around him, but there was only one big face he wanted to see.

Then Bazil emerged from the stall with a happy roar and almost crushed the life out of him against the huge wyvern chest.

When he'd gotten his breath back, Relkin demanded to be set down again.

"Good to have boy back."

"Good to be here."

Bazil hugged him again, despite his protests.

"I missed damned boy! It has been a long time."

"Seemed very long, old friend. I've been wishing I was back here ever since I left."

Relkin's practiced eye took in a few developments that made him frown. Bazil's hide didn't look as if it had been rubbed down in a while. . . . The claws were trimmed, but not very well, there was a scrape on the upper right thigh that hadn't been treated at all!

"How did that happen?" he said at once, pointing to it.

"Same old boy!" Bazil sounded very happy. "That happen in training. It healing now."

Curf stumbled into the cell a few moments later.

"Welcome back, Relkin."

"Curf!" They gripped hands.

Relkin's practiced eye took in the sloppiness in the cell. The joboquin was hanging on the wrong hook. The bunk bed was badly made. Relkin could see that the joboquin needed a lot of work. He winced at some of the damage he could see.

"So, how's it been here? Any major catastrophes, wars, battles that I don't know about?"

Curf and Bazil exchanged a glance.

"No, it's been real quiet," said Curf.

"How's Cuzo been treating you?"

"Oh, he was rough at times. You know I don't do too well at getting places on time."

"Yeah."

"But lately it hasn't been so bad."

Relkin glanced at the wyvern and saw a glimmer of amusement in the dragon's eye. Curf was probably stretching the truth a little here. Ah, well, Relkin had expected things to be even worse. But that joboquin really distressed him. At least the dragon didn't have any major wounds or infections.

"Well, I'm back. It's been a long time away, much too long, but I'm so glad to be back here. By the gods, it's good."

Curf frowned slightly. Although he wasn't much of a dragon-boy, Curf was a good worshiper of the Mother Goddess, like most young people, and Relkin's calls to the Old Gods were up-setting to true believers. Relkin didn't notice and wouldn't have cared. He'd learned way back that the gods, all of them, were capricious, at least where he was concerned.

Bazil kept silent. He was not about to praise Curf's work as a dragonboy. Nor would he complain, though there was plenty to complain about.

Curf clutched his hands a little nervously. "Well, I'll get my stuff packed up. I'll have to go back to the spare stall."

"Sorry, Curf, but that is the truth of it." Relkin stowed his pack on the shelf.

"I was going to suggest getting in some beer," said Curf as he was on his way out.

The dragon's eyes lit up at that suggestion. "Good idea."

"Be good to sing with everyone again."

"Yeah, I suppose so," Relkin muttered while still cataloging in his mind all the work he had ahead of him to get things back to shape. What he really wanted to do right then was take care of that scrape on his dragon's hide, then get out the brush and then take the joboquin apart. But he knew that the sentiment in the squadron would demand some kind of libation.

In short order the trip to the Legion Brewery was organized. Alsebra, Gryf, and Chektor were chosen by lot to fetch the bar-rels back, since after a pass of the hat in the unit they rounded up enough for three barrels of Legion Plain Beer.

Three barrels were just about enough, for ten thirsty wyverns could make short work of astonishing quantities of beer.

The wyverns were in a good humor that evening, and after the boil and the usual huge portions of noodles with akh they fell to singing all the old songs, with the dragonboys on the higher notes and the dragons rolling along, as usual, in their bass and deep tenor.

Visitors dropped in from all over the barracks. Dragonboys from the resident champion dragons, even the champion dragon himself, great Vastrox, came by for a moment to sing and chaffer with the 109th. He and the Purple Green had to be measured to decide which was the biggest, with the Purple Green ahead by a small margin when the measuring was done. Great hoots came from the 109th.

Then a toast was made to welcome Relkin back, and they all downed a mug.

General Hanth himself came by, as did two commanders from the First Regiment, First Legion, Prikkel and Leems. Captain Kesepton came to visit, and was joined there by his wife Lagdalen and their daughter, Laminna.

Laminna was a little wary of the giant wyverns. She had had dragon freeze once or twice, and was unusually quiet and subdued throughout the visit. Lagdalen pointed this out to Hollein, who grinned at her.

"We all find the limits to our powers of autocracy somewhere along the line."

They laughed together.

Throughout the singing and the welcoming Relkin kept up a cheerful exterior. He refused to dwell on the tedium of the last few months, sitting in rooms in Andiquant answering questions.

Cuzo came by early and officially welcomed him back, then joined in for a couple of songs before withdrawing. Cuzo knew the protocols well. It was right for the Dragon Leader to come by, but not to stay too long since his presence would inhibit the party.

Later, when they were sung out a bit, there were questions for Relkin about his travels. He answered as best he might. Swane was sitting near, with Rakama and Jak. Relkin drained his mug and leaned back.

"So, Quoshite, what were the witches like over there in Cunfshon? Lots of sweet novices? Bet they'd have gone for a dragonboy."

Relkin laughed with the rest of them. They all knew he was affianced to Eilsa Ranardaughter.

"Sorry to disappoint you, Swane. Didn't get to see many

young women. Mostly saw old witches who asked questions the whole time. Not a lot happens in Andiquant at the end of the working day. They work night and day, they take shifts. It's a very serious place."

"What's Andiquant like?" said Endi. "Does the emperor really ride in a golden chariot?"

"No. It's all business there. Burn so many candles they have wagonsful brought in every day More scrolls than you can imagine. Wagons full of scrolls go by all the time. These buildings are really big, mind, bigger than anything on Foluran Hill. All offices of one sort or another. I slept in one part of it, I ate in a refectory with about three hundred others, and I answered questions in another part. I got to exercise and to visit a library. I read all the Argonath history. It's amazing, so much has happened here."

Relkin still had the awe in his voice that he'd felt the first time he understood just how huge and complex the history of the world Ryetelth had been. Relkin was unusual among dragonboys in that he could read well enough to enjoy it.

"Where do all the people live who work there?" wondered Endi.

"There's apartment buildings, all around the edge of the city. And others come in from outside the walls."

"Does the emperor have a big palace?"

"No. He doesn't even live in the palace building. He has an apartment nearby. It's a very nice apartment. Great views of the sea."

"You went there?"

"Well, yes."

"You visited the emperor himself?" said Swane.

"He invited me to dine with him on three occasions." Relkin said this as calmly as possible.

"Three times! The Quoshite's gonna be in the Imperial Family next!" said Swane loudly.

"I wish," said Relkin. "Or maybe not. They all work real hard. I almost think I'd rather be a dragonboy."

"See the world, right?" said Rakama.

They all laughed. They knew how true that one was. The 109th had fought on two continents and some islands in between!

"Three dinners with the emperor! What did you eat?"

"The first time we ate crabs dipped in butter. There was white wine and fresh rolls."

"Did you eat off gold plate?"

"No. Just white china."

"What did you talk about?" said Endi, who was always curious.

"What didn't we talk about, you mean. He's a great man, the emperor. You can feel it as soon as you're in the room with him. He sees very far, and he gets information from all over the world. He showed me a globe that has the world painted on it, a map wrapped around a world."

They were all boggled by this thought.

"The Padmasans are fighting the Czardhans in the west and there may be war with Kassim again. So when we captured Ax-oxo we raised the pressure on them to breaking point. The emperor is hoping to force Padmasa to sue for peace and end the war in his lifetime."

They were all staring at him, thoughtfully. Relkin had been on the inside of the high command. Had seen the global strategy laid out. Dined with the emperor three times.

"So you're just damned glad to be back with us," said Rakama.

"Right."

"Hey, well welcome back."

"Yeah, welcome back," said a chorus of voices.

They sang one more round, and the party broke up.

Later, in the stall, while he worked on the tattered joboquin, he and the dragon spoke in more detail of the months he'd been absent. Eventually Relkin got around to Curf and what had really happened. Bazil thought for a moment.

"Curf boy is unpredictable in some ways. Never know what side of the door he going to push."

"You survived though?"

"So did Curf. It was close once or twice."

Relkin could imagine. He'd heard about the joboquin disintegrating and causing Bazil's armor to fall to the dust in a drill.

"Curf not a dragonboy. He leave soon, he think."

So even Curf had realized he didn't have it to be a dragonboy. It was just as well. No dragon should have poor care.

Relkin was looking at the joboquin and whistling in horror to himself.

"You know, just about every strap here is loose and needs stitchwork."

Relkin worked away for a few minutes. Finally Bazil spoke again.

"And how is boy?"

"I survived, that's about all I can say."

"They ask questions?"

"Endlessly."

"Now it's over."

"I hope so."

Bazil absorbed this quietly. He hadn't thought too much about what it might mean to him if Relkin were sent to Andiquant permanently. Now he realized just how much he had come to depend on Relkin's planning for their life after the Legion.

"Anyway, I'm damned glad to be back here, and I'm really sorry that you've not had the best care these past months."

The dragon's eyes glowed softly. "This dragon thanks boy for his concern. This dragon very glad you're back."

Big talon, badly trimmed, was clasped for a moment by human hand.

Before he fell asleep, Relkin lay awake in the dark listening to the familiar sounds of the dragonhouse. The Purple Green was whirring and whooping in his stall across the way. Bazil snored with the deep, low, rumble of contented, well-fed wyverndom.

He was back. He prayed he was back to stay.

Of course he did have a mission that would take him away from Marneri. He had to get to Widarf somehow. With or without leave. He had to see Eilsa. All these months apart, worrying about her, reading her letters over and over, had left him with a burning need to see her. She had been getting better in recent months, but even a couple of weeks ago she was not yet sure if she could travel.

Relkin gave a silent prayer of thanks to the gods, and then another one to the Mother for insurance. He prayed that Eilsa slept well that night and was not troubled by dreams filled with fear and horror.

Later, he even slept himself.

The following morning he had a short visit with Dragon Leader Cuzo, who was warm and affable, apparently happy to see the famous dragonboy back. Cuzo confided that he thought Relkin would receive a promotion very shortly. A new dragon squadron was to be formed and it would need a dragon leader. Cuzo was sure that Relkin would get the post once the business with the looting charges was dismissed, as Cuzo confidently expected it would be. Relkin tried not to let himself get too excited by this news, but it was hard. They discussed Curf for a few moments, who was due for a review.

"Curf will transfer to the infantry, he says." Cuzo sounded pessimistic. "But I don't think it will make any difference. I think he should become a musician.

"Right, absolutely."

"We're back to ten dragons again."

"I have to meet the newcomers properly."

"The Purple Green has been bored lately. He wants an adventure."

"I would've thought he could have used a good long break. We've had our share of adventures these past few years."

"On considering the history of this unit, I have to agree with you, dragoneer, but the signs of restlessness are there."

"Are we going to Dashwood?"

"Tell the truth I don't know where we're going next. I don't think the high-and-mighty upstairs know what to do with us. We've been installed in Marneri as a near-permanent force, and there was a long argument about breaking the unit up."

Relkin had wondered if such a move might follow after the various incidents of total insubordination, verging on mutiny, that had scarred the squadron's reputation with the high brass. Dragon units could not simply get up and roam off on their own accord.

"I'm glad to say they gave that idea up. The survival of the

109th Marneri has come to mean something all over the Argonath."

"Nice to know that someone cares. We been through a lot, all right."

"They also tried to have the Purple Green dismissed from the Legion. Some trumped-up thing about his weight and moody disposition."

Relkin sat up, surprised at this. Someone in the High Command really had it in for the unit.

"It ran out of steam. General Tregor spoke up on His Lordship's behalf at a Command Meeting, they tell me."

"They dropped it?"

"Pretty much, but we have enemies up there. What happened in Aubinas didn't quite go the way some of the powers that be wanted it to go."

"It's hard to accept. Are they traitors?"

"I don't know. I don't even know who they are really, apart from Heiss of the First Legion."

"He's the one who brought this case against me."

"Right. Which reminds me. You put in for leave this morning to visit your attorney. Leave granted."

Not long afterward Relkin headed down Water Street under blue skies in which occasional white clouds drifted north. Lagdalen had become a sort of independent Crown Attorney. Her authority came from the queen, who allowed her free rein on the suggestion of Lessis of Valmes. Lagdalen's office had grown to fill an entire building on lower Water Street, with a dozen young attorneys in that building, and several young women of high family volunteering to write up documents and keep the files. It was a hive of industry.

Relkin got a warm welcome when he walked in. The receptionist came out to take his hand, and Lagdalen greeted him with a hug. Back in her office he took a seat across from her desk, which was buried under paperwork. She searched in a scroll box for a few moments.

"Ah! I have good news for you." She pulled out a scroll.

He saw the seal and recognized the ornate "W" of Wattel and his heart leaped in his chest. His fingers broke the seal nervously and he read the scroll and felt his spirits finally soar. Eilsa was coming to Marneri. She would be there in two days. He told this to Lagdalen.

"Oh, that is such good news. Thanks be given for her recovery. Widarf is a beautiful place, Relkin. You should visit it yourself someday. It has a magic about it that is gentle and healing."

Relkin remembered that Lagdalen had spent some time there, recovering from her experiences during the great invasion. "I hope that I will. It has been good for Eilsa." He looked back to the message.

"Once she's here in the city, she will stay on Foluran Hill, as before. Her Aunt Kiri will be her chaperone once again. Kiri has also been staying at Widarf." Relkin looked away, and muttered, "And I hope it helped her mean old soul."

"Now, Relkin. That woman is not the sour apple you imagine her to be. She has a sense of humor. I think she even likes you, in a strange way."

Could some of Aunt Kiri's venom toward a certain dragonboy be drawn? It was nice to imagine the possibility. The problem with the Wattels was that he was just an orphan, and Eilsa was the heir of Clan Wattel. Until she married him, of course. Then the title would pass elsewhere in the clan.

Relkin forced himself to smile. Eilsa said she wanted only to live with him and raise a family together. She wasn't concerned about the leadership of the clan.

"We'll be reunited once again. You must both come to dine with us. Just Hollein and me, so we can talk without an audience."

They laughed together, thinking of the occasions Relkin had been invited to grand dinners by the Tarchos and then subjected to an interrogation by the guests. Folk like the Tarchos didn't get many opportunities to hear what a dragonboy had to say, especially this dragonboy, who had been taken up into the most dreadful battles with sorcerers.

"I would be honored, Lagdalen of the Tarcho."

"And so would we, Relkin of the Legion Star."

They laughed again at her riposte. She was a Tarcho princess, but he was the only dragonboy ever to win the Legion's highest award.

"Seriously, Hollein would be very pleased. He didn't really get to see you before you went to Andiquant."

They were interrupted by a knock at the door. It opened to reveal a young legal aide who brought in several scrolls for Lagdalen to read.

Lagdalen accepted them with a groan and dumped them on the scroll reader. When the girl had curtsied and left, Lagdalen picked up some parchment from her desk.

"Relkin, I'm afraid we also have to go over this case."

He groaned softly.

"It is still being pursued," she said quietly. "There is a group of senior officers, identified with the Aubinan interest, who are pressing it. They might have been arrested except for the amnesty proclaimed by the emperor. I'm afraid they have a certain amount of support here in the city."

"But the rebellion's over, isn't it?"

"It still sputters. Many wealthy men have lost their estates, forming a pool of bitterness. There are some bandit groups in the woods up in Biscuit-Barley. Our old friend Porteous Glaves roams the Forest of Nellin. General Neth and his riders are up in the Crimig Hills. So there are still embers aglow, even though the people at large have turned against the whole thing."

"What about Wexenne?"

"Serving a life sentence on the Guano Isles."

"Well that's good news, at least."

"Yes. But this case against you, on the other hand, has a problem. We have still never received any response from our message to Mirchaz."

"But we did from the king."

"Yes, Choulaput responded very favorably. That letter clears you of most of the charges and leaves that gold safe. The gold from Mirchaz is another matter."

"Ah, the tabis that fell out of the wall of Mot Pulk's house. You know, I thought me and Baz deserved them, frankly, after what we been through."

"Yes, that may be, but they are still technically loot."

"Those were strange days. The city was burning. The slaves killed the elf lords, just threw them on the fires. I thought the gold was meant to be taken. I guess I wasn't thinking very clearly at the time."

Lagdalen had read the deposition several times. Relkin had been through the end of the world there in Mirchaz, and she wondered just how much he had been changed by the experience.

When she had first met him, he was still a rosy-cheeked boy, too wise for his age and too wily for his own good. Was there anything left of that boy she remembered? That young rogue who almost got a birching for stealing orchids off a balcony garden? She smiled to herself. Even then she was looking out for him.

"I have moved for another delay in the case, but the high court turned us down. I think there has been some pressure behind the scenes from the Aubinan interest, forcing us to trial before we can get a reply from Mirchaz."

"What can we do?"

"The best we can. The judge will allow us to present the letter from King Choulaput. You and the dragon will provide testimony as to what took place in Mirchaz. We can show that you registered the gold upon your arrival and paid the appropriate taxes, and that may be what saves you."

"Right. If I'd thought it was wrong to have the tabis, why I would have registered them. I would just have smuggled them in and hidden them."

"They will give you a very harsh cross-examination. All the details about Mirchaz will be raked over for any discrepancies between you and the dragon. Nor can we coach you, for that is forbidden and the court will notice it. They'll be watching for the signs."

"Well, it'll be a long hot day or two in court then. But the dragon has a good memory. He fought the elf lords that day and brought down their city. He will tell them the truth. That's all he knows."

Chapter Eight

Warm weather blew up from the south, and the next few days were blistering hot in the city of Marneri. Heat shimmered off the cobbles in the streets. The white walls glowed in the sunlight. Folk shed their jackets and socks. The trees on Foluran Hill began to wilt. When the tides ran out, the gray mud along the fishermen's dock stank in the hot sun. Up on Tower Hill, the fine shops rolled their awnings down as far as possible.

On the third day of the heat, little Fanny Nurriat was taken ill around noon. Her home was a run-down old tenement on Fish Hill. Just that morning she had been sobbing over her cat, Dego, who had died that morning of a mysterious illness. She was seven years old and very attached to the cat. Still, she didn't even get to bury Dego. Her father took his body away and sold it for a farthing to the ragman. It would go as food to the guard dogs at Penchem's Wharf.

Fanny came down with fever a few hours later and complained of feeling very ill indeed. Her mother put her to bed, startled by the sheer heat of the fever in the girl. Then Fanny began vomiting, and continued to vomit even when there was nothing further to be brought up. Around the middle of the afternoon her mother found black buboes growing in Fanny's armpit and groin. An hour later, Fanny died.

Her mother was already sickening, and so was her brother Walter.

Fanny's father, Elben went to the dispensary for the poor. Unfortunately, he was not taken very seriously there by the acting clerks. Elben drank too much beer and was well-known for it. His family lived half-on and half-off the public purse, since Elben had never managed to keep a job for very long. He got by with occasional labor on the docks, and was a known malingerer.

Elben was desperate and would not give up this time. He stayed there in the dispensary, arguing with the clerks for half an hour. Then he was suddenly taken ill and within a few minutes began to vomit. He was taken up and carried back to his house.

It was discovered that the Nurriat house had become a place of death. Fanny's body lay in the parlor. In the bedroom lay Mrs. Nurriat, plainly dying. On the floor in a corner they found little Walter Nurriat, curled in a fetal ball. The clerks from the dispensary panicked, but it was already too late. All three of them would be dead within a day and a half.

Meanwhile Fanny's Aunt Gikla had staggered out of the Nurriat house and made her way to the Broken Hat, a local drinking parlor popular with the older generation. She didn't feel good, and a pint of rice wine ought to do the trick, she thought. She ordered the wine, but never drank it. While it was being brought she went into sudden convulsions and then began the vomiting. She expired there about an hour later, surrounded by friends and acquaintances. When they opened her garments, they found the glistening black buboes all over her body.

That evening Relkin and Eilsa, reunited again, were visiting in the great Tarcho apartment in the Tower of Guard. Lagdalen and Hollein had a small suite of rooms entirely to themselves on the interior side of the apartment. Aunt Kiri was in the kitchen with old Habu, the maid.

It was a warm night, the windows were open, and they could hear the happy shrieks of the children playing around the fountain down in the interior courtyard. The narrow parlor room was used for dining by pulling out an old table from beside the wall. Some chairs were borrowed from other rooms, and they all sat down to a fine dinner—baked guinea hens, poached salmon, and a wonderful bottle of Spriani wine from Arneis. The food, the wine, and the joy of being together like this kept their spirits high, even as they fell into reminiscences of the past.

Eilsa appeared fully recovered. She and Relkin held hands all evening, obviously in love. Since Eilsa's arrival in Marneri, she and Relkin had spent as much time as possible together. Aunt Kiri had mellowed a few degrees while at Widarf, but she remained a constant presence, which forced them to keep apart physically except for a few stolen kisses now and then. It was intensely frustrating for them, but exhausting for Aunt Kiri.

Still they were obviously happy, deliriously happy. Lagdalen wished them joy and exchanged a sly smile with Hollein. He grinned back.

By the Hand! Lagdalen said to herself. The Mother Herself must have been watching out for them. Hollein might have died in the gladiatorial ring in Tummuz Orgmeen. Instead he sat there, alive, strong, beautiful, her husband and the father of her children.

Relkin wore that same air of rediscovered purpose that she had seen on him after his return from Eigo. The child in him had almost disappeared. Behind his laughter she sensed deeper, darker concerns.

Outwardly Eilsa seemed calm and almost back to her old self, but Lagdalen sensed that there was still trouble under the surface. The girl from the hills had spent only a short time directly under the physical control of the Dominator, but in that time he had raped her mind and taken something of her self-confidence.

And Lagdalen, herself? How was she? She was an overworked mother of two with an extensive law practice and too many social causes to fight for, she thought, grinning ruefully.

"Well, to change the subject from those bad old days," she said, after Relkin and Hollein had finished reminiscing about the fighting in Ourdh. "How are things with our mighty friends in the 109th?"

"Oh, they've been in the city too long, but that's all. Even Gryf seems to have settled in. No one even complained about him when I got back. Jak and Endi made some money gambling, so they've been living the high life. New clothes, new boots, new equipment for the dragon. Alsebra was pleased by that, of course. The Purple Green is bored with the food, and he's impatient for some time in the country. We're due to rotate out to Dashwood in three weeks time. He's hoping for some game."

"Why are they keeping you in Marneri?" said Eilsa. "I thought by this time that you would have been sent to Kenor. You were due to go there."

"I don't know. When I went off to Andiquant they thought they'd be sending us to Axoxo."

A nightmarish thought came to him of Curf trying to be a good dragonboy up in the mountains in constant cold and windy conditions. The dragon would never have survived. "But no one seems to know what they'll do with us now."

The cook brought in the kalut and sweet biscuits to finish off their meal, then announced that Lady Lacustra, Lagdalen's mother, was bringing grave news.

Lacustra came in with a face gone wild with panic.

"Lagdalen, oh my child, my child. We must get out!"

"Mother, what is it?" Had a fire broken out? Lagdalen went over to Lacustra to take her hands. "Mother? What is it?"

"Listen everyone, I have terrible news. We must flee the city at once. This very night."

"Why, Mama?"

"Plague! There is plague down on Fish Hill. There's a dozen dead down there already and many more that have fallen sick."

The four friends whirled to each other. Crystal clear in their memories were those awful scenes in the laboratories of the Dominator.

"What kind of plague?" said Hollein, praying that it was something harmless that had just alarmed Lacustra.

"The sickness of rats," she sobbed. "Buboes in the armpits and groin."

Their faces turned ashen. This was the black plague, the most terrible affliction in the world.

"What is being done?"

"The witches confer. That is all I know. The message I received was brief. Expect quarantine tonight. Leave at once.

Tommaso must be told, but I don't know where he is or how to contact him."

"Leave the city?" said Lagdalen.

"Before it becomes impossible," replied her mother. "None of us are infected, we can be sure of that. There are no rats in the tower."

"Where would we go?" said Eilsa.

"Shall you go back to Widarf?" said Relkin quickly.

"No. I hadn't thought to do that."

"How can we leave the city at such a time?" murmured Lagdalen in shock.

"If it's the black plague, then we have to kill all the rats. That's the only thing that will really stop it," said Hollein, citing the historical precedents.

"We don't have plague in Clan Wattel. Or not that I have ever heard of."

"Aye," Hollein nodded soberly. "It doesn't often affect small populations because it's spread by rats. We've had it in the cities before now, but not for a hundred years or more. Not since before King Wauk."

"What can we do to help?" said Eilsa.

"Leave the city." Hollein was clearly decided.

"But what about the sick and dying?"

"The witches and the temple are taking care of all of that. They will have had the training for it."

"It seems heartless to leave when people are sick and in need of aid."

"Believe me, it is best to leave. You cannot help without becoming another victim and thereby make more work. If volunteers are called for, you will be informed."

"Oh, no, my dears, once we are out of the city I forbid you to return." Lady Lacustra was determined to prevent her daughter from risking exposure to the black plague.

"Mother, if our city needs us, then we must give all that we have, even our lives. I have learned this lesson well. It is the price we pay for the rank of Tarcho, for the honor of our privileged lives within the Tower of Guard."

"Oh, my dear, I know, but I couldn't bear to lose you now."

Lacustra was on the point of tears.

"Mother." Lagdalen put her arms around her and took her to an inside room.

Everyone took that as the signal for departure. They made hurried farewells and left the Tarcho chambers and set off down the main staircase of the tower. Outside, despite Aunt Kiri's protestations, Relkin escorted Eilsa to the house on Foluran Hill. All the way there he tried to get her to agree to leave the city at once. She asked where he was going to be. He admitted he would be in the dragonhouse. Then, she said, she would remain on Foluran Hill. She doubted that there were many rats on Foluran Hill. There were far too many cats about for that.

On the top step by the gate to the house Relkin sneaked a kiss right in front of Aunt Kiri's outraged eyes.

"Please leave the city, Eilsa."

She made no reply other than to kiss him again and then hurry inside, tearing herself away from him.

He left, not seeing anything too clearly in the first hundred yards since his eyes were unaccountably hot and moist. Peculiar anger built up in his heart.

Passing back up Tower Street he noticed the sense of emergency that was in the air. Carriages were loading hurriedly. Several men rode past on good horses. The North Gate was already busy with traffic. Several carriages were waiting at the bottom of the Tower of Guard.

The guards by the dragonhouse gate were men from the First Regiment, First Legion.

"Hey, dragonboy, what news have you of the plague?"

The guard was not much older than himself, and he was clearly frightened.

"No more than you, soldier. There's some carriages loading on Tower Street. I expect most of the upper city will empty before the quarantine closes the gates."

"By the Hand, but the rat plague is the worst. There be a lot of rats in the lower city with all those old wharves and warehouses."

"We've got plenty of work ahead of us," Relkin agreed.

"May the Mother look after our souls," said the other guard.

Inside the dragonhouse Relkin found that the dragonboys

were already engaged in a full-blooded sweep for rats. Swane had borrowed some terriers, and Jak had brought in some ferrets from a friend in the Elf Quarter.

"What have you found?" said Relkin as he pitched in to help.

"Just a couple so far. Under a crate in the corner storeroom. Must've been eating the leather."

"Were they sick?"

"No."

"There'll be more."

There were more; rats can hide in the most remarkable places. But it was also soon clear that the plague had not spread inside the walls of the dragonhouse or the Tower of Guard. The rats they caught were all healthy and vigorous, sure signs that they were not infected.

The hunt for rats in the rest of the city was already well under way. Where possible, volunteers from among the elvish folk worked to actually kill the rats. The black plague did not harm the green-flecked folk of the forestlands in anything like the manner in which it killed men.

Unfortunately men still became infected. They were placed in quarantine conditions within a closed-off courtyard. The dead were collected on wagons and taken out of the city at once, while plans for mass graves were hurriedly put into operation.

That night more people in the Fish Hill sector of the city came down with the plague, and more victims were recorded from other parts of the city, too, though not from the upper end of Tower Street, or on Foluran Hill.

The ratkillers went down into the sewers below the houses. They tore apart the thatch above the roofs. They went through the attics and the cellars. And they brought in terriers and ferrets.

At the second hour before dawn a desperate rider approached the West Gate. He shouted the news from Kadein. The plague was loose, and a holocaust was brewing.

Chapter Nine

Plague gripped the cities of the Argonath: first Minuend, then Kadein and Marneri, then Talion and the rest all reported the infection. The disease took very different courses, however, from city to city. Kadein saw a veritable catastrophe as one-third of its population succumbed over the next two weeks. Others escaped with scarcely a scratch. Ryotwa was saved by the Cat Witch, Nadeen, whose feline legions destroyed the infected rats before they could spread. Vo was helped by its design. One hundred years before, after fire had devastated the old city, Imperial Engineers rebuilt the central parts of Vo with a new sewer system, so there the plague did not catch on.

In Minuend the plague broke out in the camps of migrant field workers, and spread through the city with terrifying speed. By the end of the first day there were more than a thousand dying of the disease and a hundred already dead.

The following morning it began in Kadein. The first sickness was recorded from the crowded cribs of sailors in the harbor. From the beerhalls it spread to the overcrowded districts farther inland and became a conflagration overnight. By the dawn of the second day in old Kadein, every hour brought another thousand deaths.

Led by the wealthy, an exodus spread out from the cities. There was much talk of firing the cities and burning them to end the disease. That was what had been done in the early days of the Argonath. It had worked then, when nothing else had.

Others maintained that prayer was enough, that if the people were to pray to the Goddess with open hearts, She would hear them and end the plague. These believers flocked to the temples.

The priestesses pooh-poohed that sort of thinking right away. The Mother would help those who helped themselves, as it had always been.

During that second morning, beginning at the tenth hour, there came witches from Cunfshon, traveling by the magic of the Black Mirror between Andiquant and the Towers of Guard in the nine cities.

In Marneri, Lessis herself stepped out of the mirror after a trouble-free crossing.

She broke the ring of hands, embraced Fi-ice, the Witch of Standing, then shook hands with the young witches Yanna and Imlan. Signaling to the young witches to accompany her, Lessis moved to her private chamber in the tower and began to put plans into operation.

Seven floors lower down, sitting on a divan in the empty Tarcho apartment, Lagdalen sipped a mug of weakbeer and tried to get some strength back into her legs. She'd been up all night, working to organize the assault on the rat population in the East Bay area. Teams of men and elves, all volunteers, had gone in with dogs and ferrets. Wielding crowbars and axes, they'd cut their way into crawl spaces and cellars and slaughtered the rats.

The run-down area of Fish Hill had been totally abandoned, and the dockside was empty.

The rat hunters had found a sizable population in the dockside area, as had been expected. They had slaughtered rats by the dozen in various warehouses and within the grand sewer. Still, folk were falling ill and dying by the score. The disease had continued to spread. Now there was a quarantine on the city, and no one was allowed out, so refugees were spreading into the rest of the city, and they were bringing the plague with them.

Now the first victims began to appear north of Broad Street, a prosperous area which lay in the shadow of Foluran Hill. Broad Street was the center for merchants' offices and trade organizations. The buildings were relatively new and well designed.

There could be few rat nests there, and yet the plague was spreading into that precinct.

Lagdalen wondered if they were wrong about this plague. Was it spread by something other than rats? She sipped her beer and tried not to think about all the people that had fled the city and spread out into the surrounding countryside. What if they were carrying the plague?

It might spread across the entire Argonath.

Come to think of it, there was still no word from Kenor. They had sent to Dalhousie the previous day but the bird had not returned, which seemed ominous.

She shivered and hugged herself. Usually the Tarcho apartment was home to seven adults and four children. All that energy was replaced by an eerie quiet.

In fact, the whole tower was quiet. The inhabitants had fled, and there were just a few officials and guards on hand.

She prayed that Laminna was safe. And she prayed for her husband Hollein, who was at that moment riding hard for the nearby city of Bea, bearing messages to the authorities there.

Come home safely, my love. Don't leave me alone.

There was a sudden knock at the front door. Lagdalen sat up with a jerk. She'd dozed off. With a gulp, she finished the weak-beer and got up to open the door.

On the step she found a young witch, a girl not much older than herself, dressed in the minimal gray costume of their order, with her hair demurely braided and no jewelry or decoration anywhere.

The young witch bowed. "Beg pardon, Lady, but are you the Lady Lagdalen of the Tarcho?"

"Yes."

"Then the Lady Lessis asks if you would attend upon her as soon as possible."

Lagdalen gave another start.

"Lessis? She is here?"

"Yes, Lady."

Lagdalen imagined the Black Mirror that must have flashed into being in that hidden chamber at the top of the tower. There was something terrifying about the power of the Great Magic; Lagdalen knew she would never have made a good witch.

"What are you called?" she said.

"I am Yanna," said the young witch.

Yanna's face was impassive, calm, her eyes level. Yanna had probably been up all night, too, but she didn't look like it. Lagdalen thought that Yanna had probably been a star in the Novitiate schools. They tried to inculct that way of being calm and in control. Witches had to be in control of themselves at all times so they could control others if they had to. . . .

"Did she say where I was to find her?"

"In her chamber, Lady. I will escort you, if you like."

"That's all right, I know my way. Thank you, Yanna."

Lagdalen pulled a jacket around her and took the key to the apartment. It felt very strange actually to lock the apartment door behind her. Normally there were always people there and a guard on watch.

The only sound was her feet on the stairs as she climbed through the unnatural hush.

At length she reached the high floor where Lessis kept her seldom-used chambers, with bare blue blankets on the cots and bare stone flags on the floor. The Lady was deep in thought, writing at her desk, when Lagdalen entered. After a few moments she looked up.

"Lagdalen, my dear, thank you for coming so quickly." Lessis came around the desk and took her hands.

Lagdalen curtsied, awkwardly. "This plague is his work, is it not, Lady?"

Lessis nodded faintly. "Yes. To begin in all nine cities within days is too much of a coincidence. It is exactly the sort of thing he is well-known for. A byword for such horrors, in fact."

Lessis sat down again. "I must just finish this note." She scratched another line, signed with a quick flourish, then rolled the message up and melted wax for her seal.

"I have some good news. We have discovered how this plague is carried. It comes on the backs of fleas. When the rats die, the fleas abandon them and seek out blood from other animals and people. That's when the disease is passed to another person."

Lagdalen smacked a fist into her palm. "Of course, that explains so many things. By the Hand, we must hurry!"

Lessis smiled at the sudden energy in Lagdalen's face. The child was a doer, a credit to her line. A pity, in fact, that she could not be queen instead of the current holder of the throne.

"We must fumigate the whole city. I hope the stock of pyrethrum will be sufficient. More will have to be imported at once. . . ."

Lagdalen had come fully alive. Here was the hope she'd been lacking. The threat was terrible, but they could take effective countermeasures.

"Here," Lessis handed Lagdalen the scroll. "I want you to take this message to the queen."

"Yes, of course, Lady. At once." But Lagdalen winced slightly at being reduced to a mere messenger again.

Lessis read her expression accurately.

"I'm sorry to ask this of you, my dear, I know how busy you must be. But I know that the queen will not ignore you. Besita is often unwise in a crisis."

"Yes, lady. She has been better lately."

"She fell to pieces during the rebellion in Aubinas."

"Ah, yes."

"She must order a massive effort. We have to fumigate the city. All supplies of pyrethrum leaves, flowers and powder, have to be handed over to the crown and used to the maximum effectiveness. We need metal cans for the powder and long-handled brushes so that the powder can be applied in corners and crevices where fleas might hide. I have some drawings that must be shown to designers."

"The people in my office could help you. We are still open and working. On Water Street, as before."

"Your people stayed despite the plague?"

"Most of them."

"Then we are beholden to the noble young ladies of Marneri."

"Praise be the Mother, we've had no sickness there yet."

Lagdalen ran down the steps all the way to the bottom. In the stables she commandeered her favorite horse, a gray mare called Beety. Soon afterward she trotted out of the North Gate and headed up the road to Rinz and the Royal Hunting Lodge in Rinz Park.

Chapter Ten

⫷ 〰 ⫸

Lost Buck Woods was a small wood of oak and beech set about a mile from the North Gate of Marneri. Usually it was a quiet spot. At Stag's Pool there would sometimes be a fisherman, patiently casting with fly for the resident trout, and in the glades there would be mushroom gatherers, and in the winter woodcutters, but that was about all you might expect to find there.

On this day, though, it was a scene of terrifying activity. One of the long glades had now been completely dug up and turned into a great pit, eight feet deep, ten feet wide, and one hundred feet long. Five huge dragons wielded shovels in the pit, and five more worked above, shoveling the loose dirt into neat piles.

More dragons, along with an army of men and dragonboys, worked nearby on clearing and laying a road through the woods. A logging trail had been broadened over its entire length all the way back to the Marneri road.

This activity had begun the previous evening with the arrival of a group of Imperial Engineers. Soon they were joined by gangs of workmen, then by dragons and dragonboys. All night the first teams worked to clear and prepare the ground. Teams of dragons, usually five strong, dug, or hauled out trees and stumps.

The 109th Marneri Dragons had been in the second wave, replacing a team made up of the resident champions, lead by Vastrox the Great. Normally such an occasion would have been the cause of much banter between the two groups of mighty wyverns. This time, however, little was said.

The ground was strewn with rocks, and some were the size of

boulders. This slowed things down, but wyverns are tremendously powerful animals and not even fair-sized boulders could resist when two or three of them were working with pry bar and pick.

By the tenth hour the pit was finished.

The engineers passed word to Cuzo that sufficient depth had been achieved. Cuzo gave a sharp blast on the cornet, and the dragons downed shovels. The wyverns in the pit called up to their colleagues for a hand in getting out. The Purple Green reached down to help Alsebra up.

"Sometimes I wish you not freemartin," rumbled the giant one as he admired the athletic form of the green freemartin, who was certainly more supple than he was. She noticed the gleam in his eye.

"I think you have fertilized enough eggs for one life."

"Alas, this may be true. Certainly I get little opportunity in life as a Legion dragon."

"We'll all get the chance for that, when we retire," said Vlok, who was extending an arm for Bazil Broketail.

"Not you, surely not. This would be a mistake," said the Purple Green.

"This dragon as good as any other," growled Vlok defensively.

The Purple Green snorted. "Complete delusion."

Bazil hauled himself up, his big feet digging into the sides of the pit. "You leave old Vlok alone now," said Bazil. "We don't need any trouble today."

"Make life interesting."

"Only for you, old friend, only for you."

"Bah."

Vlok was making angry snorts, but stood fast. The other dragons stacked their shovels and picks on the big wagons that would carry them back to Dashwood, breaking the tension. Dragonboys appeared among them, anxiously scanning their joboquins for damage.

Cuzo came by, giving everything a cursory examination.

"All right, everyone, listen close. We're moving out, going back down the logging road to the highway. Then back to the city. I don't want to see any straggling."

At the pit they were already unloading the first carts, tipping them over to topple the corpses into the pit. The men doing this work were dressed in tightly wrapped clothing that had been treated with pyrethrum to discourage fleas.

The cornet sounded up ahead. Cuzo gave the order and they began to march. Lost Buck Woods soon came to an end. Up ahead lay the broad road from Marneri that headed north to Rinz and then to Camp Dashwood. At the junction, they had to pull over to the side for a stream of wagons and carts laden with the dead. Mounds of bodies shifted and shuddered as the wagons turned the corner, their horses or oxen straining with the load. It was a sobering sight.

The dragons waited patiently. They tried not to think too much about a big cauldron filled with noodles, lathered with akh.

"Good thing dragons not affected by plague," said Vlok.

"Very good," said Alsebra.

"No one know if that true or not," said Gryf.

"How?"

"It not known, is all."

"I never heard of dragons getting plague," said the Purple Green.

"Nor this dragon," said Bazil.

"Dragons caught plague in Eigo. You remember ancient forest. Disease there almost killed all of us," said Alsebra.

"That is true," said the Purple Green, and the others fell silent.

The carts and wagons rumbled by with their load of dead, many, many dead. Cuzo passed the word that they should get ready to march when the wagons were past.

No sooner had the dragons got onto the Marneri pike than they had to march in single file as another convoy of wagons went by carrying more bodies to the pits.

"How many have died, do you think?" said Jak.

"I'd bet a thousand at least," replied Endi.

"What? You counted 'em?" Swane said scornfully.

"Nope, but there were at least fifty wagons. Some of them were small, but they were averaging twenty bodies or so, I'd say."

"What about all the people who died yesterday? Where did they put them?" said little Jak.

"I heard they used an old quarry over in Quave," replied Endi. "Tommo in the stables told me."

"You want to watch what you believe from that Tommo," said Swane.

Relkin had been quiet all morning, his spirits depressed by the morbid business of digging the huge charnel pit. He marched alongside the dragon, his eyes on the countryside here, where large villas were visible among the trees. His thoughts were all with Eilsa.

She had left the city and gone to Rinz, a crossroads town ten miles north of the city. As far as he knew the plague had not reached Rinz. He prayed that it would not either.

They passed some more carriages, this time carrying the living determined to flee the city. Then came a trio of horsemen, one a woman. Relkin was familiar with the horse she rode: Beety, the pretty gray mare from the tower stables.

As they came closer the boys of the 109th recognized Lagdalen of the Tarcho.

"Hail, Lagdalen!" shouted Swane.

Lagdalen waved back at them and called out as she passed. "Hail, my friends. Keep your hearts strong, the Mother is with us!"

She rode on and disappeared behind them, overtaking the carriages.

"What d'you think that's about then?" said Swane, dropping back beside Relkin. Relkin shrugged, not wanting to get caught up in Swane's eternal speculations. "No idea."

"I heard there were witches arriving from Cunfshon."

"First I heard of it."

"I bet she's gong to Rinz. Going to the queen."

Relkin nodded. If the queen was in Rinz, then that would be good reason for Lagdalen to be riding out there in such a hurry.

Chapter Eleven

Kind Adem had built the house at Rinz Park on the ruins of a grand villa. From afar the house looked like a birdcage made of white columns, perched on its bluff overlooking the park itself.

Besita had always liked to come to Rinz. Pleasant memories from her childhood were set in this old house. With its pine-paneled walls and carved-log staircases, it was a place out of time. The servants were mostly elderly, and they remembered the times of her father and her grandfather and so were quite content with her. Compared to the tyranny of King Wauk, the incompetence of Queen Besita was of little consequence to them. There were none of the hidden sneers that she sensed all around her in the Tower of Guard in Marneri.

She was not a happy queen, nor a very good one. So be it. The damned witches had murdered her brother to make sure the crown came to her, but she had never asked for it.

Lagdalen found the queen sitting out on the belvedere, gazing at the park. There was a bottle at her elbow, and at first Lagdalen's heart had sunk. Then after her bow and curtsy she noticed that it was just a bottle of water. Besita had not lapsed into her drinking habits.

"Your Majesty, it is good to see you looking so strong and well."

"Well? What leads you to that conclusion? I am not well, Lagdalen of the Tarcho. My back is a horror of aches, my left leg is numb, and I have the recurrent head spasm. The doctors are all at sea with it. One says take the oil of turmeric, the other recommends black draughts of pimsey, disgusting stuff. None of them know anything." Besita's mouth settled into its usual pout.

"Your Majesty continues to look strong and well regardless of such suffering. My heart goes out to you, Lady."

Besita sniffed, then looked back. This girl was Lessis's creature, but at times she did seem to have a little empathy. More than that ancient hag had ever shown.

"And I have no wine or brandy to help my poor soul in these terrible times."

"Yes, Your Majesty. I know. Unfortunately that cannot be. You are too vital to your people."

"Vital? You say that, but here I am, cast out to Rinz at the first hint of trouble. Then I hear nothing. I am starved for information. I tremble to think of the horror going on in the city, but no one will tell me anything. Am I the queen in my own house or am I not?"

"Of course you are, Your Majesty. I bring you greetings from the Lady Lessis."

"I would have expected nothing else. You have always been the messenger of the War Bird. Always bringing her unwelcome invasions of our lives."

Lagdalen frowned, but bit her tongue and made no response. The queen studied her for a moment.

"So? What is it this time, girl?"

Lagdalen passed Besita the scroll. She snapped it open and read it in a single glance.

"All right, I will order all stocks of chrysanthemum petals to be made available. The chancellor will draw up the necessary royal order."

The queen's voice had changed. The whine had gone out of it. Lagdalen wondered if Lessis had put a spell on the scroll itself, but in fact Besita was suddenly recovering hope. The doom-cloud of the plague no longer covered all the sky, and she had found new strength in that news.

"Tell me, dear, what was it like in the city when you left?"

"Ah, Lady, it was piteous to see. So many dead and dying. Fish Hill is empty of people now. All the harbor area is filled with the dying. There won't be many fishermen left when this is over."

"Terrible, terrible, I ache for the people. How I wish there was something more I could do for them."

The queen rang her bell. An aide appeared and brought her a scroll, pen, and ink. Besita wrote her instructions to the chancellor, then rolled and sealed the scroll with wax, impressing her ring to it.

"You may as well take this order back with you. I presume that is what you expected to do?"

"That would be the optimum thing to do I think, Your Majesty."

"Optimum" was it, now? Besita pursed her lips.

"We will have to fumigate the whole city," continued Lagdalen. "I doubt there will be enough chrysanthemum for that."

Besita nodded, thinking carefully. "Every city will be needing it, too. The price will shoot sky-high. The merchants will be very angry when we deny them the opportunity to make the maximum profit."

Lagdalen was shocked by the thought that the merchants would even think to make a profit from such circumstances.

"Your Majesty, surely no one would seek to take advantage of this dire distress to enrich themselves."

Besita favored the child with a weary smile.

"My dear, there are always a few who will stoop to any depths to make a profit. You will see. There will be great pressure for a while on this issue." Besita knew about pressure. It came all the time when you were queen. Every interest wanting something, often something they should not have. "But we will stand firm. The merchants will be paid in full, but only the price they would have got before the plague struck."

"That is fair enough, Your Majesty."

She chuckled. "Oh yes, we think so, but not everyone will agree."

"How quickly can fresh stocks be obtained?"

"I think very quickly. Minuend is the chief commercial producer of pyrethrins. Even as we speak we can rest assured that an enormous effort is being made down there to send out shipments of all they can find."

Besita rose to her feet.

"Come, Lagdalen, walk with me and tell me of your family. I will have some tea sent up. And you should eat something, of course." Besita rang again, and a servant took her request. She turned back to Lagdalen.

"Now, how is your father, that wonderful man, Tommaso Tarcho?"

Lagdalen dutifully accompanied the queen in a leisurely stroll down the belvedere to the far end, where they went down the steps and into the exquisitely complex flower garden that lay below.

Yellow spikes of foxglove rose above pink towers of lupines, while carnivolva and bellusa threw clouds of white and yellow florets across the ground. Stabs of purple from juice lilies broke through the dark green foliage of the esmerelda.

Lagdalen barely noticed this wild summer display, so concerned was she about getting back to the city as swiftly as possible. Every minute might mean the saving of lives. Also there was the matter of a fresh horse. Beety was worn out from riding so hard from the city.

To her surprise she found that Besita was also thinking about these things.

"I have a good horse for you, very fast and very strong. His name is Hero, I will have him prepared for you."

"I thank you, Your Majesty, as does Marneri."

"If only I could do more in this time of need. I feel cut off from everything out here."

Lagdalen knew that the queen had insisted on leaving the city when she heard that plague had broken out. She made no mention of this, however. Besita's pride was a delicate thing.

Tea was brought to them at the edge of the lawn. Servants brought chairs, a table, tea, and a slice of hunt pie for Lagdalen. Eagerly she accepted both. The pie was good, freshly made and rich with meat and onions.

While she ate, the queen talked about more pleasant things: the gardens, her horses, and her plans for the future. Lagdalen was encouraged by the queen's display of fortitude. It seemed she had given up her habit of drinking to excess whenever she was faced with a crisis.

Soon the young aide came running up. The horse was ready. Lagdalen bade the queen of Marneri farewell.

Hero was an immense animal, black and ferocious. Lagdalen's heart quailed a bit at the sight of him. He looked strong, but he might be a handful to control.

Hero eyed her and snorted loudly then shook his head vigorously as if to assert that he would not be an easy ride. Lagdalen stood there a moment considering him.

"Is he going to give me trouble?"

"Oh, no, Lady, Hero's a happy horse. He'll run for you, won't you, Hero?"

Hero flared his nostrils and whinnied. Lagdalen was not reassured, but when the boy gave her a leg up and she swung into the saddle the horse responded perfectly.

"Go light on the reins, Lady, he won't give you any trouble."

She flicked him with the crop and they were through the stable gates and out on the city road. Hero soon showed his mettle and settled into a steady swift canter that ate up the miles. As they drew closer to the city Lagdalen tried to keep the dread out of her heart. The charnel wagons were still in motion, still bringing out the dead. The bell atop the distant tower of the temple seemed to ring out the dying of the white city.

At the gate the guards were muffled in tight clothing, another precaution against fleas bearing disease. They stayed clear of any wagons coming out of the gate. Not very many people were going into the city on this day.

Lagdalen rode in with just a nod and a hail. They recognized her at once.

At the inner gate to the barbican she was hailed once more and given a cursory inspection. The guards there were also wrapped tightly in puttees, with long gloves.

She found her way immediately to Lessis's chamber, arriving a little out of breath with the scroll from the queen.

She found Lessis hard at work with the Birrak and the tomes on spellsay as she practiced the Flea Spell. Fleas were unusually difficult creatures to control.

Four young witches were hunched over their Birraks, reciting and memorizing. Lessis left them and came to Lagdalen.

"My dear. You were very swift. I thank you."

"Is there anything else, Lady?"

"Not now. Rest."

Lagdalen left Lessis's chambers and went down several floors of the great tower to the Tarcho apartments, where she found Hollein waiting for her. She collapsed in his arms with a glad sigh.

Chapter Twelve

The men and women of the Ennead cities continued the struggle against the plague, volunteering despite the knowledge that most of the first wave of workers had succumbed to the plague and nearly all had died.

The forest elves, with their mysterious origins in their sacred groves, were much less at risk from the plague. Many came out of their workshops with trained ferrets, joined with gangs of men who brought their dogs, and together they began an intensified assault on the rat population in the crowded alleys of Fish Hill and dockside.

This was where the gates of hell were wide-open. Where vomit coated the streets and the stench of death hung over everything. There were still bodies in there; some of the older tenements were warrens of small rooms and cubbyholes, where poor folk lived crowded sometimes two or three to a room. Death had swept through their number like a scythe through the corn. Now the stench of the bodies rose in the hot air. The ratters checked their cuffs and seams and tightened their collars even more. One bite from a tiny flea could be a mortal wound.

The wagons rumbled through the streets, bearing away the dead. The bell of the temple rang gloomily as funeral ceremonies were held for one notable after another. The charnel pits began to fill.

In the wake of the rat-killing teams came the cleaners, men and women, armed with brooms, mops, shovels, and scrapers. They brought with them a stench of soap and bleach.

Every four hours the funerals stopped and the bell of the temple rang for service, summoning the faithful to prayer. But for many it sounded like the hollow tocsin of death, ringing over an increasingly empty city.

Still the plague continued to find new victims, and the frantic struggle went on.

Soon fires were set in every possible grate, and thick smoke was made by adding piles of damp leaves. Among the leaves were burned chrysanthemum flowers and the smoke was bitter and acrid and filled the city with its stench. But, as was often remarked, at least it helped to cover the more noisome stink of putrefaction.

Wielding brooms and shovels, brushes and fans, the people attacked the old tenements, cleaning out filth and dirt wherever it lay. To stop the plague in its tracks you had to annihilate the flea population, and that was where it bred.

Day and night there burned great piles of bedding and clothing, carpets and rubbish. Through the hellish flickering light, by lantern and torchlight, the teams worked on, raising the dust of decades and digging out every rattery in the city.

Dragonboys, of course, knew about rat killing and they knew about fleas and that you could get fleabit real bad when you killed out a nest of rats. So they went in wearing tight clothing, gloves and grease on their faces. This had kept casualties among them to one, a youngster named Arnol. Curf was now managing his dragon, Wout.

The great wyverns were employed for digging the charnel pits and a certain amount of demolition work on Fish Hill, where they pulled down old warehouses. Beyond that there was not much call upon them. Mostly they stayed in barracks, aware that disaster was in the air and restless as a result. Of course, the dragonboys were exhausted at the end of their shifts with the ratkillers and had little energy to spend on dragons.

Relkin had become one of the smoke men. He lit fires in the downstairs fireplaces and stoves, getting them hot with kindling, then he damped them down to make them smoke furiously. Then they threw on dried chrysanthemum flowers and sent up a toxic cloud of smoke that permeated through the rooms above.

When the building was smoked out, then the cleanup crews would go in.

Relkin had made more than a hundred fires and smoked at least half of the houses afterward when he had to give up and take a rest. His lungs were hurting from the smoke, and his eyes were weeping and red. He reported to the sergeant in command of the smoke team, who gave him leave to recover.

He turned his weary legs up the hill. The tower loomed there at the top, normally a symbol of the strength of the great city. Now it seemed diminished, shrunken somehow, despite its bulk. A new kind of weapon had bypassed it in the night. For all its high walls and defensive engineering, it had been helpless.

Passing shuttered shops, he came up the street to the intersection with Foluran Hill, and paused while two heavy carts rolled around the corner from Tower Street. The plague had found its way here that very day. Now, the families of the Hill were sending all their clothing and bedding out for burning, just like everyone else. Teams of privately hired cleaners were at work in most of the big houses.

He crossed the road and as he stepped back on the pavement he was accosted by a woman with staring eyes and long gray hair gone wild around her head. She wore an expensive robe and silvery shoes.

"Please, young sir, you must help me. For the love of the Mother, you must help me."

"What's the problem, Lady?"

"It is my mother. She is terribly ill."

"You want the doctors then, Lady. I'm just a dragonboy."

"No, you don't understand. It is her mind that is unwell. She's up on the roof, and she's threatening to kill herself. She listens to no one." The woman broke into sobs, but put out a hand to him. "The poor lady is unhinged. It is most piteous to see."

Relkin chewed his lip.

"Oh, please, kind sir, help me in this most desperate hour."

He sighed. "What do you expect me to do?"

"Speak to her, plead with her."

"Why would she listen to me?"

"I think she will. Please just come quickly."

She led him up Foluran Hill to a tall house on the north side of the street. Within the house they met a frightened servant woman, wringing her hands as she dried them on her white apron.

"She is still up there, madame, still talking."

"Thank you." The woman looked at Relkin, then looked up the staircase.

"On the roof, you said?"

"Yes, young sir. I'm sorry, I completely forgot to ask your name."

"Relkin, Lady, of the 109th Marneri."

An expression of shock spread over her face. She stepped back and put her hand up to her mouth. Relkin hesitated, taken aback.

"Are you all right, Lady?" Receiving no response, Relkin headed up the stairs. There were six floors to climb. The first three staircases were broad and made of stone. The upper three were narrower and entirely of wood. By the sixth flight Relkin was really feeling his exhaustion.

The door to the roof was open. A stream of words flowed on and on, from which he caught occasional phrases repeated over and over again, like snatches of prayer.

"The darkness is coming, the darkness."

"We must be vigilant, but it is too late."

"We are destroyed within our fortress."

Relkin stepped out. The wind had died, and the air above had darkened with the smoke of countless fumigations. Over all hung the stench.

A woman with a regal pose and long white hair braided with golden thread was standing by the gutter. Her hands were pressed together beneath her chin and she looked fixedly out into space. Below was a drop of six floors to the cobbles of Foluran Hill.

The houses on the far side of the street looked back in stony indifference. A few people had gathered down below, but tragedies were too common now for most people to take the time to stop and gawk.

Relkin took a breath, slid down the roof tiles, and got a footing on the outer course of bricks before the gutter.

The white-haired woman suddenly turned and looked at him.

"Who are you?" she said sharply.

Relkin kept his tone as even as possible. Being so tired that he was close to falling asleep on his feet helped a lot. "They asked me to help you. That's all, Lady." He approached her very slowly and held out a hand.

She pulled back and turned to the drop.

"The city is dying, and they don't know why."

"I'm just here to help," he said, and lowered his hand. She put up her hands as if to deny it.

"No. I cannot come back now." She threw out her hands toward the city. "Everything is gone, everything is dust and ashes. We are all dying."

"Not so, Lady."

"My boy Efen is lost. Taken to the Mother's Hand too soon. He was sent to Eigo, and he survived that. But he has not survived the black plague."

"Your son would not have wanted you to take your life. You can be sure of that."

"My son . . ." the woman sobbed. She wobbled on the brink, then steadied herself. "Efen served in the Legions like yourself. He was in the first rat team."

"He will be honored by his death, Lady. Marneri honors its dead. His name will go on the monument and be looked to for a thousand years."

Head slightly askew she looked at him quizzically.

"You are a dragonboy?"

"Yes, Lady. How can you tell?"

"Your boots, the bits of your real uniform that I can see. I know the Legions, child. My father was Commander of the Third Regiment, First Legion. I grew up in Dalhousie."

"Aye, Lady. I am a dragoneer. 109th Marneri is my unit."

"You have a sad face, child. You have seen a harsh side of life."

She was staring at him with a fixed expression. "I know, you see, I know what it was like. Efen saw battle and survived. I know what hell that is. I knew what you must have faced. Like my son, Efen, you have seen enough war."

"Yes, Lady."

She turned back to the drop.

"My son is gone. I see only the darkness."

"The city will need all of us before this is over. I think we will win."

She stared at him, not really focusing.

"What is your name, child?" she said.

"Relkin."

"Relkin? That is a Blue Stone name. Are you from Querc?"

"No, Lady, Quosh."

"I spent part of my youth camping in the hills around Quosh and Querc. That's wonderfully pretty country."

"Aye, Lady, that it is. And I hope to see it again before I die."

Her face sagged. "But now you are doomed. We are all to die."

"It is not ordained, Lady. The plague is spread by fleas. So we get rid of fleas. We know how to do that."

She stared at him. "No. We are doomed. I have seen it in the signs."

"Not so, Lady. We're stopping it. I heard the number of new victims had dropped to almost none in the past hour."

She shook her head. "How can this be?"

"We're winning the war, Lady. I been smoking out houses down on Fish Hill. That's why I'm so grimy and all. See these cuffs, so tight they hurt, and that's how my collar was too when I was down there. We wear knit helmets, too, and grease our faces. You don't want to be bit by any fleas down there. And they're quick, but we kill them all and the cleaners sweep them up and throw them on the fire."

She peered at him intently. "What are you? You are no simple dragonboy. There is something in your eyes that speaks to me; I do not know you and yet I feel this attachment."

"I would not lie to you, Lady. I am just Relkin of the 109th Marneri Dragons."

She leaned closer, trying to read something written in a script beyond her comprehension.

"What have you been? In other lives, I mean. Your aura is strange, child. You have been marked."

Relkin shivered. This he did not want to hear.

"Tell me, child, who are you?" She insisted.

Who indeed? He thought to himself. He'd been the Iudo Faex, he'd made love from the banks of the Oon to the twilight world of magic inhabited by Ferla. He'd felt the hand of the mind mass press upon him.

"I am just a dragoneer, ready to sleep, Lady."

She stared at him blankly for a moment, and a new expression came over her face softening it.

"You never knew your mother, did you, child?"

"Correct, Lady. I never knew my mother or father." A bastard, an orphan, the unwanted, Relkin had lived his life with these designations.

"Poor child, what a life you have led."

By the gods, thought Relkin, there was something in what she said. But the Lady was no longer peering into the drop. Relkin hoped that was a sign of progress.

"Efen died here, you see. His wife died, too. Now their children are orphaned."

"The worst is over, Lady. We will win."

"No, the worst will be later. When we weep over our dead."

She said this, but she turned and wrapped her arms around him and sobbed on his shoulder while they teetered on the outermost course of bricks. Moving very carefully, he backed up and started the climb up the slates, holding on to the woman all the way to the door that led back into the house. She came without protest, and proved quite agile enough.

"We will take a glass of wine and some biscuits. That is what we must do," she said, pausing in the doorway.

"Anything you like, Lady," he murmured. Just go through the door, he willed her.

With a last look at the roof, she went in.

He followed her down to the first floor, where she rang a gong and bade him seat himself at a long table in a room lined with magnificent tapestries.

"Rest here, child. I am sure you are very weary."

Relkin sat down with a groan.

The woman disappeared in the direction of her kitchen A few minutes later a servant brought almond biscuits and sweet white wine. She found Relkin already asleep, slumped over the table, his head on his arms.

Chapter Thirteen

He awoke and for a long moment thought he was still dreaming. He was in heaven—naked and freshly bathed and lying under fine cool linen in a huge, soft bed. Someone had even shaved him.

A chill ran through him. Heaven? Or was this how one awoke in the Halls of Gongo? Had he joined the legions of the dead?

He spread his hands out. The linen was very smooth. After a moment it began to feel too real, too cool. He sat up and found himself in a large, well-appointed bedroom with walls freshly painted white, and black oak beams and doors. There was a piece of fine Marneri lace on the back of the sitting chair which told him he was still in the city. Gongo, although Lord of the Dead, wouldn't bother with touches like that. There was a blue-cloth rug on the floor, too, which confirmed his continuing mortality.

The feel of smooth linen on his bare skin was a very unusual, very pleasant sensation. Normally he slept wrapped in a blanket in a cot set high up the wall in the dragon's stall. In the field he slept on the ground or in a hammock strung between trees. This was astonishing.

Then he blushed. Someone had bathed him and put him to bed the previous evening. He'd slept through it all and then right through the night until the first rays of the morning. Someone had bathed him and shaved him, and he'd never known about it.

There was no sign of his clothes. He wrapped himself in a sheet and tried the door. It opened easily, and he went through into a smaller room, lined with twin chests of drawers. His clothes, freshly laundered, were laid out on a small table.

As he dressed he wondered how he was going to explain being absent all night from the dragonhouse. He was sure Cuzo would have noticed. By the gods! they might have already posted an alarm and started a search for him. The trouble he was in had suddenly magnified itself to major proportions.

Another door led him out into a larger interior hall. Stairs took him down another floor, and there he was met by a servant woman wiping her hands on her apron. She was all smiles and welcome.

"Young Master, it is good to see you up and about, again. Can I get you some kalut? Cook has just boiled some."

Hot, steaming kalut sounded wonderful. And while he sipped it, he chatted with the servant woman, Elzer. He learned that the Mistress Selima had not yet risen and the Mistress Marda, the younger woman, had already left the house and gone to the temple.

Elzer had a cheery familiarity that made Relkin just a little embarrassed. The cook and Elzer were the only servants remaining in the house. Everyone else had fled the city.

He sipped the kalut, already thinking of how to play this roll of Caymo's dice. He would have to be open about it all with Cuzo. Explain and hope for the best. He was too clean and presentable to get away with claiming he'd slept in the streets.

"Uh, Elzer, tell me something. If I have to get a confirmation of the fact that I slept here last night, will you give it?"

"Well, of course, young Master. And it was me and the Lady Selima that put you to bed, so I well know you did sleep here. And the whole night through."

"Ah."

Elzer gave him a sweet smile. In truth she had much enjoyed bathing the young man. He had a beautiful body, albeit one that bore a lot of scars.

Relkin couldn't look her in the eye, suddenly struck with a strange bashfulness. He lived in an all-male world of dragonhouse and military unit. He had lived with women, but only in distant surroundings, such as the ruins of Ourdh or a boat on a river in the ancient jungle lands of Eigo.

Elzer patted his hand.

"Ur, well, thank you, Elzer."

"It was a pleasure, young Master."

He left the tall house and hurried up the hill. The guards nodded him through routinely, so he took it there was not yet a general hue and cry out for him.

Bazil was awake and in a bad mood. Worst of all, he was hungry.

"Ah," he said at the sight of Relkin. "So boy live!"

"Look, I'm really sorry. I fell asleep at this lady's house. I was just worn right out by the end there, yesterday."

Bazil snorted. He knew what Relkin had really been up to.

"Even in plague time you have to fertilize the eggs?" Truly humans were a sex-crazed species, driven far beyond dragons in this regard. The dragon rampant was a spectacular force of nature, but his ardor only lasted for a brief moment, a breath of great flame against the dark, then it was over. For the humans it went on and on, with enormous complications of emotion that Bazil had to struggle to comprehend. Dragon life was simpler in these areas.

"No, it wasn't like that."

The huge eyes just blinked at him, obviously in complete disbelief.

"Really. I was asked to help talk someone's mother down from the roof. She was going to jump to her death."

"That sounds like work for witches, not dragonboy."

"I was the best she could find."

"Search must have been short."

Relkin scratched his head under his cap. The dragon was well sulky, and he had a right to be. Dragons had to depend on dragonboys for everything when they lived within the Legion system.

"Look, I know I let you down. Things are a little confused these days, right?"

"Very. Dragon go hungry. This not right."

"Look, I'm sorry. I'm gonna get enough hell from Cuzo."

"That's absolutely correct," said a familiar and unhappy voice from just outside the stall. Cuzo stuck his head around the corner.

"I'd like a word with you, Dragoneer Relkin. You know where my office is."

"Yes sir! Dragon Leader Cuzo."

Cuzo disappeared. The whole horror was working out as if choreographed by his worst enemies. Relkin sighed. The Old Gods never made it too easy on you.

"So, you talk to woman on roof?" The wyvern was still angry.

"Right. And it worked. She decided not to throw herself off the roof."

"Then you fertilized her eggs?"

"No! She was an old lady." Relkin was aghast that the dragon could even think like this about him. Had he really been that much of a ladies' man? It didn't seem that way to him. The opposite, if anything

"Why that stop you? Nothing else ever seem to stop you before."

"Oh go ahead, kick me when I'm down. It helps."

"Bah. This dragon hungry."

"Yeah, right. Just a moment."

Relkin went to the galley and wheeled back a potcheen of stirabout. Then he went to see Cuzo for what promised to be an unpleasant little meeting, which it was. His fate hung with the ladies at that house on Foluran Hill. Cuzo would ask for a certification of his story. If it came through, then probably he would escape full censure.

He wandered back to the stall. The dragon had gone for some morning exercise, lifting half ton weights in the weight room. Relkin got about a minute to himself before dragonboys began drifting in to quiz him.

"So what was she like?" said Swane, never known for subtlety.

"She was about seventy years old, and her hair was as white as snow, if you really want to know. And I stayed there because I just fell asleep when I sat down. You remember yesterday, we worked all bloody day long. I just went out like a light. I woke up this morning."

"Where was this?"

"On Foluran Hill." Relkin told his story once again, noting to himself how implausible it sounded.

"A likely story," groused Swane. "You just don't want us to know what really happened."

"Hold on, you think I'd cheat on Eilsa? You know me better than that, Swane."

"The dragons know something about you. Must have come from the Broketail."

"Oh this is great. Now you believe dragon gossip. You know that's worthless."

"Come on, Relkin, everyone knows you. You must have been well taken care of, you're all clean and so are your clothes."

"It's like I keep telling you, I talked this old lady out of jumping from the roof. They were going to give me some food and something to drink. I just conked out as soon as I sat down."

When it became apparent that they wouldn't pry anything more out of him, they tired of the sport and went back to the ever-present topic of the plague.

The news overnight had been sensational. A complete cut off in cases for six hours . . . a few cases in the morning, but then no more. It looked as if the witches were right. The campaign against fleas was succeeding.

"Jak's back," said Swane. "What's it like up in Lost Buck Woods?"

"They're still digging. I heard there's ten thousand buried up there so far."

"By the Hand," muttered someone.

"Well I can tell you this," said Manuel. "There's not a flea left alive in the dragonhouse."

"Hey, not that many left in the whole city by now," Curf chipped in.

"I bet there are some. There are always going to be some," groused Endi.

"But the plague has stopped . . ."

Cuzo's voice cut through the conversation, calling them to a parade. The day's assignments had come down.

With sighs and groans they tumbled out and formed up.

* * *

The rest of that day was much like the one before. They worked over the lower parts of the city eliminating rats and smoking out houses. When they finally could take no more they were sent back to take care of their dragons and then sleep.

Thus it went for three more days, by which time there had been no new cases of the plague for two whole days. It was over.

The black plague had been stopped in its tracks in Marneri, but there had been a loss of 13,155 poor souls, most of them buried in the huge charnel pits in Lost Buck Woods. Another 9,406 were infected, but survived the disease, though many of those died within a year or two.

After a citywide ceremony the monument to the dead was begun in Lost Buck Woods. Another was begun on the row of monuments which decorated the parade ground before the Tower of Guard. On it would be engraved the names of those who had died in the effort to stop the plague. Among the names would be that of Efen of the House of Debune.

And life went on. The tenements of Fish Hill and dockside were pulled down, and city planners began to work on their ultimate dream, clearing away the whole warren of slums and putting new commercial avenues through that would allow for expansion of the mercantile areas of Broad Street and Tower Street.

Marneri had taken a heavy blow, but had shrugged off the worst aspects and stood there with head unbowed.

Elsewhere in the Enniad cities the plague was also brought under control. It took longest in Kadein, of course, where more than a hundred thousand bodies were interred in ten enormous pits dug along the Kadein-Minuend road.

Ryotwa and Vo, both of which had been spared the plague, produced an unprecedented outpouring of resources to help the stricken cities. From Vo ships went to Vusk and Talion. From Ryotwa help was sent to all the southern cities, even to Marneri despite the legacy of hard feelings that still existed in Ryotwa toward the larger city on the Long Sound.

In the summer night Lessis the Gray Witch stood with Lagdalen on the moor outside Marneri. The bodyguard Mirk hovered in the darkness of the trees behind them. Standing under the lantern at the mile marker, they awaited the arrival of the witch Krussa. In the near distance glowed the lights in Lost Buck Woods.

"The news is good, Lady?" said Lagdalen, as Lessis rolled up the tiny scroll she'd been reading.

"Yes. The plague is over in Minuend. No new cases have been reported in three days."

"Thanks be given for that. The Mother has heard our prayers."

"But this was a warning. Our enemy struck with a deadly weapon, and we were almost overcome."

"He has a long head start in this evil kind of work." Lagdalen shivered. "Waakzaam has not finished with us. We must be ready for his next blow."

Chapter Fourteen

Once more Relkin walked into the high court of Marneri. By the Gods, he thought, but he'd spent too much time in this place.

It had started with the long trial for the killing of Trader Dook up on the Argo River. Then there'd been the long-drawn-out proceedings concerning Porteous Glaves, the former Commander of the Eighth Regiment of the Second Legion. Now he was on trial himself once more on the serious charges of looting the fallen city of Mirchaz.

Looting was regarded as a serious offense, although the provision was relatively obscure, number 545 in the Legion Rule Book. It came long after such important items as theft of camping equipment, or spoliation of cavalry sawdust.

Five hundred and forty-five, "the illegal possession of stolen goods gained in theft during a period of service abroad." Such service was a rare event in a soldier's life in the army of the Argonath, which perhaps explained the low priority given to such a regulation.

There were other charges, which came under the Legion's laws of financial regulation, concerning the accounts he had opened at the Royal Land Bank of Kadein during a brief stay in the big city. These charges, however, were lesser ones and unlikely to be pressed if the first charge was denied.

As he took his place on the front bench he noted the wry look he got from the Usher. They knew him all right. Here he was again, the famous scapegrace Relkin. Innocent on murder charges in his first trial. Dragon testimony got him off. The law itself had been changed as a result of that case. Dragon testimony was now taken in many kinds of cases. But now he was back, and this time it looked like the prosecutors had got him cold. They had an admission of guilt. The Ushers and the Guards ran a finger down their collective nose; once a criminal, always a criminal.

Lagdalen came in and sat down just behind him. They had prepared him thoroughly for the trial. Lagdalen had chosen the Lady Bertonne as his barrister: she would speak his case and conduct the examination of witnesses. Lagdalen preferred to prepare the case, but not to argue it. Very few advocates were as good as Bertonne. She was expensive, but well worth the cost.

Quite a few people filed in and took seats in the courtroom. Relkin's case had aroused some interest, it seemed. There were one or two older men identified with the Aubinan cause. They had not committed treasonous acts and were thus still free, but their sympathies were known. They sat toward the back.

Just behind Lagdalen were a couple of dragonboys. The cast of dragonboys would change through the day, but there would always be one or two of them there. The 109th wanted to have its own observers on this trial. They had a vested interest in it after all. King Choulaput had given the gold to set up retirement funds for all the dragons who had campaigned in Og Bogon. There were two thousand gold pieces at stake, a sizable fortune.

The military prosecutor for the case was Captain Plake, a smooth-voiced man with olive complexion and a bright, artificial smile.

Relkin looked up to the polished wood of the judge's bench as the door opened and the judge appeared.

For a moment it failed to register in his brain, and then he realized that the face under the judge's cap was that of Marda Debune, the woman who had approached him on the street and begged him to speak to her mother.

He was stunned. He recalled that look she had given him when he'd told her his name. She'd looked as if she'd seen a ghost. She'd known then that he would come before her in the court.

Judge Marda did not make eye contact with him. She acknowledged only the advocates as she gaveled the court into session.

The advocates rose, and the oath was spoken by the sergeant of the court. Prosecutor Plake moved to have the court take up the case of the Legion versus Dragoneer Relkin of the 109th Marneri.

In support of this request the prosecutor produced a copy of what it termed the defendant's "confession." In fact, it was the Customs Form that Relkin had filled out on his return from Eigo, listing all the gold except for a handful of tabis that he'd had the foresight to keep secret. If only he'd listened to the dragon, he would've never told them about any of the tabis. They hadn't even searched him for contraband when he stepped ashore in Kadein. He could have smuggled that gold through easily. But no, he had to go and fill out the forms and get himself into this nightmare situation.

Prosecutor Plake continued in his presentation in a deceptively bland manner and style.

"We already have the defendant's own testimony to the effect that this gold is loot. Thus there is no reason to put off any further the inquiry into the crime."

Bertonne was quick to rise and to approach the judge's bench.

"Your Honor, the prosecution has neglected to mention many pertinent facts. They have done so in a way that I find disheartening, even dishonest, and certainly disreputable. I must ask why the presentation was skewed so oddly. For instance, only a part of the gold in the defendant's possession is claimed to be loot. The majority of the gold was freely given by the King of Og Bogon. And we shall enter as evidence his letter to that effect. This letter was shown to the prosecution weeks ago, so their failure to mention it is even more astonishing. One can only conclude that before any evidence has been presented they seek to blacken my client's name and prejudice the court against him."

Judge Marda had a thin humorless smile.

"Yes, Bertonne, I rather imagine that Captain Plake has been painting an overly dire picture of the situation. Still, that does not answer the question he poses. Why shouldn't the trial begin on the gold that is admitted to have been looted?"

Bertonne compressed her lips for a moment and smoothly changed track.

"Indeed, my lady, such questions abound in this case. Some of them we hope to answer, such as why this case has even been pursued in the first place.

"Furthermore we shall prove that though Relkin did take the gold tabis from the house of an elf lord in the city of Mirchaz, he regarded it as payment for services rendered. We are also confident that in time we shall have a signed statement from the current government of Mirchaz that will officially designate the gold tabis as payment to the defendant and his dragon, the Broketail of the famous 109th squadron."

"In time? What does that mean? Please explain, Advocate Bertonne."

"Mirchaz lies at the end of the world, you understand, Your Honor. Our first messenger perished on the route and never reached the city. Our second messenger sent word from Eigo that he was traveling south by sea from Sogosh and hoped to round the Cape of Winds by the end of last month. It will take longer for him to reach Mirchaz itself. He must then return with the reply of the rulers of Mirchaz."

"We could be waiting for a year or more."

"That is possible."

"Do we even know who these rulers of Mirchaz are?"

"No, Your Honor, we do not."

"Thank you, Advocate Bertonne. Indeed, there are many questions to be answered in this case, and I hope that we shall see some answers before it is over. However, by his own testimony before me, the defendant did identify part of the gold as loot. We are dealing, therefore, with an immediate plea of guilty, are we not? Therefore, there is no reason not to have the trial on that charge begin at once. The regulation is clear."

Behind him, Lagdalen sucked in a deep breath.

"Therefore, I find in favor of the prosecution. Trial to be held shortly, at the whim of the trial calendar. Speak to my office to set a date."

Judge Marda looked up and nodded brightly to the advocates.

"Court is adjourned." The gavel fell.

Relkin shook his head slowly. So much for any help from the mighty Debune family. He might have saved Marda's mother, but the judge wasn't going to do him any favors.

Outside the court Lagdalen tried to be consoling, but he could see that she was worried.

"Judge Marda was harsher than we had hoped. She has always seemed a sympathetic judge in cases involving dragonboys before. I had hoped she would see our point."

"Now there'll be a trial?"

"Yes. And we have to prepare our defense without any message from Mirchaz concerning your innocence. The judge will demand that we plead guilty. Her mind seems made up, at least."

"If we plead guilty?"

"Then we would go straight to sentencing. It could be anything up to ten years hard labor on the Guano Isles."

Relkin shivered. Ten years of digging birdshit off those rocky islands and living on gruel and onions.

Lagdalen rallied and tried to raise his spirits, but it was an unequal task. He left her at the door to her office on Water Street and made his way up the zigzag on the hillside to the dragonhouse.

While Relkin made his way unhappily back to the dragonhouse, he was not the only one concerned about his legal problems. In fact at that very moment he was the subject of discussion by four very important personages, on a high place far in the east.

In the Imperial city of Andiquant, on the Isle of Cunfshon stands the Tower of Swallows, a graceful structure known to mariners across the world.

Atop the Tower of Swallows the greatwitches met in conclave. Presiding was the oldest of the old, Ribela, the Queen of Mice. Beside her sat Lessis, the Queen of Birds. Irene, Queen of Oceans wore her usual brown tweeds, and beside her the mystic Belveria, one of the Queens of the Higher Air, who wore a simple white surplice and gown. Irene maintained a separate Office of Inquiry from that of the Unusual Insight, with informants placed in every major port around the world. Belveria worked under Ribela's direction in the gathering of information concerning the higher realms and the worlds beyond.

Irene and Belveria were not as familiar with Relkin of Quosh as the older greatwiches, but they knew all about his troubles with the law.

"He has been charged with looting," said Irene in a prim voice.

"Ah, yes," murmured Ribela. "He is a fairly larcenous sort, our young hero. He is a dragonboy after all." Ribela's relations with Relkin had lasted almost as long as Lessis's, and had included the most bizarre of interpenetrations. Since her near death in Eigo she had exhibited signs of emotional conflict whenever she spoke his name. Lessis had long wondered what it meant. Something had happened in Eigo, something connected with the appearance of the liberated gestalt mind of the mind mass of Mirchaz. But that was all she knew, and Ribela would not discuss it in any detail.

"Indeed," murmured Irene. "It would be silly to expect a saint to survive in the legions."

"This one has been marked, we all know that," said Lessis.

"They want him, that is certain," confirmed Belveria.

"So he cannot serve a sentence on the Guano Isles."

"No, he must be brought here and kept out of sight while we work with him to try and understand these things that have happened to him."

Lessis said this with the sad knowledge that she was passing a sentence of sorts on poor Relkin. His life would be snatched away despite his ability to survive so many perils.

"Can we use the sentence to hard labor as the justification for keeping him here?" wondered Irene.

"If we have to, yes. The emperor will order it so if necessary."

The emperor, too, knew this particular dragonboy.

"Is this what they want?"

"Who can say?"

"With the Sinni, it is not our place to say." Belveria's frank use of the name of the High Ones brought stares from the others.

"They are preoccupied. The Dominator threatens them. He knows they have violated the ancient convenant."

"He has violated it himself and far more grossly."

"True. That has never mattered to Waakzaam the Great."

"Say not that name in this place," muttered Lessis, casting a spell of dispersal.

They nodded quietly.

"The plague was his work, we are certain of it."

"The plague has been met and defeated," said Irene.

"The cost was high," Lessis replied. . . .

"It never reached our islands, praise be to the Mother," said Belveria.

"No ship from the Argonath was allowed to dock here," said Irene. "And we instituted the most extreme clean out of rats and fleas ever seen."

"Great business for the brush makers," murmured Lessis. In her hometown of Valmes there was a large brushmaking firm. They had taken on two dozen workers to cope with the sudden boom in demand.

"Good exercise for everyone, too, I'm sure," said Ribela with a thin smile.

"All his work," said Lessis. "His shadow still hangs over us. Whatever is happening in the higher realms, he will return to us before the end."

"What do we know of his whereabouts?"

"He remains in Haddish. But some emanation of his has penetrated the high planes quite recently. This is what has upset the High Ones."

"Will we know if he comes to Ryetelth?"

"Not at first, but in time his absence from Haddish would be noticeable."

"We cannot detect him here?" wondered Irene.

"Not at a distance, not without knowing where he might appear."

"In Padmasa, I would imagine," said Belveria.

"Then we might have word," said Lessis. "Our network is restored in the Masters' dreadful realm. If the Deceiver were to return there, we would know quite soon."

"But we cannot have agents in all the possible places that he might choose to appear on our world, so in all likelihood he will return before we know he is here."

"And then?"

"A good question. We must try and anticipate his next move."

"It is a great pity that we could not eliminate him entirely in the fighting at the Manse of Wexenne."

"A great pity," agreed Lessis, who recalled that the dragon was very close to slaying Waakzaam just before his escape. "We came close, very close. He will not have forgotten that, either."

Chapter Fifteen

⌒⌒⌒

The 109th Marneri had completed another month of duty at Camp Dashwood, cutting and hauling timber from the wood-lots. By the time they started back to Marneri they were an inch or two lighter in the waistband department and a degree firmer all over their bodies.

They swung down the road at a strong Legion pace that ate up four miles an hour, hour after hour, through dust and rain and a sharp little wind that blew in through the morning and tapered off by noon. At the crossroads by Rinz they met a cavalry detachment heading the other way, and they exchanged a crisp salute with the troopers.

Relkin noted the frowns here and there among the riders. The cavalry disliked ceding the prime role on the battlefield to the dragon squadrons and the infantry, and sometimes there were "moments of conflict" between the two arms of the service. It was usually out back of a brewhouse, and troopers and dragoneers would go at it barefisted. This didn't work well for dragon-boys since they were younger and smaller for the most part, but now and then there'd be one like Rakama and the situation would change. It was a tradition of sorts throughout the Legions.

The dragons themselves were indifferent to the presence of the cavalry, except for the Purple Green, who was eyeing the horses with another thought in mind.

Perhaps because they could sense his interest, the horses were nervous, even though they were trained to tolerate dragons in close proximity. The skittishness of their mounts upset the troopers, who wanted to pass the dragons as casually as possible. Dragonboys grinned rather obviously at the horsemen and received stony stares in return.

When the horses were past, the 109th were ordered forward by Cuzo, and they resumed the march, soon passing the entrance to the Royal Hunting Lodge in Rinz Park. On the order they went by with eyes left and their best parade march.

The sleepy guards at the gate stiffened hurriedly to return the salute. Off through the trees they could glimpse the white columns of King Adem's old house. It was well-known that the queen had passed the plague time at her house here. In the city this was accepted as both inevitable and a little sad. The queen was not much loved by her people.

Later they passed the turnoff up to Lost Buck Woods and relived the memories of the nights of digging in the plague pits. Any merriment went out of their minds until they were well past the place.

Relkin thought it was a pity that the woods lay close to this road. It ruined this march for him, which they had made a hundred times or more over the years. It was a good march, accomplished in a single day, on mostly flat terrain and past several alehouses. If they kept up a firm pace they would usually get into Marneri in time for the dragons to have a huge dinner and a splash in the plunge pool afterward. For some reason this combination had always appealed to the great beasts, and they always kept to a brisk pace on the way back to Marneri. Now the march was tinged with the shadow of the plague.

But Relkin refused to dwell on the charnel pits, or the plague. He was thinking of Eilsa Ranardaughter, who would be back in the city now.

After the plague struck the cities she had moved to Widarf, where she had worked with the sisters of the temple caring for the sick and dying. Relkin gave thanks to the Old Gods, and also to the Great Mother that she had lived through it all. He knew only too well what hell she must have been through.

She had survived it all, and now she was back in Marneri for a short while, before undertaking the journey back to Wattel

Bek. She had been away from her home for far too long. Her elders were demanding that she return and take part in the life of the clan. She remained Ranardaughter, and therefore heir to the chieftaincy. Unless, of course, she married outside the clan, in which case it would pass to another branch of the family. Her cousin Derryn, most likely, would be chieftain.

Of course Eilsa would suffer an immense loss of status, and so would her close kin, who were all, therefore, very angry with her. She faced this with sorrow in her heart, but determination, also, to seek her own way. A way that included Relkin.

Relkin felt the forces that tore at her. He had felt the dislike, bordering on hate that came from her kin as a threat to their social standing. He knew how tormented she was by it all, but she stuck with him. For this he would have died for her willingly a thousand deaths.

Relkin had his guilty secrets. His love affairs, if that's what they were, with Lumbee and Ferla during his long sojourn in Eigo. He had never spoken of them with Eilsa, and she had never appeared to suspect anything of him. It was as if she believed that he was too pure of heart ever to have actually broken faith with her.

To Relkin's credit, the truth was nothing quite so stark, or black-and-white, and what had happened had come out of strange, unique circumstances. At the time, it seemed quite possible that if he survived at all, he would end his days lost in the heart of the dark continent. He would live among the Ardu folk, the tailed people of the remote jungle in the heart of the continent. His sense of dislocation and the tug of emotions in that time had simply overwhelmed him. He had made love to Lumbee and later to Ferla, the spirit queen of Mot Pulk's magic grotto.

Now it seemed as if it had all happened in another life.

He loved Eilsa more than ever, as a sinner loves the true saint. And he loved her for the way she was prepared to give up so much. Their plan had only grown stronger with time. They would wed in Marneri, then move to the Bur valley with the dragon and horses and hired workers and build their farm.

Unfortunately, Relkin might well be going to the Guano Isles for the next ten years.

The 109th marched in with a fairly crisp salute to the gate guards, arriving at the dragonhouse with a mighty whoop. Dragons tucked into their food while beer was rolled out. Dragonboys saw to the stowing of kit and equipment and then grabbed their own dinners. Relkin took a loaf of bread as he headed out the door. He ate on the move and reached the top of the zigzag on Water Street with just the heel of the loaf left. He ate the rest while going down hill at a clip.

Fortunately Eilsa had many excuses for visiting Lagdalen's law office. Aunt Kiri would sit in the anteroom while she met Relkin in Lagdalen's inner office. It was the only place they could ever be alone together.

Relkin jogged half the way and rapped on the door with mounting excitement. The door opened and a leathery-faced guard looked him over carefully, then motioned him inside.

Relkin was glad to see that security had improved since the days of the Aubinan rebellion.

Eilsa was waiting for him in her clan tweeds and square-cornered hat. She tossed the hat into a chair when he came in, and they fell into each other's arms with a tigerish embrace.

Aunt Kiri frowned and groaned and began praying, as much to distract herself as to affect them.

When the emotion had subsided a little he found his voice.

"I missed you," he said.

"So much," she replied with tears in her eyes.

This time the embrace lasted even longer. Aunt Kiri was forced to count rosary beads while she prayed for the Mother's protection for this wayward girl she was trying to protect. At length they gave it up.

"Oh, Relkin, my dearest, what are we going to do?"

The trial date loomed just two weeks away.

"We fight the case. Maybe the gods will finally look down on me with favor and we'll get justice."

"They should have waited. There is still no word from Mirchaz."

"Nor will there be this year."

Eilsa, while overjoyed to see Relkin all in one piece, indeed as healthy-looking as ever, was burdened by the thought of the trial.

"And you helped that woman, too," she hissed. "You helped her get her own mother to come down from the roof, and she repays you by unfairly opening the trial too soon."

"Yeah, well she's a judge. I suppose she has to be above kindness."

"So far above it, for I know you are innocent. How could they send you away for ten years for this, without even letting all the evidence be heard?"

"It might not actually be ten years."

"But you will virtually have to plead guilty. They say you admit taking some of the gold. That constitutes looting."

"When I saw those gold tabis just sitting there in the smashed-up wall of Mot Pulk's house I thought it had to be a gift from the gods. Now I think it was perhaps a curse."

Lagdalen appeared at that point and brought them some good news. The judge had agreed to hear a motion to put the trial on hold until a higher court could rule on the question of whether the trial should wait until a message had been brought back from Mirchaz.

"We have many grounds for appeal, I'm glad to say. The judge recognizes that there's a chance of that, so she will be reasonable and let the high court examine this decision."

"Will the high court be any better?"

"I hope so. It's hard to be certain, but I think two of the judges are likely to rule in your favor. Ronymuse will not, of course, but he is Aubinan. This kind of sneak attack, which is all this trial is, is all that's left for them to do at this point."

"Have you heard anything from Aubinas lately? We don't get all the news up at Dashwood."

"Well there are small groups of rebels in the Running Deer valley. Porteous Glaves is loose and appears to be a leader of sorts, but for the most part Aubinas is at peace. Outside of Nellin there wasn't that much support."

"Do they campaign to have Wexenne pardoned?"

"No, they don't. Many of them realize they've been spared a terrible tyranny under the dread one that Wexenne awoke. There has been little concern expressed about Wexenne's sentence on the Guano Isles."

"For life?" said Eilsa.

"No hope of parole. Many wanted to see him hanged."

"Perhaps the emperor will pardon him someday."

"Perhaps, when he is very old. A great many lost their lives as a result of his foolishness."

"A foolish man, indeed," murmured Eilsa as she relived for a moment that terrible time during the rebellion.

"No man would willingly subject himself to Waakzaam except a fool."

Her listeners could only agree. They had not suffered directly as she had, but they had witnessed the cold malice of the Dominator. They had seen the rooms filled with tortured children, whom he used as laboratory animals. They understood what he would do to the world were he to gain possession of it.

Chapter Sixteen

On the road to Marneri's great Tower Gate a lean figure on a tall dark horse rode beside a black coach. A pair of drivers rode atop the coach, while the windows were shuttered and the doors were locked. The horseman had a thin face, dominated by a long, straight nose that reached down past his upper lip.

The rider was Higul, called the Lame since childhood. His limp was the result of a terrible beating from a cruel master. Two years later Higul slew that master in his barn, with his own pitchfork. Higul's early life lamed his spirit as well as his body, but spared his intelligence. He applied himself to crime with a cruel industry of purpose and by an early age had established himself in the criminal underworld of Kadein. Known for dealing out vicious beatings and causing people to "disappear," no trace of his victims was ever seen. The witches were said to be increasingly interested in him, which, of course, was not healthy in his line of work.

Then, one day, he was recruited to the service of the Master. A line was drawn across his life at that point. He had adjusted well to the loss of independence and dutifully educated himself in the nature of service to the great power. He was still free to indulge his hedonistic streak, but when called to serve he put himself completely into his work.

What the Master insisted on was absolute efficiency. Mistakes were unacceptable. Higul had seen others of his guild, for there were usually four or five of them, disappear suddenly. No questions were asked, and the Master never mentioned them again. Higul understood the rules.

This particular mission was extremely important, and Higul had taken great pains, traveling on back roads, often by night. Now with the walls in sight and guards at the gate, the city's formal defense systems were all that had to be dealt with, and that would be easy enough. The hook would soon be baited.

They were about a mile from the gate when Higul lifted his hand. The walls were visible in the distance, straight down the road. No buildings were allowed any closer to the city than this to maintain a clear field of fire for the catapults on the towers.

"All right, that's far enough." The coach came to a halt. Higul reined in his mount and scanned the road. No one was coming, though this close to the city that would not be the case for long.

The drivers got down and unlocked one of the doors, to the sounds of whimpering and a scrabbling at the wood. The door opened and a large, almost naked man, chained at the neck, clambered out, blinking in the light of the sun.

The drivers stood back, well clear.

Porteous Glaves stood there, the cords standing out in his neck, his eyeballs bulging, his mouth contorted but making no sound. Higul pointed to the long chain that hung from the collar around Glaves's neck, and one of the drivers picked it up and handed its end to the mounted man. Higul made a mental note to throw away his gloves when this task was completed.

"Do you want us to wait for you?" muttered the driver.

"No. Leave the coach. Take the horses and get out of here."

"Leave the coach? What for? It's worth money."

"Believe me, you won't want it. You won't want to have anything to do with it. It probably should be burned now."

The drivers had gone pale. "Plague?"

"I'd not say that again if I were you," said Higul. The Great One was capable of the most extraordinary feats of "farsightedness" as he called it. Higul had seen things since he'd undertaken the service of the Master that had challenged forever his concept of what was possible or not. And he'd seen men die for opening their mouths unwisely.

The drivers looked at each other for a moment, then began hurriedly releasing the horses from the stays.

Higul took a good grip on the long chain and spurred his mount forward toward the city. Glaves responded by breaking into a shambling run. The fool had to be delivered, and Higul wanted to make absolutely certain that he was. Failure was not acceptable.

As his horse trotted toward the city, he was careful to keep a good fifteen feet clear of Glaves. Security around Marneri's gates was fairly impressive, he noted. The spyglass teams scanned the road every so often, looking for signs of trouble. If they happened to be watching him at that moment, then they'd have picked up that he was hauling someone along on a chain. That was sure to draw their interest. So he was gambling that he could cross this last mile to the gates, riding alongside a fair amount of wagon traffic that would provide a little cover, without drawing a patrol.

Glaves stumbled and staggered along, and Higul was careful to keep his horse well clear of him.

Death to breathe his breath, was what they'd said. Death.

The minutes ticked by, and there was no sudden activity at the great gates up ahead. So far, so good. It appeared the men with the spyglass were not watching.

Near the city the road filled with traffic, drays and wagons for the most part. Higul tugged Glaves to the side of the road and trotted by on the grassed margin, bypassing the traffic. A few oaths and catcalls followed them from the wagons.

When he got close to the gate, the guards watched his approach with slit-eyed intensity. What they saw was not a normal sight in Marneri, where such aspects of slavery were illegal. They had already called for a couple of mounts to be sent up. Troopers had been summoned.

Higul rode right up to the guards. "Behold, I bring you the notorious Porteous Glaves,"

Higul pulled on the chain, and the witless figure of Glaves danced forward, red-faced from the exertion of running a mile.

"Get him behind bars where he belongs!" hissed Higul as he

tossed the chain to the nearest guard. The others had come forward with suspicious eyes, spears ready.

Porteous stared at them with an empty face, as devoid of intelligence as a sheep.

Higul turned his horse and spurred away, passing curious-eyed drovers and coach passengers, cantering at first and then pushing his horse for full speed. He galloped up the road, passed the coach, and carried on up the rise. He had a fresh horse waiting in Rinz, knowing that there was bound to be pursuit.

Behind him the guards had hustled Porteous into the guardhouse and sent for orders. He was then taken to the cells, processed, and put in solitary confinement in the tower.

Eventually a pair of troopers set out in pursuit of the rider who had brought in Porteous Glaves. There were questions for that gentleman that needed to be answered. The troopers pursued him vigorously, but they missed him at Rinz, and he lost them on a lane outside the town.

In the city the word that Porteous Glaves had been captured spread swiftly. Glaves had escaped the city at the beginning of the Aubinan rebellion, aided by traitors within the Legion. Since then he'd become one of the most wanted men in the Argonath.

On that day General Hanth was in command of the tower. He was notified within minutes of Glaves's arrest. He notified the legal officer to request a court hearing at once. In the meantime Hanth ordered the prisoner to be cleaned up, examined and fed, then read his rights under the Common Weal of Cunfshon, the basis for the rule of the law in the Empire of the Argonath. He was also to be allowed to consult with an advocate of his choosing.

Hanth almost went down to take a look himself, but family matters diverted him. His wife's aged parents were visiting that day from their country home. General Hanth was due to make an appearance for tea and scones. Hanth did not enjoy such occasions, but he endured them for the sake of family life.

On his way out, he paused for a moment, nagged by something that he'd forgotten to do. Then remembered the message from the Office of Unusual Insight that had come several weeks earlier. He scratched his chin, whirled back into his office, and quickly wrote out a message scroll and rang for an orderly.

"Take this to the Reverend Mother at the temple. Top priority. See that she has it in her hand within half an hour."

The orderly disappeared and Hanth set down his pen and gathered himself to face the ordeal of tea with Uril and Yaena.

While General Hanth was sitting down to a pot of tea with his parents-in-law, another drama was playing itself out in the bailey yard behind the stables.

A dragonboy was running from three men armed with rods and flails. He carried a guitar, which slowed him down a little. When he reached the end of the yard and turned for the gate, he was met by another man of hulking aspect who stepped around the corner and brought him down with a solid blow to the midriff.

Curf was doubled up and dumped on the ground. A second blow drove him onto his side. His guitar fell beside him. The other three men came up and took turns smashing the guitar over his body until it was in fragments. Then they kicked him for a while until he was thoroughly bloody and covered in mud.

"Remember this, you little bastard, you stay away from Emelia of the Radusa." The speaker was Rogo Radusa, a dark-faced, haughty young buck of the aristocracy and, at twenty-five, the oldest of the Radusa boys.

"Yeah, we catch you near our sister again, and we really will break your legs," said his cousin Evic, the second-in-command.

A watchman gave a shout from the far end of the yard.

"Uh, oh, here comes the watch," muttered Evic. "Better get out of here."

The young men were arrogant, but they knew better than to be apprehended by the watch. They ran through the gate and on into the long alley that lay between the northern wall of the dragonhouse and the south wall of the stables. The Radusans, Rogo, Evic, Big John, and Kale, the biggest of them all, sprinted for the doors set in that wall. Once there they would mount their horses and soon be back on Foluran Hill.

Taking the alley proved to be a mistake, however for the stable lads had passed the word to the dragonhouse. The young men in the stable were not fond of the young aristocrats from the House of Radusa.

The reception committee was waiting by the time the Radusa boys reached them. In the middle were Swane and Rakama, the biggest boys in the 109th Marneri. With them were most of the unit, excepting Relkin and Manuel, who would probably have disapproved of the whole thing. Swane didn't want to risk telling either of them.

"And where would you fellows be going with clubs and flails in your hands?" said Swane in an innocent voice as he planted himself in their way.

"Get out of my way, you damned orphan bastards!" snarled Kale.

"Oh, and aren't we the haughty men!" said Rakama with a slight smile.

"They think they can beat up a dragonboy from the 109th, and we're not gonna do anything about it," said Jak.

"You'll get yourself seriously hurt if you involve yourself in our affairs," warned Rogo.

"Now, now, don't come all high-and-mighty with us. You just dusted up our friend Curf. You can lower yourself to that, you can lower yourself to this."

Kale suddenly made play with his flail, a rod with iron chain. Swane and the others drew swords and dirks with a clatter of steel.

At the sight of steel in the hands of eight dragonboys, the Radusa boys hesitated.

"Yeah," said Swane. "You don't like that thought, do you?"

"You would hang."

"You wouldn't be there to see it."

The Radusa boys drew back a step. Dragonboys knew how to fight with edged weapons and they had no intention of getting gutted by these orphan bastards.

"That's right, you think about it. And then think about this. One of you has to fight one of us. Bare-handed. That's all."

Kale looked to Rogo and Big John. Their cousin Evic grinned. "One of you to fight Kale, eh?"

Kale was two inches taller than any of them and fifty pounds heavier.

"Who's it to be then?" he said, grinning evilly.

"Me," said Rakama, moving to the fore. Swane let him go without a word of comment. Though Swane had beaten Rakama in the one real fight between them, he had come to accept that in a fistfight, Rakama was the top boy in the unit. Rakama had also been the champion light-heavyweight boxer in the First Legion at the last Legion Games.

The Radusa boys didn't know about any of that.

Kale and Rakama pulled off their shirts and took their stances. Kale was a burly fellow with a hairy chest and massive round arms. Pug-nosed Rakama was sleek and highly toned with intense muscle definition on his upper body. Rakama had heft through the shoulders and back muscles that betrayed his power with a punch. His hands were already taped and now he pulled on a pair of lightly padded gloves.

They came together between the two sides.

Rakama was hunched low and kept constantly in motion, head moving from side to side, shoulders bobbing as he shifted around, measuring the bigger man.

Kale looked to grapple and bear the smaller youth down. Failing that, he would go for roundhouse punches and kicks to the lower part of the body.

Rakama bored in. Kale kicked at him and missed. Rakama tried a jab and scored a stinging blow to Kale's nose. The pain shocked and enraged Kale Radusa, who jumped forward swinging wildly with both hands. Rakama ducked, weaved right, and came up inside Kale's left arm to deliver a stunning left-and-right hand combination that rocked Kale and sent him staggering back into the wall of the stables.

The Radusa boys exchanged looks of consternation.

Kale shook his head and paced backwards, keeping out of Rakama's range. Then he feinted and swung a foot. Rakama seemed to fail to read it, standing there until the very last moment, then slipping aside like an eel. He came in close again and Kale tried to grab him by the wrist. Kale grasped only at air as the youth shimmered away from him while bestowing another stinging left-hand jab to his already battered nose.

They were apart once more. Kale was breathing hard, feeling blood flow freely from his nose while he shook his head to try and clear the pain.

For a moment or two they circled, then Kale tried to grapple again, throwing himself forward, only to catch a powerful uppercut to the chest and another straight right to the jaw.

Kale sagged sideways and went down on one knee.

Since they were not fighting by any recognized rules, Rakama could have leveled Kale with his boot, but he held off.

Kale took a full half minute to get back on his feet. He was a little unsteady now. His brothers shouted encouragement, but could not keep the uneasiness out of their voices.

Kale crouched low and angled in crabwise, looking to stay out of Rakama's range until he could get a hand on the dragonboy. Rakama circled Kale, then suddenly bounced forward and connected with a right hand to the jaw. Kale sat down hard. Rakama stood back, resumed his stance.

This time Kale came to his feet really mad. He was seeing double, but his anger overcame his caution. He lumbered toward Rakama and swung a haymaker with his right, missed and received two powerful shots in the belly. He spun away and took another jab that mashed his lips against his teeth.

Kale's temper evaporated in incandescent rage. He tried to hurl himself on Rakama, but the younger man seized his arm, turned, and threw Kale over his outstretched leg. The heavier boy went down with a cry and landed hard on his back. The air went out of his chest, and he struggled to breathe.

"The watch!" shouted a dragonboy from the stable end.

"Go!" shouted Swane. Boys melted back into the dragonhouse, pulling Rakama with them. Swane came after and pulled shut the gate before ducking through the pump-room door.

The men of the watch, a pair of stern-faced guardians of the law, approached at a run. Kale Radusa was dragged to his feet by his brothers and pushed into the saddle just as the constables of the watch came up close enough to snatch at him. They missed, but the Radusa boys were well-known to the constables, and they had been identified. As they rode across the parade ground the watch called after them that they would be hearing more of this before the candles were lit that night.

In the dragonhouse, Relkin found Curf barely conscious, lying on his side swathed in bandages on a bunk in the sickbay. They'd put liniment where it would do some good, cleaned all the cuts and treated them with Old Sugustus and bound his broken fingers up with nice fresh bandages.

Swane was still there, going over Rakama, who had hardly picked up a scratch in his bout with Kale Radusa.

"Cuzo's gonna be mad about this for a long time," said Relkin.

Curf had been warned by everyone to stay clear of Emelia Radusa, and he had ignored the warnings. It was not as if Curf had a lot of points in his favor as it was. Now he was sure to be out of action for a week or more. Other boys would have to pick up the slack and look after Wout.

"We couldn't let them beat Curf like that and get away with it."

Relkin nodded. "Yeah, you're right," he admitted with a shrug. Relkin understood that the Radusans had gone too far this time. "And Rakama taught them a lesson."

Rakama looked up, a gleam in his eye.

"Didn't hurt him too bad, but sure busted his nose."

"I can imagine all too well." Relkin had watched Rakama box in the ring. "Made an enemy for us in the Radusa boys, though."

"Yeah," said big Swane, "but they sure weren't going to be our friends, anyway."

Relkin looked back at poor Curf, huddled on the bunk. Curf wasn't going to have many friends left in the unit if he kept on as he was, either.

Chapter Seventeen

Porteous Glaves, in his cell below the Tower of Guard, was visited by a young doctor, who then went home to his wife and family. A nurse washed him and put his imbecilic body into a clean shift. He was left on a pallet in the cell. Uneaten food was left beside him.

Through the night he ripened like a deadly cheese and the undetectable odor was in itself deadly to all men who breathed it.

The fever began in the first hour of morning. Glaves twitched and muttered and huddled on the pallet, his flesh shaking as the fever began to rise.

An extraordinary thing happened. The spell that had virtually stripped him of his intelligence broke asunder as the fever intensified. It was as if he had been asleep for a long, long time, and had dreamed his life rather than lived it. Now he lived again, felt in control of his own mind and body. Now suddenly he saw all that he had been through in the past year, since that terrible meeting with the sorcerer in the cellar of Wexenne's house.

He understood that the fever would be his parting gift to Marneri, a chalice of the purest poison. That, at least, was something to salve his pride with, a blow that would level the city that had cast him out because of a single moment of weakness during the Ourdh campaign.

It had been necessary for him to take over a ship. That act had led to some regrettable killings, but it had been essential so that he could escape Ourdh. He couldn't be expected to stay there and die like a rat in a trap. There had been no reason to charge him with anything. He would have happily set up financial funds to take care of widows and orphans, anything they had asked for, as long as it would not harm the honor of the Glaves name. Would they listen? Oh no, and so it escalated to the threats of trials, then actual trials and sentences to the Guano Isles.

Well, of course, Porteous was not about to spend his life on the Guano Isles. And he had taken steps to secure his freedom.

For a moment Porteous grinned. Wexenne was on the Guano Isles, serving a fifty-year sentence with no chance of parole. Porteous had heard this news while hiding in Aubinas, but then it had meant little to him since at that point his mind was in thrall to the will of the Master.

Porteous's mood changed as he recalled the Master himself. Wexenne was getting off lightly. To serve the Master for a day was far more onerous than a life shoveling bird excrement under the hot sun.

But the Master had taken pity on poor Porteous. He'd decided to use him as a weapon and allow him the freedom of death. He had made him into a missile which he cast into the tinder of the city of Marneri. The fire that burned in Porteous would soon be a conflagration.

The malice of the Great One had never wavered since that moment of ignominy when he'd been forced to flee Ryetelth. Stewing in his rage while he slowly recovered his health, he had carefully considered his revenge. He had studied the people of Ryetelth closely and had investigated them for their susceptibility to diseases.

He had prepared not one, but two plagues with which to annihilate the great mass of the people. For it was annihilation that he sought. Waakzaam had seen that the people were becoming so numerous that the world Ryetelth was growing beyond his power to rule. Once he had conquered it, which he still regarded as inevitable, there would be endless problems controlling the unruly hordes. Beyond that concern was his aesthetic distaste for such hordes. He preferred an emptier landscape, devoid of cities and population centers. It was best in fact when the cities were but empty shells, broken pinnacles beneath the bleak light of a cruel, dead moon.

Glaves felt tears leak from his eyes even as he accepted the crumbs of his Master's dread vengeance. His wailing brought in the guard, and Porteous made sure to breathe over him when the man came too close.

"My breath is death," he said with a giggle. Porteous sat up, although it took a great effort in his condition. He leaned forward and put his arms through the bars and caught hold of the guard's belt.

"Get off me, you," said the guard.

Porteous released him and wailed again.

"What ails you, prisoner Glaves?"

"I want to see a priestess," he hissed.

The guard turned away with a curse. It was the one request he could not refuse.

Porteous sagged back on the pallet. The fever swelled and madness burned in his heart. He saw them dying, their faces consumed by the raging fever, their eyes bulging in their heads, their breath stinking as they rotted and died. By the hundreds they would fall, then by the thousands until the city stank of death and the survivors wandered witless in the forests, their ears stopped forever from hearing the very name Marneri, for it would be the name of death.

Later a young woman in plain gray cloth with a light blue surplice came to see him.

"You said you wanted a priestess," she said in a quiet voice.

"Shrive me, sister, shrive this sinner."

"Is it that you are dying, son of the Mother? Are you ready to go to her Hand?"

"Dying?" He emitted a ghastly chuckle. "I am death, sister, death come before you in all his glory. I bring you the light of the grave and the air of the tomb."

"These are fell words, son of the Mother. Perhaps She would hear you better if you softened your words."

"I have sinned, I know it. I have killed and ordered others killed. I have lied and cheated and I have got my revenge on you all. You are all going to die because of me."

"These are grave matters you speak of, son of the Mother. You have killed?"

"It was necessary." Fever's delirium was settling over him. He walked in the shadowland.

"Such matters can never be so described, son of the Mother." Porteous's eyes glittered with malice as he looked up at her.

"Lean closer," he hissed in a gasping whisper, then he spat on her when she bent her head. "Die, bitch, and take all the other bitches with you."

He fell back to the pallet with a groan. The priestess, Kemily of Marneri, wiped her face and left him, greatly troubled by his words.

In the temple, Fi-ice had acted at once on receiving the message from Hanth. The spell was difficult to cast, and precious time was lost when the thread was broken on the first attempt. Eventually it was found that a volume had been cast incorrectly and fresh lines had to be forged to reshape it on the second pass through the spellsay. It took hours, but at length they managed to send out a simple alarm call on the psychic plane. A call that could be heard by the listening greatwitches in Cunfshon.

Within an hour the city's witches were summoned to the Black Mirror chamber in the tower and Lessis herself came through the mirror shortly thereafter.

Lessis hurried to confer with Fi-ice, who told her of Kemily's troubling conversation with Glaves. Lessis realized that a new plague had most likely been loosed on them. General Hanth was rudely torn from his morning routine and hurled into action in a desperate bid to stay the progress of the new plague.

Cornets shrieked through the tower and its outliers. Men were hurriedly mobilized in a desperate attempt to find and quarantine all those who might be infected. At the same time great efforts had to be made to prevent panic and any attempt at a mass evacuation by the people of the city.

The guards who had been at the gate when Higul the Lame rode up, the men in the lockup and the women who hosed Glaves down and tried to feed him, all of these were found and quarantined, along with their families. The young doctor, the elder advocate, the nurse and the priestess, these too were found and confined.

And still the plague spread. Even as the guards began to grow feverish, soon followed by the men in the lockup and the nurses, a flower seller on Tower Street who had sold some chrysanthemums to the young doctor was incubating the fever even while he continued to sell his flowers on the corner.

The tendrils of death reached out into the city.

The flower seller, feeling poorly, stopped by at a soup shop and ate a small bowl of bean soup and some bread. He thought about stopping in at his favorite alehouse, the Fish's Head, on Dock Street but he felt too ill and turned instead for his crib in Mrs. Diggins's boardinghouse.

By a fluke he met neither Mrs. Diggins nor any of the other inhabitants of her crowded tenement building on Eastern Alley. He took to his cot and soon began to shiver as the fever took hold. In this case the fever was quick, perhaps mercifully so, and he died in the night. Mrs. Diggins had the good sense to call the watch as soon as she realized he was dead. She kept the door to his room locked. The plague did not spread through Mrs. Diggin's house.

However, the two young women who ran the soup shop, Elen and Virimi, both caught it and went home to their families on Peach Alley, all of whom subsequently caught it too.

Porteous Glaves finally passed away, gurgling for breath, drowning with the pink froth on his lips, in the first hour after dawn.

On Lessis's orders, no one was allowed near the quarantined victims. The men who shepherded them to the tower wore thick pads of cotton over their mouths and noses and took hot baths when their task was completed.

The sick and the quarantined were left to survive or not on their own. There could be no contact between them and the rest of the city. Those who succumbed and died were let be for a full day before their bodies were taken up for swift burial in a mass grave hurriedly dug in Lost Buck Woods, not far from the other mass graves due for the victims of the bubonic plague.

But Porteous Glaves was not the only deadly missile flung at the Argonath that night. Other men, their eyes staring from the fever, were delivered to the gates of cities and towns. All across the Argonath the authorities roused themselves to heroic efforts to prevent this new contagion from catching fire.

Kadein, the great city of the Argonath, had been struck hard by the bubonic plague. This time it escaped virtually untouched. The fever plague was contained within the Great Gate where the initial victim appeared. The gate was sealed off from the rest of the city and no further penetration took place.

On the other hand, in the small city of Ryotwa, which had survived the bubonic plague so well because of the efforts of an army of feline ratkillers, the new plague escaped and took hold in the general population.

In Pennar the plague virtually wiped out the city. In Bea it was contained and suppressed with small loss because the infectious agent was late in arriving and was a well-known local criminal who was executed soon after being taken into custody.

In the northern cities it went badly. Talion saw the plague get out of control and sweep across half of the city. The southern half of Talion was spared because the bridges were blocked by archers when the word of the outbreak spread.

Vo was almost wiped out and Vusk, too, losing perhaps half its population. The rest scattered into the surrounding countryside where few pockets of the plague erupted, then subsided.

In Kenor the fever hit Dalhousie and the other main Legion camps and towns with hammerblows. The death toll was heavy.

In the white city on the Long Sound the fuse burned on, fitful, sometimes seeming to go out entirely, but reigniting again soon afterward and dashing their hopes.

From Peach Alley to Corner Row it hopped. Then it slid west onto Randol's Court. Suppressed there, it popped up again two blocks north on Linden Street, almost to Broad Street now. Enormous efforts were made to contain it at every eruption. The rules of the quarantine were merciless. No exceptions were allowed, on pain of death. Anyone emerging onto the streets was to be shot down by the archers stationed on the corners, the only human beings allowed out. The sick were simply to be left to themselves as they died. Because it killed so quickly, it burned out of a neighborhood very quickly as well. The rate of survival was no better than one in three in crowded areas. In Ryotwa it had fallen to one in five in the worst areas.

The tension on the streets of the city intensified as the wailing of mourners began to ring out in the poorer quarters. Then from Temple Street there came an alarm. Another customer of the soup shop had come down with the plague. His extensive family had been infected, and they had passed it on widely.

Once more the witches and the Legion made frantic efforts to contain the widening pool of infection. The city had already been cordoned off into sections, with troops at the corners and barricades on the streets. Now the whole dockside area, everything from Broad Street to the bay, was cordoned off and effectively quarantined.

The harbor had long since emptied of shipping. All business activity had ceased; everything was committed to halting the spread of the new plague.

Relkin, along with just about every dragonboy in the house, had been drafted into the containment effort. The result was that he was placed on the corner of Lower Templeside and Broad Street with a full quiver and his Cunfshon bow.

On the opposite corner was a tall, brown-suited archer from the Pioneers, the crack archery unit. He recognized Silas of Lucule, the champion archer with the longbow a few years before.

It was a neighborhood of hatmakers, clothiers, and buttoneers. Relkin could look up Templeside past their shopfronts to the corner with Foluran Hill, and sent off another prayer that Eilsa be spared from this plague.

The bow rested in his hands in its familiar way. He fervently hoped he didn't have to kill anyone. The quiet in the street was uncanny. Not a soul abroad in the middle of the day. Silas had moved to the middle of the street and continued to keep a careful watch up Templeside.

"I don't know why they'd put a dragonboy out here with a bow," he said suddenly, without a hint of a smile.

Relkin was more amused than angered by the condescension from great Silas. "Oh, I guess they ran out of better bowmen."

Silas gave him a long steady look. "Damnable work, to kill civilians if they step outside. I don't like it."

"Me too, but there isn't much choice. You heard what happened in Ryotwa?"

Silas of Lucule looked off along Broad Street. At the corner down by Tower Street they could see other men with bows.

"In Ryotwa," said Relkin. "There's hardly anyone left."

"Don't need to be reminded of my duty by a dragonboy."

"If you say so." Relkin looked up the street toward Foluran Hill. It was empty, not a soul was abroad. He looked both ways on Broad Street, equally deserted, except for bowmen. Over the temple's great dome he watched pigeons circle in the sunlight. There was an unnatural quiet, broken only by distant wails of mourning from somewhere south of Broad Street.

"I suppose you do know how to use that bow," said Silas after a minute.

"I've had some practice."

"Think you could hit a man as far as the corner up there." Silas pointed up Templeside, past the shop signs.

Relkin squinted for a moment.

"Yes. Probably."

"You'd be lucky. By the hand, you dragonboys are natural braggarts, ain't you? That's a good pull with the longbow, so you can forget your little windup bow."

"I'll be happy to leave the long-distance shooting to you, then."

"Damn you, I don't want to shoot anyone."

Relkin shrugged. What choice did they have? The quarantine was the only effective thing that stopped this fever. And if they didn't stop the fever, then they were all dead and done for. He glanced up Templeside again. What was Eilsa doing now? Was she safe? Please, keep her safe, gods, please keep her safe.

The streets were empty until a gray tabby cat appeared out of an alley up Templeside. It came out and sat on the middle of the road and looked up and down as if astonished by the sudden peace in the busy city. Cats, for whatever reason, didn't catch this plague. Then it scratched itself and shifted and crossed the street and vanished into another narrow side alley.

Eventually Silas came to regret his initial haughtiness. It was tiresome to simply stand there in silence looking up and down the street for potential targets. He looked over at the dragonboy with the Cunfshon bow. Good enough weapons for close-in work. Silas had tried one, and he'd learned to respect it. Of course it wasn't like a longbow, but then what was?

"Name's Silas, out of Lucule," he said when the dragonboy looked his way.

"I know."

Silas stiffened.

"I saw you win the longbow competition at Dalhousie."

Silas's brow furrowed. "You've served a while in the Legions then?"

"Aye, we have."

"Then you know how to use that Cunfshon bow."

"I reckon."

Silas looked up and down Templeside; not a soul stirred. "So what did you do in the first plague?"

"I lit fires and put up smoke. You?"

"Dug pits, moved bodies. Hard work, that was."

"The dragons dug in the pits."

"Thanks be to the Mother for the wyverns, friends-of-man. I salute them."

"They'd be glad to know that, Silas, dead-eye of Lucule."

Silas was beginning, just ever so slightly, to change his opinion of dragonboys.

There was a loud noise from a house just a little way up Templeside. Someone was screaming inside the house. There were smashing noises, then the door flew open and a man tumbled out. He fell to his knees with his hands on his head.

Windows were opening up and down the street. Relkin and Silas spread out and drew their bows.

"Lucy!" cried the man. "My Lucy, dead. My Lucy!"

The man was on his feet. A child's face appeared in the doorway behind him.

"Father," cried the child.

"Lucy!" screamed the man, getting to his feet and staggering toward Relkin and Silas.

"She's dead, she's dead, she's dead," he mumbled. He went to his knees again, then rose back up. His shirt was torn open, his mouth gaped wide as he screamed inarticulately.

"Get back!" said Relkin.

Silas had drawn an arrow, but had not yet released. "I cannot kill a helpless man like this," he muttered.

The man kept coming. Relkin looked over to Silas and saw him talking to himself.

The man kept screaming, his eyes those of a maniac. The windows above their heads opened, someone up there screamed a name.

The man kept coming, arms windmilling, mouth open, eyes crazed from the fever.

Silas had frozen. There was nothing left to be done.

Relkin's arrow took the man in the right eye. He was dead long before his head slapped the cobbles.

Chapter Eighteen

The High Gan stretched away under the light of the moon. A desolate region, ruled by the cruel nomadic tribes of the Baguti federation. On a stark hilltop, the only eminence in miles, a great fire blazed.

The sky filled with giant wings, and the air above the hilltop became alive with the sound of great batrukhs coming in to land. Waiting for them were a column of guards, backed by a second column of imps. Great drums beat out a sullen, insistent rhythmn. Torches blazed, held aloft by albino trolls nine feet tall.

Waiting by the log fire stood a tall figure, that of a mighty lord of elven kingdoms, fair in feature and form. Behind him stood a handful of men.

Dismounting from the batrukhs they came, the Four Doom Masters of Padmasa, in person. Long had the Masters remained in their cold vaults in the deeps below their vast fortress. Yet here they were, come to meet the one who promised to complete their original configuration as the Five. He promised a powerful alliance that would rebuild their great pattern, which had been ruined by the fall of Heruta in the uttermost south, lost in great violence in the heart of a tropical volcano.

Without Heruta they had become fractured, at loggerheads, and eventually indecisive. On all fronts they faced disturbing challenges. Something had gone very wrong in the southeast, where the mighty fortress of Axoxo had fallen. Now both defensive bastions in the east of Ianta were in the hands of the witch-ridden Empire of the Rose. Meanwhile, the Czardhan knights had defeated the army of General Haxus at Gestimod-den. The western frontier was looking fragile. And in the south, what was going on in Kassim? Was the Great King daring to raise his head once more? They could soon be beset on all three frontiers at once.

The Masters had become desperate. Any more defeats like Gestimodden, and the armies of the east and west might march in simultaneously and meet at Padmasa. Only fear like this had the power to bring the Four to degrade themselves by leaving their fortress to meet this stranger on this remote ground. Only fear and the lure of the Lord Lapsor, the lightning master, the Dominator of the Twelve Worlds, Waakzaam the Great.

They came, therefore, as if at his summons, to this naked rock in the middle of the hostile steppe.

Defeat and near despair may have driven them to this humili-ating exercise, but they were still determined to make a power-ful impression. They were all Enthraans of their Magic and they used their power to levitate a few inches above the ground and float slowly toward the tall figure by the fire. Occasionally they touched down with a foot to change direction, but otherwise they had no contact with the ground as they floated along.

Once they had been men. Now they shone with a faint green fire and were sheathed in horn. They appeared like a row of gar-goyles with inhuman beaks and eyes of black fire. Heavy brows swept up into spines that trailed back over their shining pates.

They were an awesome sight to most, but they did not par-ticularly impress Waakzaam the Great.

As he watched this bizarre exercise in futility, he considered the strange frailities of the human spirit. Men were weak, both in the flesh and the spirit. They were plastic things, easily molded by more powerful forces. And yet, they grew in numbers until they ruled the world. These Masters, although considerably trans-formed by their system of magic, were weak. Yet they possessed great power, which he would need to borrow to complete the overthrow of the Argonath cities.

He indulged them. While he needed them.

They slowly moved into a line facing him beside the great

fire and settled onto their feet. He thought to clap his hands, then decided it would seem too condescending.

The Masters had set themselves into the Nirodha trance state, their minds coalesced in temporary gestalt consciousness. Their power blazed forth on the psychic plane, and all the men on the mountain quailed and felt the huge gestalt mind gazing in on them.

Only the figure of the elf lord remained still. He smiled calmly, his blue eyes raking theirs.

At once their thrust on the psychic plane encountered the gate to his thoughts, vast, steely, adamant. They thrust against it to no avail. A dreadful thought came home to all of them: Waakzaam was stronger than they.

Then the gate opened a crack and He emerged with fair countenance and open arms.

"I bid you welcome Lords Enthraan! Great have you become in your study of the deep magic. Wide and deep is your art, beautiful and astonishing, your power."

They stood there, irresolute.

"Once more, welcome, be assured that I mean you no harm." He spoke Intharion, his words were sweet and honeyed.

"Our interests coincide, and our differences are minor. Let us converse among ourselves as equals and allies. We have no need for this sort of sparring with our minds. I acknowledge your powers; you have come far down the road of your system. You acknowledge my own, I'm sure. We have no need to try and prove ourselves against each other."

The Four recoiled for a moment, then their gestalt accepted the situation. What else was to be done?

They fell out of the Nirodha trance and opened their eyes. These horn-covered demons came up only to the elf lord's shoulders and seemed slight, almost diminutive in comparison. Yet few observers would have been amused, knowing the dread power these four now wielded.

Far away across the steppe, lightning flickered beneath vast clouds.

"Speak then," said Gshtunga. "For we are here to listen to your words."

"Good. I see that you are the greatest power on this world and that you should rule it. And yet you do not. You have been defeated by the treachery of the High Ones, themselves."

This confirmation of their worst suspicions brought a hiss from the Four.

"They did intrude. We suspected this, but had no definite proof."

"I have detected them. They have left traces here and there among the under men and their creatures."

None of the Four thought fit to mention Waakzaam's recent humiliation at the hands of such, though it was well-known to them.

"They have interfered more directly yet. They have given information to the witches of Cunfshon."

The black fire eyes of the Four flickered momentarily with hatred. But for the accursed witches, the power of Padmasa would have conquered the world. But Mach Ingbok had failed, and the Six had become the Five. Then Heruta was brought down and they were four. The witches had triumphed again and again and now threatened Padmasa directly.

"This is against the treaty that long ago the High Ones signed with me. In that treaty I gave up my claims on this world entirely, and they withdrew themselves to the higher planes and promised never to interfere here again."

The black eyes stared at Waakzaam.

"They have broken the treaty; therefore, I am here to reassert my claims."

The Four said nothing, but a giant question seemed to form above their gleaming heads.

"What are these claims?" said Prad Azod, eventually.

"I will take half of this world. You will take the other half. We will share evenly."

"Which half do you claim as yours?"

"The southern half will be fine. I will reside in distant Eigo, far from your concerns."

"Eigo is a pestilential land filled with monster reptiles of the ancient times. You are welcome to it."

Waakzaam made no rebuke to this impertinence. He knew well when it was best to dissemble.

"Ah, then we shall have no conflicts. I rejoice. And as for pestilence, the Argonathi are dying by the thousand even as we speak. We have infected the nine cities on the coast and also the large military towns inland. Soon they will be sufficiently weakened for our stroke. In time, my friends, we shall burn their loathsome witches at the stake."

"That is wonderful news. You are to be congratulated, friend Lapsor," said Gshtunga.

"Thank you." Waakzaam smiled upon each of them in turn. "Have you considered my proposal for the next step?"

"We have," said Prad Datse. "We have readied a force of fifty thousand imp, five hundred troll, fifty ogres, and twelve thousand horsemen, massed not more than a hundred miles from this spot. General Munth will command."

Waakzaam the Great's perfect features remained fixed as marble, but he experienced a tremor of surprise, and even a twinge of concern. How had they moved such a huge force so quickly and so quietly?

"Wonderful. If you cross the Gan and fall on the western frontier, they will have to meet you in the lower Argo valley. When you have engaged them, you will hold them tight while I come in behind them."

"And what will you invade with?" asked Gzug Therva with a chilly whisper.

Waakzaam laughed heartily.

"Oh, my friend, great Therva, do not worry yourself that I will come in without sufficient force to do the job."

"We sent you a force before. What has happened to it?"

"I used it, as you will recall, to strike at the empire."

"You failed in both endeavors. Our force was destroyed."

"Ah, not entirely. I have retained more than half of it. It was hidden in deep fastness."

"We are relieved to hear this."

"I have also begun to awaken the Irrim Baguti. They have been neutered by the policies of the witch empire. When I give them back their manhood, they will fall on the cities of the Argo and sack them."

Gzug Therva laughed soundlessly. "Baguti are indifferent troops for conducting siege operations. We have long experience with these nomads."

"My own men are in charge of the siege train. Rest assured that they know what they are doing. They have broken into cities on more worlds than you can imagine, dear friends."

The Masters fell silent, a ring of sullen horned faces with smoldering eyes.

"Where is General Haxus, by the way?"

"Haxus is no longer an officer," said Prad Azod tonelessly. "General Munth will command."

"That is good," said Waakzaam. "Munth is a skillful commander. We will work to coordinate our blows. At Gestimodden Haxus failed to use all his forces. What did happen to Haxus, by the by?"

"Haxus went to the bloodworms."

"Ah." The Masters enjoyed a certain reputation for not accepting failure. Waakzaam could see that they fully deserved it.

"I must admit that I have had my doubts about this operation," said Prad Azod. "We have had heavy losses for several years now. Once we put more than three times this force into an invasion of the Argonath, but it failed."

"I have studied that campaign, as you might expect. We must not underestimate the Argonathi. Their Legions are a formidable military system. But they will be weakened severely by the pestilences I have set among them. With my force in their rear, we shall overwhelm them."

"All very well, but it is our army that will be confronting the Legions on the banks of the Oon. Unless your pestilence works its magic, we will be faced with thirty thousand or more men, and their damnable dragons."

"The Argonathi will not give up without a fight, but they will not have anything like thirty thousand. The witches will not go easily to that fiery death, my friends. But if we play it correctly we can defeat them in the Argo valley this time. Then we will pour over the passes and down on Marneri."

"This sounds wonderful," murmured Prad Datse.

"But only if it is true that the pestilence levels their Legions," said Prad Azod.

"It is doing so even as we speak."

"You have seen it, yourself?"

"No, but I have a witness here." Waakzaam turned slightly and raised a hand. "Higul!" he called.

Higul the Lame stepped forward. Higul had made a long journey on the back of a batrukh, a process that had astonished and terrified him. He had learned, however, that such astonishing experiences were just part of his service to the Lord. One just had to grit one's teeth and accept them.

"This is Higul, a man we can trust. Speak, Higul. Tell us what you saw in the cities of the Argonath."

"Death, Lords, nothing but death. They die by day and night, in their thousands."

"But enough to weaken them on the battlefield?" said Prad Azod.

"Yes, Lords, for the plague is loosed in Dalhousie and Fort Picon."

"The first plague had spotty success, did it not?" said Prad Azod.

Waakzaam held back any rebuke to this further impertinence. "It did its job. They were gravely weakened, and many thousands died."

"Only in Kadein did it really get loose. It hardly affected some of the other smaller cities."

"Ah, but there is more than one way to skin a cat, my friends. The second plague has devastated Ryotwa. Even their shipyards are stilled. Is this not true, Higul?"

"It is, Lord. Ryotwa is an empty shell."

"And what of Marneri, that troublesome city?" Gshtunga brought up a sore subject among the Four.

"Marneri was hit, but not like Ryotwa. An older part of the city was devastated, but it did not spread beyond that."

"And the city of Talion, too, how did the horsemen's city fare?"

"The northern sector was emptied, but they held the bridges at bowpoint, and the south was spared."

"It is most unfortunate that Marneri could not be destroyed utterly," husked Gzug Therva.

Prad Azod was troubled, still. "This is not enough to allow us to be sure. We cannot afford to lose this army."

Gestimodden had been a severe blow, Waakzaam could tell. The armored knights of the Czardhan heavy cavalry had found a way to slay trolls and break the Padmasan formations.

"You will only engage if you judge their numbers manageable. That is understood. If necessary I will revisit them with the plague. We will not be moved from our implacable aim."

"And if their force is depleted enough for us to engage, then you will invade through the north and envelop their right flank?"

"That is the plan. Then we will pour over the pass and down into Marneri and Talion. In six months the Argonath will be ours."

"Actually," said Gshtunga, "all these lands will be ours, not yours. You will be confined to the southern hemisphere."

"Of course, but to rid this world of these witches is the first essential step. I pledge all my strength to it. They are the contacts of the High Ones and represent their interest. We expunge them and cut off the High Ones' contact with this world."

"Excellent," rumbled Gshtunga. "This amplifies my own thinking."

"I, too," contributed Gzug Therva. "Heruta always said that they interfered here despite their solemn oath."

"Oathbreakers is how we have named them," said Prad Azod.

"They are that, and more. But once we cut their connection to Ryetelth, their strength will begin to fail."

"With the Argonath removed from our path, we will be able to turn all our attention on the impudent knights in Czardha," exulted Prad Datse.

"And the Isles?" wondered Prad Azod.

"Not possible," muttered Gshtunga.

"To win the Isles we will have to master their fleet," said Gzug Therva.

This produced a pause. The fleet of the Empire of the Rose

included a dozen or more immense ships, the great white ships of trade and war. They carried catapults capable of sinking smaller vessels with a single missile and were faster than anything else afloat.

"It will take us time to ready a fleet capable of matching theirs."

"This has always been their ultimate security," said Waakzaam, "but perhaps there are other ways of attacking their precious islands. Mmmm?"

The black eyes blazed again. What was this? Their minds became eager, questing for the slightest scrap of information.

"Yes," hissed Gshtunga with sudden realization. "We understand the magic of the Black Mirror."

"Good. Our thrust will surprise them when it comes. And, as for Marneri? I will take Marneri myself."

The black eyes glanced at each other for a moment. Waakzaam had something special in mind for the hated white city on the Long Sound.

Later, when the great ones had left, Higul the Lame prowled by the embers of the fire. It was cold up on the top of that hill in the night wind, and Higul wore a thick nomad coat, buttoned tightly to the neck. He pulled up the hood to ward off the chill wind. The Masters' emissary would join him here, so they had said.

The moon was partly hidden behind silvery clouds, but there was enough light to see the land spread out below, dark folds in a sea of grass. The batrukh came in suddenly, beating up from the Gan on enormous wings, then folding them and landing with a single mighty spring. It eyed Higul and snarled at him in open hunger. Higul really didn't care for the red glow in the eyes of the thing.

Down from its neck stepped the Mesomaster Gring.

"I am Gring."

"Higul."

"You were here during the meeting?"

"I was."

"And now you return into the east?"

"You ask many questions, great Gring."

"Of course, you are to be my guide in the eastern lands. There is much I will need to know."

Higul stepped closer to the batrukh, which was eyeing him hungrily. "I hope it has had its dinner today."

"He ate a young pony an hour ago on the Gan."

"You watched, I suppose."

Gring remained impassive. "You have ridden a batrukh before?"

"Once."

"Then you know what you must do."

Higul ignored the look in those wicked eyes and stepped up to the stirrup and hoisted himself over its neck and into the small saddle. The Mesomaster followed, climbing into the second saddle just in front.

The batrukh stood up and sprang forward a few times as the wings unfolded. Then it bounded up and beat its way into the sky with sheer brute power. Higul gripped the monster's huge neck as tightly as he possibly could and tried not to look down. The immense body warmed as the huge wing muscles beat furiously, hauling them into the sky. Soon the ground was no more than a gray enormity spread to the far horizon under the moon.

Chapter Nineteen

The man's face contorted in a scream. The eyes bulged in the head; the skull deformed and became something else—a rising serpent, a giant moth, a thing of webs and tissues that hissed death at him. He felt himself turn, gliding across the land and saw drifts of the dead, heaps and windrows, huge mounds of corpses rising into the sky.

The very land breathed in sorrow, the gods shed their tears in gray torrents, but death marched on victorious, riding his pale horse, carrying the long scythe with which to cut men down and stack them like the corn.

He wished there was something he could do, but there was not. He notched the arrow. He raised the bow. The man's face was open wide, mouth a black circle, eyes bulging, lungs screaming. Wil, was his name, Wil Fansher.

Relkin drifted toward a dream shoreline littered with bodies, which thickened occasionally into drifts, moving backward and forward in the shifting surf. The oceans were gray and greasy, the skies ominous. Death rode over all.

And then again Wil Fansher came on, still screaming, and Relkin raised his bow. Fansher's face became the target, his right eye the bulls-eye. With a sick feeling in his heart he prepared to release.

And woke up to the nudge of a large, well-tended talon against his ribs. There was someone sobbing for breath, and after a few seconds he realized it was himself.

"Boy have dream again."

The dream. The same damned dream. It still haunted him, even now, months after the plague had died out.

They were in Razac, at Camp Fairwood, on their way to Fort Dalhousie. Having survived the plagues without loss, the 109th had been immediately pressed into service. The High Command had ordered all available troops to head for the Argo valley. This was the old, dilapidated dragonhouse in Razac. It was night, and it was warm and muggy.

"Sorry." He shook his head sadly. "I don't know why I keep having that dream."

"Boy kill men before, many times. This was just one more man you killed. You were ordered to kill man. It was your duty. Why it haunt you so?"

It seemed crazy. Bazil was right. Dragonboys soon lost that elemental guilt from killing another being. It happened too often in their lives. And yet, poor hysterical Wil Fansher tormented his dreams.

"He wasn't an enemy, you know? It's not good to kill Marneri folk."

"You say this about Aubinans. I understand what you say. But you not sweat in night for Aubinans."

"His name was Wil, and his wife had just died and he had lost his mind. I could feel his insanity, feel his pain." Relkin willed the dragon to understand. He'd felt that poor man's mind, torn to shreds by grief and fever. Felt it right inside his own, and then he'd shot Will Fansher dead.

"I've changed, Baz, I'm not who I was. Sometimes I think I'm losing my own mind."

There was a reassuring chuckle in the dark.

"You not only dragonboy to do that. Half of them are lost, thinks this dragon."

Relkin sighed wearily. "Yeah, well it's no wonder considering."

"We fight again soon. That will settle your mind, if you live."

Relkin chewed the inside of his lip and hugged himself against his fears. He wasn't who he'd been. Something in his core had shifted on that great and terrible day in Mirchaz. To be the vessel for so much power could unhinge a man's mind,

Relkin had no doubt of it. He had stood before the great gates of the city of the elven lords. He had raised his hand, and fire had blasted the gates asunder bringing down the dynasty of the Lords Tetraan.

How was he supposed to stay the same after that?

He shivered, but not because he was cold. For solace he turned his thoughts to war. The dragon was right, there was bound to be fighting in their future once again. The plagues had been intended to soften up the Argonath. Now the enemy would take the field to try their strength. It was the perfect way for Padmasa to retake the offensive. With both Axoxo and Tummuz Orgmeen occupied by Legion troops, the Argonath was stretched thin on the military end even before the plagues. Now Legion numbers were drastically reduced. A program of recruitment had been begun, but it would be months before the new recruits would be trained. For now they would have to hold their lines with what they had, which was barely enough.

The enemy was sure to attack, and soon. And considering that the Argonath still held the great fortresses at either end of the White Bones Mountains, the attack would be sure to come across the Gan toward the mouth of the River Argo.

Relkin was already convinced that the fighting would be in the old battleground of the lower Argo valley. Fort Kenor sat up on the flank of Mount Kenor and commanded the whole region. Below the fort the Argo River wound across the flat land like a silver-gray snake toward the enormous silvery mass laid across the horizon all down the west, the Oon, the great river, several miles across at that point in its course. The winter winds whipped across the Gan and over the river before coming up against the mountain with a wicked snap that could cut through two free-coats and a sweater and leave you chilled to the bone.

"Got to take freecoats, it'll be cold up there."

"Where?"

"Fort Kenor."

Bazil remembered Fort Kenor. A cold winter with boring duty for the most part.

"That's where the fighting will be."

"Of course, dragonboy knows this. Dragonboy knows more than general, right?"

"No. But I know that there'll be fighting down there. Even a dragonboy can see that."

The dragon did not respond. Dragonboy think he know everything, it was always the same.

While the dragon began to snore, Relkin lay awake for a while thinking of Eilsa, and then of the village of Quosh. The village had come through the plagues pretty well. Quosh was fortunate there, making up for the misfortune of being caught up in a wild battle the year before, which was a precursor to the rebellion in Aubinas. They were still rebuilding, down by the village green where the fires had burned just about everything.

His thoughts fluttered back to Eilsa, as they usually did at this time of day. He prayed that she was well, and healing and recovering. He prayed that they would be reunited for good someday soon, if he should live through the upcoming campaign. Finally he slid back to sleep with the image of an extra freecoat in his mind. And blankets!

Chapter Twenty

The plagues had devastated Dalhousie, the big military town on the Upper Argo. The 109th debarked from the barges from Razac at the Dalhousie dock and marched up to the fort through the town. Empty shopfronts and boarded-up houses were common. The crowds were sparse and gaunt-faced. By some estimates half the population had died or fled from one or the other of the plagues.

It was painful to see the old town so down on its luck. The older dragonboys had served plenty of time in Dalhousie, and they were shocked by the state of the place.

The fort was similarly half-empty, except for the dragonhouse, which was full of the dragons of the 145th Marneri. The 109th marched into the fort under the pennon of the Eighth Regiment, with the cornet shrieking a welcome. Much of the housing in the lines, where the soldiers lived, was empty. At the kitchens the crowd was more manageable than usual for a soldier's camp.

First out to greet them were the pack of young leatherbacks, with Hep, Kapper, and Jumble in front. Then three big brasshides, Rudder, Chepmat, and Vaunce shouldered through the mob. Vaunce was a rarity, a pale purple wyvern, a color only seen on brasshides, called "crullo." Nearly all of these dragons had lost their dragonboys to the plague.

Once he'd seen Bazil into quarters, Relkin went down to the kitchen for a wheeled tub of noodles, slathered in akh. The fires were blazing, but not all the ovens were lit. Still, there was the smell of fresh-baked bread and frying chicken. Noodles were dumped out from enormous cauldrons and akh was poured from five-gallon jugs. Dragonboys from all over the Argonath were milling around.

Standing next to him was a beanpole, at least a head taller than Relkin. He nodded and stooped a little as he introduced himself.

"Welcome back to Dalhousie. I'm Ralf, 145th Marneri."

"Thanks. I'm Relkin of the 109th."

Ralf's eyes got wide.

"You're Relkin?" he said, as if surprised.

Relkin smiled. "You were expecting a giant, seven feet tall?"

"No, of course not. Sorry. But if you're Relkin, then they sent the 109th up from Marneri to replace us."

"Right."

"By the Hand, but, well, I think it's an honor."

"I thank you, Ralf, for your kind words. What's the situation with the dragons here?"

"Not so good, really. I'm the only dragonboy left. We've got the services of five stableboys, part-time, plus the Dragon Leader, who has pitched in with a will. Dragon Leader Hussey is one of the best, but it's not enough. We've got a lot of little nagging problems. Vaunce, the crullo, has a soft plate that needs skin toughener a lot of the time. Stableboys don't know how to do these things. They can't cut talon either. We've got three split talons now. Rudder has a bad one; I think it might infect."

"Well, we've got ten dragonboys, so we'll pitch in. Let's get together right after they finish feeding."

"Over by the pump, then."

Relkin rolled the tub of noodles back to the dragonhouse and saw that Bazil was set up for dinner. Once again he marveled at the flexible natures of the wyvern dragon's appetite. Wyverns would eat anything that moved, of course, but they also enjoyed man-made foods like bread and pasta. Relkin had half a loaf of fresh-baked himself, with some salt pork and sour pickles. He washed it down with a cup of weakbeer, then roused himself to go out to meet Ralf. He took his kit bag with Old Sugustus, needle and thread, cutters, scissors, and the rest.

Along the way he passed the word to others. Jak came out with him, as did Manuel and Endi. They met Ralf in the pump room and accompanied him down to the 145th's row of stalls.

There was a lot to do.

Rudder was a big, healthy-looking brasshide, in the usual tan to ocher shade. However the second talon on his right front hand was badly split and already swollen with infection. Rudder's dragonboy had succumbed to the plague on the first day. Rudder had been in the care of stableboys pretty much ever since, and he looked it. In addition to the split talon, he had a dozen scrapes and untended bruises and rips all over him. Wyvern dragons were big and boisterous, and they exercised hard. Dragonboys always had work to do.

Manuel and Jak mused together about the danger while they looked in their kits. Rudder was in pain, but hardly showed it. Typical brasshide behavior, of course. Brasses could be tricky. Just because they were big and a little slow didn't mean they weren't complicated.

Jak saw the need for stitches to a cut on the left shoulder. Manuel decided to lance the infection around the talon and bleed out pus before soaking with Old Sugustus and packing the wound with honey under a clean bandage. Rudder listened with keen attention, big eyes going from one to the other.

Relkin, meanwhile, had gone down the lines and found Jumble with a split talon on the left hand that had just started to get serious.

"That talon has to go, my friend."

"You are dragonboy?"

"Yes."

"By the fiery breath and the red stars above, that is good to hear."

Relkin got the heaviest cutters he could find and removed the whole talon down to the quick. Jumble's hand was a little larger than Bazil's, Relkin noted, while he filed the stub flat. Jumble was a young leatherback, and Relkin noticed a few things about the dragon's skin that reminded him that Bazil was no longer quite so young. Most of all, Jumble didn't have the marks of the hundreds of stitches that Bazil had received in all his years in the Legions.

"We're going to fix you up, all of you," said Relkin in an effort to reassure.

"That good, because horse boys not too good at this job."

"Yeah, I can imagine."

Relkin filed the stub until it was smooth, then he treated the surface with a hardening agent.

"You arrive today?" the dragon inquired politely.

"Yes. Came up on the barges from Razac."

"We been here a year now. They were going to send us to Aubinas, but then that fighting stopped and they didn't need us, so we stayed here."

"That's the way the military works, there's never much reason for how things work out."

"You have been in Legions for long time, you know more than this dragon."

"This your first posting?"

"Yes. Me and boy Sui, we came from Seant. Did our training in Blue Lake camp. Then came here. We from village of Keesh. You heard of it?"

"Sorry, never have. Haven't spent much time in Seant, though there's boys and dragons from Seant in our unit. Big Hurve, that orange brasshide, he's from Porthouse."

"Keesh is very small village. We leave there and go to Marneri. They send us up to Blue Lake and we train very hard. Then we go to Razac and ride in the boats all the way down to very big river."

"Yeah, we've done that. Years ago, now, we went down that big river a ways and came out in the land of Ourdh."

Jumble was staring at him with big dragon eyes, obviously impressed. "Well, then they brought us back up the river, and we stay here. When the sickness came, boy Sui was one of the last to die."

Relkin looked down. The 109th had been lucky with the plagues, and by a combination of luck and skill he had been spared the loss of his dragon. He knew that for dragons the loss of a dragonboy was just as traumatic. The sorrow was plain to hear in young Jumble's voice.

"You will get a new boy, soon."

"This dragon very sad. Sui was a good dragonboy, good dragonfriend."

"Yes, I'm sure he was."

Relkin went on to put a few stitches into a wound on the back of Jumble's neck. Jumble hissed when the Old Sugustus was applied, but he understood how necessary it was. Relkin's needlework was fast and efficient. Jumble scarcely noticed that part of it.

Later, when he'd finished with Jumble, Relkin went looking for more work. He reckoned he had just enough time for one more dragon before he had to get back and see to Bazil before they bedded down for the night. But boys from the 109th were all through this part of the dragonhouse, doing what needed to be done.

Manuel and Dragon Leader Hussey were talking in a corner. Jak and Endi were dividing up a pile of dirty bandages for washing. He looked into the end stall and saw the big, light purple brasshide, Vaunce, on his side while Curf worked patiently on the sore place, located on the flank, behind the left arm.

Curf looked up, but never stopped rubbing liniment into the sore plate.

"How's it coming?" said Relkin, thinking that Curf had made progress since the plagues.

"This is Vaunce, Relkin. He's amazing. I never dealt with a crullo, before."

Relkin noted how different a shade of purple this was from the dark tone on the Purple Green's huge body. Vaunce was a lovely pale color, with darker tones around the base of his talons and the edges of some of the plates of fibrous armor that covered a brasshide.

"Beautiful," said Relkin with frank admiration.

Vaunce lifted his head to give them a stare.

"You the Broketail's boy?"

"That's right."

"This dragon heard about the famous Broketail leatherback."

"Yeah, he's famous all right, and he'll be wondering where his dragonboy is by about now. The boil must be going. I heard the first gong a while back."

Curf nodded. "I'll be back soon to tend to Wout."

Relkin trotted back through the huge passage that ran down the spine of the dragonhouse. The plunge pool doors were open, and there was no noise from within. Relkin quickened his stride. Dragons were waiting in their stalls, hungry after a long splash and romp.

Relkin went straight into the kitchens and took a huge potcheen of soup and wheeled it up to the stall along with a dozen full loaves of fresh bread. Bazil was waiting, and devoured the lot in a matter of a few minutes. He had questions.

"How are the young dragons?"

Relkin shrugged. "They were a bit of a mess on the outside, and still very upset about losing their dragonboys."

"Yes. We come close to losing a partner many times."

"Yeah, but we made it through alive."

They clapped hand and talon.

"How is the blue one?"

Wyverns saw purple as blue generally, another thing that distinguished them from wild dragons. The Purple Green, himself, had excellent full-color vision.

"He has a sore plate, along the ribs under the arm."

"Ah, soft plate they call that."

"Yeah, that's it. Curf was tending."

"Curf?"

"Hey, Curf's been getting better. No complaints lately."

"Glad to hear this." Bazil swilled down the last of the soup and scratched his belly. "This dragon sleep, then in the morning this dragon meet with the young dragons."

He pushed back onto the mound of clean straw and settled himself for sleep.

Relkin understood that the older dragons felt it was necessary to establish their superior rank by virtue of age and experience, but that too much age was not a good thing either. Bazil would feel fresh and vigorous in the morning, and after a plunge in the pool he'd be looking his best, a leatherback in his prime. It would be a better time to deal with boisterous young dragons.

Relkin found a small group of dragonboys down by the hay chute. Jak had a jug of ale and they were taking a sip.

"Long day," said Swane, handing the jug to Relkin when he joined them. Relkin took a sip and passed it back to Jak.

"Too long, and tomorrow will probably be the same."

"Too right," groused Rakama.

"Where's Cuzo?" wondered Jak. "I haven't seen him since well before the boil."

"He went up to see base command," said Rakama. "I saw a messenger tag Cuzo just before the boil. I was coming back from the armory, had to get that shoulder plate fixed I told you about. Messenger came belting down the passage and into Cuzo's office. 'Right,' I said to myself. 'What's the betting we're going to be moving on tomorrow.' "

"Yeah, well the harbor's full of shipping," said Jak. "We could be back on the water tomorrow, just like that."

"Back down the river again. Just like when I was first in the unit," said big Swane. "Hey, remember going all the way down to Ourdh?" said Swane with a sudden snort of amusement.

"No tall tales about the whores in Ourdh, not tonight," said Rakama.

"Seconded," said Jak.

Swane's face clouded over. He liked to tell those tales of the exotic realm far to the south.

"And we'll be going to Fort Kenor, not Ourdh," said Relkin.

The memories of the whistling winds at Fort Kenor in the winter came back to them all.

"Got to get an extra freecoat."

"You already have two."

"Three is better than two."

"Better than that is an extra wool lining. Double the linings in one coat and double the coats on the very worst days."

"Trust Manuel to come up with something that elaborate," said Swane.

"Just a little bit of sewing, that's all it takes. Saves space in your pack."

"We'll need everything we can get come wintertime," groused Swane.

"Hey, quit your griping, at least we ain't going to Axoxo for garrison duty," said Jak. "Those poor devils, they're the ones who need our pity."

"Brr," rumbled Rakama.

"Hey, enough of that talk. Where's that ale? If we don't go back on the river tomorrow, maybe we'll have time to get the dragons set up for a sing. Get in some ale, buy some beef, let them have a good time before, well, you know," said Swane with a shrug.

They knew.

"Well, we haven't had a sing for ages."

"Yeah, get some ale at the Traveler's Inn, best in Dalhousie these days."

"Yeah."

Curf came into sight, loping down the main passage from the north end.

"Heard the news?" he said as he came close.

"What news?" said Jak.

"Enemy on the move out west. We're going to Fort Kenor, to-morrow morning, first thing."

"Oh right, we knew that already."

The top of the rock was a cold bleak spot, scoured by winds out of the Hazog. Munth's men had scouted the rock, seeking signs of an ambush, but found nothing. No one else was there. The rock itself was a solitary, jutting up like the fin of some giant fish out of the flat Gan. From its top one could see for many leagues in all directions. The Oon was visible in the west, a line of silver under the light of the moon.

Munth ordered his men to climb down again. He would wait alone for the meeting. They were to signal him when the other party had arrived.

Munth was a hard man, yet he was sensible enough to be afraid. This meeting was at the command of the Masters, and Munth was their man. Yet he knew that this prince of power, the Lord Who Burns Men, would test him in some way or other. To be a mortal in the company of the Masters and their like was to risk being ground up like a potato between millstones.

Munth had been born to a Hazogi herding clan and was inured to pain and suffering by the age of eight. He'd gone to Padmasa at sixteen and excelled in the training for the officer corps. Tall for a Hazogi, he was battle-hardened by twenty and had risen rapidly in the ranks, developing into a methodical, steady commander, with an intimate knowledge of cavalry. Munth was a master in the use of nomad cavalry in support of heavy infantry. Other Padmasan generals did not understand the strengths and weaknesses of nomadic tribesmen. They failed to use their endurance capability and their speed of maneuver to full effect.

Munth had survived Gestimodden. His formations had been virtually the only ones that had withstood the crushing charges of the Czardhan knights. Later Munth had witnessed Haxus's demise with little emotion. Haxus's contempt for the nomads had kept him from using them to blunt the effectiveness of the Czardhans. Instead they cooled their heels out of sight of the battlefield where the steel-clad knights broke the Padmasan line. Many friends had perished at Gestimodden because of Haxus's incompetence.

Now Munth was in Haxus's place. He commanded a force of fifty thousand Padmasan infantry, mostly imps. In addition, he had the tribal army of the Gan Baguti, which numbered around thirty thousand men, all nomad cavalry. Ahead of him, however, he faced the Argonath Legions, a rather different proposition from the Czardhan knights.

The Argonathi had been hammered by plagues, he knew. But he also knew that the troops of the Legions were exceedingly well trained. They boasted a skill at warfare far above that of anyone else in the world.

For the first time in his professional life, Munth was seriously worried.

To gain an edge therefore, he had equipped himself with fifty new, powerful catapults mounted on wagons hauled by teams of oxen. These, of course, added enormously to his feed problems, and increased his supply columns appreciably. Munth was a nomad at heart and disliked being held to a heavy supply train. It put the army at greater risk and slowed things down.

However, the catapults could break up formations, even dragon squadrons.

"And what I would give to know your thoughts at this moment," said a deep voice from behind him.

Munth whirled, hand on the hilt of his sword. He was confronted by a giant of a man, no, an elf, with the pointed ears of his kind. He stood there, hands clasped, in a surplice of white silk over silver chain mail. His face was perfectly formed, surmounted by the silver curls of the elven kind.

"Welcome, General Munth. I believe you know who I am." The mail-clad giant put up his hands. "I hope you're not really going to draw your weapon."

Munth caught himself, took his hand off, and stood back a step. "You took me by surprise."

"My apologies, General. I didn't mean to startle you with my sudden appearance, but I wanted to be here first and to observe you without your knowledge."

Munth stared at him. The giant had been here all along. Sorcery of such a high order was frightening, even to Munth.

"There are various ways to achieve invisibility, Munth. Some are more complex than others. I am a master of all of them."

"I am not versed in these things. You are called Lord Lapsor, they told me."

He maintained an external calm, but inside Munth was still shaken.

"That name will serve. Munth, I have followed your career. I have heard that you are an effective commander and can use the nomad cavalry better than any other."

Munth was recovering now and found his voice. "I think it is possible to use them, let us say that."

The Great One smiled disarmingly. "I concur completely. Padmasan general officers have usually looked askance at nomad cavalry. An elitist response from an officer caste molded at an elite academy. A response that has not served them well."

He brought his hands together and rubbed them gently. Munth immediately felt a soothing sensation run down his spine. Sorcery! The Masters had told him to expect it, and he tried to shake it off. Still, the effect was there.

"And yet, Munth, you are also a product of that academy. You have always served this army. What sets you apart?"

"I am of the Gan. I am Hazogi."

"Yes, I can see it, you're one of those slitted-eye horsemen. A hard people, the Hazogi, a hard people from a hard land."

"If you are hard, the life feels good. If you are not, you die."

"Frankly spoken, Munth. Tell me this, General Munth, do you like beautiful women for your bed?"

Munth's eyes narrowed.

"Well, do you?"

"Yes."

"You shall have a dozen of the loveliest from me when this battle is won."

Munth cracked a tiny smile. "My mother would not approve."

Lapsor laughed and extended his huge hands. "Perhaps she shouldn't be told about them, then."

They both chuckled.

Lapsor put a hand on Munth's shoulder. Munth felt dwarfed by the towering knight. "General, I think we will work well together."

Munth did not allow men to put their hands on his shoulder, or lean over him in this position of superiority. His sword would be in their guts first. But Munth had just allowed the Lord Lapsor to do these things, and he knew it was due to some act of sorcery.

"General, I have an army gathering just north of Fort Kenor. When the time is right we will come in on the Argonathi flank and rear. We shall envelop them and destroy them piecemeal."

Such was the force of Munth's anger that he managed to shake off the elf lord, coming back to himself with an almost audible snap.

Lapsor smiled broadly, twirling the hairs he had lifted from Munth's collar together between his thumbs and forefinger and Munth felt his anger melt away just as quickly as it had come. With those hairs, Lapsor could control him unknowing.

"This is most welcome information. I thank you, great Lord."

"Thank you, General Munth. Now, the most important thing during this campaign will be maintaining good lines of communication. Our attacks must be coordinated to have the maximum effect, but we will be operating over a considerable distance from one another; in effect the enemy's army will lie between us."

"There is the batrukh. The Mesomaster Gring will be there to help."

"Excellent. That was just what I was going to propose."

Lapsor rubbed his huge hands together and leaned forward with a conspiratorial gleam in his blue eyes. "Munth! General Munth, you seem to be a lean and hungry fellow. I wonder sometimes if you are more ambitious than you seem?"

"Lord?"

"Munth, consider, you served your masters all your life and what do you have to show for it?"

Munth's forehead furrowed. "What do you mean, Lord?"

"Let me describe your life for you. You sleep on a narrow cot under a tent. You have no lands, not even a house. You eat humble fare and drink bad wine. Once a week you are allowed to go to a brothel. You endure constant scrutiny by spies and informers. Really, Munth my friend, life can offer so much more!"

Chapter Twenty-one

❧

It was seven years since Bazil and Relkin had passed down this river exactly like this, in flat-bottomed sailboats designed for river work. Seven years before he and the dragon had been one-year veterans on their way to Ourdh and the campaign to save the ancient riverland from conquest by Padmasa.

In the interim both boy and dragon had seen a great deal of the harder side of life. That sixteen-year-old had been almost carefree compared with the worn-faced young man of twenty-three.

This time around they were aided by a cool wind out of the north that kept the sails taut as they sped downstream. They rounded Pine Point and bade good-bye to the middle Argo towns and settlements. In seven years, the small towns had grown considerably and there were dozens of small places that had just sprung up out of nothing along the banks of the river.

The towns thinned out quickly as they entered the Baratan swamps, forty miles of meandering shallow channels. Bulrushes and reeds grew at the margins and the waters were dotted with islands bearing groves of small trees.

That night it was clear with a faint hint of the coming winter in the air. The fleet moored at Gideon's Landing, a spot graced by three buildings. Gideon's Inn overlooked the river with a dock jutting straight out into the water. This structure consisted of about a dozen ramshackle rooms on two floors, with an extensive stables in the back. From Gideon's onward, the swamp waters were shallow at this season and would require daylight to negotiate safely. River traffic often chose to pause here overnight.

Water was boiled and dragons were fed. A keg of ale was broached and everyone had a single mug. The fiddler, ol' Henry, had passed away, so Gideon's was no longer the jolly spot it had once been. Gideon himself was not one for conversation, or company for that matter. So after a desultory round of conversation, everyone drifted away from the main room.

The great beasts took dips in the river and bedded down early in the inn's stables. Dragonboys slung hammocks in the stalls. Outside the swamp was quiet but for an occasional mournful cry from some unidentified bird. Far to the east, on the hills of Esk, a light burned on a watchtower.

Relkin washed himself down under a sluice outside the inn. Endi and Swane were next in line. He moved over, shook off the worst, and dabbed himself dry with his shirt.

"Brrr," said Endi under the sluice.

"It'll do you good," chuckled Swane.

"By the Hand, you wait 'til you're in here, you big ape."

"Who are you calling an ape, Endi?"

"Beg pardon, but that's all we've heard from Rakama and you for I don't know how long."

"Yeah, well that's between me and him, then."

"Yeah, and you owe me five gold pieces," said Endi, reminding Swane once more of his gambling debts.

"Hurry it up, Endi," said Manuel, who was next in line. Rakama had come out now to join them.

Relkin ran in place to warm himself and took a few deep breaths from the nighttime air. The familiar humorous squabbling of a squadron went on between the others, but Relkin hardly listened. He heard the sounds of the swamp instead . . . the occasional splash of a fish breaking the surface . . . the croak of a heron . . . the whine of insects. He wondered if he would ever get to live somewhere as peaceful as this.

Suddenly there was a blaze of green fire in the north, far away, beyond the horizon. It burned very bright for a few moments, then vanished, to leave them all with dazed eyes, stunned with afterimages.

"That was never lightning," said Swane.

Nobody disagreed. It had lasted far too long for lightning.

And then came the sound, a swelling roar that shook the heavens for half a minute before finally dying away. They stood there looking to the north, ears cocked. Would there be more? No further flashes came, and the afterimages began to fade from their eyes.

"Something's different," said Endi.

The swamp had changed. They heard cries and whispers, wails and chirrups as a million creatures rose to the surface. A strange breeze cut across the river, and the swamp sang to its tune. They rose in disbelief at the uproar as every frog, bird, and animal gave out its particular cry, over and over.

"What's goin' on?" said Swane.

"How the hell should I know?" replied Rakama.

The uproar built to a crescendo, then stopped abruptly. There were a few last croaks that slowly dwindled away, and all was quiet.

Everyone was now out on the dock or up on the porch, wearing a general look of astonishment. They looked to one another and shook their heads. The night was peaceful once again, although a wolf started to howl way out in the swamp. It seemed an uncertain omen at best.

After a few more minutes they broke up and, in a somewhat subdued mood, went back inside.

Wolves were calling in the north, back and forth for a long time afterward. Relkin lay awake in his hammock and listened while he wondered about that green light. He knew their great enemy was easily capable of such manifestations. Relkin recalled the final moments in the labyrinth beneath the big house in the valley of the Running Deer when they'd battled Waakzaam. He remembered the blows the monster had struck him with, blows of pure mental power, blows powerful enough to drive a man to his knees, stunned and stupefied.

Could that enemy have returned to their world?

They had not slain him, and perhaps no mortal could slay such a being as Waakzaam the Great. His goal was the conquest of their world, and as long as he lived, he might well return.

In a room on the second floor, Hollein Kesepton, acting Commander of the Eighth Regiment, looked up from a table covered in maps and saw the bright flare blaze in the north, then suddenly blink out.

Later the thunder came and shook the skies for a half minute or more.

Dread sorcery at work? Hollein feared so. He offered a prayer for the witches and their efforts to end the rule of overmighty mages of the dark spirit. Even as he muttered the words, he doubted their effect. Hollein had served many years in the Legion. He'd been to Eigo and Ourdh and had a formidable array of battle stars on his formal uniform. He knew that sorcery would never be stamped out completely. One had to get on with life, despite that overhanging dread.

He sighed, then looked down to the maps under the small, wavering lamp. Their journey through the swamps was half-completed. By late evening the next day they might be in sight of Mount Kenor. The day after that they would arrive at the landing below Fort Kenor.

He'd begun to gnaw at the problem of the tents once more when the swamp suddenly erupted with sound. He leaned out the window with his hands on the sill. Every bird, every amphibian, every insect even, was shrieking its head off.

Sorcery? It had to be, but to what end? Was there a threat out there? Should the men be called to arms? Hollein listened carefully, then the sound dropped away suddenly and was gone. A shiver ran down his spine.

Men were shouting out on the dock, but more in complete wonder than alarm.

Lieutenant Breff came in, bearing cups of hot kalut. "What the hell was all that?"

Hollein shrugged and shook his head slowly. "Nothing I've ever seen or heard of before."

The wolves in the northland began to howl from pack to pack across the steppes.

"The men are spooked. They're all talking about wizards now."

Hollein took a cup of hot kalut and sipped it. "We still have to get ourselves down to Fort Kenor, no matter what the wizards are doing out there on the Gan."

"Right," said Breff, taking up a writing tablet. "As far as the tents are concerned, I think we got poor treatment from the quartermaster in Dalhousie. We've got nothing like enough. I checked every boat."

"If we have to, we'll make our own. The sailmaster at the landing will have plenty of canvas."

"I'll warn the sergeants. A regular sewing bee it'll be."

"Volunteers will be rewarded with good leave when this is all over. Make sure they all know that."

"Yes, sir. Moving on to weapons, I checked and got the totals from each unit."

Hollein grimaced as he read the figures. "Ten men who don't even have swords?"

"Their replacements are being brought up from Marneri. Held up somewhere down the line."

Hollein tossed the scroll down, leaned back, and sighed.

"That wasn't lightning, Commander," said Breff.

"I know, Lieutenant. But I'm not going to speculate about what it might have been. It was a long way away, for which I'm thankful. We're going to have to cross a lot of streams and marshes. That isn't going to be easy. We have to concentrate on preparing for that. Have to leave the wizards to themselves, at least for now."

"Right, sir. Still, the men are all talking about it."

"I expect they'll talk about it for weeks. I don't expect I'll ever forget it myself. I never dreamed there were that many frogs in the world."

"As for the situation regarding the dragons' gear. We have most of it, but there's a shortage of some items, especially blister sherbet."

The next day the cool breeze out of the north picked up again and they ran on through the rest of the swamp and out onto the Lower Argo. In the early afternoon they glimpsed the cone of Mount Kenor as a slight bump on the western horizon. Soon it was a distinct cone. It was a fine day, and the top of the mountain glittered every so often from its crown of ice.

The mountain ruled alone here. For a hundred miles in any direction the land had been worn down to a plain by the mighty Oon and its tributaries. And yet here was the volcano, eight thousand feet high, towering over the low hills and swamps of the region.

The River Argo wound across the flatland in snaking lunges that generally took it westward, toward the confluence with the enormous Oon. The rushes in the swamps and the grasses on the prairies had turned brown from the summer heat and rattled in the north wind, a constant sussurration in the background.

Now they had to beat up into that northern breeze sometimes, tacking across the broad, shallow river as it wound around on itself in great loops and whorls.

There were a few new settlements down here as well, and inland to the south the grain towns were expanding. Despite the upheavals of the invasion six years before, the settling of Kenor was continuing at a rapid pace.

Relkin and Bazil watched the mountain grow larger as the fleet wound its way across the floodplain.

"Remember that winter?" Bazil asked, thinking back to their days on Mount Kenor.

"Who could forget, never been that cold before or since."

"Ach! Those winds were invigorating for dragon."

"Made dragons hungry, as I recall."

"That is right. Not good to remember this."

Chapter Twenty-two

Late in the afternoon of that day, General Tregor met with the regimental commanders in his office at Fort Kenor. Tregor had been on the scene for only a week, having hurried down the Argo himself.

A large map of the Lower Argo region was pinned to the wall.

Commanders Dirken, Clumb, Fellows, and Rush were already seated when Hollein Kesepton arrived, fresh from the quartermaster's stores, where he'd been squeezing out supplies.

"Kesepton. Take a seat, Commander."

"Yes, sir."

"How did it go at the quartermaster's?"

"Well, sir, we've got everything we need now, except a bit more rope. Quartermaster and I have been talking a lot about rope."

"Ah yes, the perennial, no quartermaster likes to give away rope and yet that's what we're always asking for. Especially here!

"We will be maneuvering across terrain that is little better than swamp, pulling wagons out of the mire all day and night. Good work with ropes and bridging can make life a lot easier. Get all the rope you can and hoard it carefully."

Tregor turned to the map for a moment, then back to them.

"Dragons will be essential in helping us through this. Their strength makes the difference, believe me. So they must be well fed, and you know how much food they can get through in a day. You understand the kind of wagon train you're going to have to have. We'll even need to haul in firewood."

The commanders absorbed all this calmly, their sergeants already on the job.

"I have some better ideas of what we'll be facing, too. Scout reports indicate the enemy will arrive on the Oon bank within a couple of weeks. His force runs to fifty thousand imps, with perhaps twenty-five thousand nomad horsemen, and at least five hundred troll, perhaps more. There are also some ogres and quite a few war machines, catapults in particular."

The commanders nodded thoughtfully. Padmasa had learned at last that trolls could not take the battlefield from battle-dragons with legion support. Not even the addition of a few superheavy ogres had changed that equation. Wyvern dragons with dragonsword and shield were unbeatable.

But dragons were vulnerable to thrown spears and to catapults, particularly the latter, which could hurl a heavy spear over a considerable distance, as much as three hundred yards with the right wind.

"The enemy will try to set battle on a field with good line of sight for the catapulters. We cannot risk exposing the dragons to catapult fire. So! We shall have to build field defenses, to force the enemy to close with us on ground of our choosing."

His audience murmured in agreement. They had trained for this.

"A parapet made of tree trunks at least six inches in diameter will stop catapult fire even at short range. Of course, this means a lot more work for your men. We will be digging and logging and sawing trees right up until we actually make contact with the enemy."

Tregor turned to the map. The crossings of the Oon were numerous at this stage of the river. Here, in the middle region of its long course, the Oon became a vast sheet of shallow water, moving slowly through a thousand braided channels at the end of the long dry season.

"It would be best to stop the enemy from crossing, and we will make our stand on the bank of the Oon. But, being realistic, we have to expect that he will get across, either here or above the Argo. There are too many places where the enemy can cross easily for us to stop him. But we have some advantages. A Padmasan horde army is poorly disciplined. Imps are volatile and prone to chaotic behaviors. We know if we can hit them before they get themselves sorted out, we can break them."

"Sir?"

"Yes, Commander Clumb."

"Will we remain organized in two legion corps? There was a rumor to the effect that we might go to divisions, two regiments in each."

Divisional commands would therefore become available, something of no little import to men such as Clumb, twelve years in the Legions and a commander only since the plague.

"The rumor is ahead of the facts, Commander Clumb. No decision has yet been made."

"Yes, sir."

Tregor tapped the map. "The Red Rose Legion is already in the field. I want your regiments to join them as soon as possible."

He looked over to Hollein. "The Eighth Marneri will be paired with the Bea regiment that is due to arrive in a few days. Your regiments will eventually be set up in mobile array behind the shoreline, keeping watch on the enemy's movements. Initially we seek to frustrate his attempts to cross. Later we will work to destroy him if he crosses the river successfully, which—realistically—is likely to occur."

Tregor gave them a tight smile.

"We will have about fifteen thousand men and three hundred dragons. This is smaller than the accepted critical mass for a Legion disciplined force, but it's the best we can do. As always, we know we cannot afford to fail."

After the plagues it was a miracle they had any army at all.

"He couldn't be here today, but General Urmin will be. my second-in-command. He will command the Argonath Legion. General Va'Gol is in command of Red Rose."

Tregor swung back to Hollein.

"Commander Kesepton, I believe you know General Urmin."

"Yes, sir, I had the honor of serving under his command at Avery Fields."

"He did a marvelous job with very slender forces. I superseded him on my arrival, but by then the tough part was over. Everyone pulled together very well."

Kesepton marveled at how selective a commanding officer's memory can be. Back then, General Tregor had been near-apoplectic over the sudden disappearance of the 109th Marneri Dragons.

"So." Tregor clapped his hands together and faced them. "Our first priority is to see that all units are equipped as fully as possible. Second is to be ready to move in a few days' time down to positions closer to the shore. Fortification parties will be sent to particular locations where a ditch or bank might be useful later on. Of course, a lot has already been done at these places. Certain materials are kept there as a matter of course. The men stationed here at Kenor don't spend too much of it sitting about in the fort. Commander Keezar sees to that."

Hollein and the others chuckled. Outside of Oratio Keezar's presence, it was safe to chuckle at the older officer's famous energy and zeal.

"But there's still much to be done, so I think you will understand me when I say that I will eviscerate any of you who don't give me your last ounce of energy! We are in a perilous situation here, and I will not accept anything but your absolute best effort, every waking moment!"

For a moment there was a silence.

"Good," said Tregor.

The talk moved on to more detailed matters, such as the routes to the staging areas behind the Oon. When the meeting broke up, Tregor asked Kesepton to stay behind.

"Commander, I read your report; strange incident there in the swamp at Gideon's Landing."

"Yes, sir. Everyone who saw it will affirm that it was not lightning."

"We will make note of it. The witches have been informed, of course."

Hollein said nothing, which was the wisest course when witchcraft came up.

"So, Commander, tell me something. You have the 109th

Marneri in the Eighth Regiment. You may remember that I made certain intemperate remarks concerning the 109th Marneri after they absconded outside Posila. At the time I was unaware of the gravity of the mission for which they had volunteered themselves."

"Yes, sir, I remember."

"Yes, I expect you might. Well, the 109th will be under my command again. I would not want to have any bad blood between us. Were the wyverns made aware of my remarks?"

"Yes sir, I'm sure they must have been. I don't think they would have expected anything else, sir. They did desert their posts, and they expected trouble. The dragons are like that, you see. They expect the rules to be applied. Very orderly in their ways the dragons are, sir."

"I expect they don't care much for me, then."

"They're not known for bearing grudges, sir. If anything, I expect that particular bunch would like an opportunity to show you you were wrong in your estimation of them. They seem confident and ready for anything."

Tregor chewed his lip a moment.

"Well, that is good of them. It was a very difficult moment, and I'm afraid I spoke before I knew all the facts." Tregor rubbed his hands together and nodded to himself. "That is a relief, then. One thing less to worry about."

The 109th were to fortify a narrow neck of land in the Big Side Swamp, behind the mouth of the Argo. On either side of the spot lay deep mires and bogs all the way to the river. For an enemy army, the neck would be an essential route if they were to get off the riverbank and further inland. Excellent maps had been prepared of all of Kenor by the Imperial Cartography Institute, and Hollein took another copy of the area map, in which each inch represented a mile. The terrain beyond the fort was broken up by swamps and lakes that verged into swamps. Tregor's words about rope came back to him. He would redouble his efforts to prise more out of the quartermaster.

As Hollein was about to leave, Tregor picked up his report of the incident in the swamp.

"And so, Commander, what did you make of the disturbance you witnessed out there?"

Hollein considered for but a moment. "It was no natural phenomenon, sir. Sorcery of some kind, very great sorcery indeed."

Chapter Twenty-three

For the thousandth time Lessis wished they still had the batrukh Ridge Eyes that she had ridden across the distant dark continent of Eigo. It made travel so swift to fly by batrukh. Of course, it was a little heart-stopping as it hurled itself through the skies on immense wings, but it got you places in a hurry. Much faster than traveling on horseback.

Lessis was still saddle sore. It was always painful getting reacquainted with the saddle after a long absence, and at her age it took even longer. They had been riding for two weeks, all the way from Marneri. They had paused briefly at Dalhousie to re-supply before heading on north and west, past Mount Ulmo and onto the Gan, the vast steppes that occupied the flatland all the way to the distant mountains of the White Bones.

For days they had ridden deeper into the grasslands, pushing their horses to the limit, searching for elusive landmarks and a meeting at Widows Rock with a witch spy who dwelled among the Baguti of the nearer Gan.

Lessis traveled with a party of six and a string of twelve horses. Beside her was Lagdalen, once more her assistant, despite all the promises that her service in this way had ended. Behind them rode Mirk of Defwode, Lessis's grim-faced body-guard. Ahead, halfway to the horizon, rode three tall young men from the Imperial Guard, named Beruyn, Ward, and Mellicent. The emperor had insisted she accept them, the pick of two hundred volunteers. And there was a new sensitive, a willowy young man named Giles of Corve, a youth of seventeen summers, quiet and unobtrusive, with a diffident manner. You would hardly imagine that he could track almost any person across a bare desert, following some scrap of the pursued's aura. It was uncanny, this power.

In this region the Gan was a tawny sea of tall brown grasses, softly whispering in the wind. The land was not absolutely flat, for there were ripples and low hills. The golden light of late afternoon flecked the land in crescents. Where the rivers cut the land there were stands of aspen, dwarf oak, and bogs full of white birch.

Lessis had borrowed a sextant and chronomoter from Irene to keep track of their position. She took readings every so often, and made annotations in a small leather-bound notebook, tracing their progress on the map, which she carried in a small leather tube in her knapsack.

Lessis knew they were about thirty-five leagues due north of the volcano, Mount Kenor as it was known to the men of the Argonath. The plains tribes called it Ashel Veerath, "Fire of the Earth"—for they remembered that long, long ago, the mountain had spoken in flame and lava and torn the world around it for forty days and nights. The horsemen of the plains had been driven to the edge of starvation before the mountain finally quietened. The lands across the Oon had been buried under the ash, and nothing would grow for three seasons. No good grass grew for seven. And thus Ashel Veerath was always seen as an angry manifestation of the gods and was much feared by the tribesmen of the plains.

Lessis was headed south and west, into a wide tongue of land that stretched westward where the Oon curved its mighty course, slowly snaking across its vast floodplain. Somewhere ahead stood the Widows Rock, beyond the edge of the frontier. Far from the centers of power where Lessis normally operated.

And all for the sake of a rumor, but one that spoke of green fire, like lightning that blazed for a minute, and of a thunder that shook the Gan for a hundred miles.

The word had come from outposts on the River Argo, and also from the Baguti, the wild nomad tribesmen of the Gan. Fierce warriors, great horsemen, they spanned the steppes in their constant migrations with their herds. The witches had placed many informants within the Baguti peoples in the last few years, and they all spoke of a great Master, a being from the ancient aeons of the past who had appeared in a blast of green fire and passed among the Baguti. He had the powers of a god, and had stirred up a great storm among the fierce clans of the horsemen.

The Office of Insight was well attuned to such stories from beyond the frontier. In the time it takes an eagle to fly from Dalhousie down to Marneri, the word had reached Lessis. Her reaction was immediate. She gathered up Lagdalen, Mirk, and the new sensitive, just arrived from Cunfshon, and headed northwest for Razac.

At the Hollow of the Dead Elk, they met with a spy who brought them new stories, very strange tales. Monsters had risen out of the ground. The horses of a Baguti clan who had refused to serve the Master had been devoured, the people enslaved.

Many Baguti clans, genuinely terrified, had fled the Gan and were seeking shelter in the fort towns along the Argo. After pledging their swords and bows, the Baguti were allowed to set up their tents in designated areas, under Legion watch, and always outside the walls.

The Lord Who Burns Men, they called him, for he was said to throw men, alive, into blazing fires and extract their very souls to use in his tremendous magic. He called down the thunder and lightning, as if he were ancient Asgah, the Great God of the heavens and of war, and lightning.

Of course the green lightning had been enough to instantly capture Lessis's attention. Such sorcery was far beyond the powers of any mere wizard, or even the Padmasan Masters themselves. Waakzaam had returned.

And so they rode on, through the endless whisper of the grasses, heading toward the setting sun as it became a ball of gold sinking in the uttermost west.

Ahead appeared a sliver of black on the horizon, the Widows Rock, a single jut standing above the grassland.

They pulled up at dusk under the lee of the towering rock, a remnant of an ancient volcano chain, of which Mount Kenor was the most recent. Mirk found a water hole where they watered the horses, then hobbled and fed them enriched oats from their saddlebags. They made no fire in this hostile land. It was the third day of dried meat, dried fruit, and dried biscuit, washed down with canteen water, but after another long day in the saddle they ate it with the usual ravenous hunger.

Ration devoured, Lessis laid her blankets down and, with a little groan, settled onto the ground, determined to rest as much as possible. Sadly she recalled the comfort of her own bed in her house in Valmes. That was another thing that was harder to do as one aged, sleep on the cold, hard ground.

"Lady, would you like some more water?" Lagdalen had brought out their larger water jug.

"Of course, my dear. Thank you."

Lagdalen was also saddle sore and weary, but she was still a young woman and far more resilient. She, too, gave a groan as she sat down on her own blankets.

"I wish we had Ridge Eyes."

"So do I, dear, by the Hand! So do I, but alas, we had to leave him in his own world. He belonged in Eigo. It would have been unjust to take him."

"We'd have been there days ago."

"Travelling on the back of the batrukh can spoil a person, I'm convinced." They exchanged a small smile.

"And Ridge Eyes is free now, whereas before he was slave to the Masters. I remember when we were on the Gan before, Lady. It seems a long time ago, now, eight years I think."

"Yes, my dear, I remember, too, but for me it does not seem so long ago."

"We passed to the north of here."

"Considerably. I think the grasses are longer here. We are close to the great river."

There was a short whistle and a hail from Beruyn. Mirk had returned from his reconnaissance of the Widows Rock. He squatted beside them, grim-faced in the moonlight.

"Someone was here within the last month. A big fire was made on the north side of the rock. I found scorched bones."

Mirk handed Lessis a piece of a man's thigh bone, blackened and cracked in a great fire.

"Take Giles to the spot in the morning. See if he can pick up a trace."

"Yes, Lady."

"Witch Shuneen is coming. Her signal was seen."

"Shuneen is prompt, good. You can turn in now, faithful Mirk. The Mother Herself commends you."

The Witch Shuneen came out of the dark about an hour later. The men were all asleep, except for Mellicent, who kept watch.

"Approach, Witch," said Lessis. "Sit with us and tell us your tale."

"Thank you, Lady," said Shuneen, a cowled figure in the dark. She pulled back her cloak and revealed a face browned by the sun and the wind. She was clad as a Baguti squaw, with leather apron and jacket, hide boots to the knee. At her hip she bore a long knife with a high, horn handle and an iron hilt.

"It is an honor, Lady," began Shuneen. Lessis hushed her with a raised hand in gentle protest.

"You have word for me, I hope?"

"I have, but I know not if it should be given before the youngster here."

"You can speak freely. This is my assistant, Lagdalen of the Tarcho, from Marneri. Do not be taken by her youth. I can assure you that she has wisdom far beyond her years."

Lagdalen bobbed her head, embarrassed by this encomium.

Shuneen stretched out her hand, brown and callused from woman's work in the tents of the Baguti. Lagdalen's was pale and soft in comparison.

"Honored to meet you, Witch," said Lagdalen.

"Likewise, Lady Tarcho."

"So?" said Lessis.

"I have bad news. The Irrim Baguti, you know them?"

"Big tribe on the eastern side of the Gan. Have been neutral for much of recent history. Didn't join the invasion armies."

"They are hostile now. Their horde is massing. They will aim to fall upon Fort Kenor."

"They will have to cross the river first. The Argo is low now, but still it cannot be waded across like the Oon at the crossings."

"The Lord has a force of Padmasan engineers."

"The Lord? The Lord of Evil is all he is. I have heard it said they call him the Man Burner."

"That is him. I believe he is known by many names, but I do not know them, nor do I wish to repeat them."

"It is better not to, for such names give him his strength. We call him the Deceiver, for it is treachery that is his true hallmark."

"Then I shall use that name. Ten days ago he burned a man, right here at the rock. He brought down the thunder and the lightning beyond all lightning ever seen. The Irrim fell prostrate and worshiped him. They think he is Asgah, the ancient god of war returned to the world."

Lessis nodded faintly. He had been here! Once before she had been close enough to kill him and missed her chance. This time she vowed she would not fail. In her mind she carried the lethal spell, provided by her sisters.

"He has godlike powers. I am but a lowly woman." Shuneen grinned. "So I was not allowed to see his work from close at hand, but even in the camp the lightning was astonishing. A column of green fire into the clouds that continued for a minute. The thunder deafened everyone and drove every horse to panic.

"Now the men are his to lead. He has sent a force of Padmasan mercenaries to work with the Baguti. They have talked of nothing but war since that night. They envisage war and rapine from here to the ocean, with fat pickings in the rich cities of the plain."

"We must get a warning to the fort."

"Warn them that the Irrim will fall on them within a few days. Already the signals have gone out, and the war drums are thundering on the banks of the Great River."

Chapter Twenty-four

It was a hot day in the Big Side Swamp. The sun beat down from a cloudless sky and there was no wind. The dragons of the 109th were digging that day. Wielding immense shovels, they heaved muck out of a trench that already stretched across the narrow neck of land thrust out across a lagoon.

They had piled the dirt up into a neat bank, now standing six feet high, all along the inland side of the neck. Forty men from the Kadein Second Legion were at work on the bank, tamping it down and hammering sharpened stakes into the seaward side. Dragonboys assisted with the hammering, or else resharpened the stakes after they'd been hammered in.

A cornet sounded for lunch, and, with a few groans and sighs, men and dragons put down their tools and gathered around the cookshack. The usual big boil was on, three to four hundred pounds of noodles, gallons of akh, hogsheads of beer, a hundred flat loaves of bread, big jars of fish paste, and some steamed herbs gathered out of the swamp by the surgeon's staff. It was imperial policy to encourage the men to eat some kind of green stuff several times a week.

At the lineup everyone was pretty subdued. This was their third day of backbreaking work. The men had few jokes left to tell. The dragons, at least, were holding up well. As long as there was plenty of food and some beer to wash it down with, they could throw themselves into a huge, energy-intensive task. Here, they'd dug three hundred yards of deep trenches and hurled up enough dirt for an impressive fortification at the base

of the Neck. Dragonboys were pleased with the general tone
and condition of the dragons, but they were hot and sweaty from
scrambling around on the bank all morning. They fed the dragons, grabbed some bread and akh for themselves and took off to
the riverside for a quick swim.

They had to go down the Neck to the far side and around the
lagoon to reach a bank of gravel that skirted the river itself. The
Argo here was a broad flat expanse of water, slowly flowing
toward an even larger one.

The water was murky, but still cool and refreshing after hours
of labor in the hot sun. They ducked, dived, swam, and strode
out feeling a lot better than before. They'd kept back most of
their ale ration, and they drank this down, warm as it was, and
prepared to hike back to their dragons.

"Sail ho!" cried Jak, still out in the water, splashing around.

A trio of sails, in fact, was now visible, rounding the bend
about a mile upstream. Within a few minutes they drew level,
but still way out in the water, for there was no landing here. The
water was far too shallow for the riverboats to come close to
shore.

"Ahoy there," came a cry from the leading vessel.

"They've got dragons aboard," said Endi.

"Hey, there's a crullo!" said Swane, spotting a dragon with a
bluish hide.

"Then it must be the 145th," said Endi.

Suddenly dragons started jumping off the sides of the riverboats, which heeled over dangerously while splashes rose to
their topmasts. Sailors cursed generously. The dragons simply
swam to shore while boats were let down behind them to bring
their equipment.

Jak and Relkin both reached the same conclusion and looked
up into the other's eyes a moment later.

"Hope they've got dragonboys now," said Jak.

Relkin scanned the boats. There were just a group of rowers
and a steersman.

"Uh-oh," said Rakama.

The dragons walked out of the river shortly afterward and exchanged greetings with the dragonboys of the 109th. Dragon Leader Hussey came ashore on the first boat.

"We've been seconded to the 109th," said Hussey in explanation. "Our dragonboy replacements died of the plague when it stuck Razac. You boys are going to have to take on an extra dragon for a while."

Dragonboy hearts sank a little at the thought of the extra work, but they rose a bit at the thought of getting to know another dragon.

Hexarion, a hard green, and dragonboy Ralf were the only surviving pair in the whole 145th, so virtually everyone in the 109th would have to pair with a new dragon.

Back at the new fortification, the 109th rose up to greet the new dragons with cheerful roars and slaps. They concealed any concern they might have about having to share dragonboys. One look at the shambles into which the kits of the 145th dragons had descended and everyone knew they'd be working into the wee hours for weeks.

When it came to pairing, this was something best left to the dragons themselves, and Dragon Leader Hussey understood that. Hussey, himself, would be outranked by Cuzo, who was a Dragon Leader of First Rank. Hussey wore only the single oak leaf that designated Second Rank.

Fortunately, Hussey had gotten along perfectly well with the dragonboys of the 109th at Dalhousie. He was a thoughtful type, tall, gray-eyed, almost gaunt in feature. He and Cuzo knew each other from previous terms of service and shared a mutual degree of respect.

Jumble, the leatherback, selected Relkin. Vaunce took Curf, Swane was picked by Hep, a leatherback from Marneri. Kapper chose Endi and Rudder took Jak. The big brass Chepmat chose Manuel, but Mono promised to help since he was a brasshide dragonboy all his life and Manuel also had the Purple Green to tend, who was a handful.

Soon all the dragons were paired with 109th dragonboys, and the process of boy and dragon imprinting on each other began. They walked together up the beach, Relkin lugging some of

Jumble's equipment while Jumble carried the rest, including the heavy items.

Jumble was a leatherback, like Bazil, but there the resemblance ended. Jumble was a little bigger all over than the Broketail, except in the heft of arms and shoulders, where Bazil was exceptionally built up for a leatherback.

"Has everything healed up tight?" said Relkin, thinking of all the stitches he'd put in this dragon back at Dalhousie.

"Think so, but stitches itch."

"Then they're ready to come out. You've healed quick. That's a great thing if you're a battledragon."

Jumble clacked his jaws. "This dragon think you know what you talk about. I know you been in Legions long time, ever since I was a sprat."

"It seems that way sometimes, to me, but it ain't true. Been seven years since Bazil and me joined up. Just seven years, we'll soon have served our term. And then we'll muster out."

"The Broketail is a legend."

"He's the best, you'll see. He hardly ever complains."

"This dragon will never complain."

Relkin chuckled. "You better, 'cause I might miss something otherwise." Relkin checked Jumble's left hand, where he'd cut the talon down to the quick. Everything was healing well.

"The Broketail is best dragon with sword in all the legions, they say."

Relkin nodded. "They're right. Only dragon that might beat him is old Burthong. You ever seen Burthong fight?"

"No, but this dragon hear of him. Brasshide, but very quick with the sword."

"That's him. He'd have been champion years back if it wasn't for Bazil."

The dragons chaffered merrily until the cornet blew for the resumption of work. Then they took up tools and worked the rest of the day together. A small boil-up at three was added to the schedule since the 145th had missed their lunch. With the aid of a passing fishing boat, the cooks came up with a hearty fish chowder and stacks of fresh-baked loaves that were dispensed to the hungry horde.

All too soon it was all gone, and they went back to digging and building fortifications. With the 145th added to their numbers things went very fast. Later, when the cornet blew to officially end the day's labors, they all tramped up together to the camp, set a mile back behind the new wall on the Neck. It was fortified with a ten-foot ditch and stockade.

The fires were already going and a huge dinner boil was soon under way. The dragons relaxed with a plunge in the lagoon, except for Jumble, who sat patiently while Relkin removed stitches from some of the wounds he'd stitched up at Dalhousie.

When the noodles started coming out, the dragons ate together in a big circle around the fire, while dragonboys gathered at a smaller fire to exchange thread and needles as they took up a long list of repair jobs. Cuzo and Hussey earned respect by rolling up their sleeves and tackling some of the worst joboquin work. Ralf, the sole boy from the 145th, had been trying to keep as much of the unit's kit from disintegration as possible, but ten dragons were too much for one pair of human hands to take care of, and the joboquins had frayed badly.

The dragons finished off their rations and took themselves to their tents. The 145th had no tents, but Kesepton had had the foresight to bring extra supplies. With a bit of ingenuity, they raised tents of some description for everyone. Relkin saw that Jumble was bedded down, then headed up to the tent he shared with Bazil.

The Broketail was already stretched out on a bower of branches and reeds gathered from the swamp.

"Jumble is a good wyvern. Young, but he willing to learn."

"I think so."

"Just hope he is good with sword."

"Yeah," sighed Relkin. "I hope so, too."

"Also hope boy can cope with two dragons."

"Likewise, my friend."

Chapter Twenty-five

In the Baratan swamps, the hush of night lay over Gideon's Landing. A single light showed, from an office on the second floor, where many an officer had worried the night away poring over maps of the Lower Argo swamps. All around were set up Legion tents, rows of white rectangles, ghostly in the moonlight.

This night it was the Bea Third Regiment, under Commander Hugo Fesken, that was asleep in and around the inn and its outbuildings. The smaller boats had been pulled out onto the riverbank while the main ships were moored out in the stream. A guard of twelve men was on watch, two together on the dock, five on the south perimeter, and four on the north, plus one more perched on the roof of the stables. There was also the presence of Gideon's guard dogs, Fang and Brown, both young and keen of hearing. Sergeant Kemster placed the sentries himself and assured himself that the perimeter was tight before he turned in.

In the office on the second floor Commander Fesken and the pilot for the fleet, old Hundswide, were going over the charts together. Fesken, recently promoted because of the plagues, was young, ambitious, and somewhat anxious about his command. Old Hundswide wasn't a completely reassuring sort either. He'd seen too many young officers with arrogant airs and ignorant ways when it came to the river.

"No suh, the waters down to Pillow Creek, they be too dry for your bottoms. Those big bottoms got to go way around by Black Lake and come down to Strett's Channel, that's the only one deep enough now."

Fesken's heart sank. To go the route proposed by Hundswide would take them miles off to the north and west, where the swamp gave way to broader channels that looped around in a great circle before turning southwest.

"That's a terrible long way out of the way. Sure there's nothing better?"

"Sure. Unless you want to try Cracktree Reach."

"That's marked 'inadvisable' on the map."

" 'Xactly, my point, if'n you don't mind my sayin' so."

Fesken rubbed his chin. "What about keeping to the main channel?"

"Ah, young sir, you'll be digging your big boats off the bars before an hour is passed. After Gideon's Reach, the river splits again, and both streams are shallow. You get past the point above Crab Creek and water drops to a fathom this time of year."

Hundswide brushed the map with a weathered old hand. "I know you be in a hurry to get down there, Commander, but believe ol' Hundswide, you'll be a lot slower if'n you try any route other than Strett's Channel. Only place that's deep enough for those big boats."

Fesken gloomily foresaw that it would be another day before he could get his fleet to the landing below Fort Kenor.

Sublieutenant Gink stifled a yawn as Fesken ordered the purchase of an extra day's worth of supplies from Gideon. Gink had had a long day.

"Pay from the regimental account, sir?"

"Yes. On my seal."

"Yes, sir."

Gink produced the regimental account book and immediately began the process of writing out a promissory note to Gideon, to be drawn in gold pieces from the Marneri Legion accounts. He turned the page and detached a clean sheet of high-quality vellum. Then he took out his fountain pen, an ingenious invention from Cunfshon, which allowed for a pen stylus to be attached to a rubber balloon filled with ink by confining both to a stout tube of wood or horn. A small valve between balloon and pen nib ensured a slow, continuous flow of ink to the nib. While Gink wrote out the requisition Fesken looked out the window and prayed they didn't have any ships run aground the next day. This would be the trickiest part of the trip down the Argo, which at this season was shallow and prone to shifting sandbars from the position they'd last been charted.

Fesken's preoccupations with the morrow kept him from fully noticing the change in the swampscape out the window.

A faint green luminescence was spreading slowly across the surface of the bogs and pools of the swamp. At the main channel it slowed, then resumed its onward creep, slipping forward like a moving shadow beneath the moon.

The night was filled with the sounds of grasshoppers and field crickets. Far away a great bittern unleashed its cry. Occasionally a fish slapped the water out in the channel.

Burk and Hudge were in the final hour of their watch. They were awake, but not at their most alert. They didn't notice the eerie green sheen until it had reached the dock. The bittern boomed again.

"That be a big, randy cock bittern," said Burk, a country boy.

"I'll believe you, sounds very randy, to me," said Hudge, who'd grown up in Bea town itself and didn't know a bittern from a chicken, or even a pigeon.

Hudge raised his arms and stretched his legs, then his back muscles. Finally he moved his head from side to side while he kept his hands on his hips. At which point he noticed something funny about the water. There was a soft green glow over everything as if the whole swamp had been coated with pixie dust. It seemed alive almost.

"What's that?" he called out.

Burk looked up. On it came, a slow-flowing tide of that eerie sparkle. There were tiny gleams of brightness in the depths, sprites in motion, forever at the very edge of vision, like minuscule green lights in the water.

"Better tell the sergeant," said Burk.

"I think so," said Hudge backing up. Sergeant Kemster would bitch about being woken up, but he would also want to know about this. They were supposed to be on a high alert, even with only a modest watch being set.

"Yeah," said Burk, noticing that the weird glow was brightening. "Hurry!"

As Hudge ran up the dock, Brown and Fang started to bark from their sleeping places in the stables. Their barking soon became frenzied. Hudge looked back. The whole swamp was glowing, and there were yellow nodes of light darting about like insects above the water.

"What the hell?" said Burk. There was a sound like a buzzing, or the chirp of a million crickets. Something briefly stirred the surface of the water out in the river. More circles appeared. Movements, swift movements, were taking place beneath the surface.

"Sergeant!" called Hudge, knocking at the command post door. "Sergeant, come take a look!"

"What is it, Hudge?" Kemster stuck his head out the tent.

Sergeant Kemster was out of his cot and down on the dock a few moments later. The glow was brighter than before, and the noise had increased until it was as loud as a storm in full fury.

"What the hell is this?"

"Don't know, sir," muttered Burk. "It just came out of the swamp, just started to glow. And the crickets are going like mad."

"I never heard of lights like this in a river."

They looked over the edge into the waters. The dogs were insane up in the stables. Everyone in the camp was waking up by then.

"Something very strange about this. Go tell the captain, Hudge, at once!"

Hudge turned and started ashore.

"What's got into those dogs?" said Sergeant Kemster, pacing out onto the dock toward Burk.

The waters beside the dock suddenly seemed to explode. Huge shapes, a great many of them, erupted upward. Massive arms swept up Sergeant Kemster and Burk, whose screams rang out briefly as they were thrust headfirst into enormous red maws, gaping wide. In a moment only their legs till hung outside the champing jaws of the monstrous swamp beasts. In another moment their feet were sucked in and gone forever as the beasts swallowed them down.

The dogs had woken everyone within miles by then. Men poked their heads out of their tents and gaped at the unthinkable. The shore was suddenly filled by a herd of monstrous shapes, hulking things, shaped like huge frogs but with the habits of crocodiles, that had sprung from nowhere. They were coming out of the river in an endless flood.

Commander Fesken was one of the first to comprehend. He grabbed a cornet and blew the alarm.

Tents were going down under the things, men were being devoured, torn to pieces and the fragments flung high as the brutes came on. Panic set in. Some men bolted, and ran for their lives into the dark woods. A few ran straight into packs of the swamp beasts and were seized and devoured.

The dragons of the Bea 77th rose up with dragonsword, checking the tide of monstrous creatures. A mound of corpses soon grew across the dragons' front. Dragonboys held their positions behind the dragons, Cunfshon bows in hand.

Elsewhere the camp disintegrated; boats were smashed and men devoured. Here and there men held their ground, veterans whose training kept them alive. They grabbed their spears and shields and prepared to fight even these monstrous foes. The spears were enough to keep the things at a slight distance, but they continually edged forward, despite being jabbed. The men retreated, keeping the swamp beasts off, but only just. The brutes were simply too massive. The swelling chaos threatened to become total.

Fesken had seen this, and also saw that his dragons were holding their line.

"To the dragons," he ordered. "Form up on the dragons, in square." The building shook as more and more of the things crashed up against it and wedged themselves there while yet more piled in behind them.

Sergeant Turgan blew the command for forming a square while Lieutenant Ballard and Lieutenant Shakes ran to take command of two clumps of spearmen.

By dint of great effort, they were able to bring the clumps together. More men joined them. The brutes needed to get close in to seize men in those massive arms and bring their jaws to bear, but the spears jabbing at their eyes kept them at bay. Their clumsy brachts waved and their jaws snapped in frustration and they emitted chilling wails. Cornets screamed, sergeants bellowed, men screamed and either ran or stood their ground with spears raised.

With a clatter the front portion of Gideon's building collapsed onto the horde of swamp beasts that were packed against it, pinned there by the pressure of those behind them, who were still emerging from the swamp.

Columns collapsed along the side of the house, and the dock, meanwhile had already splintered. In the stables the monsters tried to eat the horses, which resisted with flashing hooves.

Out in the dark, many men had slowed their steps as the initial panic subsided. They heard dragons roaring and the thud of terrible blows. They heard the dogs barking and the cornets shrieking. They came to a halt, then almost every one of them turned and ran back to the fray, swords in hand.

Filled with rage where before there had been simply fear, the recovered soldiers came up to reinforce the line, and the swamp beasts were stopped. The tide of battle swayed back and forth for a while, but the swamp beasts could no longer break the Legion line. For several minutes they continued to die on the line, then there came a sudden change, a howl came from the swamp as if from the throat of a giant. A blast of cold air swept over them and the monsters turned as one and hopped and staggered back into the river and subsided beneath its surface.

The men and dragons on the line stood there, chests heaving, sweat running down their bodies, staring wide-eyed while silently giving thanks that they had been spared. Dead beasts were piled in windrows along the front of the dragon line. The bodies of men and horses were spread around the stables. More dead beasts were pinned under the ruins of Gideon's main building.

Commander Fesken found old Hundswide's body in the ruins. The pilot had been caught by a falling beam when the main hall came down. He was added to the casualty list written down by Sublieutenant Gink. There were almost two hundred names on that list. The Bea regiment had been struck a hammerblow. It would be days before they got down to Fort Kenor.

Chapter Twenty-six

Giles led them now, through the long grass growing down to the banks of the river Oon, just visible at the edge of vision in the west. Giles led them, though he was afraid. Each step brought them closer to their quarry, and this terrified him. He could not even carry the charred fragment of a man's thighbone that bore the mark of the Great Being that they tracked. Lessis kept the bone in her satchel. Giles sensed him though. The Lord Who Burned Men left a trail that was seared into the world like a brand, openly visible for those, like Giles, who were sensitive to such things.

The nights were terrible. It was hard for Giles to sleep, knowing as he did what they were seeking, whom they were following. Giles was not a timorous fellow, nor physically inept, but he was very much afraid of the power he had felt when he touched that bone. The dark powers always left such traces, for they burned the very stuff of the universe to do their work. For Giles, the touch was like that of red-hot iron.

And yet he fought down his fears. Lessis helped him. Sometimes he detected her sly little spells. They were visible to him, of course, things of wisps and threads too fine for his sensitivity alone to pick them out. But he knew they were there. She burnished his courage, letting its gleam keep him focused on the great task he faced.

He had trained since childhood for this role, which had always promised to be dangerous. Sensers like himself, that tiny minority gifted with the power, were sought out and employed by the Office of Insight. Often they tracked criminals for the witches. It was his misfortune to be called to the service of a greatwitch, one of the most powerful of them all. He had thought he might track evil men, murderers, and the like. He had never dreamed of following this sort of malign power.

"Can you follow him?" said the witch.

"Yes." He could follow such a power to the ends of the world.

Once or twice he would say that it was madness to follow the Great One. Lessis would smile sadly, but she did not accept his plea.

"We must find him and destroy him," she would say.

"How can we destroy him? He bestrides the world like a colossus. He burns with power beyond our imaginings."

"He is vulnerable, child."

At his look of disbelief, Lessis's anger would spark. "Do you think my sisters have been idle?"

The young man stared at her. "Lady, I know very little of these great secrets. You know that."

"You were trained in Andiquant. You were given classes on history, including recent history. You know who this thing is that we follow."

"Lady, he moves as a mountain in this world. He will trample us and suck our souls from our very bones."

Lessis's eyes would flash at this. "I have fought this demon before, child. I am still here." A shrug. "Alas, so is he."

Giles stared at her, sudden realization blossoming in his eyes. Normally, witches seemed imbued with power. He detected very little projection from her, and had assumed that the quiet exterior was all there was to her.

Giles mastered his terror. "I was trained for this mission; I will not abandon my duty."

"I understand your fear, young Giles. This is no man, no wizard, nor even elven lord that we go up against. This one is a part of the world that was never laid in its place. It was never meant to live like this, separate from the world it created. It has become a fell spirit, grown dark and evil over the aeons. It is indeed terrifying to imagine bringing down such a mighty foe."

Lessis fixed him with her pale eyes. "But, Giles of Corve, I say we can dare the worst, we can extinguish the fear with our courage. We can surprise our enemy who thinks we are weak and easily terrified. That is what our enemy always fails to grasp. In his heart, fear and calculation rule, and courage knows no part."

Giles had taken some renewed heart from her words. The witches knew of a way to destroy the Great Being. Lessis knew his weak spot. They would not fail! Could not fail. Could not.

Still Giles rode ahead, to stay away from the bone that he felt in her saddlebag. Lessis rode beside Lagdalen, with Mirk just behind.

Lessis knew her great enemy far better than she had during her first encounter with him. He had first tried to decapitate the empire, then helped fan the flames of rebellion in Aubinas. Both attempts had failed, and he'd seen that it would be futile to try that route again in the Argonath. So he had released the plagues. It was a move they had expected, and they had done their best at countering it. To some extent they had succeeded. Marneri and Kadein were still functioning. The others were in worse shape, indeed Ryotwa was almost destroyed, but the Legion armies were still in the field, and the white ships ruled the seas. True, the ranks of the Legions were severely depleted, but they were still there. With the help of a Legion from the Isles, they would hold off the Padmasans. Or so it was fervently hoped in Andiquant.

But with the addition of the Baguti of the Irrim Gan and the fell Lord Waakzaam, the equation became more tricky. Birds with warnings had gone south already. She prayed that General Tregor would take action to shore up his northern flank.

And beyond her immediate concern for Tregor's flank, it was a little shocking to her to find their enemies cooperating like this. After the fall of Heruta she had thought the remaining Four Doom Masters would deadlock, two on two, and lose all decisiveness. That would ensure they would stay on the defensive and eventually be destroyed. She had never thought the Four would bury their pride and truckle to Waakzaam. Yet they had, despite their legendary hauteur. They had recognized that they needed a fifth, to break the deadlock, and they had made a devil's bargain with Waakzaam. Fools! He would suck their very souls from their bones before he was finished with them!

They continued due south, hours passing slowly as they rode on elk paths through the tall grass. As they traveled, the grass was changing character; shorter varieties were taking over, the horses' bellies were above the grass for the first time. Away to the right, Beruyn came riding up. Mellicent and Ward were ahead and on the left.

Once every couple of hours a hawk would circle down out of the sky to alight on Lessis's arm and giver her a report on movements around them. Large bodies of horsemen were abroad and moving parallel with them, but closer to the Oon.

They drew together at the noon hour. The trail food was tough and chewy, and their water was low. Beruyn thought there would be water ahead, perhaps another hour. Mirk was not so sure. They drank carefully, aware that finding water by the end of the day was essential, for the horses were in need of a long drink.

Lessis contrasted her current situation, chewing pemmican and dried herbs and washing it down with stale water, with her brief period of retirement. She had lived in her own house in lovely old Valmes, a beautiful house, built of the Valmes white stone, with blue-painted shutters and a pear tree in the backyard.

She sighed. It seemed that it was not to be her lot in life ever to live in that house and enjoy its peace. Only once in the last nine years had she been there to enjoy the pears. She had so enjoyed using the skills of witchcraft to help the crops and the animals. Caring for the sick and the elderly. Living in her house, meditating on her pear tree.

Alas, the necessities of the state had intruded once again. Her work was not yet done.

They had barely remounted before Giles turned, with concern on his face. "I sense something, Lady. Many men, I think, riding this way . . ."

Lessis turned to Mirk, who exchanged a look with the others. Beruyn jumped down and put his head to the ground. He listened for a long while before rising. "Yes, there are hooves, but distant still."

"We'd better move up to the rise and hide over the crest. We don't want to be seen by Baguti."

The movements reported by the last hawk had accelerated, it appeared.

"They must have crossed the big river," said Beruyn.

"They're not of the Irrim tribes, then," said Mirk.

They turned away from the Oon and rode hard for the eastern horizon. By good fortune they topped a long shallow rise and found a small watercourse, trending south toward the Argo. There they pulled up, tucked the horses down out of sight, and went up to the crest of the rise to watch.

After an hour or so, a dark smudge appeared on the far western horizon. The smudge grew swiftly, and soon they caught gleams of metal and the movements of individual horses as an army approached, moving across their front at a distance of about four miles. A torrent of horses and men flowed past them for another hour before all were past. It was even longer for the last of them to disappear over the horizon.

Eventually they remounted their horses and rode south, following in the wake of the Baguti army, moving slowly and cautiously. Lessis had a hawk constantly hovering above them, changing birds as she rode every few miles, taking reports every few minutes.

The Baguti kept on due south, moving swiftly.

Mirk conferred with Lessis, and they decided to swing away to the southeast. They had to find water, and the Baguti wouldn't leave much for them at any water holes directly ahead.

Lessis dispatched another bird to Fort Kenor.

They rode through medium-length grass all afternoon, and Mirk's horse smelled water an hour before dusk. They followed a small stream down to a narrow lake that had contracted to little more than a pond. Wild animals had been to the water in great numbers. The tracks, of bison and deer for the most part, cut up the soft mud along the shoreline.

A turtle plopped into the water. The horses drank. Mirk refilled their canteens by pushing out into the middle, where the water came up to his neck and it was still clear.

Lessis and Lagdalen bathed together to one side, behind a

willow tree for modesty's sake while the men bathed on the muddy shore. The water felt delicious after the long day in the saddle.

After they were dry they gathered near where Mirk had tethered the horses and ate pemmican and flat biscuit. Lagdalen also carried lime juice, and they each took a drop on their biscuits to prevent scurvy. Later they wrapped themselves in their blankets and slept on the hard ground while Mirk kept watch.

Chapter Twenty-seven

The Bea Third Regiment had finally staggered into Fort Kenor, a badly shaken formation. Tremendous casualties had reduced them to barely six hundred effectives. Many of the survivors were exceedingly nervous and found it next to impossible to sleep.

Even the Bea dragons were nervous. Mumzo, an older brass, had some bad slash wounds. Web, the leading leatherback, had bruising where he'd been stomped by the beasts as they tore down his tent. His dragonboy Lammi had a broken leg as a result of the same moments of terror and confusion. The unit was emotionally battered and physically beat-up.

The 109th had done its level best to welcome the 77th, and the Bea men, too. They all knew they faced a grim test against an army two and a half times their own size, and that it was vital to keep a sense of élan. Each night a few kegs of legion weak-beer had been squeezed out of the fort's commissary and after a big dinner, all the dragons and dragonboys milled just outside the fort's main gate, where they drank the beer and did their best to raise their own and each other's spirits.

There had been much speculation, some of it indecent, on the subject of how the swamp beasts had been generated. The guffaws were dying away from Roquil's remark that not even turtles would mate with crocodiles, who were infamously ugly in the eyes of dragons, even though they shared a few common characteristics. Crocodiles, of course, were cold-blooded dimwits, but successful ones that had outlasted most of their competitors in the history of the world.

"Still they have scales, they have four legs, big mouths."

"They not be dragons," said Zed Dek, the freemartin from the Bea 77th.

"They must have hatched from egg, this dragon know that much," said Vlok.

"Yes," agreed Zed Dek, who had already sized up old Vlok, who was not known for quick thinking. "They definitely not like cattle or mammoths, not live birthers."

"Big eggs though."

"Have to be. Not enough crocodiles in these swamps to produce all the eggs you'd need. There were hundreds of the things."

"Maybe they use giant eel?" wondered Vlok.

"What is this eel?"

"Giant eel only lives in the sea," said Alsebra before Vlok could inflict on them his idea of what a giant eel might be.

"Giant eel does have many eggs. Maybe they combine giant eel with crocodile and then with something else."

This concept made dragon eyes get big with anger. Vlok had hit a nerve somewhere. Dragon jaws shifted angrily, huge hands grasped involuntarily.

"Best we find them soon, kill them before they get much further with this."

"By the fiery breath, you right about that," agreed Vlok.

Vaunce joined the group. Vaunce, the crullo, was a quiet sort for the most part, a wyvern of a sweet temperament. He had a middling speed with the sword, for a brass, which meant he was slower than almost all leatherbacks and greens. But he had been taught great technique and used the shield well.

"This dragon still doesn't understand how you can be blue," said the Purple Green with his usual tact. "Blue color only seen on flying dragons, like me."

Vaunce shrugged.

"Well, I am blue, as you can see," he said calmly. "And I am wyvern."

"I see, but I don't understand."

"Not many crullos in the world," replied Vaunce. "The dragon master try to explain to this dragon and I think I understand, but it very complicated. First you have to have a green female from a mating between leatherback and a green. That green female then mates with a brass. Result is usually a leatherback, but sometimes like me, the crullo."

"Astounding."

"Leatherback and green is unusual pairing. Leatherback and leatherback is the rule, though greens are mated with brasshides. Gives you quick, light brasses."

"You know a lot about this," said Alsebra.

And why wouldn't he? Even as a sprat in the dragonhouse, he'd known he was special, almost unique.

"So why do they not breed more like you?"

"We are free beings, not animals. Dragons choose whether to breed or not. But every dragon know that one in three sprats from a leatherback and green mating will be freemartin."

And freemartins were sterile.

"I have heard this," said the Purple Green, casting a wary eye Alsebra's way. The 109th resident freemartin seemed unperturbed.

"That is the way it happens," she said. "Sometimes green and leatherback want to mate, so they do and wyverns like me are the result. I kill my share of our enemies. I just cannot mate."

"Yes, this dragon understand that. But if you were a green and you mated with a brasshide, then you would have leatherbacks?"

"Leatherback is the commonest type. All types breed to leatherback."

"But once in a while there would hatch a blue one?"

"That's it."

The Purple Green absorbed this in silence.

Zed Dek erupted in the strange noises that was the wyvern equivalent of laughter.

"Why is this so amusing?" asked Alsebra.

"When they put this force together the gods must have been

drunk. We've got a crullo, a wild, winged dragon, two free-martins, and the amazing Bazil Broketail."

Rumbles and subdued laughter followed this remark.

"There is also I, Hexarion," said the big green from the 145th.

"There is you, this is true," said Zed Dek.

"Another green," rumbled the Purple Green. "We already have Gryf. He have enough attitude for all of us."

"You are partly green," said Hexarion.

"And mostly purple," said the Purple Green, with arched neck and flashed fangs.

"And mostly purple," said Hexarion, with unexpected meekness. Alsebra breathed a sigh of relief. To have a big green with a bit of good sense would make a pleasant change.

Vaunce had been listening to it all while idly pondering his own question. "When wild flying dragon mate with wyvern, what happens?"

The Purple Green whirled around, big eyes wide.

"Wild flying dragon would eat wyvern, better than mating."

"Well, in your case, perhaps you're right," said Alsebra. "But didn't the Broketail mate with flying dragon?"

All turned their gaze on Bazil, who until then had been quietly standing by, having drunk up all his beer ration early.

"Well?"

"Well, what?"

"Well, did you or didn't you mate with a flying dragon?"

As if uncomfortable with the thought, Bazil replied in a sober-toned voice, "I mate with High Wings. I have two young; they have wings like their mother."

The Purple Green was scowling, eyes blazing. With a snort of uttermost displeasure he lurched up from where he'd sat by the ditch and stalked inside. The wyverns watched him go with astonished eyes.

"This dragon fail to understand why you had to go and say that," grumbled Bazil. "Now he will be prickly for days."

Alsebra checked her first response. Having the Purple Green sunk in a depression or a bad mood could ruin the morale in the unit. "You're right. I shouldn't have said anything, but one thing to be said, I didn't bring it up."

They all looked at Vaunce, who stepped back, tail low. "I only ask because I . . ." He looked at them all focused on him. "I didn't think it would upset the wild one so."

"The Purple Green and the Broketail fought for High Wings, and the Purple Green lost."

"This dragon meant no harm. I didn't know about all that."

"Too late now. The Purple Green will be dangerous company for a few days. Try not to say anything when he's around."

As this disaster among the wyverns took place, the dragonboys were off at the other side of the gate, sitting on a bench brought out from the fort.

Swane and Rakama were telling a complicated story about the twin daughters of the landlord of the Blue Post Inn at Dalhousie. Most of the others gathered around them, but Relkin sat apart, with Manuel and Mulian, the dragonboy for Zed Dek. They discussed what the Bea boys could do to help cope with the load of tending the boyless 145th.

"With Lammi down because of his leg," said Mulian, "we're having to cover on Web, but we can still pull extra details to help you."

"We'd appreciate it. Keeping two dragons going full-time when they're working so much outdoors is overwhelming."

"Joboquins going like crazy, I can imagine."

"Well, everything's going. At least we ain't been fighting yet, nothing chews up kit like fighting, but there's been a lot of extra things to do. Did your joboquins get torn up in this swamp fracas?"

"Most of the dragons never got the joboquin on, just had time to take the swords and then we were fighting."

Relkin nodded. In hand-to-hand fighting every moment lasted too long, but the dangers and exertions to meet them annihilated time simultaneously. Exhaustion or death was all that could end it sometimes, and often they came together, hand in hand.

"It was sorcery, Relkin." Mulian's voice had changed. "Pure evil. The water in the swamp was glowing green. It sounded as if every bug in the world was there, and then these things just came out of the swamp. They were almost the size of dragons, and they just ate men left and right."

"I guess it shows us why we're fighting."

"Well said, Relkin," spoke Manuel.

"The dragons are moving," said Jak.

When the wyverns straggled back to their tents, the dragon-boys soon followed. They slept soundly for the most part, though many in the camp were disturbed in the second hour of the morning when something passed overhead, leaving a single shrill screech in its wake.

The batrukh that let out that scream was guided by Gring, the Mesomaster. Behind Gring, in the second seat of the saddle, sat the fair form that Waakzaam preferred to take.

The batrukh powered its way through the air until they spied campfires by the banks of a lagoon.

"Land!" said the tall elven lord.

With wings beating to slow itself, the batrukh swept in to land on the beach below the fires. It came in with a thump, lifted, and landed again, this time slowing to a walk and then halting.

Gring was still recovering from the violence of the landing when he saw that the tall figure had already descended to the ground. It stood like a statue in complete silence. The batrukh turned its huge head to the elf figure and seemed to purr. Gring had never seen a batrukh do this before. He shivered.

Gring dismounted and dropped to the ground. The batrukh ignored him.

The Lord Lapsor was already striding toward the Baguti who were gathered around the biggest fire. He had long since learned how to handle Baguti troops. They responded to greed, and also to fear.

"Welcome!" said one of the squat, muscular tribal chieftains. "I am Ugit. What are you called?"

The Lord Lapsor brushed past him. These Baguti in their leather armor and skullcaps were westerners, devotees of a cannibal cult called the Ulq Murqh. This meant they would be ruled by their Skulltaker, in this case Najj. Therefore, it was Najj that the tall serene elf lord approached. Najj, a muscular sort in black-leather armor, set his hand on his sword.

"Who are you?" said another Baguti. The giant stranger made no response.

Najj raised a hand. "Be quiet, Jihj. The stranger has come to talk with me. I am Skulltaker."

The elf stepped to the fire and suddenly stooped down and threw in all the wood that was stacked there. The fire had already been stoked up, now it blazed at once, and sparks flew over campsite. Men scrambled back from the intense heat.

The giant turned back to Najj.

"You are the one in command here."

"I am Skulltaker."

"You have not fulfilled the plan. You were supposed to be far north of this position."

The Baguti chieftains hissed at this, and several reached for their swords. He ignored them. "General Munth wonders why you haven't made better progress."

"General Munth commands the Padmasan army. I am Skulltaker here."

"Nonetheless, General Munth has a plan. You have not done your part."

"General Munth can go fuck himself," snarled Najj the Skulltaker, slapping his palm on his massive chest. "He ask too much of us. This country is not good for Baguti. Too wet, too much quicksand."

The elf lord struck so swiftly that they were all stunned into action. He reached forward, seized Najj neck and crotch, and swung him up high. Najj belowed and struggled, kicking and swinging his arms, but he was helpless. The lord held him high, stepped forward to the blazing fire and hurled Najj directly into it.

Najj fell among the embers and burning logs and rolled out screaming, smoking, flapping his arms. He writhed onto his hands and knees, but the tall elven lord seized him again and dragged him to his feet. Najj struck out at the demon lord, but achieved nothing. He bellowed with unaccustomed fear as he was lifted off his feet again and swung up high.

Najj screamed as he was cast once more directly into the center of the blazing fire. The rest of the Baguti were watching in stunned horror, but none lifted a hand to help.

Najj thrashed, but failed to escape the flames. His screams cut off after a few seconds.

Over the fire the Man Burner had raised his arms while his eyes calmly surveyed the astounded and horrified Baguti. He lifted his eyes to the heavens and raised his voice so it rang off the hillsides.

"Aah wahn, aah wahn, gasht thrankulu kunj."

A strange sense of unease permeated the scene. The men felt their stomachs flutter in their bellies, and their hair stood on end.

"Tshagga avrot!"

There was a huge flash of green fire that seemed to suck the blaze out and consume the very soul of poor Najj the Skulltaker.

The green fire shot down from the skies and onto the erect figure of the giant elf, standing with his fist clenched above his head. He stood there for several long, incredible seconds, while the green blaze continued.

Thus was the life force of Najj the Skulltaker totally consumed.

The clap of thunder broke over them and continued to beat back and forth in the hills for long minutes afterward.

The fire had gone out and there was nothing left of Najj at all.

The elf lord faced the Baguti.

"I am now Skulltaker, understood?"

The mumbled their fearful assent.

"You will know me as Lapsor. Tomorrow you will reach the designated place."

The Baguti mumbled. Jihj dared to mutter askance.

The Lord Lapsor raised a fist and called again that strange and terrible cry.

"Aah wahn, aah wahn, gasht thrankulu kunj."

A green bolt of fire leaped off the giant's fist and spat across to strike Jihj in the chest. His scream was accompanied by his body tossed backwards ten feet to land in a smoking heap.

The other chieftains exchanged a slow glance.

"Tomorrow you will reach your designated position, or I will burn your souls to dust."

Chapter Twenty-eight

The morning dawned bright and clear over the volcano, with that chill in the air that warned of winter approaching. Dragon-boys were among the first up, and tureens of kalut were soon being wheeled to the dragons. Smoke rose by the cook pit, the early-morning wood splitting details were starting up, and the familiar "thwack, thwack, thwack" of mauls on wood soon filled the air. A supply wagon creaked down the line to the cooks' tent.

Hollein Kesepton emerged from his tent with his blue blanket over his shoulders in time to grab a big mug of kalut from the passing orderly. All the officers were standing out there, some more dazed than others as they began another punishing day. The generals were keeping them very busy with work. Every sandspit and peninsula would be fortified before they were satisfied, it seemed.

General Urmin appeared, already fully dressed, from the headquarters tent. Hollein had slung the blanket and got into his coat and pulled up his boots by the time Urmin reached him.

"Morning, Commander. I trust you got some sleep."

"Yes, sir, the bare minimum. At least that's how it feels."

"It's only going to get worse, it always does. I don't know if we'll ever satisfy the engineers."

"Not possible, sir. No such thing as a satisfied engineer."

Urmin smiled, then turned serious. "Kesepton, I've been wanting to ask you something, something sensitive."

"Yes, sir?"

"It's Fesken, I'm worried about him. Does he seem quite himself to you?"

"Well, I don't know him, sir, but he seems fine. I haven't heard of any complaints."

"You've read his report?"

"Yes, sir. Harrowing. Sorcery, sir, and of a high order. You remember that great flash of light while we were at Gideon's? I can't help but think the two events were related. Maybe we were just lucky."

"Sorcery, eh?" Urmin shuddered with loathing. "I suspect you may be right. What they went through might shake any man. Do you think I should send him home? Have him reevaluated?"

Hollein was loath to answer. Fesken's efforts at Gideon's had helped stem the panic and saved many lives. And yet since joining them at Fort Kenor he had been morose, shut up in some inner gloom. It often happened that young officers blamed themselves for casualties, and the Bea Regiment had been hurt at Gideon's. The choice really was whether to jeopardize one man's career, or risk hundreds of men's lives if their commander came to pieces in the heat of battle. Being an officer of similar rank to Fesken and well aware of the pressures that came with active combat, Hollein hated the choices.

Before he was forced to commit himself, there came a welcome interruption. A short cornet shriek from the watchtower announced a rider. Men were in motion pulling back the gates. Two riders came thundering in, then pulled up sharply. One ran to the headquarters tent to deliver his message to General Tregor while the other held their horses, both blowing hard and sweating after their ride.

Cornets blew immediately, and kept blowing as units were called straight to parade formation. In full battle regalia they marched out soon afterward, without even their breakfasts straight down the road to the Oon. Ahead of them went the two riders, on fresh mounts, with messages for the officers at the front.

The news filtered down. The enemy was making straight for the shallows below Crescent Island. Baguti cavalry had already crossed the river in several places. More Baguti on their steppe ponies had already crossed the Argo and were operating in the rear. They were at the center of a huge coordinated attack that was aiming for a double envelopment of the Legion's flanks while their center was held in place by repeated attack.

"It's exactly what I'd do if I had their numbers, and they had mine," rumbled Tregor as he studied the maps with his staff.

Tregor had less than five thousand horse and would be hard-pressed in a cavalry engagement. What he had included the great Red Rose Regiment from Cunfshon, the two-thousand-strong core of the Red Rose Legion itself. But not even the Red Rose Regiment could be expected to defeat twenty times its own strength on the battlefield.

In his favor was the fact that the enemy customarily misused the wild nomad cavalry, distrusting its anarchic shortcomings. Still, the numbers were daunting on all fronts. The current estimate of the horde approaching the river crossing was thirty thousand imp, two hundred troll. There was even a party of ten ogres, the enormous ultratrolls bred from tormented mammoths. That was almost twice the size of the force under Tregor's command. Then there were the Baguti. The northern force came from the Irrim tribes of the near Gan. The estimates were of perhaps fifteen thousand riders. Those to the south had come from the far west and were Baguti of unknown tribes. The estimate was that their strength was about ten thousand.

Fortunately the southern force was also cut off by trackless bogs and quaking sands. It would take them days to affect the southern flank, or at least so Tregor hoped. He also hoped that his flank forces could slow the Baguti long enough to let him deal with the main thrust across the river by the horde of imp.

The Oon River had wide flats on either side, culminating in dunes farther back. The 109th, along with the 145th and the Bea 77th, were set out in a fortified line dug down behind the dunes, with a staked barricade along the top. They were hungry, but dragonboys soon appeared with carts full of big flat loaves of bread. Dragons tore into the meal hungrily. They were hot under the bright sun, and uncomfortable in full armor. They had been allowed to remove their helmets, which were stacked with their shields, but wearing many huge pieces of metal hooked to the joboquin was inherently hot on a sunny day.

Still, it was good to have something to eat, even if there wasn't enough akh. They washed the bread down with pails of water fetched from the river by bustling dragonboys, who were working especially hard since many of them were taking care of two dragons. Relkin went down to the river three times before he'd satisfied both the thirsty wyverns.

Each time he went down to the water's edge, he observed that the smudge marking the enemy's horde had deepened and darkened on the far side of the Oon. The enemy had also made an appearance on Crescent Island, a low green feature slightly upstream. Imps and trolls became visible on its shore.

The catapults erected by the engineers started to fire at the trolls on Crescent Island, and after a couple of spectacular hits from hurtling nine-foot-long spears, all trolls were removed to safety behind adequate cover. Dirt was flying on the island from many shovels, and men in black could be seen in the spyglass as they went about erecting their own catapults. Shortly thereafter, catapults from the island began seeking the range of the defensive line. With a clatter heavy, ten-foot spears began to strike the stakes of the stockaded barricade. The dragons were urged to keep down as an occasional spear burst through a weak spot in the stockade.

Tregor frowned. He had not expected such expert catapult work. The enemy had improved their battlecraft since the last major conflict.

The rest of that day passed in a duel of catapults, with huge spears flashing over the heads of either side as they crouched behind cover. The Legion crouched behind well-prepared barricades, however, while the Padmasans were far more exposed. The Argonathi catapult crews took a toll on their opponents.

That night cookfires blazed high behind the lines, and a huge boil-up was distributed to the men and dragons along with some legion weakbeer. This improved everyone's spirits by the time they turned in. Tents had been pitched during the afternoon, and the place was quickly becoming a proper Legion camp.

The enemy's camp was visible as a line of distant fires, etched along the horizon. There were also a few fires on Crescent Island, but these were hidden as much as possible, for the Legion catapults were quick to home in on any fire within range.

A strong watch was set, and the flank forces were instructed to be particularly vigilant. Excused watch, dragons and their dragonboys slept soundly.

Meanwhile, General Tregor and his senior commanders were gathered in the general's tent, confronting potential problems. Tregor pointed to the large map spread on the table.

"The Irrim tribes have crossed the Argo up here at Poot's Point. They have about fifteen thousand effectives and can either swing down to blanket Fort Kenor behind us or try to envelop our flank. However, to get on our flank they will have to pass through three choke points, two of which we have fortified and can defend quite easily; here at Brownwater Lagoon and here at the neck of land at the bottom of Falze Bay. That's the only way for horses to get through the swamp there. Provided we can hold them on those lines, we can continue to hold this position."

"Won't the enemy come around by the Military Road, sir?" Commander Lenshwingel had raised his hand early.

"Most likely, and they will have to be met in the swamp and stopped. Probably at Angle Pond."

"Which we fortified years ago," said Lenshwingel, a young know-it-all out of the Marneri Military Academy who had been suddenly promoted after the plagues and given command of the Marneri Fourth Regiment, First Legion. "The ditch is ten feet deep now, and the stockade is reinforced, plus there's two twenty-foot-tall towers in the center, over the gate."

Commander Clumb of the Kadein Eleventh Regiment raised his hand. "What word do we have from the south, sir?"

Tregor tapped his pointer on his hand.

"Red Rose Regiment is down there, following their progress. The Baguti are making little headway so far. They don't know the country, and that makes them cautious. Plus, it's all bogs and quicksands for miles down there."

"So it will take them more than a day to reach the Little Fish River?"

"All estimates are that it will take them at least two days, By which time we will have met their thrust at the crossings and denied it."

"And in the process let them winnow their own ranks attacking us in prepared and fortified lines."

"We can prepare a warm welcome for the Baguti, too, though I'm sure that once they see us waiting for them they'll back off and recross the river. Baguti are not irrational, and they don't usually fight with the black drink in their veins. They are not imps to be driven like cattle to the slaughter."

"Sir." Lenshwingel again. "What if the Baguti in the north move down against the Fort? We'll be cut off from supply."

"Right, Captain, excuse me, that's uh, Commander Lenshwingel, yes?"

"Yes, sir!"

"Of course if he moves down to the Military Road he will cut our supply line. The road is fortified, though, at every major bridge. But ten thousand riders can cause a lot of problems nonetheless. So we have been stocking up. We have almost four days' full provision in hand, am I right?"

He turned to Sublieutenant Gink.

"Yes, sir, four days, at a stretch."

"But we'll be able to feed the dragons, right?"

"Yes, sir."

"So," Tregor wheeled back to the others. "We will stand on this line and hold it and let them splinter their army on it."

"Sir, do you anticipate that we will fight here for three days?"

"Well, look at this way, Lenshwingel. We can hold them off, but they must overwhelm us if they wish to invade Kenor. So they will come right at us, hoping that their Baguti flanking forces will help them envelop our force. We will kill them on this line for as long as they come."

Lenshwingel thought he understood. This was his first experience of combat. He was anxious to be seen as useful and performing well. He was afraid, but he was told that it was normal for men to be afraid.

"Yes sir, I see it now."

"About the position at the Angle, sir?"

"Yes, Commander Kesepton."

"Have we worked out the new dragon rotation for that position? You wanted one unit at a time there, primarily to rest up from the line here, but also for the defensive role, if the enemy come in on the Military Road at our rear."

"Gink?"

"Yes, sir, it will be posted shortly. The big problem is the 145th Marneri. Since they don't have dragonboys, they're being taken care of by the boys of the 109th, with some help from the 77th Bea. If we move them up to the Angle, they'll be forced to fight without dragonboy support."

"Not good, not good at all. Hard to deputize men for that though, they'll all get killed with the tail mace."

Tregor turned to the dragon leaders.

"Cuzo, what do you think?"

"Move some boys with the 145th, take three from each squadron. It's better to have dragonboys with them, you need the archery and the protection from the occasional imp that gets through. Once a dragon is hamstrung by imps he's helpless."

"Right, sounds practical enough. Gink, write out the orders and get them posted at once."

"Yes, sir."

The officers studied the map carefully, checking it against the smaller maps they carried in leather tubes over their shoulders. The Red Rose Legion held the southern half of the position, which stretched out on a front of half a mile. The Red Rose was drawn up in a slightly curved line down to the Little Fish River at the southern end. The northern part of the levee was held by the Argonath Legion, set out in divisions made up of two regiments apiece. There were two regiments held in reserve.

The levee had been fortified with a stockade its entire length, and a ditch had been dug in front and staked. The dragons would fight from behind the protection of the stockade. Men occupied the line between the dragons. Dragonboys would fight behind the dragons as usual, and archers were set at intervals all along the line. Finally there were the catapults, set every fifty yards. It was as strong a line as could be fashioned with less than twenty thousand total effectives.

Behind them lay five and a half miles of swamps and lagoons to the higher ground at the base of the volcano. Fort Kenor was up there, high on the northern side of the cone. There was but a single road back to the fort, and it crossed a number of bridges. This was their greatest weakness, but at the same time it offered a strange strength of purpose. They would hold their line because they had no alternative. To retreat down that road, fighting their way through a Baguti army with the Padmasans behind them would be to risk annihilation.

They were Legion troops, trained from the beginning to fight superior numbers—and win.

"We have recruited two hundred of the best archers to work up and down the line, in addition to the regular troops of archers which will be stationed up and down the line. You'll always have an archer in earshot," Tregor said.

The officers, young and old, nodded grimly.

"We can expect their attack first thing in the morning. I want the maximum watch maintained through the night. There will be a mist, and they will use that to get as close as possible. Half an hour before dawn I want every man up and awake. Extra supplies of kalut will be on hand. There'll be time for sleep later in the day if they don't attack."

Chapter Twenty-nine

General Tregor was not a stupid man and his scouting intelligence was good. Consequently, he went to his cot that night reasonably convinced that he would be ready for the enemy's assault the following morning, at dawn.

All would have proceeded as expected, if he had not been facing in General Munth, an extremely aggressive commander determined to make his mark, and the power of the greatest sorcerer of any age, the Dominator of Twelve Worlds, Waakzaam the Great.

The moon set in the second hour of the morning, two hours before dawn. In the darkness Munth threw two huge assault columns across the river. To guide them were Baguti who had trained extensively for this job. They kept the lumbering trolls and imp columns marching steadily through the shallow waters, over rocky bare islets and stretches of mud.

The Great River was three miles wide at this point in its course, and in the dry season it formed a braid of channels and islets and flat expanses of rock. The guides knew it all, and they performed faultlessly. Through the hours of complete darkness, the assault parties moved swiftly.

As they closed within a mile of the farther shore a strange effect arose off the waters. A faint mist, glowing green, seemed to breathe out of the ground in wisps. As it came it laid a complete silence upon the world and all the noise of their passage, from the splashing of thousands of feet in the water, to the clank of metal, the rasp of wood and leather, all vanished.

They seemed to glide on in silence, and the very moments of time became stretched out, dreamlike, as they moved on toward the Argonath lines. A great wonder spread among them, and with that wonder came a savage hope that at last they would surprise an Argonathi army in its sleep.

Under the deep darkness the Padmasans came on, silent and almost invisible. They passed into catapult range, undetected. Then they passed the range of the best archers and then the crossbowmen and now the stockade wall was dimly visible to the vanguard, a pale barrier stretched across their front.

They were just a couple of hundred yards now from the Argonathi wall and still there had been no response. With a sense of mounting triumph the men in the black mercenary uniforms exchanged cheerful sallies, urged the imps on, even patted the vicious trolls on the shoulder as they went by, ignoring their sullen snarls.

In the vanguard strode enormous albino trolls carrying huge hammers. Behind them came blocks of imps with scaling ladders and pry bars.

They left the water behind and ascended the shingle beach. The scrape of stones was masked, not a sound reaching the sentries on the towers.

And then the huge feet of trolls trod on the petals of a rose that had been scattered there earlier by a witch.

As the petals were crushed so Hadea, the young witch attached to the front line force, broke out of her meditative trance.

There! Something was on the beach, something had broken the invisible cordon she had established. She tried to sense it and recoiled. Enormous sorcery stalked the night, the power was so vast it was stunning to contemplate.

Without further thought she jumped to her feet and ran naked to the command post. The guards almost dropped their spears at the sight of Hadea, stark naked, long golden tresses streaming behind her as she ran up, pulled the cornet off its hook and blew on it, way off note, but loud.

"What ails the witch?" said the guards, but Hadea continued to blow into the cornet with horrible results.

The guards scratched their heads, but men and dragons were

waking up. Querulous voices called out from all over the camp, mostly damning the drunk on the cornet to hell and beyond.

She blew it again and again and quite suddenly the men on the rampart felt a strange sensation pass over them, as if a soft blanket had been pulled from their heads, a blanket that had muffled the world. Hadea's tuneless cornet shrieks had broken the spell. From their front was the rush of sounds of a huge army, the stamp of thousands upon thousands of feet, the clank of metal, all coming forward at a rapid pace.

The sergeants were already up there, impelled by that insane cornet. Men were awake all up and down the line now. More cornets shrieked, but now they called the alarm and the "prepare to receive the enemy" in quick conjunction.

Hadea dropped the cornet while the astonished guards turned away. Discovering her own nakedness, she doubled back to her own tent to get some clothes on. The first men to scramble toward the rampart at that point were treated to the sight of Hadea running past them. These men subsequently reached the parapet with their eyes widened and their senses fully awakened.

In the rest of the camp sergeants ran through the lines of tents, turning out the laggards with curses and none-too-gentle taps with a cane. Dragons hauled themselves upright, barely popped an eye before they grabbed their weapons and went out to greet the enemy, some with dragonboys still arranging armor and latching straps and clasps.

The first reinforcements were just arriving on the rampart when the parapet began to shake up and down the line. The heavy trolls had arrived and were beating in the stockade walls with their huge hammers. Scaling ladders thunked up against the wall while a storm of arrows flew up into the faces of the defenders.

In the confusion, men and dragons were all mixed up on the rampart, arrows were pouring in, and the archers were firing back, when suddenly a vast green fire blazed in the west, a light so bright that it temporarily struck blind those who glimpsed it. Coming from behind the Padmasan horde it did the imps little harm, but it flashed directly in the eyes of the Argonathi defenders.

Unable to see, the archers stopped firing. Imps scrambled up the ladders and onto the wall, driving home their crude swords against men who could barely see them to fight. Unhindered by the bowmen or the catapults, the trolls were pounding down the stockade and scrambling in. Men gave way before this mighty assault. Dragons managed to engage the enemy, and the clangor of dragonsword on troll shield and helm began. But the dragons were still reeling from the light, which continued to pour in from the west, out of a blazing orb low in the sky. They fought tentatively, with their shields up and trolls scored unusual successes early on.

By the time Relkin got his vision even halfway sorted out, he was hammered to his knees by an imp with a sword blow that knocked off his helmet and just about left him unconscious. Somehow, he got back up and found the Purple Green coming with the big Legion-issue sword in motion. He dived below it and felt the wind of its passing. Imps were cleared brutally from the scene, but the sword got stuck in the parapet. A troll forced its way through a gap smashed open with the hammer. Imps were prying it wider, more imps were coming up the ladders.

Men were recovering. The Purple Green was heaving his sword free, but an imp was coming for him. Relkin hurled himself bodily into the imp and knocked it down. The Purple Green stamped on it even as he heaved his blade clear. Relkin ducked aside as an arrow flew past, and he heard it go thunk against the Purple Green's massive shield. Then Manuel was there, firing straight into the troll's face, allowing the Purple Green to hew it down.

Bazil swung by, sword high, pitching into two trolls that had burst clean through the parapet and onto the rampart. Troll shields were riven by Ecator as Bazil brought the fell sword over and down.

Arrows were still coming in, and now the enemy catapults on Crescent Island were firing. The enemy would happily sacrifice its own if it would help kill dragons. Shalp, a leatherback from Bea, was killed by a ten-foot catapult spear. Trolls broke through where he'd fallen. The stockade was disintegrating.

A brasshide from the Kadein 144th went backwards off the

rampart with another of the terrible spears through his guts. Trolls hewed down old Gungus, the wise old leader of the Kadein 64th. These trolls were fighting in trios, one of the giant albino brutes, one of the more usual black-purple kind, and one of the new, more slightly built sword type, which had enough intelligence and speed to wield battlesword almost as well as a dragon.

General Tregor, awake and trembling, found himself with a nightmare on his hands. The terrible green light in the west was blazing again. And the enemy were breaking through in several places on his front. Cornets all up and down the line were shrieking insanely over the roar of battle and the deep bellows of massed trolls that were pushing through the breaks.

"Orders, sir?" said Sublieutenant Gink.

Chapter Thirty

The light cut off as suddenly as it had begun. Everyone was now fighting in what seemed like pitch-darkness.

Dragons, accustomed to hunting by darkness, recovered from this more quickly than men or trolls. At once wyvern swords were in motion, and in moments trolls were separated from their heads up and down the line. The dragons took heart, and their roaring built up to the usual formidable pitch as they resumed the fray.

At one point Relkin glimpsed the monstrous bulk of the Purple Green, unmistakable with the wings strapped tight to his back. He had picked up a troll and held it over his head as he strode deliberately to the parapet, then hurled it down into the oncoming imps.

Then Relkin lost track as imps poured in, and it got very hot for the dragonboys and men on the rampart. An imp arrow bounced off his helmet with a stunning blow, driving him to his knees. Shaking his head, he brought up his bow. An imp was almost on him, leading with its spear. He aimed instinctively and fired almost at the same moment. The spear caught on the end of the bow and though the imp fell past him, the spear was deflected down to the ground just in front of his foot. Relkin looked back and saw the imp was dead while he reloaded without pause. He caught another imp at the rampart's edge, then a third as it tried to spear the dragon from behind.

A huge catapult spear suddenly sank into the uppermost part

of the parapet in front of Bazil. The wood splintered apart, and the spear ended up projecting through for half its length. Relkin's heart skipped a beat. The big leatherback had covered with his shield, though not even a shield could stop some of these catapult projectiles.

"Keep down!" Relkin shouted.

"This dragon is keeping down."

Bazil had slain three trolls and cleared his front. Alsebra was occupied with two trolls, unfortunate Vlok had three. Swane had missed his imp and was busy fighting on the ground with another.

Their neighbors pitched in to help. The Purple Green knocked one troll senseless with the flat of his sword. Manuel shot the imp that almost got Swane. Bazil engaged the sword troll that was climbing through the broken parapet in front of Vlok. Bazil's stroke was held, the troll was strong as well as quick. It made a cut and then a return that Bazil could only take on the shield and deflect with Ecator. Vlok helped out some more by tripping on a dead troll, falling, and knocking the sword troll down to its knees. Bazil finished it with a flash of the sword. A huge albino troll, its yellow tusks exposed in a savage snarl, went belly to belly with Hexarion, the green from the 145th. Hexarion was actually borne back a step, though the troll was barely two-thirds his own weight.

He shook off the thing's grip and smashed an elbow into its hideous face. It shrieked and they wrestled, snarling and spitting in each other's faces until Alsebra leaned over and slid her blade into the troll's side and finished it.

Hexarion stood over the body. "Thank you, that was a hell of a strong troll."

"You're welcome," was her response as she engaged with some spearmen in the black-leather uniform of Padmasa.

The fighting was chaotic and intense, but Legion training came to the fore. The men formed into triads, then coalesced into a short line. Lines connected to one another. Dragons fought in front, men stayed out of the wyverns' way.

The imps pressed against them, but the trolls could not break the wyverns' line, and any imps that got past them were swiftly dealt with by the men. Where a wyvern was speared or cut down, the line of men would move forward at once to engage at the parapet edge, where they worked with spears and arrows against the trolls. That could hold them back for a while, but eventually a new dragon would be needed in that hole.

The line along the much-damaged parapet stabilized. The Legion force had almost been shocked off the rampart and into flight, but had held after that first fierce struggle. The battle see-sawed a little more, but it was starting to settle into a pattern. The Legion, with the dragons on the rampart, could not be broken. Dead trolls mounded up at the edge of the parapet. Imp casualties ran into the thousands.

Still the Padmasans had not given up. They regrouped, more black drink was passed among the imps, and once more they came on against the battered stockade. As before, the powerful green light flashed on just at the moment of impact. The Legions were better prepared this time, but it still had its deadly effect, and the imps and trolls broke through once more.

Relkin felt his sword ring against another imp's blade! He turned inside, and rammed his knee into the imp's midriff, where the armor was slight. The imp gave a gasp, Relkin got past its guard, and slew it in the next moment. Another was coming, almost immediately.

And then Jumble was there, swinging with nice crisp strokes, wielding his village blade, Chantceer. He disabled a troll, spun it around, and sent it crashing back into the ruins of the parapet. His tail sword came over and sliced its throat with a nicely timed move. The troll thrashed in the broken timbers.

Jumble then swatted some of the insurgent imps and kicked others back. They retreated to the parapet, past the still-thrashing troll. Relkin shot one as it went. Jumble caught another one with his sword. The troll was dead at last, and the imps were gone.

For a moment their front was clear. Bazil had killed everything that had come over the parapet on his front. He had also unwittingly brained a poor soldier from Bea, who had failed to duck the tail in time. The Purple Green and Alsebra had cleared their fronts, too, and now the parapet was back in the hands of the 109th all along their front.

Catapult spears were still whipping into the position. Wynelda, a lively freemartin in the Kadein 144th was killed as a spear passed clean through her upper body. Officers, tongue-lashed by Tregor, were out there with the engineers, dragooning men into repairing the stockade. Their efforts were hastened by the sounds from the enemy. The trolls were starting to roar again, and the imps clashed spears on shields as the black drink took effect once more.

Bands of copper wire and stout rope were employed to tie back together the broken sections of the parapet where it was possible. Where the damage was too great, the timbers were hastily hammered across the gap horizontally and bracing posts were rammed into the rampart behind them.

And still arrows and spears from the enemy catapults flashed through breaks in the stockade. Several engineers had fallen during the repair work.

One ten-foot spear smashed through the stockade between Vlok and Bazil, who were hunched down behind the parapet. The spearhead quivered about three feet inside the wall, directly between the two leatherbacks as they faced one another.

"This dragon hate these catapults."

"This dragon agrees."

They shifted back several feet. The dull horns were blaring again, and the enemy was readying for a third assault on the lines.

At that point they heard a sudden crescendo of cornet calls from the south. Sharp shrieks announced trouble on the southern flank, past the Red Rose Legion from Cunfshon.

General Tregor heard the cornets and bit his lip. The Baguti had reached their flank? But they had been miles away. How had they driven themselves to get this far so soon? They must have traveled through the night, across the bogs and swamps. How? It seemed so unlike the usual pattern of warfare from the nomads, who avoided arduous conditions and hazardous attacks whenever possible.

More cornets told him that it was indeed the Baguti, and that a crisis was building on the flank of the Red Rose Legion.

Tregor was on his horse and riding for General Va'Gol's command post in the next moment. Sublieutenant Gink was on his mount just a few moments later.

Tregor found Va'Gol's command post a scene of anxiety and confusion. The Legion line had broken under an assault by dismounted Baguti. Then mounted Baguti had followed and now the nomads were pouring in, thousands of them. The entire left flank had been broken down and turned off the ramparts, forced to fight ad hoc in the woods behind the beach.

The Legionaries' iron discipline had held, they were fighting well now, but the rampart was compromised, and there were ten thousand or more Baguti engaged on the southern flank against less than two thousand defenders who had no defensive works left.

Tregor immediately ordered some of his slender reserves to hurry south and bolster the Red Rose Regiment. Dragons were shifted south, too, a scramble of heavy bodies moving down behind the rampart.

The enemy charged the stockade once more. Horns blaring, trolls roaring, and imps howling, they came on, threw up their ladders, drove home with their hammers, and once more the green light threw everything into stark, hideous relief.

The line shook all along the front, but this time the Legionaries held firm. Men and dragons ducked behind their shields at the crucial moment and avoided the blinding light. Then they took on the enemy, despite having the fierce green light in their eyes.

At which point Tregor received the news that the enemy had assaulted the Legion positions at Brownwater Lagoon and also at the Angle on the Military Road. The Baguti had moved with far less lethargy than they'd ever shown before, and as a result Tregor's army was bottled up on the beach with no clear road back to the fort at the volcano.

He had expected something like this to develop, but not this early and not with his left flank broken off the rampart and in extremis in the woods.

Tregor faced the prospect of annihilation and the loss of the empire's main surviving army after the two plagues that had struck the lands of the Argonath. He put his head in his hands for a moment and prayed for strength and guidance from the Great Mother of all things.

Chapter Thirty-one

The fighting petered out toward midmorning, leaving the Legion position damaged but unbroken. The imps were simply exhausted. Not even unlimited black drink could kick them forward in another charge. The enemy retreated back across the river, leaving only the catapults on Crescent Island to continue hostilities.

Catapults sniped all day while the Legions worked to repair their battered lines. On the beach, mounds of dead imps and trolls began to heat up in the sun. On the southern flank, in the woods north of the Little Fish River, the Red Rose Legion dug itself in with a furious effort. A ditch, a short rampart, and a stockade were going up in record time.

Relkin had time to examine the two wyverns under his care. Bazil had some scrapes, some bruising from a troll hammer, and plenty of damage to his shield. The secondary strap on the third lumbar had come loose on the joboquin. Lots of other straps were stressed, but his cross-stitching had held.

Behind the dirt rampart, safe from catapult fire, all the dragons that hadn't been recruited to work on the southern flank fortifications were sitting down, working over their weapons. Bazil took up a whetstone to work on Ecator, which had certainly lost some of its edge after the work of the dawn hours. It felt heavy and full, as if the fiery spirit that inhabited the blade was sated in some grim way.

Jumble had some serious damage to the straps for his breastplate. He also had a pair of nasty cuts on the right flank, where something had cut into him twice. Relkin cleaned these wounds and sewed them up as quickly as possible. Jumble let out a few whistles as the disinfectant bubbled in the cuts, but Relkin was quick and deft, and the sewing was done in little time.

Jumble took the whetstone to his sword and went to work beside Bazil. There was some soreness on his right side, but he worked through the pain.

"Boy is very quick with stitching," he rumbled.

Bazil had to agree. "Boy is one of the best. I have few complaints."

"I miss Sui, we grow up together back in Keesh. But he was not this good with stitching."

"Boy Relkin is very good at close work. This dragon always impressed by results. Men work very small, little hands in constant motion, and yet work they do is enormous in every way. Far too complicated for this dragon to understand."

Jumble nodded. He, too, had once thought of this, but had not mentioned it to the other young dragons. "That's the difference," he agreed. "Dragon not need joboquins for wyvern life."

"Only for war, always war."

Relkin was down behind the fortification where he'd found a useful flat rock on which to work on the breastplate straps for both his dragons. Working as swiftly as he dared, he rethreaded the fastenings of the straps with seasoned thong and tied off with neat knots known as shoebows.

He recalled for a moment how old Macumber used to teach them this knot, with that constant refrain, "Tie them shoebows neat, boys, tie them very very neat. . . ." Well, old Macumber would be proud of these shoebows, he thought. He tied them without conscious thought and produced an even, neat, very tight knot every time.

From the breastplate straps he went to the helmet strap and then finally got to Bazil's joboquin, which required heavy needle and yarn.

Some men and dragons came in from the Angle on a relief. They spoke of fierce fighting against the Baguti on the Military Road. The Angle had held, though. As had the line at Brownwater Lagoon.

Three dragons from a Kadein squadron tramped past with cheerful waves to the 109th and 145th where they sat together whetting their blades. A messenger came running past and stopped at Dragon Leader Cuzo's dugout in the rampart. Everyone watched with interest. The messenger reappeared after a few minutes, then ran back past them at the double, not responding to their cheerful inquiries.

A few moments later Cuzo burst out of his dugout and told them to get ready to move out.

"We're rotating up to the Angle. There's a Kadein squad that's going to Brownwater. More Kadeins coming up to take this position. So let's move it, everyone. Get our bags packed and on our shoulders as quickly as possible. I want to move out within twenty minutes."

With a few groans from dragonboys who were still completing repairs to joboquins and straps and equipment, they moved.

The dragons set down the whetstones and sheathed their giant blades. The wagons were brought round, nervous oxen shifting restlessly in their yokes. The whetstones were loaded up, along with helmets and heavy pieces of armor. Tents, axes, and miscellaneous tools went into the big chest on the second wagon. Cuzo was up and down their line making sure that nothing important was left behind, particularly rope.

They were finally on their way after half an hour of struggle. The wagon teams were six-oxen strong, so they moved at a good pace through the scrub forest on the margin of the dunes. Cuzo intended to be up at the Angle well before dark, it being only a few miles away.

Meanwhile Tregor met with the commanders of the Argonath Legion, but without General Urmin, who had been shaken up in the morning fighting.

"I have just returned from meeting with General Va'Gol. He assures me the Red Rose Legion can hold the southern flank. His preparations are well under way. We must make sure that we can do as good a job as the Cunfshon men."

The Argonath commanders rumbled lightly at that.

Commander Fesken of the Bea Third wondered if there were

any new supplies of posts and stakes or building timber in general.

"Down to brass tacks, hmm? Over to our Quartermaster," and Tregor turned to Commander Hare, Divisional Quartermaster, and discussions of posts and stakes soon turned to requests for rope. Eventually Quartermaster Hare was obliged by Tregor to give up more of his precious stock of rope.

Later, when the others rose to leave, Tregor asked Kesepton to stay behind. Kesepton was necessarily privy to that world of secrets, witches, and bizarre magic, since his wife was Lessis's assistant, and Tregor needed reassurance every so often about that world.

Hollein knew the signs by now. Tregor was rubbing his hands together in an anxious manner.

"Captain, sorry to hold you back like this, but I've had another message from the Gray Witch. Came in the form of a scroll on the leg of a raven. Apparently there are more Baguti pouring down from the north; not just the Irrim tribes, but western Baguti, Skulltaker tribes."

"Well, that means more pressure at Brownwater Lagoon. We've made the line there very strong already. Six catapults on the second rampart."

"Yes, I'm not worried so much about that. She warns us that the new enemy, that fell spirit we fought at Avery Woods, is involved here."

"Yes, sir." Hollein had expected that.

"She says that he has been lurking up there to our north, and the Witch Hadea, she told me that the business at Gideon's Landing was likely his work."

"I have feared so, sir, since that green fire shone in the north. I knew then that he would be back."

"In Avery Woods he attacked with imps and those special trolls of his with the funny name."

"Bewks, sir."

"And we just about lost everything. It was touch-and-go there for a while. What we have to think about now is what he might do that we haven't planned for. What trick he might try."

Tregor's haggard eyes betrayed the raggedness that was

creeping into his thoughts. The responsibility was heavy; the fighting on the southern flank had worried him all day. Disaster might come at any point. The anxiety tore at one's mind.

Now, added to everything else was this baleful elf lord, some mighty wizard of old, who possessed tremendous powers. This was no figure of fun, this enemy.

Unsure for once, Hollein said nothing.

"What might he do? You see, that's the question."

Hollein shrugged. "We can only prepare for what we know, and those lines at Brownwater and the Angle are as well built as Legion soldiers can build them. I would not care to assault them myself."

"We have to prepare for anything he might throw at us. Commander Kesepton, I want you to ride up there to Brownwater and take a good look at the position. Then go over to the Angle."

"Yes, sir. Do I have time to issue some orders to my own command, sir?"

"Yes, Commander, of course. Take care of any immediate business, but then take a look at those positions to see if anything might be improved, then have it done."

"Yes, sir."

"Before you go, give me an opinion, Kesepton. I'm being asked to mount a surprise counterassault on the south flank to push the enemy back to the Little Fish."

"Yes, sir, it might be a better line to hold."

"Let's say we could push them back to the Little Fish. Are we sure we could hold that line when they counterattack?"

"It was well fortified before."

"They may have done some damage to those fortifications."

"Do you think they've had enough time to do much damage? I think the trolls have been too busy over here, sir."

Tregor smiled, but was unconvinced. "With reinforcements we have twenty-five hundred effectives on the flank line now. There are at least four times that many Baguti. I could shift men and dragons down from the main line, but they're getting valuable rest right now. And if we should attack and fail? Then we will have taken unnecessary casualties that we cannot afford.

No I can't risk the army on those odds. We will stand on the defensive and make him pay for attacking us."

Kesepton saw that Tregor had had his mind made up from the beginning. He had just been used as a sounding board. One mistake here could cost them the only sizable army that the Argonath could put in the field. Defeat here might mean the loss of Kenor. The enemy might even break through the mountain passes and ravage Arneis and Aubinas, burn Kadein and Minuend. In short, the entire Argonath endeavor was at stake.

"I understand, sir. Neither would I."

Any attack would be too risky at this point. They would need every man, every dragon.

Chapter Thirty-two

Darkness was not yet complete when the batrukh, bearing two passengers, landed between the north bank of the Argo and the east bank of the Oon. Lessis had been hiding there, waiting, ever since she'd seen the huge beast fly away several hours earlier.

On the foreland, about a mile from the shore of the Oon stood a cluster of tents and pavilions, made of hide in the Baguti manner. Lessis had watched the place all day sending several birds to inspect it more closely and report. It was full of men; not even crows could count the numbers. There was also something that was not a man, nor an animal ever seen before by these birds.

The tall figure left the batrukh with its Padmasan controller and strode into the camp. Lessis moved closer.

Mirk and the others were hidden half a mile back, in a deep gully cut by a stream. Mirk was back there on her express orders and much against his will. She didn't want him with her on this mission. Only a greatwitch had the requisite strengths for this. If she did not return, they were to move out before dawn and ride north as quickly as possible. With the strong string of horses they could probably distance the Baguti pursuit. The batrukh might pursue, of course, but then it would come in range of Mirk and the other bowmen. Once out of immediate danger they should circle around and make for the Argo towns to spread the dread news. That Lessis had failed, and Waakzaam still lived.

The spell she would use was Great Magic, something created

by Ribela and Irene. They believed they had found his secret weakness. Lessis prayed that they were right.

Lessis used no overt magic in her approach, since that might alert Waakzaam, but there was a bustle to the place which would aid her. After all, she reasoned, the Master had just come back. Men would want to seem busy.

All in all, there were two dozen tents pitched up above the high-tide mark of the Oon, which was now a mile away since it had shrunk in the dry season. A long dune rose just behind the camp. There was a corral full of horses on the far side of the dune. Beyond the tents was a fire with a number of men gathered around. She counted twelve, perhaps thirteen, most of them in the distinctive garb of the nomads.

There were a few sentries posted around the perimeter, but they were not skilled in the detection of a greatwitch working subtle magic. She was able to slip silently past one of them, who was distracted by a fierce itch that began between his shoulder blades. While he slipped a hand down his back to rub the irritation, she made her way into the central space between the tents.

In this space there were Baguti, mercenaries, and slaves clad simply in gray and brown. Lessis could pass easily as a slave. The problem was that she dared not use magic to locate the Deceiver's exact whereabouts. He would sense such use and be on his guard at once. That meant finding him by more direct means.

There was one obvious choice, however. A large square tent, slightly off to the side.

As she passed one of the other tents, the door flapped open and a man in the Padmasan uniform emerged. He walked right past her, barely noticing a slave woman in gray. Inside the tent, she glimpsed men throwing dice by a lantern's light.

The guard outside the big square tent was the giveaway. Lessis shivered as she saw once again a bewkman, one of the Dominator's obscene creatures, made from the stuff of life with vile magic. Bewkman were seven-foot-tall, four-hundred-pound brutes, with almost the agility of men.

The bewkman was far too alert for her to just walk past; nor could she wield magic. Lessis knew that Waakzaam had many tricks for detecting assassins. If she touched the wall of that tent, she was sure she would set off some inner alarm for the Deceiver.

She waited, lurking behind a guard tent, remaining unobtrusive amongst two empty wagons that were drawn up there. More wagons were parked a little farther down. Men came and went from the other tents, but this centerpiece of the pavilion they ignored. The seven-foot-tall bewkman in front of the big tent was wide-awake and staring around itself with an active eye.

Lessis moved quietly around to the other side of the pavilion. Here the tents were lined up in a row, with the dune directly behind them. The dune's crest kept the camp from being seen by anyone to the west or the southwest.

The dune's sand had been stabilized by stringy grass, now yellowed by the long dry season. Lessis crept up the side of the dune, but the slope was steeper than she had imagined, and she struggled after the first few steps. Finally she stumbled and slid down feetfirst, windmilling her arms to keep herself upright. Some sand was dislodged and tumbled down the slope and rolled across toward the tent.

Had any grains of sand made contact with the tent wall?

Lessis lay there absolutely still for a few moments. There was no reaction. She picked herself up very quietly and moved a little farther down the dune before trying to climb over again.

She heard rather than saw the approach of the sentry and instantly crouched behind a clump of tall grass and held her breath. The guard came steadily along the top of the dune. He did not see her and went on past the big tent and farther down the dune.

She arose in his wake and scaled the dune, moving very carefully. There was a wind rising in the east that tore at her cloak and hair, and she pulled the cloak tighter. At the top of the dune she was aware of the dark prairie out beyond. A horse whinnied in the corral and was answered by another.

Lessis crouched there, studying the square tent guarded by the bewkman. Something was missing, she could sense it.

From the fire came the sound of harsh male laughter. Another horse whinnied in the near distance. She began to wonder if the Deceiver had gone into that trance state she'd witnessed once before. If he had, then he might be vulnerable to a less subtle form of attack.

They had almost had him that time! To come so close and fail was heartbreaking.

A bittern's loud ringing cry echoed up from the west.

Then Lessis noticed a tall figure, standing alone on the far side of the hillock, seemingly lost in thought. It had appeared silently out of the deeper shadow. Unnaturally tall, with wide shoulders, it could be no other. It was him, the Dominator. This vast physique was an immediate, simple giveaway, and a pure expression of his enjoyment of a life with power, enormous power.

She nodded, hearing Irene's wisdom. Such brutal strength invites the gentle counterstroke, the needle from the dark.

She examined the shadows at the rear of the tent. There were no guards that she could detect. She wondered at this lack of concern for assassins, then recognized that he felt almost invulnerable to mere man. What could a man, even Mirk, do to such a monstrous strength as his?

She pursed her lips. Mirk was deadly, he would find a way to kill anything. But this dread figure was imbued with fantastic power. And with that power had come arrogance. Arrogance always lead to blindness, and that blindness could be exploited.

She slid closer. It was important that the spell she carried be delivered as a surprise. Its effect depended on the sudden blankness of the mind that surprise delivers.

The tall figure still did not move, wrapped as it was in its own thoughts.

Another few shallow steps, her boots barely touching the ground, not a sound escaping. Now Lessis stood right behind him, almost close enough to have driven in her blade if that had been their plan.

She tossed a pebble by his feet.

The huge figure whirled, and she raised her arms, palms forward and invoked the final volume of the spell she carried. It came out with a strange backward shriek, and she felt it go home, sinking into his face.

Waakzaam was truly taken by surprise. There, right behind

him stood a figure that he recognized at once with a snarl of
hate. And then it was as if a mirror had been thrust up before
his eyes, and he looked himself in the face and saw himself as
he really was. The spell Irene and Ribela had concocted had
sparked self-insight in a blinding flash that could not be denied.

The glossy patina of conquest and dominion was stripped
away. All pretensions, all evasions were laid bare, and the horror that he had inflicted on the universe was revealed to him.
His hatred of the world had undone him. He who had brought
this beauty into existence had failed his duty, which was to undo
his own existence in order to end the corruption of magic and let
stability rule the universe.

To buttress his position he had gone on, and on, in one effort
after another, to establish that he had been right not to sacrifice
his life! The universe was great, and he was not only enjoying
it, he was adding to its splendor. He had to prove that he was
right! No matter what the facts might say.

Now he saw that such things as the splendor of his palace on
Haddish, the Heptagon, were rendered trivial beside the evil he
had wrought. He had become small in spirit, fearful to everything, and cruel beyond understanding.

At first it had been his contention that conflict was inevitable
among the creatures of the worlds of the universe. The Great
Game of the Sphereboard of Destiny determined the players
and the play. This occasioned war, and war was hell, but sometimes it had to be fought. From that concession to war had come
other things, leading in the end to the determination that only
when his rule was absolute could he bring his vision to the
worlds. His own cities would be bathed in brilliance.

But to get to those brilliant cities he had had to end billions of
lives.

And now, everything was annihilated by the withering eye of
his own former self. All lies were eradicated, all attempts to
avoid the truth were rendered useless. He saw himself with peculiar clarity. He had been consumed by his hatreds, dishonest
and deceitful even with himself. There was no escape, no way
to pretend that it wasn't true.

Tears formed in his eyes for the first time since Puna's body had fallen to the floor before him in ancient Gelderen, long, long ago. That first murder, strangling the beautiful Puna who had seen through him and denounced him to his face, that was the crime that had set his subsequent decline in motion. Tears ran down his face, and he wept for the horror of what he had become. He, who had once been so noble, so pure, such a shining spirit of creation. Now, he was tarnished and corrupted beyond measure.

His shoulders slumped, his great thews bent, and he sank to his knees there on the dune beside Lessis. Even kneeling, he was taller than the slight figure of the witch. A vast sob racked the huge body.

"I have erred," he said in Intharion, the ancient elf tongue.

Lessis simply watched, astonished at the sight of this mightiest of enemies reduced to this incapacitated misery simply by the gift of insight.

"I only wanted to improve the worlds."

The voice was spiraling, wavering. It was as if it spoke from out of the deep past and had all strength gnawed away by time.

"On Haddish, from the earliest days of my realm there, I tried to make life a paradise for the Glem, the bright and restless Glem of Haddish.

"But they were never satisfied. They warred with each other continuously over strips of ground. I struggled to find some way to change them, to get some sort of use out of them! My creatures farmed them like cattle and drank their blood, but still the Glem were proud. Still they were insolent! So I exterminated them. I ground them out of existence!"

The huge figure sobbed and sucked in air loudly. Then it spoke in a different voice, almost as if from a different being.

"That turned out to be a mistake. Because I was still building the Heptagon, and I needed more labor. The Glem had to be replaced. So I went to Orthond, where the Eleem had bred the remarkable Neild. I brought Neild to Haddish and made them thrive."

He paused. There was something else working in his eyes now, a strange glitter of irrationality.

"But, you see, in the end I had to have Orthond, too. I held off for a long time, because the Eleem world was so perfect in its way."

There was another huge sob and a long silence.

"They had to be exterminated, don't you see?" He was entreating Lessis, begging her to understand why he had been forced to annihilate the peoples of so many worlds.

She made no response. All of the spell's work had to come from within, that was the key requirement.

One possibility the witches had discussed was insanity. Waakzaam the Great had lived far too long and had grown strange and fell in that time. Perhaps his mind, great as it was, would be unable to stand the shock of self-realization.

But Irene and Ribela thought that the most likely course would be suicide. So painful would this self-awareness be that he would at last lay down his stolen life and pass into the fabric of the Sphereboard of Destiny. It would be the only way to end the agony that his existence had become.

The giant figure hunched down, sobbing. The groans and heavy breaths continued while he apologized to Lessis, babbling about the slaughter of Geft and the emptying of Bar Ob. Terrible things had happened on Geft; he had gone too far, altogether too far. But there were simply too many Gimmi. They had carpeted Geft with themselves.

The nightmarish end of the Gimmi seemed to snap something in the sobbing voice. There was a change. There was now a whine of complaint.

"*They* came, they decided to interfere. After all the time of peace between us. Long aeons without their interference had passed. They broke the treaty!"

They were the Sinni, of course. The High Ones, the Golden Elves of the earliest times, when Gelderen had been the golden city of the most high and completely uncorrupted.

The complaint quickly intensified, because once they broke the treaty and began interfering, they raised up insurrections and rebellions. No sooner had he conquered and settled Armalle, then They were at work there. The trouble was endless. For a while the Ixin, the folk of lovely Armalle, came together in a revolutionary army. They threw down the rulers he had set over them and took the field against his own army.

It was Their work. And after he crushed the rebellion he boiled the leaders alive and slew one in ten of the general population before reducing the Ixin to the level of animals. To show them, the golden ones, the children of Los, what would happen if they dared to interfere again.

And it was their fault, therefore, that he was at war! Their fault. If they had just left him alone, he would have solved the problem, and achieved those brilliant cities that he dreamed of. They denied him the opportunity to create his masterpiece! And after all that he had put into it and all the lives that had been sacrificed.

How dare they! How dare they interfere with his work!

The great face raised itself slowly from abasement. Lessis found herself staring into perfectly golden eyes, all blue extinguished. The face was slack, the elfin beauty cold and unstirring. With slow crawling skin, Lessis felt the madness that now governed the creature before her.

The powerful blow that knocked her to her knees took her by surprise, still.

"Witch! I will have you . . ."

North of the foreland, hidden in the gully, Lagdalen and the others were suddenly shaken by a great blast of green light that lit up the south. A clap of thunder shook the sky.

Giles, the sensitive, suddenly gave a gasp and put out a hand to steady himself.

"What is it?" said Mirk.

"The Lady did not speak of this," whispered Lagdalen, her face turned ashen.

Giles felt the hot eyes of the Lord searching for them. "He lives! He has taken her."

Chapter Thirty-three

The moon rose late, yellow and huge, low along the horizon. It threw its light across the dismal swamp to create stark shadows. The lone pine and clump of aspen, the fallen tree and bank of rushes, all were etched silver in the moon's light.

On the rampart at the Angle, Bazil and the Purple Green were keeping watch. Relkin and Manuel were standing together out of earshot, discussing the Purple Green's uncertain temper. The great wild dragon was still out of sorts following the unfortunate conversation concerning High Wings and Bazil's mating, years back.

So far, Bazil had refrained from mentioning any of this. The fighting at the beach had been intense enough to put everything else out of mind. Afterward they had barely had time to put the edge back on his sword before the order came down to move out. On the march, though, the Purple Green of Hook Mountain had been a withdrawn, moody presence, radiating ill will. Everyone had grown silent, even Alsebra, who usually refused to be cowed by the Purple Green. They were all depressed by the time they reached the Angle and took up bunks in the row of available spots behind the line.

Bazil had received his posting with the Purple Green for watch duty with resignation. Then again, perhaps it would offer an opportunity to broach the subject and get this over with.

Out in the swamp coyotes called. From farther away came a long sobbing cry from a night bittern. Bazil sneaked a glance in the Purple Green's direction. The huge wild dragon was sunk in on himself, his neck tucked over and his head almost resting on the breastbone. He was staring out into the dark, lost in gloom.

"You are still angry."

The Purple Green hissed, but made no reply.

"It is foolish to be still so angry. Whatever happened then, we have passed beyond it since, many times over."

"Foolish?"

"Yes."

"Foolish!"

"Yes. What is the point? High Wings hunts in the northlands. I not see her again, ever. I see you all the time."

"I had never been defeated until then."

"I had dragonsword, and you did not. How could you have defeated me?"

The Purple Green knew this truth, but at some level he could not accept it. Just as in some deepest part of him he remained wild, forever at odds with Legion discipline, social rules, and order.

"That was the beginning of the end of my life."

"The end of that life. Now you have another life. This life is not too bad."

"I went to heal up on the mountain and those damned filthy imps came."

The horror of imprisonment returned to the huge dragon. His eyes began to glow with sheer hatred. "They destroyed my wings."

"You and I, we met again in the place of death. They try to make us kill each other, but we refused. We fought back-to-back then, and ever since."

"You are groundbound; you cannot conceive of wild dragon life."

"We swim," said Bazil defensively, proud of the wyvern dragon's adaptation to the coastal life. "It is not the same as flight, but we not groundbound as you like to say."

"It is not same."

"Even so it helps me understand your loss."

The Purple Green muttered to himself, then took a new tack. "You break their rules. You swim in ocean."

"You don't have to bring that up all the time. They not supposed to know."

"You hate rules, like me."

"I have always known these rules. I am not wild dragon like you."

The wild one had slipped back to his global gloom. "You cannot understand."

"Yes, you right. I was lucky, the witch could fix my tail. But your wings were too damaged for their magic."

"Too damaged. Filthy imps . . ."

"Think of this, though. You have plenty of opportunity for revenge in this new life. And you eat well, too."

"Food is bland."

"But always there. Don't go hungry very often."

The Purple Green had to accept the truth of Bazil's words. Unlike the wild life with its all-too-frequent hungry spells, the life in the Legion was a settled, well-fed one. He cast around for something to complain about.

"You call that tail fixed?" he said.

They both looked at Bazil's odd tail, with the last few feet crooked and a bit too small. The leatherback flexed it—it worked well enough. It had never been beautiful.

"It better than not having a tail. I can wield tail mace."

"You have tail. Wings too badly damaged. I useless now."

"You have learned to wield sword. You have fought in many battles, killed many, many imp—trolls, too. You not useless."

"Useless. Cannot fly."

"Not useless. You kill enemy, get revenge. This dragon impressed by what you have done. This dragon learn to wield sword as a sprat. It easier to learn when dragon is young."

The huge head had risen well off the breastbone now. "Yesssssssss," it hissed like some enormous snake.

Bazil heaved a quiet sigh of relief. That was an improvement. This happened every so often, and eventually the Purple Green exhausted the tunnel of sulking and bounced back. It was always like this with him, the long sulk, the grief at his bitter loss, then something would break him out of it, sometimes days later.

"Yessss!" the wild dragon said again even more loudly. Then

he switched to dragonspeech in an accent so thick that Bazil could barely follow him. "We take revenge on the brasska*, cut their filthy heads from their filthy shoulders."

Relkin and Manuel heard the sudden excited hiss from the Purple Green and looked up.

"He's back," said Relkin.

"No doubt of it." Manuel sounded relieved. He had come to take enormous pride in caring for the great wild dragon. The witches of the Insight regularly took depositions from him for the library of dragon lore. But the wild one could be very trying at times.

"Heads says you go tell Cuzo." Relkin pulled out a coin, an imperial penny from the new mint in Dalhousie.

"Why do I always get tails?" Manuel groused.

"All right, you want heads?"

"Yes."

Relkin flipped the coin. It came up tails. With a sigh, Manuel got to his feet. "Why do I always lose with you?"

"I gave you the choice. You took heads. It came up tails."

"You blasphemer! Away with your Old Gods."

"Go tell Cuzo."

After Manuel slipped down the steps behind the rampart, Relkin gave quiet thanks to the Old Gods, in particular Old Caymo, who ruled the worlds of commerce and gambling.

A raised voice in the tower turned his head. The men in the tower were laughing over some sally or other. Their laughter carried out into the swamps, dark and quiet. The sea of reeds hardly stirred. The lone pines, standing tall, were stark against the grasses under the moon's amber light. Relkin turned back to contemplate the dark swamp.

Since he and Bazil had worked on seven different construction sites in the swamp, he had a good idea of the general geography of the battlefield. He understood that the army was in effect surrounded, but that if they had to they could smash through any force of Baguti that got in their way and retreat to the fort on the volcano five miles away. Still, it was unnerving

*brasska—less than edible enemy, not worthy of eating.

to be cut off like this. The enemy on the riverfront greatly outnumbered them and possessed a great many trolls. They faced a hard, bitter-fought struggle before they could truly claim a victory. Tregor expected a long campaign, one reason he'd been so keen to fortify every possible defensive line and height in the area. They had to keep their own casualties very low, while exacting a heavy toll on the Padmasans.

Relkin was confident that it could be done. Legion troops were just that much superior to the imp-and-troll mixture that Padmasa relied on.

He put war out of his head for a moment and thought of Eilsa. Her face floated up in his memory while he prayed that she was well. Prayed that they would eventually be together again, wed and raising their family in the highlands of Kenor.

He'd barely finished his little prayer, this time to the Mother as he'd been taught at the dragonhouse, when there was a great flash of green light way out in the swamp, miles distant. The green fury blazed for ten seconds or more before it sank and then was gone. The thunder boomed over their heads for half a minute afterward.

Relkin was on his feet, his hand automatically reaching for an arrow as he took up the bow.

The camp had awoken. Cornets screamed. Men dressed quickly in the darkness, grabbed their weapons and helmets, and formed up behind the rampart. There were two companies of men and one dragon squadron, a fully sufficient force to hold such a well-built fortification.

Sharpshooters were up on the rampart aiming over the parapet, eyes sharp for the slightest movement. The catapults were loaded and wound up tight, their ropes twisted hard, ready to fire.

Captain Beeds made a hurried inspection, running up and down the rampart, with Sergeant Glep in tow. Beeds had seen action before, but like many men, he had a horror of sorcery, and the story of what had happened at Gideon's Landing had left him uneasy in his mind.

Dragon Leader Cuzo took up his station on the rampart set halfway down the line of dragons. Only five dragons could fight from the rampart at a time.

They waited for a short while, tense, expectant, ready for battle.

Then it began. First came a sudden shiver down their spines, like a draft of a sudden chill wind. Even the dragons, usually impervious to magical spume, noticed the effect. Though the reeds never moved, they all felt as if a cold wind blew over them.

"What is it?" snapped Beeds.

"I have no idea, sir," replied Sergeant Glep calmly. There were a few chuckles among those who were in earshot of this exchange. Glep was famously phlegmatic.

Still, everyone was thinking about what had happened to the Bea Third out at Gideon's Landing. That business began with the green light.

Now came occasional wisps of weird sound, haunting twisting keens and moans, always at the edge of the inaudible. And with them came little stings on the skin, as if there were a sudden cloud of biting midges. Men slapped at themselves, but the gnats were noncorporeal.

Then suddenly it ceased. Silence returned to the bogs and swamps.

"Well, that was a strange one," said Sergeant Glep, turning to go. "But it seem like it be over now." Glep didn't sound impressed.

"I see something," yelled a man on the nearer tower.

Everyone strained into the dark. The moon was still low on the horizon, and its light continued to be the color of old ivory. The scene remained fixed; no movements could be detected. The man in the tower was arguing furiously with the others up there. Yes, he had seen something. Yes, it wasn't moving now.

Again they stared at the swamp, but the scene seemed frozen in place. Not even the reeds were stirring. After a minute or so, Sergeant Glep gave up in loud disgust.

"I aim to get some sleep while I can." He clumped down the steps.

Others gave up as well and turned away.

"So that was it?" said the bowman Ortiz somewhat disappointed. "Just a big light and a lot of thunder?"

"So it seems."

"Ah, well." Ortiz put up his bow and placed the arrow back in the quiver.

With a huge gulping sound something surfaced in the nearby slough. Heavy sucking sounds followed, as if something enormous was being pulled from the mud. A shape began humping out of the ground and rearing up.

By then, even Sergeant Glep was on the rampart, staring out into the murk.

"What in all the names of hell?" said Captain Beeds.

A cylindrical mass, twenty feet high, perhaps eight feet wide, had risen out of the mud of the slough. As mud fell away the dark hide was revealed to be streaked with glowing green lines.

The top four feet of the barrel-shaped body was occupied with the roots of a dozen or more muscular tentacles that whipped around the top of the tube with a sinister energy.

"It moves!" cried someone in astonishment.

The huge bulk was sliding forward on a caterpillar-like body. As it came it made a strange, terrible noise, akin to singing, but in an eerie key that put their teeth on edge.

Behind the thing, way back in the swamp, lights began to appear. Men bearing torches were gathering farther out on the neck of dry land between the swamps. The Baguti were out there.

The thing came on, directly against the stockade. It was enormous, a hundred tons of flesh. As it drew closer the tentacles began to whip about excitedly. These tentacles were between fifteen and twenty feet in length, and tipped with pads covered in red suckers. The strange singing filled the air, cut by the sudden crack of the tentacles as they snapped like whips.

"Fire catapults!" came Beeds's order.

The catapults began to snap and whine in response and their big eight-foot spears were hurled into the body of the towering thing as it moved toward them.

The spears had little visible effect. The mountain of flesh came on. It looked up over the rampart, and the tentacles reached over and seized men and dragged them screaming from the wall, even still hewing at the tentacles with their swords, before they were lifted up and tossed into the gaping maw on the top of the central barrel. The mouth opened to reveal rows of peglike teeth.

The screaming men were dropped into this milling machine and quickly pulped and swallowed.

Arrows and spears stuck in the tough outer layer of the thing's hide, but didn't penetrate deeply enough to cause it any visible discomfort.

It brought its caterpillar body up to the wall and surged up to the nearest tower. Tentacles wrapped about the tower and the thing heaved and tore the entire top part of the tower free. Men dived from it as it disintegrated in the grip of the thing. Dragons hewed down with all their strength and drove their swords a foot or two deep into the creature, but not even this was enough to stop its advance. The Purple Green crashed into it and succeeded in getting its attention. Tentacles swung down and seized him. He roared and cut at them with his sword. The sword sank in but not all the way through, and the flesh rehealed the moment the sword was pulled back.

Bazil had fought against creatures with magical flesh before. "Have to cut all the way through," he grunted as he hewed into the breast with Ecator. Ecator went deep and momentarily the bright green lines on the monster's flank went dark. Then it screamed with astonishing violence and rammed the wall with its huge body. They all felt the shock. The rampart itself had moved. The parapet was shattered.

Bazil had a foot up on the thing's side, heaving Ecator free. The blade came out, aglow with its own angry energy. Globs of dark fluid flowed from the wound for a moment before it shut and healed itself.

The Purple Green was being tugged off the rampart by three massive tentacles wrapped around his huge form. The wild dragon was bellowing and struggling. A tentacle snatched at Cuzo and barely missed. The Dragon Leader pitched backwards off the rampart with a wail.

Like everyone else, Relkin searched for eyes on the thing, but could not find any. There were no obvious targets for his arrows, except, he noticed a pale patch underneath each tentacle where it joined onto the main trunk of the thing.

Like armpits, they might be weak points. He raised and fired, and saw his arrow jutting out of the paleness in the next moment.

The monster reacted with fury. The tentacle twitched and the pad coated with scarlet suckets slapped down where Relkin had been standing the moment before. Relkin had dodged aside, however. He crouched, aimed, and released, putting a second shaft next to the first.

The thing's terrible singing gave way to a dreadful shrieking, and tentacles tore wooden beams out of the gate supports. A tentacle slapped down again and Relkin dived for his life.

Its grip on the Purple Green loosened. He was tugged back to the rampart by Jumble and big old Chektor, the heavy veteran brasshide. Jumble was smacked backwards by a tentacle slap and the leatherback went down with a heavy thud. Other dragons charged forward for the place, and the rampart got crowded with wyvern bodies.

The tentacle snaked in to get at the Purple Green, and Haxarion and Alsebra hewed at it, then trapped it with their bodies and held it down.

More tentacles came for them. Part of the rampart was breaking up as the caterpillar body tore at it in its frenzy.

Vlok swung and brought down Katsbalger in a two-handed overhand that finally did the job and severed the tentacle held down by the two green dragons. Black fluids gushed briefly, but both the main body and the severed tentacle healed in an instant. Even separated from the body, the tentacle continued to live, wriggling like an enormous worm. It wrapped around Hexarion in a flash and began to choke the green dragon. Alsebra grabbed the tentacle and tried to pull it off, but could not. Hexarion fell over, still struggling with the thing, until Vlok got both hands on it and heaved it free and thew it over the parapet.

Bazil dodged a dragonsword on the backstroke and thrust home with Ecator, driving the elvish blade deep into the monstrous magical flesh. A second terrible cry erupted from the gnashing maw above their heads. The huge thing trembled while it pulled back, freeing itself from Ecator's deadly metal.

It hurled itself at Bazil, tentacles snapping. Arrows sank into the pale undersides of the tentacles as dragons threw themselves on the tentacles to hold them down. Others hewed into the tentacles with all their might, here and there succeeding in severing one.

Writhing tentacles then had to be peeled off the dragons and cut into chunks that were unable to move.

The monster screamed again and again, still tearing at the fortifications while Bazil stabbed home with Ecator, driving deep. Even now a man was dragged aloft, crying for his mother as he vanished into the gnashing maw.

But finally the tentacles moved more sluggishly. Dozens of arrows were jutting from the thing's armpits. Ecator had gone home again, too, sinking four feet into the bulk of the thing.

Dark body juices gushed down and soon the rampart was slippery. More and more arrows sprouted from it until it was encrusted in them and its tentacles had slowed significantly. In some cases they were barely moving. More were hewn off. The Purple Green was driving his sword into the barrel of the monster with greater success. Ecator's deep thrusts had weakened it in some way.

Its wails grew continuous and its movements weakened further.

Several dragons worked together to carve a huge chunk from the front of the beast. The Purple Green cut off the last moving tentacle, then the main body fell across the rampart. They lined up to hew it in half and then to cut the thing to small pieces. Black fluid and evil-smelling gas bubbled from the dying flesh.

The torches of the Baguti remained where they'd first appeared. The monster was supposed to break the wall. It had failed. They were not interested in throwing themselves against a wall, even a battered one, that was still held by dragons.

On the rampart, the Legionaries gave up a great cheer while the cornets shrieked exultant. Dragons roared and slapped their shields.

Meanwhile an anxious Captain Beeds took stock of the casualties. Forty men were either in the thing's belly or incapacitated with broken limbs. The east-side tower above the gate was gone, and the wall alongside was badly damaged where the beast had torn down the palisade. The massive dirt rampart itself with its huge bulk had been gouged and cracked. But the gate was still strong and so was the west side of the fortification.

The Purple Green had pockmarks all over his body from the scarlet suckers, and most of the other dragons had a few of these. The young witch named Tessi came to look. Relkin thought she looked no older than Lagdalen had the first day he'd met her years before. Tessi kept her pale hair tied back, and she wore a perpetual frown on her serious little face. Manuel welcomed her warmly enough, though, and she burned herbs and prayed beside the Purple Green and then the other dragons with wounds from the monster's suckers. Finally she smeared unguent on their wounds after they had been treated with Old Sugustus by the dragonboys.

Eventually they stood down and got some sleep, arms weary from the effort of bringing down the monster.

With the dawn, repairs on joboquins and kit began in earnest. Fortunately the Baguti showed no sign of interfering. Scraping sleep out of their eyes, dragonboys jumped to it and brought up kalut and noodles for the dragons, then ate their own hurried breakfasts while darning needles flickered in their hands.

The sun gradually climbed into the sky while the men and dragons worked under the direction of an engineer to repair the shattered palisade and parapet.

The seventh hour was past when a dust-covered rider came galloping in from the front line. He jumped down and ran to report to Captain Beeds. His message was grim. The same kind of attack they had faced down in the night had occurred at Brownwater. But there the tentacle beast had broken the wall open, torn down the gate, and let the Baguti ride in.

Four dragons had been slain, two more badly wounded during the subsequent rout and retreat. More than a hundred men had been left to the mercy of the imps, to be roasted alive and eaten.

More important, the Irrim Baguti were now through the last barrier and could envelop the northern flank of the main position. Already Baguti riders were active in the rear areas of the main army. The messenger had been delayed by having to hide in the swamp twice when parties of Baguti went by.

Beeds knew that he could not abandon his position. If the army had to retreat, then it would have to come through the Angle, across the Neck, and onto the Military Road that ran to Fort Kenor. Along that road there were three well-fortified positions that would offer some degree of shelter for the retreat. But at all points they would be enveloped in clouds of hostile Baguti cavalry. It was vital they hold the Angle.

Chapter Thirty-four

That day was one to test the strongest nerves. General Tregor found himself racked with nightmare visions even as he worked to stem the Baguti on his flanks and keep the front line organized and steady.

The enemy launched probing thrusts around noon, then in early afternoon committed to a mass assault on the front of the Red Rose Legion. The assault lasted for hours as the imps were hurled forward with the fumes of the black drink rising through their brains. At the same time the Baguti attacked the new, hurried fortifications on the south flank. They made a few breaks in the line, but were thrown back each time, and in the end withdrew with little to show for their efforts.

Far in the rear of all this, the Angle was quiet. The 109th and 145th combined squadron were ordered to stay put and hold their position. Baguti cavalry came to take a look at them, but by that time the defenders had created a short rampart and parapet wall on the inside of the main line facing toward the river. The rampart was only five feet high, and the parapet was assembled from what they could fetch out of the nearby swamp, but the Baguti showed no interest in attacking.

At the northern end of the line the Argonath Legion was also left in peace, although just a little father north, in the scrub around Mud Pond, the fight to contain the Irrim Baguti grew extremely hot. Tregor's cavalry were involved in a daylong struggle with the nimble Baguti ponies, while companies of foot soldiers fortified positions on the northern flank and also along the road to the Angle. These positions served as bases for the Talion troopers. Dragons were kept for the main line, in case the enemy did decide to give up on the Red Rose Legion and shift the assault columns to the north.

Late in the afternoon General Va'Gol of the Red Rose Legion reported that the enemy attacks on his front had ceased. The dark masses of Padmasa had slipped back across the shallows, leaving mounds of their dead behind. The Red Rose Legion had suffered relatively few casualties. Va'Gol was confident he could continue to hold his line.

The sun slowly sank in the west while the catapults picked at each side's positions. The Legion boiled food while men and dragons stood down, except for the cavalry, who would get no rest for the foreseeable future.

By dusk Tregor had encouraging reports from both flanks, and his nerves began to settle. In the south the Red Rose Regiment had managed to inflict a sharp reverse on the main column of Baguti. In the north the Talion troopers had checked the eruption of the Irrim Baguti and largely pushed them back to the northern sector, close to the break-in point at Brownwater Lagoon.

Tregor went to sleep that night, totally drained, but feeling that he had a good chance of just fighting it out on the line. The Padmasans would either have to attack or give up and go home. If they attacked, he felt sure he could hold them and take a heavy toll. Eventually they would have had enough and the horde would move back across the Gan for the distant mountains. Then the Baguti would slip away, too. They'd raid on their way out, before recrossing the rivers and returning to their normal haunts on the Gan. By then, however, the emergency would be over, and winter would be in the offing.

And yet he was still deeply troubled by the business at Brownwater. Sorcery was something you simply could not plan for.

Kneeling by his cot he said his prayers and called for blessings for his distant wife and their children. He got into his blankets

and wondered if he really could sleep, but then exhaustion turned
out the lights and his snores filled the tent.

The night hours passed quietly. Tregor dreamed for a while,
gentle dreams of the hills of Seant, rising above the Long Sound.
His mother at the door of a whitewashed stone cottage in the
golden rays of the late-afternoon sun.

He awoke suddenly, disturbed by a sound inside the tent. It
was pitch-dark, but there was a skittering on the fieldcarpet, and
something leaped up into his face.

With a shriek of alarm he warded it off. It landed on his bed,
between his legs, and he jerked back with a yell.

The guards were in motion, the tent flap opened. Light flashed
in from a lamp. The thing on the bed was shown to be like a
monkey, but with the head of a dog. It bared yellow fangs and
sprang at him with a hiss.

Now that he'd seen it he was even less eager to let it touch
him. He swung desperately and knocked it away while rolling
out of the bed.

He landed on his hands and knees, but the thing leaped onto
his back and sank its teeth into his neck. He reached up to tear it
away and was bitten on the hand as well. The guard struck it
with his spear butt and kicked it aside.

The creature was not easily deterred. It bounced from the
floor and climbed the tent pole before leaping onto the guard's
head. The guard fell over with an oath, crashing through the
map table.

Tregor saw the thing leap off the guard and turn right back to
him. It sprang for him, with those weird black eyes fixed on his
throat.

Instinctively he got the fallen guard's spear up and knocked
the thing aside. Another guard had entered the tent, the first still
struggling to rise. The thing sprang at Tregor again, and this
time he knocked it down and speared it before it could get away.
The second guard dropped on it and stabbed it again and again
with his dagger. It was slow to die.

By then Tregor was quivering on the floor, his mind lost in
nightmarish hallucinations. The injured guard was similarly

disposed, wailing through clenched teeth. The animal's fangs were poisoned.

Kesepton was one of the first on the scene. General Urmin was summoned from his tent and found himself in command of not just the Argonath Legion, but the entire army. Tregor was trembling, unable to speak. The witch was with him, along with the surgeon. The body of the dead monkey, if that was really what it was, was being examined. The fangs were hollow, having discharged their poison. Tregor was obviously unfit for command of the army.

General Urmin took command. Tregor and the injured guard were taken away on a stretcher, twitching, their faces puffed up as they gasped for breath. Urmin immediately made Kesepton Field General of the Argonath Legion, then turned to the maps and charts, when they'd been rescued from the wreck of Tregor's table.

Urmin had to shake his head wearily. He had been looking forward to retirement, a hero at the end of a long but otherwise undistinguished career. Then the twin plagues had struck the Argonath. Urmin found himself promoted to general and sent to take command of a combat Legion under Tregor. Bewildering as all this had been, Urmin had kept his head. His country needed him more than ever. And serving as a Legion commander beneath Tregor had meant he had only the tactical concerns of his Legion to worry about. The strategic responsibility was Tregor's.

Now the whole burden rested on him.

Staff workers rebuilt the map table, and Urmin had a hurried conference with officers. He informed General Va'Gol of what had happened and received confirmation from Va'Gol accepting his actions and his command for the duration of the battle. Urmin gave thanks for the cooperative nature of the Cunfshon men.

Newly promoted, Hollein Kesepton went down to the tent Urmin had been using just a few minutes before. Once he'd taken a look at the situation there and informed the staff of what had happened, he went back to see Urmin.

"Well, General," Urmin said the word softly. "What d'you think of the position?

Hollein smiled, wanly. "Serious, sir, but manageable; we have control of the battlefield despite the Baguti on our flanks."

"So we should stand here and hold the line?"

"Yes, sir."

"What about the attack at Brownwater? What d'you put that down to?"

"The sorcerer, sir, the same one we defeated at Avery Woods."

"A close-run thing that day, Kesepton. You credit this tale of a giant octopus?"

"I don't know, sir. It sounds fantastic, but there was a similar attack at the Angle which was beaten off. They cut the monster into pieces."

"Yes, yes, of course. So we might expect more attacks like that?"

"Anything is possible. You saw what happened to General Tregor."

Urmin pursed his lips. "Tregor is in the medical section. They couldn't tell me much about his condition except that he's hallucinating."

"Let's hope there aren't more of them."

"I've doubled the guard. We'll be looking more carefully from now on."

The day dawned eventually, and the Argonath army waited behind its fortifications. The catapults picked away at the enemy's catapults on Crescent Island, and the Legions worked on their defenses while they waited. The flank defenses in particular were thickened that morning with ditches and stakes.

The Padmasans stirred eventually, but though they marched up and down on the distant bank of the Oon, they did not attack. Unknown to Urmin, the Padmasan army was quiescent because its general, the great Munth, had been called to a conference with Lord Lapsor.

These two now stood on a barren hillock a dozen miles north of the battlefield, overlooking the Oon from the west. The batrukh waited nearby, with the Mesomaster standing beside it.

Munth's eyebrows rose at seeing a Mesomaster reduced to little more than a batrukh handler.

Waakzaam approached with the man Higul at his side. Munth had noted Higul's rise to prominence. Higul was like himself, a hard man with no sorcerous pretensions. Waakzaam preferred Higul to the Mesomaster. Munth understood, it made sense. Mesomasters were a pain in the ass.

"Greetings, General Munth," said the elven lord.

"Greetings, Lord."

"We have driven in his flanks and tested his line. But we have not broken him yet."

"The Legions are stubborn opponents, we have always known that."

"You have absorbed casualties."

"Too high, much too high. We are attacking them in a well-fortified position. I begin to think I may have to move south and try to cross farther down."

"Except that we have their army surrounded."

Munth nodded. "That is so, but a screen of tribesmen is not going to halt them if they wish to march to the volcano."

"I will thicken that screen with other resources."

Munth had heard reports from the Irrim Baguti about the monsters raised from the muck of the swamps.

"Ah, yes, well that might change things. If we can exert more pressure on the flanks, we might thin out that line. I have kept the ogres back, in case an opportunity for a breakthrough might come. If they had to pull dragons off the main line, then I would throw the whole army at them with the ogre force to break their line."

"Good, that is what I expected of you. I thought you were a combative type. Why we pushed for your appointment, y'know."

This was a surprise to Munth, who blinked, silent.

"You have friends in high places General," purred Waakzaam the Deceiver.

Munth was captured by the sweet words and sorcerous seduction of the Deceiver. "Thank you, Lord, that is a great relief to hear. I would not want enemies there."

"So you will drive home with your army while I tear into the flank. Good, we will break him on this line, and then invade the Argonath."

Waakzaam beamed down at the Baguti. Munth might rise high under the rule of the Dominator. He had the right attributes.

Chapter Thirty-five

By nightfall the catapults on both sides had virtually ceased firing. Dusk settled over a quiescent battlefield. Cookfires blazed up and men and dragons got down to their evening meal. Despite the adversity, the arrival of a hot meal produced a degree of good cheer among the men.

General Urmin made a hurried inspection of the lines. Much of the damage caused the previous day had been repaired, at least partly. New defensive works had been thrown up at Mud Pond, south of Brownwater Lagoon, where extensive quicksands constricted the approach to a strip of sand barely a hundred yards wide. Dragons and men had labored through the afternoon to dig a ditch and throw up a rampart.

Urmin had increased the strength of the flank force. A full regiment, the Marneri Fourth, First Legion, under Lenshwingel, now held the place, along with two squadrons of dragons. This had reduced the dragons on the main line to the barest minimum, but Urmin knew that almost anything could happen on the swamp flank, and he had to lay in significant force to deal with it. The 109th and 145th together had brought down the monstrous beast that attacked the Angle. Two full squadrons of dragons seemed the minimum required to deal with such a large and difficult opponent.

Commander Lenshwingel was bubbling with excitement and adrenaline in equal measure. His first taste of combat had left him in a strange state of exaltation. The fighting had been hard, furious for much of the time, but their lines had held, and they had piled up the enemy in drifts. Now Lenshwingel's responsibility had risen to command here at this vital point. He was virtually babbling about ditches and parapets. Urmin thought the commander needed a good night's sleep.

And all the time, hovering in the air was the thought of sorcery. Every man in the army now knew they were facing more than just the Padmasan horde. The previous night's fighting had been the work of land squids or some such madness. It sounded laughable, except that men had died under the assault, and the position at Brownwater was broken open. Prayers were said every hour, and many more men than usual joined the prayer groups.

Urmin wished he could take the time for prayers himself. Instead he rode back to his command post and found General Hollein Kesepton waiting to report that all was quiet on Argonath Legion's front. The river mists were thickening, but no enemy lights had been reported beyond the distant shore, where a city seemed to glow as the enemy sat by its campfires.

The first change in the situation came on the southern flank. An hour after the fall of night, suicide squads of Baguti came out of the swamp and up against the flank line. Here and there they broke into the lines. Fierce fighting was eventually required to kill them or throw them out again.

Urmin read the reports as they came in very carefully. No hint of sorcery about it. The attack had been made by roughly two thousand Baguti, who had crept through the swamp and swum the lagoons. There had been no backup assault by the main mass of the Baguti. It looked like a feint, except that the Baguti had paid with hundreds of lives. This was unusual behaviour for the nomads, who were hardly ever as suicidal as imps.

Uneasy, Urmin decided to hurry down there and take a look at the position himself. This took ten minutes or so, working down the narrow track that lay behind the main line camp, two miles altogether. He met with Commander Fina and then with General Va'Gol. All seemed quiet. Parties of men were still adding abatis, working in the swamp by the light of small lanterns.

"What d'you make of it?" asked Urmin.

"I think it must have been a feint, sir," replied Fina. "There was no support."

"These Baguti are acting strangely."

"We are fighting a sorcerer of immense power," murmured Va'Gol. "Perhaps that is the source of this unusual energy among the nomads."

Urmin concurred and studied their detailed charts. The flank position had been thickened where possible. It looked as if it should hold.

It was while they spoke beside the brazier outside Va'Gol's tent that they first detected the sound. It was not very loud at first, like the howling of a faraway hound. Slowly though it increased in volume. The main source seemed to be north, a long way off, but now there also seemed to be a source off to the east, behind their lines, somewhere out by the Angle.

"What the hell?"

"Wolves?" said Va'Gol.

"Those're not wolves," said Fina.

"I must return to my command post." Urmin hurried to his horse. "Keep me informed, General," said Urmin as he spurred his mount north.

The howling continued, each time taking half a minute or so to rise very slowly from the lowest to the highest note. If it was a dog, it was a dog the size of a bull.

As he rode Urmin felt a deep sense of dread creeping over his heart.

He hurried his horse northward along the line. His staff followed with heads lowered, as if before a storm. It was hard to talk, hard to concentrate on anything, since the howling never stopped and kept getting louder.

While they were riding up to the command post they observed huge clouds boiling out of the north and blocking out the stars. These clouds moved with an extraordinary rapidity. Lightning flashed and flickered in the north, and soon the thunder was booming over their heads.

Still the howling could be heard throughout, getting louder by degrees. Dragons roared back every so often, and these short, heavy sounds could obliterate the howling for a few moments, but then it recurred.

Everyone on the line was up and awake and looking off to the north, where the storm clouds had piled up in a huge anvil cloud.

Urmin found Kesepton waiting in the command post. The howling continued as before, rising steadily to a pitch that set men's teeth on edge.

"Location?"

"Not sure, yet." Kesepton turned to Hadea, the witch, who was trying to fix the direction from which the sorcerous noise was emanating.

"What is it, sister?"

"A power, sir, a very great power. He is just a few miles away, to the north."

"The howling?"

"It is his work. There is a field, a bed of sorcery, that seems to encompass all the swampland around us. He is the source of it."

Just then there came the lightning blast, a pillar of green fire that shot down from the leading cloud edge into the swamps north of Brownwater. The fire continued to flare, a line of brilliant green stark against the dark night. Thunder cracked and rolled, and the whole sky seemed to quake with the power of it.

After a long half minute the green bolt cut off, leaving them startled and temporarily blinded. The thunder roared over the land for a long time while they swallowed and stared around them blinking. At last it shook itself out.

Silence returned. They blinked and rubbed their eyes.

"Was that what it was like when you saw it, Commander?" said Urmin.

"Much more powerful, sir. When we saw it at Gideon's it didn't last so long, nor was it quite that bright."

"Have you noticed that the clouds have completely disappeared?" said the witch, with no little wonder in her voice.

They looked up and saw the stars visible in the north again, where so recently there had been clouds.

"At least that damned howling is over."

"There's always a silver lining. . . ." Urmin said with a tight smile.

There was not long to wait. A rider came galloping up within the hour. The man was wild-eyed, his uniform in disarray. Urmin's hands shook as he read Lenshwingel's report.

The beast. . . .

A creature of enormous proportions had arisen out of the swamp. It stood on four ten-foot-tall legs that were like pillars beneath a huge blunt body and a massive, spade-shaped head. The brute had tramped up the middle of the sand causeway and smashed into the main works. The palisade had collapsed, the ramparts of sand had given way, and the monster had broken through. Behind it came the Baguti, an army of ten thousand, driven by a fanatic passion that had never been seen in Baguti before.

The dragons attacked the beast, but even dragonsword could scarcely cut deeply enough. Baguti overwhelmed the Legion soldiers, and in the cramped, confused surroundings they managed to get onto the dragons. Two were slain there, cut down by a multitude of men with spears and swords.

Lenshwingel had been forced to pull his survivors back, but they were being pursued hotly by the enemy. The flank position was destroyed. They had killed hundreds of Baguti, but the rest were as crazed as imps with the black drink in their systems. The Marneri Fourth Regiment, First Legion was in flight.

The huge beast had then vanished; some said it had simply sunk back into the swamp and disappeared, others that it had been consumed in green fire. Either way its work was done. The Legion position was unhinged.

Cornets shrieked up and down the line. Men fell in and were dispatched to the northern flank, dragons under way behind them. The Talion cavalry was already at work there, fighting desperately to delay the Baguti. On this occasion, however, the nomads were unstoppable. When the solid ground was blocked, they took to the waters and swam across to infiltrate behind any position. Their archers climbed trees in the darkness and sent their arrows thudding down into men and horses below. Other Baguti archers used fire arrows to spread fear and confusion.

Urmin and his soldiers turned themselves about to face the oncoming Baguti. The dark woods suddenly blazed with the green fire and the Baguti swarmed out from the trees and were on them in the next moment.

The fighting grew up and down a temporary line established at the edge of the woods skirting the military road that led east to the Angle. The Talion cavalry riding that road had orders to keep it open. If they had to retreat, that was the only way out.

The Baguti fought like maniacs. They fought more cleverly than imps ever could, and their use of feints and sudden rushes caught many dragons by surprise.

The casualties were far too high for Urmin to accept, though his lines held firmly. The dragons and men of the Marneri Four Ones under Lenshwingel got word out that they were cut off and surrounded about a mile from the line. A force of volunteers was sent in to break them loose. After some fierce fighting they succeeded, and the Four Ones rejoined the army. They had lost 230 of their number and four dragons. Lenshwingel was ashen-faced, reduced to mumbling. He had personally slain three Baguti, fighting hand-to-hand on several occasions during their flight through the dark swamps and forest.

Appalled, Urmin had orders drawn up for a retreat. The Angle and the forts at the crossings of the three major streams were all stoutly held. A retreat in good order was possible if necessary.

And while this phase of the battle played itself out, and the Baguti attacks faded in intensity, nobody much noticed the subtle thickening of the river mists to the west. Hidden by this dark cloaking cloud of sorcerous origin came Munth's climactic assault, two columns, each ten thousand strong, filled with the black drink and stiffened with trolls, led by teams of the huge ogres.

Now they came tramping out of the darkness and threw themselves against the northern end of the Red Rose Legion line and the southern end of the Argonath Legion line. It was the junction between the two halves of the army, carefully ferreted out by Munth's scouts during the first wave of fighting.

The lines were broken by the ogres swinging their huge hammers. Dragons were reduced in number in the units on either side of the junction, and these squadrons were unable to cope with the packs of trolls that came up against the palisade. Within a few minutes there were breakthroughs, and the junction area itself was lost completely as both Legions contracted toward their own centers, away from the point of attack.

Urmin hurried every available dragon to the breach. The 44th Kadein Dragon Squadron died to the last during this phase of the battle, all gone but for a single dragonboy, named Heraut.

The fighting stabilized, but the Baguti were pressing again on the north flank, and now there was renewed assault on the southern flank.

Urmin's head was swimming as disaster rose up in front of him. He called a conference. Kesepton and Lenshwingel joined Va'Gol and Fina in his tent.

"Either we retreat, or we die here, gentlemen," was Va'Gol's comment. Kesepton agreed and urged an immediate fighting retreat to the Angle.

"The position is untenable. We retreat, at once. Get your men out in an orderly fashion. The Marneri Eighth will cover on the north end, the Kadein Eleventh will cover in the south. Cover will be rotated when possible."

"Wagons?"

"We leave the wagons. We've eaten most of the food. The trolls will stop to eat the oxen; that will take them out of the battle for hours."

"The horses?"

"We take the horses, of course."

"Sound the retreat, gentlemen."

Chapter Thirty-six

Lessis's former companions crouched together, grim-faced. The day was ending in glory far off in the west as the sunset glittered off the distant River Oon. Beruyn was keeping watch at the head of the gulley. Their horses were muzzled and tethered nearby. Mellicent and Ward stood behind Mirk. Lagdalen and Giles faced him.

"She said we were to head north until we were sure we had not been pursued and then to turn east until we saw Mount Ulmo. From there we could go south and find the middle Argo towns."

"Right," said Giles, wrapping his arms around himself against the wind that wasn't there. "Let's go then."

Mirk and the others were silent for a moment, as if they were solemnly considering this thought.

"There is no chance of recovering the Lady?"

"I don't know," said Lagdalen, struggling to keep her voice level. "You understand who our foe really is?"

"Oh yes," muttered Giles. "I know who he is. I feel him burning in my mind. His power glows there like a dark sun. Oh yes, I know him."

"Then you can find him for us?" said Mirk. Mellicent nodded his big head at this. Ward's face was without expression, perfectly blank.

"Find him? You want to find him? He took her! Lessis the Great, just like that. And you want to find him?"

"He has powers, this ancient wight, but if he lives and breathes in flesh then he can be killed. The Lady bade me kill him once, but I was just a little too slow. I will not fail a second time."

Lagdalen put a hand on Giles's shoulder. "We must try to save her. You can find her."

"If she still lives. He may have put her to death already."

"He may have, but then again he may have wished to torment her beforehand. The Lady said that it was his cruelty that would be his weakness."

Of course, Lagdalen thought to herself, if the Dominator had not killed the Lady right away, then he was taking a serious risk, because keeping Lessis around was sure to be dangerous for him.

"You can't be serious." Giles still could not believe them.

There was no reply for a moment. Then Ward spoke for the first and only time.

"He is still in the camp."

"This is madness," Giles exclaimed. "What can we hope to do to a being like him. He is a colossus. He will rule this world and squeeze it until the pips squeak."

Mirk turned to Giles with eyes of stone.

"No. If a man lives, he can be killed. Killing is not so difficult. Getting close is difficult."

Mirk leaned closer. "You can sense him, you can guide us to him."

"By the Hand, I don't think that's a very good plan."

"You will not have to risk yourself. Just show us where he is."

Giles caught the grim certainty in Mirk's voice and wondered for the first time. Could it be possible? Mirk had a matchless reputation as a killer. But the Lord Who Burned Men, he was surely beyond the knife and the sword thrust, the poisoned arrow or the hidden syringe of curare.

Lagdalen spoke as if she read his thoughts. "He is not a man, not a wizard, nor a magician. He is an elemental of the greatest kind, and his power is indeed enormous. But the Lady says he can be slain. A knife is just as deadly to his flesh as it is to ours."

And if Giles didn't want to help them, what was the likelihood that Mirk would force him to with the threat of violence? Inside he cringed with fear; that burning power, that ferocious strength, that terrible keen eye, were all familiar to him just in the pursuit they'd made with the witch. To get even closer?

Giles's face sagged into gloom. "You really want me to take you right to him?"

After a moment Lagdalen smiled at him. "Yes."

Away to the south, beyond the River Argo, the setting sun was also a spur to the rearguard force fighting at the Angle. The battered Legions had passed through sometime before. The head of the retreating column was already on the Swampfish Bridge. They had held their lines well, but the enemy was out-flanking them on both sides with parties of Baguti who had been goaded into the most maniacal fighting.

The 109th, still paired with the 145th, pulled off the rampart during the lull and began the march down the military road in the dark. To guide them, the road had white spots painted on the center stones, and these were visible stretching away into the murk in a straight line.

They had fought well and repulsed two severe assaults with-out casualty, though Vaunce, the crullo, had taken a knock from an ogre's hammer. Vaunce was on a wagon, being hauled by a few lucky oxen that had not been left for the trolls.

The dragons were hungry; there'd been little to eat that day. The dragonboys were bunched between Alsebra and Jumble, and though they were elated at coming through without casual-ties in their own unit, the story of the 44th Kadein was dis-cussed somberly among them. Most of them were too tired to talk much. They concentrated on saving all their energy for marching.

Behind them on the Angle fortifications they had left mounds of dead imps and trolls, with even an ogre or two scattered among them. But they knew the enemy would not be stopped. Though they had killed more than their fair share, still the enemy had hundreds more trolls, dozens of ogres, and thousands upon thousands of imps, who would be on their heels very shortly.

They pushed the pace, and huge dragon bodies swayed down the road in two-legged motion, forcing dragonboys to jog to keep up. Archers formed the rear guard, moving back in ten-yard increments and stopping to take aim.

They kept the Baguti horsemen back, but bands of Baguti would pursue on foot and attempt to close on the archers. Then the rearguard spearmen would step forward and take on the Baguti. This was hard fighting, but the rear guard did the job and held back the immediate attack.

Now the Padmasan horde came on through the Angle and parties of imps, reeking of the black drink, were driven forward. The rear guard's duties became more onerous, the retreat more hurried.

Men just ahead of the rear guard eventually found themselves involved in the fighting. There was a bottleneck at Viper Swamp, and this soon turned into a battleground as the enemy came up in greater numbers and turned the rear guard into a desperate rabble. With some effort a line was formed and held, but then trolls came up and the line was broken and many men died before a few dragons were able to get back through Viper Swamp and stem the trolls.

The rear guard rallied then, and the archers took a toll of the oncoming enemy horde.

At the bridge over the Swampfish the battle was renewed when fresh forces of Baguti rode out of the dark or crawled up from the swamp, slathered in grease. For a while the road to the fort was cut off by a Baguti force that dismounted and built a barricade.

The 109th formed up and charged the barricade. The Purple Green tore the flimsy thing apart and Alsebra cleared the Baguti off the rest of it with vigorous blows of the dragonsword. The others ripped what was left off the road and drove the remaining Baguti into the swamp. Relkin and Bazil hardly got into this fight. For once they were in the rear party. Jumble, however, was forward, and he went down into the bog a few paces to thrash a group of Baguti who were struggling with their horses in a mire.

The Purple Green roared back onto the road after chasing away more Baguti, and the others turned back soon after. Bazil had never left the road, and he and old Chektor were the only ones not covered in mud. The others, dragons and dragonboys, looked at them with envious eyes.

"Very clean pair of dragons," boomed the Purple Green.

"Compared to you, perhaps," said Bazil, tired, hungry, and bruised after all the fighting of the past few days.

"It is good that the old veterans stay out of the mud. Leave that to us young ones," said green Hexarion, with the usual green lack of tact.

Bazil gave him a withering stare. "You be lucky green dragon if you live to our age, this dragon know that for sure!"

There was a whistle, and someone called, "Cuzo!" out of the dark. The Dragon Leader ordered them back on the road at the double. The enemy pursuit had not lost its impetus. They were still in a footrace to the fort.

Chapter Thirty-seven

The road became a chain of white dots stretching into the distance ahead. They set to hard marching, moving at that ground-devouring pace that the Legions of Argonath had perfected.

The 109th were well accustomed to this, even on an empty stomach. They swung along in two-legged stance, bodies leaning forward, balanced by tails, with dragonsword slung over their heavy shoulders. Marching was something that Legion units did better than any unit the Padmasans had ever organized. After the first mile or so, nine-foot-tall trolls were not able to march at much over three miles an hour. Ogres were even slower. Once they'd distanced the trolls and imps they found the Baguti suddenly more hesitant in following up.

Thus Urmin's army was able to leave the Padmasan horde behind by marching at the double through the darkness from the Angle, across the Swampfish Bridge and on to the flank of the volcano. There were two more bridges, a short wooden one at the Little Mountain Stream and a larger one built partially of stone over the Mountain Stream. The fort was just above the stream, within bowshot of the bridge.

Soon the steady tramp of Legions took them up to the bridge over the Little Mountain Stream. There was no fighting at this bridge. The Baguti probed, but they were still nerving themselves to attack when Urmin pulled off the rear guard and withdrew to the last bridge, the big one over Big Mountain Stream, just below the fort. This bridge was fortified, part of the fort's outer line of fortifications.

The 109th, the 145th, and two companies of Legion troops marched up that final stretch of road together with a defiant chorus or two of the Kenor song. They'd fought a huge battle. They'd been forced to retreat, but in their hearts they knew they were not beaten. Their spirits were high.

Not everyone was in good spirits, however. By then, Relkin had discovered that Jumble wasn't with them. He gave Cuzo the bad news at the bridge. With a curse, Cuzo called a halt. A party was sent back to look for the young leatherback, but there was no sign of him. No one reported seeing him at the Little Mountain Stream bridge either. Relkin was devastated.

To lose a dragon was the ultimate blow to a dragonboy. Relkin had not forged the deep bonds of long-term familiarity, it was not like losing Bazil, but still the loss horrified him.

"I just didn't see him go. I don't know where it happened," Relkin explained again and again, as if that would help make the guilt go away.

Alsebra tried to help. "This dragon remember Jumble step down into the swamp at the first bridge," she said.

That turned out to be the last time any of them remembered seeing the young leatherback from Seant.

"Must have got caught in the bogs," said Swane.

This thought did not help Relkin's peace of mind that much. A lone dragon in broken terrain or forest was in danger when fighting men or imps. They could easily get in behind the dragon and spear him or cut his hamstrings.

The 109th formed up again and resumed the march up slope to the fort. Rescue parties were already working back down the road, but the enemy was coming on in the rear, and that meant there was little hope for Jumble unless he could somehow get out on his own.

Behind them General Urmin rode down to the bridge to meet Kesepton. Because of their previous service together, because Urmin recognized the vast experience that Hollein Kesepton carried, he turned to him for a sounding board, as someone whose opinions he could trust. They rode out of earshot from the troops, just across the bridge.

"So, Kesepton, we marched them into the ground. But what

now? They will try to keep us under siege, then send a huge raiding party up the Argo. We can't allow that."

"Well, sir, both Legions are intact. Casualties during the retreat were not terrible. About forty men all told, split between the Red Rose and ourselves."

"Plus a dragon, damn it. And we've lost so many. Can't afford to lose any more."

"We have parties out there searching for him, but I admit it looks bleak for Jumble."

"Bad business to lose dragons when we're so heavily outnumbered, and they have ogres, too."

Urmin pulled out a silver flask and took a sip of brandy. He passed the flask to Hollein, who also took a generous sip.

"This army fought well; we bloodied them. Maybe we haven't won a victory, but we haven't been defeated either."

"Sir, I have this crazy idea."

Urmin cocked an eye. "My grandfather's brandy can have that effect, young man."

"Yes, sir, and maybe that's part of it, but still, I think we have an opportunity coming up."

Urmin's eyes suddenly popped wide open. "You mean?"

"Counterattack. And soon."

Urmin saw the chance at once. "Yes! We have the time to recuperate, get a hot meal into everyone and even a few hours' rest. By then the trolls will be up and the enemy will be in position right outside the fort. That's when we hit them, just bang the doors open and charge them. Put the dragons in front, men behind to exploit the confusion."

"You have it, sir."

"And if we can break the front elements, we might even stampede the whole damned horde. Such things have happened."

"If we hit them hard enough, sir, just at that moment when they've cooled down after coming up against our lines here, they'll be ripe. They'll be beat, footsore, and tired. We'll go in hard. I think we can shatter them."

Urmin felt his own confidence grow. "I know the men are angry that we had to retreat. This might be just what they'd like. If we can get to grips with their army, then we can smash them."

Urmin smiled grimly. "Then let them bring on their sorcery, and I'll put a hundred dragons on them and we'll see how long they last."

"'Damned right, sir," said Hollein, feeling an unusual readiness for battle.

"Never forget the dragons of Argonath."

"Never!"

They took another sip of the forty-year-old brandy of Urmin's grandfather Albimuel, then rode back across the bridge. As they went Urmin was thinking hard about this riposte. It would need judicious timing, and it would need to slam home with everything they had. He made a note to meet with the witch Hadea. She might be helpful with the matter of timing.

It could be done! If they struck hard enough.

Miles away, poor Jumble was left to play out what luck remained to him. Unfortunately, he didn't have much left. When he'd stepped down into the bog after those Baguti, he'd gotten knee deep into quicksand that had slowed him then frozen him in place. To try and get out he was working backwards slowly when some Baguti crept up behind him and cut him across the back of his right leg, severing the big tendons.

After that he was unable to walk, and could only stand there up to his knees in mud, virtually immobile. When a party of overeager Baguti rushed him, he feigned helplessness until they were very close, then swept his sword through their ranks and sent the survivors splashing back through the mud with cries of horror.

More Baguti arrived; torches lit up the swamp. Arrows and spears continued to fly his way, but the men stayed out of the range of that long dragonsword, circling around him, looking for the moment to rush him.

Then it came. At a prearranged signal the Baguti charged him from all sides, their war cries resounding from the dismal swamp. Jumble swung hard on the forehand, checked himself from falling by jamming his shield down into the mud, and came back with a return stroke that caught four men in the act of trying to spear him from behind. Their screams cut off with a mighty "thwack" as the sword sent their souls to hell.

The others scrambled back with snarls of hate.

But now his shield was stuck in the mud, and he couldn't heave it free. He was exposed to thrown spears.

The spears were out, and the Baguti were closing in when a chieftain galloped up and barked orders at the men surrounding him. The men were displeased, the chieftain barked more orders, and the men spoke back angrily.

Abruptly there was a sharp sound in the air as if a giant whip had been cracked above their heads and a green light flashed about them.

The spearmen fell absolutely silent and turned away from the trapped leatherback.

Now they waited in a ring around him. Jumble watched them with dull eyes. He was young and would not live to be much older. He knew his mistake had been to pursue too eagerly, not waiting for the dragonboy. Forgetting that with only a single dragonboy to two dragons, Relkin might not be watching his back as well as Sui might have. He'd forgotten all he'd learned and put himself at risk.

He was puzzled for a while about why they didn't spear him and get it over with. The whip sound and the green flash had frightened them, that was clear. Maybe they wanted him alive. This thought brought both hope and fears.

They waited as the sky lightened at last and dawn broke over the land of Kenor. Then Higul rode up with a huge wagon drawn by a team of albino trolls.

The huge trolls came at him from all directions and, though he killed one, they overpowered Jumble in the mud and bound him with chains. They placed him on the wagon and towed him away, back toward the deeper swamp. By midmorning he was far to the rear. In his heart there was little besides regrets and despair.

He never heard the great roar of his name, the battle cry of the 109th and 145th fighting dragons of Marneri, as they burst out of the fort and pitched into the enemy front lines. He never heard the din of battle either, for a steady cool wind out of the west kept the sound of it from reaching him. Jumble passed beyond the reach of any assistance with no idea of the furious fray that had broken out below the fort.

When the dragons broke the trolls and sent them running, the Padmasan horde trembled. The Legions poured out behind the dragons and spread the confusion throwing the imps back on their heels and catching the enemy in the midst of meal preparations. The imps rallied for a brief few minutes, but the trolls could not be turned around, and the ogres were too slow for defensive fighting against dragonsword. The Padmasan horde rocked back.

The news of the counterattack reached Munth where he rode his horse at the Little Mountain Stream bridge, a mile from the fort. At once he understood the danger, He had overlooked the recuperative powers of such well-trained troops.

He ordered the Baguti forward to stiffen the imps and help hold the Argonathi, until the trolls could be halted and given enough black drink to get them into fighting mood again.

The various Baguti hordes went forward, with the Irrim and the Skulltakers in the lead and the mountain horde at the rear. They scrambled through the thickets and down the Military Road, but they ran into mobs of panicked imps. Then columns of fleeing trolls packed the road. The Baguti could not ride through; they bunched in the road and created a bottleneck instead, and the trolls just pushed through them, trampling anyone who was foolish enough to stay in their way. The Padmasan army had become a mob, a mindless thing struggling to escape through critical choke points. The Baguti were forced to flee as well, riding their mounts into the swamps to escape the keen edge of dragonsword.

The Legions kept up the pressure and the Legion cavalry came down the road at the gallop and into the rear of the fleeing mobs of imps. Imps, trolls, and men were cut down in the tightly pressed chaotic mass.

The men in the Legion front knew they were winning, and the dragons knew it, too, and this put great heart into them and kept their swords in motion through all that long, blood-soaked day. Again and again they sang the Kenor song in triumph after bringing down trolls and Padmasan cavalrymen, the hated mercenaries who served the evil ones.

By the end of the day they had driven the Padmasans all the way back to the lines on the beach. The Irrim Baguti retreated northward through Brownwater Lagoon to the Argo shore. There, without pausing, they recrossed the Argo to the north bank.

The Skulltakers and the other western tribes crossed the Oon with the Padmasans, then pressed westward, leaving the volcano of ill omen behind. Once more Ashel Veerath had shown itself to be a graveyard for the nomads.

Clearly the Padmasan contribution to the war had come to an end.

Almost unnoticed in all the chaos, just before the Irrim clans urged their mounts to swim the river, a large boat had crossed over with a dragon chained in the hold.

Chapter Thirty-eight

The fire for Jumble and the other casualties blazed high on the parade ground below Fort Kenor. The dragons sang their death song for their dead and the great noise of it was audible miles away.

Urmin watched from the corner tower. There had been losses, but the battle of the Oon crossings would be entered in the books as a great victory. Kenor was spared; even the Argonath cities themselves breathed easier. Urmin had a stack of congratulatory messages on his desk.

Kesepton entered after a knock.

"You wanted to see me, sir?"

"Yes, Kesepton, I want you to take my report to Marneri. You deserve the chance of being the first of us back in the city."

"Why, thank you, sir. Thank you very much."

"You were right, General."

"Sir, that was only a field rank. Am I still really a general officer?"

"You are, until the Argonath Legion is decommissioned. That won't happen until I am replaced or receive an order to do it."

"Thank you, sir."

"You were damned right, and we whipped 'em and sent them running. They thought we'd be trapped in here, under siege, and instead they're back over the Oon and running for their lives. A damned fine victory. Except . . ." he trailed off.

Their eyes met.

"We took a lot of casualties out there."

"Hard fighting, sir. The army fought magnificently."

"Yes!" Urmin's enthusiasm was relit. "Caught them when they were mentally unprepared, just like you said, and they never got organized again. You will find yourself credited with the idea in my dispatches." Urmin took Hollein's hand and held it tightly for a moment. His face filled with emotion. He had never expected to command an army like this. He had not dared to dream of achieving a victory of this order, either.

"May the Mother look after you. Go at once and be with your family for Fundament Day."

"Yes, sir!"

Outside on the parade ground the pyre burned low after a while, and the wyverns set to drinking a boatload of ale and remembering their lost companions. Many a song went up in memory of this old champion or that, like great Sorik, who was cut down years before. Or Nessessitas who died in the gladiatorial ring at Tummuz Orgmeen. Or Themistok, a valiant green from a century before.

They had a great victory behind them, but for now their thoughts were only for their dead. They drank and sang the melancholy funeral dirges of their kind.

Men avoided them that night. Even dragonboys tiptoed around their charges.

In the morning, scouts came in from General Va'Gol down at the crossings. The Padmasans had not stopped in their headlong flight for the mountains. They had a long march ahead of them, and unless they got to the high passes before snow fell, they would be trapped on the Gan. With both Axoxo and Tummuz Orgmeen in Legion hands, there was no easy way out to either north or south.

Another rider came up from Kenor Landing a little later to announce that a second shipload of ale had come ashore that afternoon and would be sent up to the fort. The fort's own brewery had been struggling to keep two entire Legions and all their dragons supplied, so the arrival of ale from upriver was a source of great cheer.

Spirits were further raised by the news that two thousand

more men, scraped together from Kadein, were on their way downstream from Dalhousie. Fresh horses and riders from the Talion regiments were also on their way, coming up the Oon from the southern valleys of Kenor.

Now came a period of quiet activity. Dragonboys had the time to try and patch up the dragon's kit, as well as their own. Joboquins, of course, were a mess of stretches, burst studs, and ripped thongs. The official name for the battle was Crossings of the Oon, but for the ordinary Legionaries it would forever be the Battle of the Sorcerer's Beasts.

Relkin worked alone, in the stall. His own coat was a mess, with one sleeve torn loose and the other ripped. He'd lost a heel off a boot, which was at the cobbler's, and left him in sandals.

The joboquin was on the hook. More work was needed, but the worst was repaired. They could pass Cuzo's inspection the next morning. It was time to make sure the dragonboy could pass inspection. No chance of getting a replacement for the coat here at Fort Kenor, and Cuzo would not take excuses, so it would have to be done by the dragonboy. He took up needle and thread, small needle and lighter thread than he was used to, and started on the sleeve reattachment. It wouldn't be beautiful, but it would have to pass muster until he got back to Dalhousie and the Legion commissary.

As he worked he could not stop thinking about poor Jumble. The dragon he'd lost. The ultimate failure for the dragonboy, to lose the dragon. He sank into bitter self-recrimination.

They'd not found a body yet, but they had found tracks of a heavy wagon. So it was supposed he'd been taken captive. Relkin had all the excuses lined up, and he'd heard them all from everyone else. It didn't take the sheer horror out of the idea though.

Bazil came in after a while, fresh from a plunge in the crater lake. He understood immediately that boy was in an anguished state. He stood there awkwardly, towering over Relkin.

"Just want to say that it not all your fault. Jumble at fault, too. In fact, Jumble more at fault than dragonboy."

"Yeah, thanks, my old friend. I know he was a novice. But I

should have kept that in mind. He was a good sort, and he was young, and I should have kept a close eye on him."

"How one dragonboy supposed to fight with two dragon to watch? It not possible. It not your fault, they ask too much."

"Too much of this dragonboy, that's for sure. I must have just looked away at the wrong time. I must have been just watching your back, out of habit, you know?"

"Good habit, keep this dragon alive."

"Yeah, but didn't help keep Jumble safe."

"Boy can't fight for two dragons. Jumble broke the rules. He not supposed to go down into the swamp. Not alone. We trained to keep in line, always fight beside the other dragons, don't fight alone since we sprats. That's basic. Dragon surrounded by imps is a dead dragon, when we learn that, age three? Jumble must have forgot the lessons."

"Yeah. Wish I'd just noticed. Feel I didn't do enough."

"Death come to us all. Jumble know that."

"They never found his body."

"They kill him later, like in the city of the Evil Rock."

"Yes. Probably. I've heard they kill dragons for their magic powers."

Bazil's eyes glowed momentarily, the big hands clutched. "Someday we kill them, that for sure."

"Someday."

"When dragon die, his shade goes to the red stars. Whichever is in the sky at the time. There we all join with the gods and become one. Jumble will be there before the rest of us, that is all."

"Too many old friends up there, way too many."

"But we still live. Came close a few times, yes? Remember Nessi?"

"Yeah, of course."

"And Kepabar?"

"Oh, yeah. So many old friends. We picked the wrong time to be in the Legions if we'd wanted the peaceful life. Thirty years ago maybe, but not now."

"We got that rock though, stupid rock! Smashed it. . . ."

Bazil's words brought back that day in Tummuz Orgmeen, when the Doom had fallen. "Who could ever forget?"

"Boy throw this dragon the sword, just in time. By the breath, it was close."

"It was close, Baz, it was very close."

Hand and talon clasped once more in friendship.

Chapter Thirty-nine

Waakzaam stood on the hill above the pyre. Men and bewks were still adding wood and brush to it. The dragon was bound to a tree trunk laid across the middle. The preparations were all in order.

It was a terrible thing that he was about to do. Dread magic that tore at the heart of the very stuff of the universe. But it was not his problem, it was theirs, the oathbreakers! After Orthond he had warned them. They had definitely interfered here on Ryetelth, the oldest of all the worlds, and left him no choice. He would therefore have to take his complaints directly to them. He would show them what their oathbreaking would cost!

Their little coup on Orthond had almost caught him out, but he'd survived, by the nimblest of retreats through the dark ether of the subworlds, pursued by Thingweights, back to Haddish. The Thingweights had come horribly close, but he'd beaten them and cut the mirror behind himself a second before the first tentacle could reach it.

In Haddish he'd withdrawn to his high chamber and pondered the situation carefully.

The children of Los, the Lord of Light, how he regretted that he had not smashed them in that first aeon, when he could. But then his spirit had been larger and his humor less dark. He had signed the great treaty in that generous spirit and been repaid with nothing but betrayal.

Of course, they were usually unsuccessful in opposing him. He had marched across twelve entire worlds and brought them under his rule, and they had been unable to stop him. Still, they were an annoyance, wheedling and warring to halt his projects. They were among those who sought actively to bring him down and force him to surrender his glorious existence.

So, naturally he had been angered by this interference with his work. He had almost finished cleansing Orthond. It would soon have been time to repopulate it with beings of a more co-operative type. His work would then have been done.

All ruined now. All that warfare had been for nothing. Now he would be unable to bring Orthond back to the glory he had in mind for it. But he had told himself that he must not retaliate. At least not directly, for he had sworn not to, back in the First Aeon, long long ago. Instead he had taken himself to Ryetelth.

They had interfered outrageously here, and so he was left with no alternative, but to take the hammer to them. He knew where they were and what they most feared. He knew how to bring them low!

With the strength taken from the dragon he would be unstoppable. He would build a magical construct so huge and powerful that his enemies would quake in terror at the mere sight of it. And to build the Black Mirror he would make use of Munth. The mirror had to be of great intensity to bridge the vast gap that lay ahead. Munth's miserable life would provide just the right spark.

He scanned the sky; there were clouds in the north. That would be useful soon. But first, there was the hag to deal with.

Waakzaam strode back to his tent, a wide rectangular pavilion that encompassed a space for his experiments. He was not sleeping during this expedition, so his sarcophagus was not present.

There, hanging in chains from the tent pole, was Lessis of Valmes. On the table were several cages containing some of his current experiments. He was investigating the capabilities of certain interesting parasitic worms.

"There you are," he said with a cheerful laugh and a clap of his huge hands as if he were some kindly uncle.

Lessis made no reply, but watched him coolly. He had left her a shift, but no other covering, so she was cold. There were many burn marks on her body and many, many welts. The inquisition had made a strenuous effort to get her to talk.

However, Lessis was far too stubborn for mere pain to make her answer his questions. And he had not been able to force his way into her thoughts. He had clawed at her mind, tried to crush her with his own vast mental power, but she was elusive. She retained her own mind, and this infuriated him.

"You continue to resist me, but I think we will change your mind." He came close, examining her with a practiced, callous eye. His insanity glowed in his eyes.

"You are in contact with the Sinni. You deny it, but I know you understand the name. They are behind this, the children of Los."

He paused a moment, contemplating the distant past. "Los was my own brother, you know."

"And blessed the world long ago with his grace. Once you were fit to stand beside him. You have fallen far from those days, have you not?"

"Oh, listen to you, as if one can make revolutions without some loss of life. These worlds needed to be kicked out of their sleepy complacency. We must climb to the heights, not wallow in mediocrity."

"That is why you have to destroy entire populations?"

"You know it's necessary sometimes."

"You are not a god. We are all children in the Hand of the Mother. It is not your right to slay any being. You aren't even supposed to be alive still. You have cheated the world by not doing your duty."

"So you say. I say that I am building a more glorious world and that my great life is an inspiration to the worlds beyond worlds. They see in my gleaming achievement the life to emulate."

"Achievement? Life supported by endless killing."

"Of course, you fool. Life involves killing. We must revel in all the aspects of life, including the slaughter of the innocent!"

The Lord's perfect face broke into a malevolent smile.

"Well, I will be leaving you now. I am going to smash them. You know who I mean. They think they're above all this. Well,

I'm going to show them that interfering with my plans is a bad idea. I will finish with them for good."

Lessis struggled to speak in a calm, quiet voice. "In fact, Great Lord, the problem you have is that you have slowly weakened over the aeons you have lived. The very act of living has used up your vast strength, and you have grown weak. You have come to enjoy cruelty, and this indulgence has finally sapped your mind. You are insane."

He laughed for a moment. "Yes, I know. Isn't it wonderful?" He leered at her with his perfect lips and completely insane eyes, now gold, now blue, now gold again.

"And while I'm gone, the Neild will use you in my next series of experiments with the blue worms."

There was a poor young girl in a cage, infected with these vile things. Her body was covered in enormous purple boils, inside which the worms thrived and laid their eggs. The eggs dripped constantly from the suppurating boils. Despite her best efforts not to, Lessis shuddered. Give me the strength to serve you, Great Mother, she prayed silently.

He laughed again, noticing the sag in her expression. "When I get back, you'll be just like the one in the cage."

He left her to contemplate that and went down to the pyre.

At his command the thing was lit. The oil-soaked wood soon caught.

Poor Jumble cursed them in dragonspeech for as long as he could. The fire mounted rapidly, and a vast cloud of smoke boiled up into the sky.

Waakzaam stood forth and roared the syllables of power, his terrible voice challenging the cries of Jumble's agony. So loud did the clamor grow that men turned aside with their fingers in their ears and crouched down, their spirits utterly abased. The flames were shooting fifty feet into the air when Jumble finally expired and the Lord received the green fire from the sky. Never had it flashed down for so long. The world seemed about to be split in twain by the thunder.

Munth, formerly General Munth, stood there rooted to the spot ten feet behind the giant figure of the Lord Lapsor. Some spell held him in thrall, so that he was unable to move a muscle unless allowed by the Lord. Thus, he could do nothing except pray fervently that his end would be brief. He'd seen enough to know that the alternatives were appalling.

The Lord had absorbed the enormous bolt of lightning from the sky. The green fire had bathed him and everyone else in its heat, so that they flinched and turned away. Looking back, one expected nothing but a pile of ashes to be visible, but the Lord remained there, fist raised defiantly to the sky, now empty of clouds. For a while he stood there, shaking and quivering slightly, his face contorted into a grimace. Then he stepped back and stood before Munth, towering over him.

"General, I had such high hopes for you."

Munth could barely grunt a response.

"But you failed me, Munth. Failed me when I most needed a victory. I cannot accept failure like that."

"I'm sorry, Lord," Munth managed to say.

"Oh I'm sure you are, Munth, I'm sure you are. And a sorry sight, too!" He smiled with a strangely hateful malice. "But I intend to get some use out of you anyway."

The Lord picked Munth up as if he were no more than a child and held him high on raised arms. He turned and advanced on the fire while roaring out syllables of power. The fire was burning with renewed vigor, having just been stirred up by men with long shovels. The heat could be felt at a hundred feet. Munth looked up into the dark sky and felt the tears rolling down his cheeks. He had risen so far, and had almost won a great victory. It was hard to end like this.

But, he consoled himself at the last moment, it was probably better than going back to Padmasa. For that would have entailed a final trip to the Deeps to be quizzed by the Masters and then thrown to the carnivorous hordes of cockroaches that seethed in the bottoms of the Deeps.

Still roaring the syllables of power, Waakzaam tossed Munth onto the fire. The fire was large enough to provide an almost instantaneous death, and thus a perfectly balanced jolt of released life force on which to thrust his magic. The balance was very important, for this magic would project him an immense distance in time and space.

Waakzaam raised his hands again and uttered more syllables packed with power. There was a harsh sizzling sound, and a Black Mirror opened in the air before him.

Before the stunned audience of Baguti riders, he stepped in and vanished. The mirror swallowed him with a harsh crackling sound. A moment later the mirror vanished with a final seething roar.

For a long moment no one moved. The fire continued to blaze, sparks flying high above, but the rest of the tableau remained motionless. Then cautiously at first, but with increasing speed, the Baguti departed. Many mounted up and rode away northward. A foolhardy few tried to loot the tents. The Padmasan men stood guard over some of the tents, however, and prevented the Baguti from more than a symbolic bit of loot.

Up the slope, hidden in the grass that fringed the top, Lagdalen and Giles watched the scene.

"What was that, Lady?" said Giles when his ears had stopped buzzing. His face was slack from the shock of what he had witnessed.

"That was a Black Mirror. Our great enemy has left our world."

"I'll take your word for it." Giles hugged himself. He still had spots in front of his eyes from the awesome green lightning.

"The Lady Lessis is in that big tent. She is alive. That is all I can sense."

"Thank you, Giles. You have done well. I know it was hard for you to be this close."

"He burned so hot in my mind. Now everything is cold. I know you are right when you say he has gone from our world. But where could he go? I do not understand."

"Nor do I, Giles. Perhaps the Lady will tell us when we free her."

Chapter Forty

Mirk slid away into the dark soon after the sun had set. Lagdalen and the others waited with the horses, for he wanted no distractions. The great fire had died down considerably, and though other fires were lit, the darkness was considerably stronger than before.

"Be ready to mount and ride in an instant," said Beruyn.

"You think he must fail?" Lagdalen replied softly, not wanting Giles to hear.

Beruyn merely shrugged and looked away.

"The Great One has gone," she said. "It will not be as rigorous a place now. Trust me, I've seen these things before."

Beruyn's face filled with disbelief. What did a young lady of the Tower of Guard know about Baguti war camps?

"Just be ready to ride. It's our only hope. The Baguti will kill us very slowly when they capture us."

Out in the darkness, Mirk moved with his characteristic stealthy lope. In less than an hour he was over the rise and moving down toward the camp of the Lord Lapsor. The dying great fire threw a red light over the camp, which was yet in turmoil.

The Baguti had circled back from the Gan, looking for loot. Once their first terrified lurch for the steppes was out of their systems, they remembered the fat pickings in those tents. The Padmasan men were already taking their share, where they dared. A smaller group among them, who had worked for the Lord Lapsor before and knew how inadvisable it was to steal from him, maintained a stout guard on the tents that held the

Lord's own baggage. The Lord's main tent was guarded by the Lord's own creatures. The Padmasans left them well alone.

In the main tent there were a half dozen Neild, strange little creatures with huge goggle eyes and turtle heads. They held to their daily schedule. After dusk, the Lord would work on his experiments. When he tired he would retire to the divan for a rest. Later he would drink elixir and awaken to his full power. They waited for an hour, but the Lord had not appeared. Usually this meant he was not coming at all. With their quick, skillful hands, the Neild dismantled the experimental setup on the main table. After putting away the tools and instruments, they took down the experiments in their cages and covered them with black cloth before placing them on small carts and trundling them over to the side of the tent. Lessis was always stacked above the girl with the blue boils, who simply begged for death. Next to her was the boy's head that had been grafted on the body of a medium-sized monkey. The boy was insane and sang constantly in nonsense syllables.

Outside, in the darkness, Mirk drifted through the camp. His well-worn clothing, dark wool trousers, leather coat and hat, were much the same as that of the Padmasan mercenaries. Once he was past the sentries he managed to merge quite unnoticed among the figures moving between the tents.

The fire's red light gave the scene an eldritch cast, with dark figures silhouetted every so often against the fire. Smoke drifted up. Padmasan guards at the entrance to the tent eyed him briefly and he moved on.

He glanced down the side alley between the tents. There was no guard visible. He slipped between the row of tents and came out on a wider alley at the rear. Several tall wagons were parked behind the big pavilion tent.

Giles had indicated that the Lady was in the back part of the tent.

Mirk noticed odd-looking, two-legged creatures working around the back entrance, moving some crates down from a wagon and into the tent. These would be Neild. Mirk had seen them before in the catacombs beneath the Magnate Wexenne's grand house in Aubinas. Standing guard were a pair of enormous bewkmen. Even at thirty paces Mirk could tell what they were. There was something in the stiff-shouldered stance and oddly shaped heads that was instantly recognizable.

He turned back to the space along the side of the tent, which had no visible guards. He slipped into the gap between the pavilion and the next tent, a space about fifteen feet wide. Dodging tent pegs and ropes, he moved halfway down and took stock. There might be some kind of invisible alarm, but there seemed no other choice. He would simply have to move quickly once he was inside. With a prayer to the Great Mother he pulled out one of his razor-sharp knives and cut his way in with a single swift motion.

Inside was a realm of fantastic shapes throwing sharp shadows from a hanging lantern. A bust of the Lord Lapsor, twice life-size, stood on a plinth by the lantern. A tall table carried an array of cartographer's globes. A telescope ten feet long was standing on its mount.

Mirk sensed something moving toward him, and he slid into shadow. There must have been an alarm spell. Mirk glimpsed a powerful body as it rounded the far end of the rows of cages. It had the mass of a lion and the body shape of a baboon. Mirk had one of his killing knives in his hand, but kept inside his coat to prevent any chance of a gleam on the steel. He squeezed back into the space behind a tall wooden crate.

The thing prowled past without seeing Mirk, master of the shadows. It was blue-skinned and had orange eyes, tail twitching stiffly about as it sniffed along the side of the tent wall. It stopped precisely at the place he'd cut through. It inspected the cut, then turned and began to taste the air with a long pink tongue.

Mirk chewed his lip. There was no alternative. He would have to kill the thing, somehow.

Stealthily, he climbed a stack of solidly built crates and studied the layout of the tent. There was a massive table, thirty feet by eight, that dominated the center of the tent. Behind it was a thronelike chair and a rack of books, three shelves stuffed with leather-bound tomes. A pile of message scrolls was laid out on a platter on the table.

He watched the Neild completing their routine tasks. They were feeding the experimental animals in the cages. He caught sight of the demon, pacing down the far side of the tent, its orange eyes glowing like twin lamps.

Mirk slid down off the crates.

The demon prowled on, searching for the intruder that it sensed somewhere in the tent. The tent wall was pierced, the ground stank of a man in man boots. The demon was trained to rip such men to pieces and devour them. There were far too many who thought they could beat the odds and break into the Lord's tent and steal some great sorcerous secret that would make them wealthy beyond avarice. Such stupidity had to be rewarded, and Waakzaam thought it was every time he returned and found the demon gnawing down on the bones of some wretched, would-be-thief.

Waakzaam kept the accoutrements of such fools; their swords, bows, knives, hats, even their sandals, and over the months of the campaign had collected a chestful of treasures. The demon had proved most satisfactory as a tent guardian.

Now the blue demon pulled up short. It smelled the man. It whirled and glared down the passage between the crates. There! The man was visible for a moment and then he disappeared. The demon sprang in pursuit. At the spot where the man had been standing it caught the scent once more and followed it around a crate, then between two more and caught sight of the man ducking into the dark interior of a large crate that was open on one side.

The demon moved stealthily across the intervening space toward the entrance. The man did not carry a spear, and this made the demon abandon inhibitions. It moved inside with a bold step and found the big crate had been half-filled with small crates. The man was at the far end, the demon sprang forward, but the man slid away in the narrow space between crates. The demon could not reach him. It rocked the smaller crates around in its fury, but now it had lost all track of the prey.

Something heavy landed on the demon's back, legs gripped

its body. It gave a scream of rage and turned its head while reaching round with its right arm.

The big head turned to bring its teeth to bear. As the shoulder dipped, Mirk got a knee up on its shoulder blade and drove his razor-sharp dirk into its left eye and right through its brain.

It crashed to the floor instantly and writhed briefly before stiffening in death. Mirk pulled himself to his feet from where he'd fallen. He withdrew his knife and wiped the ill-smelling blood of the thing on its chest. It was awesomely well muscled; he could never have fought the thing for a moment. It would have torn him limb from limb.

Fortunately, there were more ways than one to skin just about anything he thought as he pushed himself to his feet and moved away from the scene. The sound of that little scuffle would have been heard; the bewkmen might come at any time. Mirk faded toward the sidewall of the tent, but there was no immediate sign of the guards.

Perhaps they did not want to come upon the demon in the process of devouring an intruder. Encouraged, he moved toward the tiers of nearby cages.

The Neild had heard the commotion, and some of them had stopped work, craning their heads in the direction of the stacked crates. Mirk slipped quietly away from the crates, around the telescope, and came up behind the row of cages.

There was no black cloth on the backs of the cages and Mirk saw more horror in those dark recesses than he would have ever dreamt possible. He averted his eyes most of the time and sent up prayers to the Mother that he be allowed to be the one to finish the tyranny of this most horrid monster.

There was a cage on the second tier, just up head, where a voice babbled endlessly in nonsense syllables. A cage below had a girl, bound at wrist and knee. She writhed and sobbed in some agony that he could not understand in the near darkness.

Above her he saw a slight figure slumped against the side of a small cage. He knew who it was at once.

"Lady, can you hear me?" he whispered.

She jumped, almost knocking her cage over and momentarily

startling the monkey boy, who screamed and jumped up and down in his cage.

"Lady?"

"Mirk?"

"Yes. I need to know how your cage is locked."

"Large key, kept on a ring. I don't know where it is kept, but I suspect it will be on the desk area of the table, where the scrolls are piled up."

"No magic?"

"Not that I can detect."

"I will be back."

Mirk slipped away back down along the row of cages at the rear of the tent.

He found that the Neild were clumped together down by the crates, jabbering excitedly over the body of the fallen demon.

He reached the huge table set five feet off the ground. The chair was equally massive. Books were jammed into a heavy bookcase nearby. There was a set of drawers and the pile of scrolls on a platter. On the table were a long delicate knife, a slab of glass, and a pile of fresh scrolls. There was also a hefty key ring.

He gathered this up and ducked back to the cages. As far as he could tell he had not been seen. The Neild remained in animated conversation over by the crate where the demon lay.

Out of the twenty keys on the chain he found the one for Lessis's cage on the fourth attempt. He pulled the door open and cut the Lady's restraints, for she was still bound at the wrists.

She climbed out, and almost fell getting down except that he caught her and set her down gently. She wobbled for a moment.

"Excuse me, Mirk, I've not been on my feet much just lately."

"Lady, shall I carry you?"

"No, I don't think it's gone quite that far. Just give me a moment to get my legs back."

Lessis sagged against the bars, and then heard the tormented moaning coming from within. She pushed herself upright again with a shiver of unease. This poor child was in constant agony.

"Mirk, I want you to open this cage and kill the girl. Be careful not to touch her, she is infected with a horrible disease."

Mirk swallowed and then set about trying the keys. The fifth try opened the cage. The girl looked at him with insane hope in her eyes, and begged for death in some Baguti tongue.

Mirk closed his eyes with a prayer and drove home the blade.

He backed out, took the Lady's arm and pulled her after him to the sidewall of the tent. His knife cut through the canvas, and they clambered through and hurried down the alley of ropes and tent pegs.

Lessis stumbled a lot at first, but gradually got a grip on things. Out on the rear alley, a wagon was in motion toward them, riders were trotting by on the far side. Baguti out for plunder. Mirk ignored them.

"Can you run?"

"I don't know. Maybe not."

"Can you keep walking?"

"Yes."

"All right, then we're going to just walk out of here. Things are pretty much in chaos without His Lordship around to keep the lid on."

"As good a plan as any, Mirk. And thank you for coming back for me. I told you not to, and you disobeyed, but I'm very thankful nonetheless."

"I would never leave you in his hands, Lady."

Chapter Forty-one

A month had passed since the battle at the crossings. The legion force at Fort Kenor had been built up to the point where the fort had had to be expanded considerably.

The 109th had been separated from the 145th, who had new dragonboys at last, and were now quartered in a row of new tents set up in the west ward that had been enclosed with stockade and towers.

Bazil was with the other dragons, noisily clanging shield and sword on the practice ground. Relkin worked on various elements of their kit that Cuzo had deemed insufficiently shining and virtuous. He was polishing the brass buttons of his jacket, which had been criticized along with his cap badge and the buckles from his new, official Legion boots.

That day he'd had a message from Lagdalen, who was upstream at Dalhousie, on her way back to Marneri. She expected to be home within the week. She was riding up to Razac because that was quicker than taking the boats up the last section of the river below the Argo watershed. After Razac she'd crest the slope and the rest of the way to Marneri would be downhill.

Marneri! More than ever he felt the call of the white city on the Long Sound. Relkin knew that he should receive notice of his retirement date sometime soon. A lot of things were backed up in the bureaucracy since the plagues, but in time it would arrive and they would have to make the journey to Marneri for the official ceremony of mustering out. Whenever possible, soldiers left the Legion from the same place they signed up.

For now, though, they were still on active duty, still posted to the Fort Kenor command. The enemy was in full retreat, and no further attacks were expected, but no chances would be taken, and that meant nobody would be getting leave or a posting to Marneri just yet.

Marneri also meant seeing Eilsa. She was in Widarf, completely recovered, she wrote in her letters. She would join him the moment he reached Marneri. They would be able to schedule a wedding.

She would give up the clan leadership then, and accept that she was out-clan by marriage. They would be together, just as they'd dreamed all these years, able to move out to the virgin lands along the Bur and start their farm. They'd have Bazil's great strength to call on, and they'd have enough money for horses, oxen, and men to do most of the hard work of clearing enough land to get in some crops. They'd build a house, a beautiful house. Bazil would live with them, in his own ample quarters. He'd specified a large plunge pool.

Of course there was one remaining fly in the ointment: the trial for the gold tabis. As soon as the emergency was over and the Legions went back to peacetime postings, he assumed the trial would be rescheduled and he would be summoned back to the court in Marneri.

And if he was found guilty? Not worth thinking about. Could mean five or ten years on the Guano Isles. At the least a fine of the tabis and maybe more.

So preoccupied was he that he never noticed when the curtain was pulled back at the door, and a slim figure stepped inside.

"Hello, Relkin," said a quiet voice that was strangely familiar. He jumped to his feet; his buttons and rag fell off the table.

"Lady!" he said, astonished by the sudden intrusion. Behind her, in the doorway he glimpsed the tall figure of Mirk. Another familiar feeling spread over him—fear. When Lessis came to call trouble was never very far away.

The Lady bent over and picked up two of the buttons.

"Those buttons are exceedingly well polished," she said, handing them to him before embracing him with a warm hug, her calm facade shattering for a moment.

"Oh my dear, my dear Relkin. I'm so sorry. I didn't mean to startle you. I just got directions to find you and came in and there you were and I just was so taken with the sight of you that I forgot my manners. I remember how diligent you always were, how all the boys were."

"Lady, this is a surprise; Lagdalen just left a few days ago."

"Yes, my dear I know. I'm sorry. You look as if you'd seen a ghost." She was smiling.

She squinted a moment, looked away, and looked back to him. "You know what happened to me, Lagdalen told you. Thanks to our friend here, Mirk, I was rescued from his grip."

Relkin and Mirk exchanged another glance. Relkin's respect for Mirk had climbed another notch when he'd heard Lagdalen's tale.

"By the Grace of the Mother and the courage of Mirk, I have survived. And my first order of priority was to find you, Relkin. I have some things to tell you, things I have only very recently learned."

Relkin felt his heart sink. He hoped she didn't notice his sudden gloom.

"First, I have some wonderful news from Marneri. The case against you has been dismissed. A message was received from Mirchaz. It was favorable to your position, and all the charges have been dropped."

"Oh! That's great news. To be free of all that, at last, oh thank the gods!"

Lessis felt her eyes widen at such bald-faced mention of the Old Gods. Relkin had obviously remained immune to the efforts of the priestesses.

"Well, that may be, but the Mother has blessed you in many ways, my dear. So that may help with the rest of what I have to tell you."

The elation faded as suddenly as it had bloomed.

"Our enemy has left our world, but he has not abandoned his war upon us."

"How can he harm us if he is no longer on our world?"

"Oh, he can return. Whenever he wants to he will come back. But he has bigger game in mind. He has gone to make war on the High Ones, the Sinni themselves."

Relkin felt his eyes boggle and his throat go dry. Whenever that name was invoked things became very dangerous indeed.

"They have called for you and Bazil to come to their aid."

"Come . . . ?" Relkin looked at her, helpless for a moment. "Aid?"

"Yes. It is a tremendous thing they ask of you, my dear. They have foreseen this crisis. It was foretold to them long ago, by the Great Bos, before he fled Gelderen the Golden and took his people to found Mirchaz. You remember Mirchaz, Relkin?"

"By the gods, I thought this was all done with. We beat them! We knocked them right back across the Gan."

Relkin remembered Mirchaz all too well; the city of the brazen elf lords with their evil game that consumed human minds for its fuel. He wanted nothing more to do with Mirchaz.

"This service will not be performed here on Ryetelth, Relkin. You are called to help them on the higher planes."

"How are we supposed to get there?"

"There are ways to accomplish the journey. You will have to receive training. I will have to give it to you, since there is no time for you to get to Andiquant."

"No, not Andiquant, please. You said that was all over."

"Well, you might prefer Andiquant to this mission."

"I don't think so." He put the buttons away in his coat pocket. He'd have to sew them on later. He wouldn't be too good with a needle for a while. In fact, he was physically trembling with all this news.

No case! They'd dropped the whole damned thing. The gold was all his. The clouds cleared from the future ahead, and the sun beamed down.

Except for this sorcery problem again. He was begged to give aid, and not even on the world he knew.

She was smiling. "No Andiquant then, Relkin. But we do have a lot to accomplish in a very short time."

"The dragon?"

"He will have to be trained as well. There are responses, attitudes, understandings that will have to be attained. And quickly. The emergency is very great, critical in fact."

Lessis withdrew a glass ball from within her robe. It was only as wide as her palm, but it glittered peculiarly in her hand. Relkin sensed at once that it was some tool of witchcraft.

"Look in the ball, my dear. You will understand better after that."

Nervously he took the ball and held it in his palm. It was warm to the touch, and there was a tiny golden glow inside it, at its exact center.

After a few minutes he felt a profound tug upon his mind. There came a feeling almost as if he were flipped over onto his back. Things opened out "under" his thoughts, though "over" might equally have applied. He was learning things that he had always known, but never understood, or something like that. It barely made sense, but he understood, that was the important thing.

A small golden face floated up in the ball. It had eyes like green glass. A voice spoke in sweet Intharion, directly into his thoughts.

"Greetings, Relkin. I am honored to meet you. I am Yeer, or Sweetwater in your tongue. You have felt us touch your life several times. All will be explained to you someday, but now we call upon you for help. Alone in the world, you and your dragon are strong enough to take on this task. All was foretold long ago, but we dared to disbelieve. We hoped that Zizma Bos was wrong, but the patterns of fate are hidden even from our sight. You traveled to Mirchaz, and there you became the Iudo Faex. You ended their cruel Game, confirming what we had already suspected. You alone have the strength to do this, as does no other living thing on your world, except Althis and Sternwal who keep their eternal vigil in Valur."

"Althis and Sternwal? I met them, once."

"Yes, Relkin, so you did. You were chosen long ago to play a great role on the Sphereboard of Destiny."

"Are you the gods?"

"No, Relkin, we are not the gods. We are the children of Los, the first comers, who tended the garden when it was still Eden. We left the garden long ago, and our stewardship came to an end. At that time we concluded the oathtaking that removed Waakzaam from the world Ryetelth. We have broken our vow. In truth we could not keep it, for we had to attempt to halt his terrible depredations through the worlds. He knows this. As I speak to you he is searching for us and when he finds us he will kill us.

"Look!"

Relkin blinked at the sudden violence within the glass ball.

Another world.

Blue lightning flashed on the steel hills. The air was as thick as lead but so hot that lead could only exist there as a liquid. The sky was alive with dark clouds writhing past like live things.

Nothing could live here, but something yet moved on the seething rock surface.

Through the canyonlands came the Intruder, a towering man-like figure half a mile high bearing an enormous hammer over its shoulder. Each step from this titan raised sludge off the patches of semimolten rock and sent globs of melt arching away in the thick superheated air as hot rock tore like taffy.

The Intruder glowed with a green internal energy. Its eyes shone like green lamps, but the metallic "face" was otherwise blank. The hills, the metal plains, all rang harshly with noise of its passage. The Dominator was come to smash the shells of the Sinni.

The scene vanished for a moment and was replaced by another.

Within a colossal vertical canyon, under blue lightning, pyramids crouched within the crystalline forest. The pyramids were slow things, their shells made of overlapping ceramic crust, their weight enormous. They crept along at no more than a man's walking pace.

This world was so huge. The clouds so deep, layer upon layer, and the sun was blue!

The voice continued.

"We are the children of Los, the Lord of Light. This is the world Xuban. We chose our world for its energy. We chose a world that could never have indigenous life forms. Nothing can live here without enormous protection. We live within these pyramids. Zizma Bos was one of us in the early days, and he warned us that the great oathtaking with Waakzaam was a mistake. That Waakzaam would never surrender his life willingly, now that he had openly rebelled. That only with his destruction would the worlds be made safe from him.

"Now, Waakzaam comes to destroy us with this terrible weapon. Against it we are helpless. Only you can help. Will you?"

Relkin shook his head for a moment, but only to try and clear his thoughts. What was he getting into? They wanted him to go to that place, where the rocky ground was semimolten?

"I will help, but I don't see how I can. I cannot live in that place. I would die in an instant. So would the dragon."

"You will be altered in the transition between your world and this one. The witch will explain. First, you will voyage to the Temple of Gold. Then you will seek out the Orb and be transformed in the pure light of Los. Eventually you will be ready to operate here. For a while."

Relkin didn't like the sound of that. "How will I find this Temple of Gold?"

"The witch will guide you."

The golden face retreated into the crystalline depths. The ball was merely glass once more. He looked up at Lessis.

"We don't know if the dragon will do this; we never asked him."

"Relkin, I think Bazil will do whatever you ask of him. His great heart will not flinch from such a duty."

Relkin knew she was speaking the truth. Bazil would fight anything and anyone, if Relkin asked him to. Except that the opponent in this case was awesome, a golem thousands of feet tall. Relkin was still not clear just how he and one wyvern dragon were going to handle a thing as tall as a mountain.

"We will train together," said Lessis. "There are things I will teach both of you."

"How can we learn enough in time?"

"It won't be easy, let me assure you."

Chapter Forty-two

Lessis wasn't joking.

It was hard work for both dragon and dragonboy. It was arduous to remember the precise order of syllables in what were nonsense words, chains of words, complete paragraphs, actual pages of rhyme and rhythm. They had to memorize these things so that they could be run out without much thought.

Bazil sweated hard to memorize what had to be said. At times it seemed impossible as he wrestled his long, wyvern tongue around the alien sounds and glottals. Relkin found the task somewhat easier and once he'd mastered his part he worked with the dragon every waking moment. Lessis worked with them both, and then with some young witches who arrived one afternoon from Marneri and Bea. They, too, would have an important part to play.

Eventually, after more than a week of intense effort, with all Lessis's considerable energies poured into the task, it was done. They performed their parts flawlessly five times in a row with Lessis and the young witches as a highly critical audience. At the finish the young women applauded with great sincerity. All were quite amazed at the dragon's performance.

Bazil was amazed, too. He stood there tasting the air, working his big jaws slowly open and shut, savoring the thing. Relkin was beaming. Lessis was obviously very pleased, looking like the cat that had got the cream.

The training was over, there was no time to waste. The moment of truth had come. That evening, in a clearing in the woods near the fort, they came together.

Seven witches were gathered by the fire to cast the spell. Lessis worked with these witches, leading them in certain chants and cries until they formed what were called "volumes," strange sounds somewhere between wails and screams, that would "break" out of the air independent of any human voice and raise the hair on the back of men's necks in the process.

It was a mighty spell, and one that required the full range of the techniques of the Witch Magic. Forging it took time and a great amount of work. The young women were sweating openly before it was done.

Bazil and Relkin said their parts perfectly on cue. Lessis worked the highest parts of the spell, and, with a harsh ripping sound, a Black Mirror opened in the air before them.

Relkin felt his pulse thudding in his chest as he stared at the evil sheen of the mirror, an eye into the random diffuseness of the chaotic ether.

Lessis spoke quickly to settle them and reviewed one last time what they must do.

"We simply step through the mirror and enter as a group. Remember to keep making walking motions and stay close to me. We don't have to physically touch, but you need to be within my reach.

"And remember to keep calm no matter what you think you see. Just look at me if you become afraid. Remember, we cannot speak to one another once we are inside the mirror."

One by one they stepped through: Lessis went first, then Relkin, Bazil, and finally Mirk.

There was a terrible cold that burned the skin. Relkin felt his hair stand up all over his body. There was a sour stench and a constant, roaring buzz in the ears, occasionally cut with sharp cracks and pops, usually in tune with red flashes that blazed far off in the distance. Hashmarks, chevrons, and starblazes of black and white broke around them like tiny fireworks.

Lessis shepherded them in the correct direction. She had an unerring sense of direction in the subworld, which made her one of the greatest Black Mirror voyagers of her order. It was a long distance this time, a vaulting across the Great Sphereboard itself. Her mind was filled with calculations and concerns.

The others were filled with vague terrors. The cold had become less biting, and they moved as if in a strange and terrible dream, walking but not making contact with any solid surface. Around them roared the sour sea of chaos, and just ahead was Lessis, leading them to solid ground somewhere unknown in the Mother's Hand.

Bazil hated the strange motionless walking, the incessant buzz and flash, the cold; it was all alien to his being.

Lessis led them on.

At one point a small predator swam in toward them, a thing like a jellyfish, many-tentacled, filled with gossamer flares of energy. It was the size of a house and ravenous. Sensing their life force, it moved hungrily forward until Lessis struck it with a spell that stopped it cold. Its tentacles shot out sideways, and it almost eviscerated itself in coming to a halt. She struck it again and set it fluttering away in panic, convinced that death was close behind.

Throughout the journey Lessis watched anxiously for more dangerous foes, but was relieved when she detected no signs of a Thingweight along the route. Their only hope was to vault the heavens without stirring such a predator's interest. Every second they covered a vast distance, both spatial and temporal. Every second they came closer to their faraway goal. Each second was vital if they were to survive the attentions of the true monsters of these deeps.

Lessis had been chased by Thingweights before and had once come very close to being snatched, right at the mirror's face. She scanned the murk ahead for the first signs, the crackling far-off lightning that would always announce a great Thingweight's approach.

On they went, the cold of chaos on their skins, the twirling gray nothingness on all sides, Lessis peering ahead.

There! A faint greenish crackle on the far, far right, away in the distant emptiness. Something approached. It was too far as yet to determine if it was closing on them or just moving across their path with no idea of their existence.

Anxious moments passed; Lessis stared fixedly at the distant flickers of lightning. Was it coming straight at them, or veering off ever so slightly to pass behind them?

Gradually the lightning grew brighter. The monster became visible as a dark smudge stretching out behind the area where energies were in play. Lessis could tell at once that this was one of the big ones, a giant even among its enormous kind. As it approached, her heart began to sink. It was vast, far greater than any Thingweight she had ever seen before.

The behemoth was coming directly toward them, its front measured by sheets of lightning, bolts and blasts coming one on the other so quickly that the flashing light was virtually continuous. It was as massive as a mountain. A rippling range of hillocks rose into the central massif—huge, dark, and ominous—behind the endless lightning of the forecurtain.

Lessis estimated how far they had yet to go. It would be close, very close, but there was a chance. Her group had gained tremendous momentum in their long vault across the vastnesses of chaos. Perhaps it would be enough.

Closer and closer drew the enormity, behind its curtain of lightning. They were almost microscopic prey for the thing, but it was their life energy that it sought, not their flesh, and in that precious resource they were well endowed, and it could sense this. Ahead of the great mass the tentacles were darting and curling, seeking the tiny, precious prey item.

A far-ranging tentacle looped past them, tracing a line of green fire. Lessis looked back; the lightning curtain was terribly close now. Any moment and it would have them.

More tentacles flickered in their direction. The great mass of the monster loomed above them like a mountain, dark and implacable. Lessis felt panic rising in her heart. Tentacles flashed past overhead, no more than a hundred feet away. Too close, the next would be among them. Prayers sometimes fell on stony ground, so Lessis had discovered.

And then with the astonishing abruptness that marked this terrible form of travel, they reached the destination coordinates and were ejected across the threshold and out of the chaotic realm though a Black Mirror that had been created by a doppelgänger spellsay effect. They emerged from the subworld about three feet off the ground and dropped onto a smooth slope covered in short grass. Bazil stumbled and fell, rolling down the slope about fifty feet.

Behind them the Black Mirror vanished with a harsh zap of static.

The grass was unusually dark in color, almost black, and it seemed to grow in tight spirals on the ground. They got to their feet, a little unsteadily, and gazed on a new world. The skies were pale purple, and prairie stretched away in all directions. Tall grasses and patches of yellow flowers covered much of it, and along the watercourses small flat-topped trees grew in dense clumps.

A wind gusted up from somewhere warm, bringing a mixture of scents. There was water nearby, and the musk of the yellow flowers was strong and sweet. The sun was orange and large in the sky.

Lygarth!

Lessis steadied herself. She had done it! The level of difficulty was off the scale, but once the dragon had memorized his parts, the rest was something she could attempt. Not even Ribela could have done better.

Bazil was still in a state of something close to shock. He stared around himself at the alien landscape. Slowly his breath came back; the terrible cold was gone; the terrifying thing that had pursued them had missed. He was still among the living dragons. It took him a few seconds to recover and begin to move his limbs. He hissed loudly, in sudden anger, pure dragon response.

Mirk stood by silently, inscrutable.

Relkin noted the dark hue of the vegetation. The sun was a huge orange disk, much greater in extent across the sky than the sun of Ryetelth. The vegetation was green, but green fading to black.

Lessis spoke. "This is the world Lygarth, the hidden world where lies the Temple of Gold, the gateway to the Higher Realms. The gateway lies inside the temple and access is controlled by the Order of the Pure and Holy.

"You will be tested before you can enter the gateway. You must pass the test before you can pass through. Only thus can you reach the world of the High Ones."

"Lady, will you come with us?"

"Alas, Relkin, I cannot. It would not be permitted me, nor would I seek it. Only you and Bazil are equipped with the resources to make the translation to the higher planes. For us it would mean instant death."

"I do not understand these things," said Relkin after a while. He stared off toward the southern horizon, "but I think we will find water in the south. Where there's water there's usually game."

That was as much as he could handle for the moment. The world had suddenly become a lot bigger and stranger by far than anything he had ever imagined.

They headed south in single file, with Mirk at their head and the dragon in the middle, the sword swaying over his shoulder as he prowled forward like the great predator he was. The dragon was just glad to be out of the strange place they had crossed. This world was solid ground, and there was water nearby. He would survive.

Chapter Forty-three

Under the blue lightning the pyramids crouched deep in the huge canyon of Eras. Eras split the great plateau at its northern apex. Above them the walls were carved in tremendous bas-reliefs, each covering many miles in extent. This was the heroic, glorious work of Eras, the Carver of the Worlds.

But the Sinni in their protective pyramids could not linger to contemplate the works of Eras. They moved on, albeit slowly, for it was very difficult to move their enormous masses. The pyramids moved solely by the use of magical power, never having been meant to move more than a few feet a day, to track the blue sun as the world slowly turned beneath it.

For aeons the Sinni, the children of Los, had dwelled thus, bathing in the abundant energy provided by the blue sun. Other than the crystal trees, which were not really alive, nothing could live in the seething temperatures obtaining at the surface without elaborate protection.

Waakzaam's dreadful Intruder, an enormous golemoid, half a mile high, was approaching from the south. He brought a hammer to smash their precious shells, to let the lethal environment into their protected catafalques. Not even the children of Los could survive here unprotected.

And so, even as they inched along with every ounce of power they could muster, they worked feverishly to try and hinder their enemy.

The Intruder was now marching up the silvery plain of Charmeesh, which covered the southern half of the great plateau.

This put it on the far side of the Chasm of Huth, which bisected the plateau. The only way across the chasm was the bridge of Huth, a light, airy span whose delicacy belied its massive strength. It had been grown from crystals worked with great magic by Elute. Of all Elute's bridges, the one at Huth was the masterpiece.

By concentrating their energies, the Sinni were able to dislocate the internal structures of the crystal and turn it to dust. The great bridge glowed for a long moment, then plunged as a cinder into the depths of the chasm.

That would halt the Intruder south of the chasm. Perhaps that would give them enough time to get off the plateau and hide in the scarlet sand sea to the north. Even there they could only prolong the inevitable. Unless their champions arrived soon, they would be destroyed.

Some hours later the Intruder marched up the plain, climbed the glittering hills of fused silicates, and strode to the edge of the chasm. The bridge was gone, leaving only the pits that had once secured its members.

The vast golemoid turned and headed back the way it had come, halting beside the Pinnacles of Eslaut. Tall, sinewy works, these statues in metalline crystals rose many miles into the hot air, filling it with grace and strange, almost startling beauty.

It swung its hammer and began to smash the base of the tallest of the Pinnacles of Eslaut, the one called Havilden the Fair. Aghast, the fugitive Sinni observed his actions through optical agents they worked from afar.

The hammer was filled with deadly energies, and it soon buckled the ankles of Havilden and brought the great piece down, crashing upon the plain of Charmeesh.

No sooner was Havilden down, face buried in the silver mud, than the Intruder turned to the tall, perfectly round pinnacle of Shorj. The Intruder swung its hammer and broke the pinnacle loose and cut it into three sections of almost equal seize. Then it heaved the fallen Havilden up section by section upon the three rollers it had made. While its limbs glowed with the green fire, the golemoid pushed the huge statue forward, removing a roller from the rear as it came to the ruined ankles, then hurrying forward to place it at the front. Then it pushed the pinnacle forward once more. In time this slow and tedious work brought the mass of Havilden to the brink of the chasm.

Now the golemoid was still while the Dominator raised his strength, summoning energy from the turbulent skies of Xuban. After a few minutes there came a crescendo of lightning bolts striking down from the clouds upon the golemoid. For half an hour or more they continued to strike and then finally petered out.

The Intruder stood behind the pinnacle, raised its hands toward the ruined ankles, and became still. A tearing, shrieking vibration built up in the ground beneath the pinnacle. The rock shuddered and leaped as if in torment, and the scene disappeared in an enormous flash of green light. The heavy air quaked and shuddered. The ground heaved and Havilden erupted skyward with red-hot sparks trailing from the ruined legs. The golemoid was blown backwards by the eruption, staggered several steps, and fell with a crash in the crystal forest.

Havilden soared, then fell back to land with another great noise aslant the chasm, spanning it with a somewhat wobbly bridge.

The Intruder slowly struggled up, molten metal dripping from its elbows, which had been driven deep into the ground. Flashes of red light were coming from various sections within its awesome bulk, indicating damage wrought to its internal mechanisms.

Stepping cautiously past the blasted pit, it found the pinnacle now stretched across the chasm of Huth with the legs resting on one side and the head and shoulders lying on the other. Carefully it tested the statue with a foot. There was a wobble, but it seemed to hold firmly enough to risk an attempt at crossing. Cautiously the Intruder climbed up on to the scorched and ruptured legs of Havilden and began to make its way across.

With desperate haste the Sinni joined their thought to concentrate upon the material of the fallen pinnacle of Havilden. After a while they found the frequency required and soon the pinnacle began to glow from within.

The Intruder noticed the glow within Havilden and was forced to hurry, which caused the statue to rock. The glow intensified, the Intruder increased is pace. The statue shifted under its weight. The Intruder gambled; it sprang forward, set down one foot, and leaped onward even as the glow consumed the material of Havilden and its cinders fell into the chasm.

The Intruder was left clinging to the edge by the hammer hooked over it. A slip and a fall was certain to destroy the golemoid, since it was more than five hundred miles straight down into the chasm.

Painfully, slowly, it hauled itself up to the edge. Its difficulties were compounded by the friable nature of the crystalline material of the cliff. The hammerhead slowly sank into the rock and eventually would cut right through the cliff face and fall free. The gigantic Intruder looked down and saw the ash of Havilden sparking in blue fury as it fell endlessly into the chasm's hot depths. It resumed its desperate efforts to climb the hammer's handle back to the top.

Slowly, even as the hammerhead continued to slip through the cliff rock, the Intruder climbed, until it got one arm over the edge. It brought up the other arm and levered itself to the top with a mighty effort and rolled over and lay flat on the top.

The Sinni were still trying to convert the material of the hammer to energy as they had done with Havilden. However, the material of the hammer was imbued with magic that protected it from their skill.

Their efforts caused the hammer to emit a cry, and so it warned the Intruder, which rolled over and thrust its arm into the cavity into which the hammerhead had sunk. Deep in the rock it found the hammerhead, moaning as it twisted in the fields generated by the Sinni.

Waakzaam's Intruder roared in anger. Slowly it heaved the hammer up, back through the cavity it had torn through the cliff top. Green fire flickering over its shoulders as it made the effort, the golemoid hauled the hammer to the surface, got both hands on it, and tore it free of the cliff.

Once more the Intruder roared its defiance of the High Ones.

Count your hours now, children of Los, for your doom is nigh!

Chapter Forty-four

The water hole lay in a deep swale below a row of hillocks. Bazil and the others hid themselves behind a screen of shrubs with black leaves. As the day progressed the huge red sun slid to the horizon, and their hiding place was obscured in deep shadows.

Animals of many kinds came to the water hole as the dusk drew on. First there were groups of large, four-legged beasts whose horns projected from their mouths and curved upward in wicked-looking tusks. They had shaggy coats of dun gray and fierce red eyes and they drank with frequent pauses to look around.

"These beasts are often hunted here," said Bazil softly. Relkin nodded.

"Do you think they detect us?" said Mirk.

"No. We are downwind. They check the air by the ground, perhaps smell traces of us, but this dragon think they fear some other enemy."

Relkin nodded.

The herd of tusked bison drank for a while longer then suddenly departed, spooked by nothing discernible to the watchers. Shortly afterward a trio of ungainly creatures with long necks and massive limbs projecting from barrel-like bodies appeared. Their hides were a dirty white, with patches of black and brown here and there. Their forelimbs were considerably longer than their chunky hind legs and equipped with claws. Relkin thought he'd never seen anything more peculiar, not even on the dark continent.

He was about to say so, when something else moved on the periphery of the scene. A darker mass crept closer.

"He over there," whispered the dragon. Mirk had already noticed. Lessis turned her head.

The dark blotch had moved to a clump of much-chewed-over spine bush. The barrel-chested beasts drank, looked up. There was a snort and several harsh braying cries as the beasts stood back, then withdrew.

The blotch of darkness remained in hiding.

After a while a herd of small four-legged animals, perhaps thirty in all, came to the water. They had the shape of deer or antelope and were decorated with white stripes on their flanks. They were joined by other herds and groups. Some heavyset piglike beasts appeared among them.

The dark mass hidden in the spine bush suddenly exploded into view and rushed toward the nearest of these huge hogs. The hog ran for its life, its feet scrabbling for purchase on the loose gravel, while behind came a squat, powerfully built beast with a toadlike head that split open to reveal twin rows of daggerlike teeth. It sprang after the hog, and both departed into the darkness, while everything else at the water hole also stampeded for safety.

In a moment the scene was empty. They listened carefully but heard no death struggle.

"This dragon think he missed the prey."

"I have never seen a beast like that."

"This is Lygarth, Mirk, not Ryetelth," murmured the Lady.

The dust settled. Soon other creatures came down to drink. Some were remarkably like horses, only half the size, while others sported clusters of horns on their heads. A few two-legged things also appeared, reminding Relkin and Bazil of small pujish from Eigo. All drank peaceably together.

Later some more of the piglike things appeared. The sun had almost completely set by then, and the light was poor. Mirk and Relkin crept close enough to shoot one. It went down with a thud as one shaft found its heart, and the other entered its throat. The others ran, and Bazil came forward to help drag the carcass away.

They built a fire out of the poor spine bush and augmented it with more dry wood they found close by in the grass. There had once been some trees here. Meanwhile, Mirk butchered the creature and cut it into roastable chops and haunches. Lessis sharpened some of the straighter pieces of wood and started broiling the meat as the fire burned down to a hot mass of coals.

While Relkin filled all the water bottles Bazil waded out into the water, drank deeply, and splashed himself all over.

The tantalizing smell of roasting meat soon drew other interested parties. Eyes glowed orange in the dark until Relkin tossed rocks, and they departed. Then came something larger, a shambling form on four legs that could also stand on two. It roared a challenge as it moved toward the fire and the delicious smell.

Bazil got up with a slight groan. At the sight of the big wyvern dragon, the creature's features split open in a baboonlike snarl. Bazil roared and rushed at it with his arms high.

The thing jammed to a halt, then retreated fifty paces and stopped. Bazil charged again. This time the beast kept going and vanished into the murk.

The roasted meat reminded Relkin of beef, though perhaps more like venison. He ate heartily, aware that it might be the only food he'd get for a long time.

More scavengers appeared, and Mirk hurled bones out into the darkness, which were snatched up and borne away by growling packs of smaller animals.

And then three huge four-legged brutes, shovel-shaped heads bristling with curved teeth, came bounding out of the dark. Since each of them stood ten feet high there was an immediate menace from them. They approached without hesitation, making loud booming cries, swinging their heavy front paws and snapping their huge jaws.

Everyone had already taken up their weapons. Now, Mirk

and Relkin put arrows into the brutes with little effect. Bazil stepped out with Ecator swinging loosely in his hand. The creatures paused, circled for a few moments, then attacked in a group.

Bazil bent at the knees and swung the sword at their legs. He came around smoothly and took down the first one, one of its front legs severed above the knee, then jammed his foot into the mouth of the next before bringing the sword up and over to finish it. The third one grappled with him and tried to bite into his neck, but Relkin was already on its back and had his sword jammed into its mouth.

It snarled in frustration and pawed at him, while Mirk stabbed it from behind. The beast emitted a cry like a steam kettle on the boil and sprang back, dislodging Relkin, who tumbled to the ground. Bazil swung around with Ecator in hand. The beast moved back, still squalling.

The beast previously reduced to three legs staggered to the edge of the brush and was almost instantly taken down by the toad-headed predator that had returned unseen. It dragged the still-thrashing victim back into the darkness of the brush and ate it alive.

The other staggered up to the top of the hillocks and lurched away, still bleeding. To everyone's surprise other toad-heads soon followed, appearing out of hiding places here and there around the water hole. The wounded beast's final mournful cries came not long afterward.

"I hope that's enough to keep them busy for the night," said Relkin.

Back at the embers of the fire they finished their own roasted meat and rested their limbs. Relkin checked Bazil's back and neck for cuts, found a few scratches that he cleaned and dressed with Old Sugustus from his kit bag. Mirk proposed that they take turns at the watch, and they rolled themselves in their blankets for sleep.

"And remember to keep an eye for those toad-headed things. Don't want one of them sneaking up on us."

Before sleep claimed him, Relkin turned on his side to face Lessis, who was taking the first watch.

"You said we would be tested at the temple. Why is this?"

"The Temple of Gold houses the maze, which is a gate to the entire Sphereboard of Destiny. Every world in the Mother's Hand is connected there. And so it is guarded by the Order of the Pure and Holy."

"I have heard you mention this order. Who are they?"

"They are the children of Erris, who infused life into the air of the worlds."

"Gods?"

"No, my dear, they are as the Sinni: High Ones, children of the seven spirits, but not gods. There are no gods; I thought you understood that. But there were seven great ones, who were created to infuse themselves into the worlds. Los it was who brought the qualities of light. Cerule brought the sky and others. Waakzaam was supposed to bring the grounding of the worlds. His refusal opened them to the dreadful sorcery that grips them."

Lessis continued, "The Order of the Pure is from Erris. Erris is both female and male in characteristic. The order are similar in that respect."

Relkin looked blankly back at her.

"They are of both sexes at once, is what I mean."

He swallowed, somewhat troubled by this idea. "Apart from that, though, they are like the Sinni?"

"Yes."

"Did Waakzaam make such beings for himself?"

"No. In his pride he retained all his strength to himself. The wizards and mage lords grew up in his shadow. They are his only children."

Lessis did not mention that she, herself, was one of the children of Cerule, the Queen of the Sky and a close ally of Erris.

"What do the order look like?"

"They are a beautiful people, tall and fair with grace and a love of life. Even-handed in their judgment, but fierce and implacable in pursuit of purity. If they find the stain on the character of a person who wishes to travel through the maze, they rend that person to pieces. Thus do they keep the passage between the worlds safe from wizards, malcontents, and other harmful ones."

"How does our enemy travel between worlds then?"

"He slew a dragon and used the life force to rip open a path."

"Jumble?"

"I am afraid so."

Relkin felt a wave of hate rise up in his heart. "I wish you'd told me about the Pure Ones earlier."

"Child, you will pass. You have no stain upon you."

Relkin wished he could be as positive about that himself.

Eventually he slept, waking only when some large animals tromped in from the dark and began to drink with lots of splashing and whistling. Relkin took the next watch, followed by Bazil, and then Mirk the watch before dawn.

The next morning opened with orange glory in the east and settled into a repeat of the day before. Wandering south through a range of hills cloaked with tawny grasses and dense clumps of thornbush, they occasionally glimpsed distant herds of animals. That night they found a small trickle of water in the bed of an almost dried-up stream. It was just enough to slake thirsts and fill their water bottles.

They found no game and slept on empty bellies.

The next day they reached a forested area. The trees were not more than ten feet tall and had marks of severe browsing upon them. The streams were dry, but clearly this was a wetter area than the first part of Lygarth they had seen.

They hunted and shot an animal not unlike an elk, except that its horn was on its nose rather than the top of its head. This time they roasted it on an exposed rock. After nightfall, yellow and orange eyes showed around them, but they ignored them and concentrated on eating well before sleeping.

Nothing chose to disturb them that night.

The following days were spent moving due south through this region of hills and forest, with crystal-pure lakes and the occasional flowing stream. They managed to make a kill at least every other day and thus kept hunger at bay. They had come more than a hundred miles by Relkin's reckoning, which had been honed to accuracy over years of campaigning, and were embarked on their eighth day of marching when they came over a rise, and saw something glittering on the next hilltop.

Through the distant trees they glimpsed a golden dome.

"That must be the temple," said Relkin, thinking out loud.

And so it was.

Chapter Forty-five

After winding up the side of the hill on a cobblestone road, they came to the simple, massive gate set into the ten-foot-high wall of white stone that surrounded the Temple of Gold.

The gate was open. No guards were visible. They entered and found themselves on a broad courtyard, paved in white-and-black stone which formed some complex pattern that was invisible to them.

Two-story buildings of stone lined either side of the court while ahead rose the temple itself, a simple square structure crowned with a glittering gold dome. A broad span of white-stone steps lead up to its entrance beneath a curving vault, decorated with inlaid lapis lazuli.

The only visible inhabitant was a small black cat sitting by itself on the steps below the temple entrance. At their appearance the cat sat up, stared hard, then turned and bounded lightly up the steps and into the shadows within the doorway.

"Where is everybody?" muttered Relkin. The dragon clacked his jaws lightly.

A breeze blew over them, sending a cool rush down their spines.

"Someone watch," said Bazil.

Mirk and Lessis had already realized this.

"Why do they not show themselves?" Relkin wondered.

"In time they will. Have no fear."

For a long moment, perhaps half a minute, the silence continued, and the cool breeze played over them. Nothing stirred in the courtyard except that breeze.

Relkin found himself thinking guilty thoughts. All the petty larcenies of his career as a dragonboy rose up to haunt him. So did visions of young women he had known at various times.

But to steal was to survive, if you were a dragonboy and faced with the demands of the job. There was never enough equipment, and it wore out fast when laced onto a two-ton fighting machine. A dragonboy had to liberate stuff like thread and thongs, metal and polish. As for the ladies he had loved, well why shouldn't he have loved them?

Suddenly there came a single deep chime from a bell, which reverberated in the silence. Several seconds went by, then out from the side doors came a dozen or more tall figures, clad in simple white robes and sandals. In feature they were akin to the golden elves that Relkin knew from his time in Mirchaz, but their faces were longer and narrower, and their skins had a faint bluish tinge. Their hair was white or silver and worn long, to the shoulders. Some had the suggestion of breasts beneath the white robes, others did not. This was the only sexual difference between them that was visible. The similarity to the elves of Mirchaz sent a shiver down Relkin's spine. He and Bazil had had enough trouble from the likes of these.

The twelve formed up in two lines of six. One stepped forward. He, or was it she? wore robes of purple silk over the white and a silver disk above its head.

"Welcome, strangers, to the Temple of Erris. I am Elory. We were told to expect a party of four, of which a wyvern and a man would seek to journey onward. You appear to be that party.

"We are also pleased to find a daughter of Cerule is among you. Welcome, Lessis, it has been many a year since last we saw you."

Lessis bowed.

"I thank you for your welcome, fair friends and children of great Erris. I am but a guide for those who would journey onward."

"Indeed, such information has been conveyed to us by your sister."

Lessis nodded to herself. Ribela had done her part.

"Normally we would not allow access to the temple courtyard to a fell creature such as the dragon, but we understand that
the dragons of Argonath are not of the ancient archetype."

Bazil's big eyes popped dangerously and he hissed quietly to
himself. He was every bit of the ancient archetype, if they really
wanted to know.

"Seeing this magnificent beast, with its obvious intelligence,
forces us to admit that we have been restricted to our temple for
too long." Bazil's hiss cut off abruptly. "There have been great
changes in the worlds that we were unaware of. Waakzaam's
folly has produced strange consequences. Dragons have ceased
to be the ravening monsters that haunted the worlds when they
were young, and it seems to us most fitting that a dragon should
be part of the quest to end Waakzaam's reign. Our cousins the
Sinni have chosen well in their extremity."

"They live still?" said Lessis anxiously.

"They do."

"Thanks be given for that. I pray that we will be in time to
help them."

"There is time, but not much room for error." The disked one
turned to Mirk.

"And this is the one chosen?"

Mirk looked back with surprise. "No, friends, I am not the
one."

Twelve heads turned as one and looked to Lessis, who confirmed what Mirk had said.

They turned in surprise to the younger man, a slight figure in
comparison to burly Mirk. "You?" they said. "You are the one
to be tested? You wish to enter the maze of gold?"

Relkin shrugged. "Well, actually, they asked me to."

There was a long silence.

"Tonight you will rest. Rooms are being made ready. Tomorrow morning we will see whether or not you may be allowed to
enter the maze."

Relkin looked up at the dragon. Bazil was expressionless.
Relkin thought the leatherback wyvern had taken it all very well.

"First though, we beg you to bathe, enjoy a meal in our refectory. There is a fresh vintage of the wine, and the cheese is very good, even if I say so myself. You must be hungry and footsore from your journey."

After eight days on the march through wild country, living off game and drinking from muddy wallows and water holes, they were all ready for the chance to bathe, wash their clothes, and sit down to a civilized meal.

The baths were carved of stone and coursing with hot water. They beat their clothes on the stone, wrung them out, and left them to dry. Robes of fine brown wool were given them by the order to wear in the meantime.

The dragon hosed himself down in the stables while a warehouse space was readied for his occupancy. A great pile of straw had been set down, along with water. A table and simple chairs of wood were brought in for the others to eat off.

Meals were simple among the Order of the Pure and Holy, but on this occasion they had outdone themselves. There was a great deal of barley and corn stirabout, to which they had added a concoction of onions, garlic, and wine. Bazil spooned this up with the largest ladle in the temple kitchen. There was bread, some sliced roast venison, and fruit for the others. Bazil had a haunch of the venison, a dozen loaves of bread, and three big pails of a curious, spiced ale that was a speciality of the temple's own small brewery.

They ate in a strained silence, each filled with their own thoughts. Relkin was thinking of Eilsa and wondering if he would ever see her again. What they were up against seemed impossible to overcome. He had no idea how they were supposed to tackle that huge thing that they'd seen in the vision.

If he never came back, how long would she wait? Would she wear widow's weeds all her life, as she had sworn that she would when he went off to Eigo? Or would she succumb to the demands of her family and marry someone approved by the factions of the Clan Wattel.

Relkin took up a goblet of the spicy ale and went out into the courtyard, where Bazil had been demolishing huge bowls of stirabout laced with onion sauce.

"This dragon very hungry. Nothing but a half a deer in two days."

"Yeah, we didn't run into much once we were in the forest."

"Almost as quiet as old forest in Eigo where we lived off pujish."

"Tough and stringy critters."

"But, boy know how to bake them to perfection."

Relkin laughed out loud. "As if anyone would want to eat them, unless they had to."

Together they laughed long and loud, then fell into a long silence as their mood turned more somber. Bazil broke the silence first.

"Tomorrow they test us; they destroy us if we fail test."

"That's what I heard. Doesn't sound good. So if I don't make it out, I just want you to know that you're the best damned dragon a man could have had. You've got me out of more jams than I can count."

Bazil put up a huge hand.

"Relkin always good dragonboy. And save this dragon's hide many time. Relkin dragonfriend."

Relkin's goblet was empty. Bazil had finished his pail. Both felt light-headed; the ale was stronger than they were accustomed to.

Quite suddenly a young woman was there, wearing a short tunic of worked hide fringed with red beads. She carried a jug of beer, and, with a big smile, she poured most of it into Bazil's pail and filled Relkin's mug.

With another smile she eyed Relkin quite frankly.

"Hello," she said, "I am Ilaren."

She was beautiful, with long dark hair brushed and glistening down her back. Her tunic was belted tightly at her waist, and, despite her youth, her figure was that of a voluptuous woman.

In fact, she reminded Relkin of Ferla, and the thought brought up a chain of complex, unwelcome thoughts, mostly about his lack of purity. Ferla had been the dream creation of the mad elf lord, Mot Pulk. Relkin had been the victim of strange, lush magic, but he had loved Ferla.

"The sisters of the order told me that your name is Relkin.

My name means, 'flower of the spirit.' What does your name mean?"

Relkin stammered a moment, thunderstruck by the deep violet eyes and stunning beauty in her face. "I don't know," he said. "I don't think it means anything. It was just what I got named in the dragonhouse. I was an orphan, you see."

"What is an orphan?"

"Someone without a mother or a father. No parents."

The ale in his cup was sweet and easy to drink. Quite suddenly, though, he felt the world reel and spin for a moment. He shook his head to clear it a little. Ilaren was still there, still smiling. He drank in her beauty. Time passed. She was now sitting very close to him.

"They told me you are a soldier. Tell me about your life."

Her eyes were so attractive, so deep. His eyes were caught by the dark, mysterious curve between her breasts. He felt the roaring in his brain of absolute primal lust. He wanted her with every fiber of his being. And she wanted him, or so it seemed.

Mysterious patterns danced across his eyes. Her opulent bosom heaved. The dark softness between her breasts seemed the most inviting place he had ever seen. He put out a hand. To turn her away? Or to make that first contact, before making love to her? He would never know for sure. For the rest of his life, Relkin would never be absolutely sure.

An image of Eilsa burst into his mind, and the thought of her was like having the sun suddenly break through the clouds on a rainy day. Eilsa was real; Eilsa was his love.

He clung to that thought. Eilsa was his true love. He had fallen when he went with Ferla, and with Lumbee, but he had resolved never to fall again. His situation in both cases had been extreme, and thus he could forgive himself to a degree. But this was different, for now he knew himself and knew what he could not do.

Ilarin continued to sit and smile and cock her head while her violet, mysterious eyes drew his in. Occasionally she said something sweet and slightly suggestive. But Relkin was no longer enticed. His lust had cooled, as if a bubble had burst. He could feel the sweat congealing on his brow and under his arms.

He was immune to her charms. Eilsa's face had been enough.

Suddenly he was tired, very tired. Drowsiness swept his thoughts away. It was hard to think properly. The dragon was already snoring.

Relkin fell asleep.

The Intruder towered into the sky, marching into the teeth of a hellish storm one massive stride at a time. Clouds of purple and black had massed above, and near-continuous lightning flashed and flickered, crowning the silver skull in brilliance.

On the hills of Varon, beyond the chasm of Huth, the Intruder came upon a straggler, the pyramid of poor Harisia, poetess of the spirits and the wraiths. Her pyramid crawled slowly through the crystalline hills, which o'ertopped the Intruder by a bare hundred feet. The pyramid came barely a third as high, its mass creeping forward under Harisia's magical impulse.

Deep in meditation when the alert was first sounded, she had received the news of the Intruder late. When she finally awoke to the peril there was only the chasm of Huth to protect her. She had delayed departure, still, convinced that the chasm was too wide for even this colossal Intruder to cross.

The others had raised the storm to help her, but the Intruder plowed right through the clouds and hot winds. The storm could barely slow it down.

Harisia saw the Intruder as it stepped around the nearest of the crystal hills. She spoke directly to the consciousness of he who controlled the monster.

"Waakzaam, you trespass where you promised never to come. You have broken your oath."

"Bah, be silent about oaths. You broke yours to me long ago."

"Waakzaam was once a name that shone with glory. Now you have become a low creature obsessed only with your own evil fantasies."

"You spit out your insults and your lies even now!"

The giant Intruder pulled the great hammer off its shoulder and hefted it in both hands. Harisia would not keep quiet, however.

"I remember Puna, Waakzaam. I remember her most of all. Puna was my friend. You loved Puna because she was the purest of all and because her beauty was like a lantern to all the worlds.

You wanted her to be yours, to be owned by you. She understood that, even then, when Gelderen was fair still, and the black cloud of your envy had not yet fallen across it.

"Puna knew of the coldness in your heart. She understood your secret weakness, and you hated her for that. You succumbed to that weakness, and you killed her with your own great hands. You walked brazenly through Gelderen, and no one knew that you had the blood of Puna on your hands."

"You lie, you filthy whore!" The Intruder bore down and swung the hammer directly into the leading face of Harisia's pyramid.

There was a flash of light; a roaring blast of sound wobbled away through the tumult of the hot air. Dark vapor exploded from the site of the strike. As it cleared, there would be seen great cracks across the carapace and a crater in the center.

Harisia's pyramid rocked back and settled to the surface, embedding in a patch of hot basaltic rock. Her scream of anguish echoed through the thoughts of all her kin.

They screamed with her.

The Intruder swung the great hammer high. Lightning struck it twice at its apex and down it came, swinging with full force into the side of the pyramid. Another flash of light burst forth, even brighter than before, and another boom rippled away through the dense gas. This time, however, Harisia's agonies brought forth no cry, but rather more accusations.

"But when Puna was missed, Los sent Lorn, the Hound of Heaven, to seek her. He found her body and brought it to Los."

"Los the liar! Los the defamer! I would crush him if he dared to manifest himself. Instead he torments me with you and your underlings, the children of the worms."

The hammer rose high and smashed down, breaking away the tip of the pyramid and tearing open the side. Blue fire sparkled in the damaged area, while dust flew away in the superheated air.

"You warred against us, rather than admit your guilt. You chose the path to violence, abandoning your duty. You fell then, and have fallen much farther since."

"I will silence you soon, you stinking liar."

The hammer fell again and again, but Harisia never ceased to praise the lovely Puna and damn Waakzaam for her murder long ago.

Waakzaam's Intruder doubled and swung and brought the hammer down. Shards of the pyramid flew away in explosions of light and dust. Stabbing beams of energy broke out of the ruined interior as its mechanisms were smashed.

Eventually the hammer cut through the final layer of the pyramid's integument and broached the catafalque. In an instant Harisia died, smothered under the heavy, scalding air.

Her death did not stop the destruction. Spewing poisonous curses, Waakzaam worked his golemoid in a passion. The Intruder continued to flail away at the shattered pyramid until it was virtually flattened.

He stopped, raised the hammer above his head in both hands, and roared out his sentence of doom.

"Beware, oathbreakers, for I am come to slay ye!"

Chapter Forty-six

Relkin awoke. He was lying on a cot in a warm room with sunlight streaming in the window. He felt fresh and well rested. He remembered very little of the previous evening. All he could recall of the final part of it was that a stunningly attractive girl had brought them some beer.

Bazil had woken up recently, too. He was outside in the courtyard, stretching his legs and working his shoulders and tail.

Asked what he remembered, he shrugged.

"This dragon have strange dream. This dragon was young again. Sitting up on the hills above the village with old Macumber. He say, 'You will have a long career, Bazil, if you keep the sword sharp.' "

"Well, I can testify to that, you've always taken good care of the blade."

"In dream, old Macumber say that dragonboy I have is a good one and that I should keep him alive."

The temple bell rang, a single note, deep and cool, echoing somewhere in the vastness of the temple.

"You know, something tells me that means breakfast."

"Good idea. We think alike."

They left the stables and investigated the temple. The smell of porridge and hot butter soon caught their interest, and they entered the great refectory. The room was large enough for the dragon to stand upright quite comfortably, and the long tables were set far enough apart for him to sit down between them.

Smiling men and women in white uniforms were soon wheeling out a huge bowl of porridge laced with butter and salt for the dragon. Wide flat loaves of fresh-baked bread were stacked on the table, and Bazil ate them in pairs, as a man might eat biscuits.

Relkin had porridge and bread smeared with a thick plum jam. Hot tea was available, but no kalut.

"No kalut, no akh for the porridge," groused Bazil.

"It could have been worse. I mean there's plenty of it, right?"

"Right."

They ate for a considerable time, for when Bazil emptied the huge bowl, the cooks immediately offered to refill it. Lessis and Mirk soon joined them. Lessis had woken several hours earlier and spent much of that time since closeted with Elory and Elory's consorts.

"How did you sleep?" asked Lessis.

"Pretty well, I think," said Relkin. "That was a heady brew we were drinking last night. I think I just about passed out, and I only had a cup or two. Funny thing is I don't feel any aftereffects today."

Lessis smiled, then impulsively reached across the table to squeeze Relkin's hand. She did the same with Bazil's enormous finger.

"I have to say you two are the most remarkable pair of fellows I have ever had the pleasure to work with."

Relkin felt himself blush at such praise. He hesitated, then he squeezed the ancient witch's hand in return. It seemed as if she was saying good-bye. This made Relkin a little nervous.

"You are going to journey to the Higher Realms, Relkin. Do not concern yourself with the how of this. You will first enter the higher planes. There you will transform and be equipped to make the transition to your eventual destination, the world of the Sinni."

"We have seen that world. You say we will transform?"

She nodded gravely.

"So we will be able to survive in that place that we saw in the vision?"

"Yes, of course."

"Oh, well then, it'll be easy, right?"

Lessis shared in his soft laugh. *Alas no, dear child, alas . . .*

"They come . . ."

Mirk's warning turned their heads. The twelve beings were filing into the refectory. They had put aside their white robes and now wore radiant armor from head to toe. They carried long spears and heavy swords. Their helmets bore plumes of red and black, and they reminded Relkin of much taller versions of Althis and Sternwal, the guardians of the forest of Valur who had once rescued him from the dwarves.

So. Now they were to be tested, and if they failed the tests, the children of Erris were prepared to slay them.

Bazil had Ecator to hand, but there were a dozen of these tall giant forms, and they would be sure to spear him before he could kill them.

A figure in golden armor stood forth. It clanked to a halt beside where they sat at the table. A visor was raised, and behind it was Elory.

"Good morning. When you have finished your breakfast and prepared yourselves, you are free to enter the Maze of Gold."

"But I thought we had to pass a test?" said Relkin.

"You have already been tested. No taint was discovered either on you or on the great dragon. You are cleared to pass into the Maze of Gold."

"Already tested?"

"Yes. You are cleared to enter the maze."

It must have been the girl, what was her name? Ilaren? She must have been the test.

"What can we expect inside?" he asked after a moment.

"Who can say, precisely?" Elory seemed to smile for a moment. "There is no center to the maze, nor any particular spot that is more active than others. You will explore the maze and then you will exit from a similar maze far, far, from here. There is no sensation involved."

"But how will we know we have gone to the right place?"

"You will be informed, never fear. The maze will know."

"The maze will know?"

But Elory had turned away. The guardians of the gate were heading back through the doors.

Now the time remaining to them seemed vanishingly brief. They washed down under a hose, and Relkin checked the dragon's hide for cuts or ticks or anything he might have missed. All too soon the time came.

At the entrance to the maze they said their farewells to Lessis and Mirk. Lessis, herself, seemed quite affected. Again, she took a hand and a talon and bade them good-bye. Relkin could have sworn that Lessis was going to shed a few tears once they were safely out of sight. He felt a little choked up himself.

Inside the temple they entered a huge room dominated by a wall of what appeared to be solid gold. The wall was twelve feet high and stretched right across the room. There was one entrance, only just wide enough for a wyvern dragon to squeeze through. Inside the space between the walls was wider, but the ceiling, a black shining surface, was uncomfortably low. Bazil was forced to move down on all fours. It would be impossible to wield sword in this confined space.

The maze extended before them, identical golden walls on either side, occasional side alleys opening up, more occasional T-junctions.

Three openings confronted them. For some reason Relkin was sure that the right turn was the correct one.

"How do you know that?" said the dragon.

"I don't know how I know, but I know. We're supposed to go this way."

Relkin didn't know where it was coming from, a tiny voice whispering guidance in his ear.

Each turn brought them to another identical view, walls of shining gold running off into seeming infinity. Sudden openings, blank spaces between the gold, and the black floor and ceiling. The dragon squeezed through the openings, went four-legged down the golden corridors.

They traveled this way for perhaps an hour, and Relkin was past astonishment at the scale of the maze. How they had all this tucked away inside the Temple of Gold was a mystery. It seemed the thing had to be enormous, spread over miles of space.

And then, quite abruptly, they emerged onto a very different scene.

One doorway opened into a passage that was rather more brightly lit than the others. They stepped forward and emerged onto a much wider space, with a silver floor and a vast vaulted ceiling above. Brilliant light came in from the sides.

Behind them the golden wall stretched across the space. They moved out onto the silver surface. It was cool beneath their feet, and yet the air was very warm.

"Where is this?" said Bazil, standing up and stretching after the confines of the maze.

"I don't know. But we're supposed to go out there." Relkin pointed to an opening on the far side of the great enclosure. "We have to find something called the Orb."

The world outside was stupendously strange. A tiny green sun burned hot and small in a sky of red ocher. A plane of flat silver stretched away in front, dotted with black blocks of all different sizes, slipping smoothly across the silver surface in an elaborate dance.

"What are all those things? What are they doing?"

"Can't see them properly from here. It's like a dream of some sort."

The plane shimmered there under the intense light of the small green sun.

"If this a dream, then we be having the same dream."

They looked at each other. Relkin shrugged. "Can't stay in here. This is a way station of some kind. I know we have to go on."

"To that place we saw, and fight that thing?"

"I don't know how. Seemed pretty big. Maybe we can think of something."

"Dragonboy good at that."

"Yeah? Nice of you to say so after all these years. Come on." Relkin stepped out; Bazil came after him. Within a few moments they felt a strange, chilling sensation pass through their bodies. The feeling of cold became very intense. Relkin felt his back arch. His lungs ached as he screamed, but he could hear nothing.

To their amazement and horror they saw their flesh and bones suddenly deform, melting like wax and shrinking. As they shrank they darkened and grew lustrous until they had completely re-formed.

They had both become crystalline. Bazil had become a triangular solid about eight feet high. Relkin was now a cube, four feet on a side. The sensation of being very, very cold faded slowly and was replaced with a feeling as if the body was asleep. Relkin felt a moment of panic, he couldn't feel his legs or arms. He couldn't move a muscle!

But he could see and hear and think. A mad whirling dance was going on out there on the plane.

"What?" the dragon was speaking, Relkin swore he could hear him.

"I hear you. How?"

"You are the cube thing I see."

"You're a big black triangle."

They struggled to absorb this.

A blue flash shot past just overhead. It slowed, curved around, and hurtled back. It came a full stop just beside them and hung in the air at the height of a dragon's shoulder.

"Ecator!" it "said" to them in the same magical voice that spoke directly to the mind.

Bazil examined the blue flash. At its heart was a small figure, a creature like a tiny elf, bright blue and shining. It had small bright red eyes and a dark line for a mouth.

"Ecator!" it said again.

"Magic, very strange, this dragon not like this."

Bazil especially did not like the feeling of having no sword. If the sword had transformed itself into this small blue sprite, then he wondered how he was supposed to fight their enemy. Then again, he didn't even have arms!

"Very strange is right," Relkin felt like a disembodied eye, floating in the cube which seemed to be his "body."

"Maybe we've gone mad; the whole thing was too much for us."

"Sword is now a blue pixie. Not much use as a sword."

The "pixie" whirred around angrily, emitting a stream of indecipherable language which Relkin thought was best left untranslated. He wondered if he was simply losing his mind. All the dislocation and bizarre magical effects really had been too much for him.

Then he recalled the magical worlds of the elven lords. Created by the energies stolen from the mind mass of the Game board, those worlds had been so perfect that they seemed absolutely real. This might be something like that, an artificial construct, an incredibly full and complex illusion.

The voice from the maze was back, whispering inside his head.

"Apparently it's something we have to do. A sort of preparation for something else."

"Something else?"

"That's all I know. Don't ask me how I do, but I know it."

For a long moment they simply stood there, absorbing their strange surroundings. Relkin wondered who, or what, was talking to him. What were these messages? Why did he feel so little panic at all this?

He shrugged inwardly. He'd seen worse and survived, that's all. It would take more than this to frighten this dragonboy. The Lady had told them that it was vital that they went through with this. Relkin and Bazil of the fighting 109th weren't going to give up.

"What now?"

"We have to go out there, travel somewhere, somehow."

Bazil suddenly gave a hoot of surprise and his tall pyramidical form slid forward across the silver surface and slowly coasted to a stop.

"What happened?"

"Don't know."

The blue sprite flew around Bazil a couple of times and resumed its position. It seemed to have calmed down a bit.

After a moment the dragon's pyramid moved again, sliding off a few feet while it spun slowly around before coming to rest.

"This dragon understand."

Relkin had to admit that Bazil had always been a quick-witted wyvern.

"What is it?"

"Try to walk," said Bazil's voice in his brain.

Relkin tried to move his legs and his cube suddenly wobbled forward across the gleaming silver surface and slowly spun around. He stopped it by trying to crouch and get both feet down on the ground. He couldn't feel the ground, but he came to a stop anyway.

The shaft of realization ran through his mind.

He tried to lift a foot for a full stride and the cube moved more quickly, slicing across the plane. He tried to stop by putting a foot down and the cube slid to a sudden stop.

There was no sensation of acceleration or deceleration. Questions flooded into Relkin's mind.

There also came a suggestion, which bubbled up from somewhere, that they move out and make good time. They had to travel to the Orb. It was a long way to the Orb. There they would pass on for the next translation.

"Where is Orb?"

"I don't know how I know, but I know that it lies in the opposite direction from the sun."

"Sun is green!"

"You noticed."

"Very strange. This dragon not care for it."

"Yeah, right."

The blue sprite spun off Bazil's pyramid and darted off away from the sun. "Ecator lead!" it said in their minds. With these brief communications there always came a kind of steely sensation, cold and crisp.

"Well, I guess . . ." Relkin started taking imaginary steps and slid forward. Bazil slid forward, too, and soon caught up, then went ahead.

"Dragon have to go slow on this world, otherwise leave dragonboy behind."

Relkin concentrated on his stepping and caught up. They slid along straight into the whirling dance of other things, all solids like themselves, heading in every imaginable direction, passing each other at great speed, never intersecting, or at least not as far as Relkin could see. The little blue figurine of Ecator flew ahead, glowing furiously, just a few feet in advance of them.

They picked up speed and moved swiftly away in the direction opposite to the small green sun. As far as Relkin could see there was no curve to the horizon. The silver plane went off in all directions forever. It was uncomfortable to contemplate such immensity.

Still the motion was enjoyable for a while. They slid along at great speed without doing much more than walking fast. Small things, brown-and-black cubes slid past in front of them harmlessly.

And then a huge shape hurtled past, just a few feet in front of them, traveling at tremendous speed. It had seemed to come out of nowhere, an enormous pale brown tetrahedron that whirled close and then sped away. If it had come a split second later, it would have smashed into them.

Then another huge shape zoomed past, this time directly across their course, missing them by ten feet and speeding on into the distance to become a dot in an instant.

These were unsettling events and left them apprehensive.

Other near collisions followed; one time a swarm of things the size of a man's fist came whipping through at high speed. Several passed between Bazil and Relkin, but none so much as grazed them.

Thus it continued for an unknown length of time, several hours, it seemed to Relkin. They just kept trying to move the legs they could no longer feel or see and they sped along on the silver surface.

Eventually, though, Relkin noticed a small change.

Ahead there was a sort of thickening in the line at the horizon. As they sped on the thick part darkened and deepened. Slowly a shape became apparent, a dark sphere humping up from the plane. Now with increasing swiftness the sphere grew in size and soon became mountainous, standing high above the plane, dominating it for a vast distance in every direction. Yet Relkin had seen no sign of it when they had first set out.

He shivered a little at the strange alien scale of the place. Close to the enormous sphere of the orb there was a great crowd of smaller objects. Many were large, towering above them. Others were the size of mice, hurtling past on the surface at the same sort of speeds that Ecator's blue figurine was capable of in the air above it.

As they moved into this dense belt that surrounded the Orb a beam of golden light flashed down from the Orb and fell full square upon them. They had barely the time to register this before they felt themselves lifted off the surface.

"We are flying," said Bazil in astonishment.

"Oh, my," said Relkin, as they rose up toward the dark surface of the enormous Orb.

He glimpsed the blue figurine zooming past and looked out below at the vast silvery surface flecked with specks in a multitude so vast they were like grains of sand at the seashore.

Then he looked up in time to see the surface of the Orb, black and glistening, approaching fast. He braced for the impact, expecting to hit a solid wall, but it never came. Instead they passed through the surface with a sensation of diving into warm water and reemerged in the next moment in a place filled with light and thus into the interior of the Orb.

At once they were dazzled in blinding golden light. The light became everything and they felt themselves filled with amazing warmth. A great tingling passed through them and they were consumed by the light, their bodies giving up their energy and being infused with new energy, cycling through the blinding light of Los.

Relkin had no understanding of the duration of time in this state. He merely accepted the blissful feeling of warmth in his bones. It was like coming in from a night on the palisade at Fort Kenor with the winter wind cutting to the bone and standing by the big brazier that was always kept hot in the dragonhouse. It was enormously pleasurable.

There was a sensation of turning in space. Their bodies, if they had bodies, were rotating, and there was a sudden feeling of compression, as if they had been suddenly placed in deep water. Pressure was squeezing down upon their bodies. The compression grew very tight, almost unbearable.

There was time for a panicky thought that he was drowning, then they were out of the golden light and deposited quite abruptly on a rough rock surface. Crystalline cliffs of amber and gold glinted a short distance away, illuminated by the blue light that poured down from above.

Relkin unwound his body and raised his upper torso. The motion took much longer than he was used to. He stared around him. The silver plane had been a strange landscape, but it had been calm and peaceful compared to this.

The light source was a searingly bright dot only occasionally glimpsed above the cloud layers that were stacked up in the enormous sky.

At the bottom, small, dense clouds of pinkish gray slithered swiftly by above their heads, fishlike in their motions. Above them was a layer of yellow haze. Above that there were white clouds, layer upon layer of them ascending upward toward the ferocious blue circle. Intense lightning blasts slammed and boomed through the thick air.

The surface was both rough and slightly plastic to the touch.

The ground shuddered. In the distance a volcano was erupting. Dark clouds were billowing up above the horizon.

Then Relkin got his first real shock. He looked down long, brass-colored arms to his hands. They were not human. They were of metal, and he was sure they were enormous. The arms were not human either, and yet he knew they were his.

What was he? What had he become? What had happened to him?

He heard a movement, a kind of throbbing rumble behind him. He turned his head, noticing as he did so that it seemed to rotate very smoothly. A huge dragonform creature was coming toward him.

It towered over him as he stood up to his full 250 feet, and he estimated it was perhaps six times his own height, built on a massive scale.

Ecator had become a sword once more, only now on the same heroic scale. The blade stretched five hundred feet in length and gave off gleams of blue fire.

"Crazy place. Don't understand, but this dragon pretty damned big."

Relkin had noticed that the searing heat and pressure of this place was perfectly normal for this thing that he now inhabited. He had his senses, and could see and hear, smell and touch, but the heavy sour odor of smoke and hot gas seemed completely neutral to him. The blinding blue light was the normal level of radiance, and the intense heat was merely a nice warmth.

Relkin had a feeling that this place was real, a world like Ryetelth, not a construct like the silver plane.

It was disconcerting to have the surface sticky and soft in many places, not because it was wet, but because it was semimolten.

"Pretty damn big," the dragon repeated while pressing one foot down into a soft patch of ground.

The dragon was bipedal, simplified. The tail was straight, tapering to a whip. The head was squared off, like a hammerhead. He had huge shoulders, was plated with armor like some vintage brasshide, and bore Ecator in a shoulder scabbard.

Relkin was equipped with a sword and a knife, both built on the same scale as his metallic form, both shimmering with energy. Like Bazil he had armor plate added to his metal frame.

He moved his arms, wondering at the transformation. How had they done this? And then they were no longer alone.

"You have arrived!" said a voice in their thoughts, the same voice that Relkin had heard before, but now audible to both of them and crystal clear.

"Oh praise be to Los, you are here in time. But hurry. You must hurry."

Another voice broke in; for some reason Relkin thought of it as female in gender.

"They are here, they are finally here. . . ."

And another voice, this time male.

"Hurry, for the love of Los, hurry."

"Which way do we go?"

"This way," called the voices in his mind, and Relkin turned and pointed out toward a range of crystal hills, standing tall amidst roiling clouds of yellow dust.

Chapter Forty-seven

Through the yellow-crystal hills they came, striding forward on their huge and unfamiliar bodies. Bazil's mass shifted forward with each step on legs of stupendous girth and musculature. His feet tended to leave tracks in the bare rock as if it were mud.

This world was oppressive in every way imaginable. The view was of bare rock, deformed by the heat and pressure. Here and there heat-resistant crystals had formed ridges and cliffs. These caught the hot blue light of the sun and flashed and flickered with unbearable brightness.

"Look at it this way; we're real close to getting a crack at him again."

"That is good. Been hoping for a rematch ever since. That one is evil. Needs to be snuffed out."

Relkin was actually getting the hang of his huge new body. His legs were metal tubes, joined at the knee by a sleeve of something that was both resistant and flexible. His arms ended in huge hands that were like nothing he had ever seen.

Bazil was more true to his own nature, closer to his own form and shape. But he, too, had had to struggle with the madness of his position.

"We find that damned wizard and we cut him down."

Relkin heard the anger in the dragons' words. Bazil rarely expressed such hate for his foes, but they had both seen the work of Waakzaam, all too much of it.

Relkin discovered that his body, huge as it was, could be made to move quickly across the strange landscape. There was a springiness to the stride, he "felt" great strength in his metal limbs. He experimented, learned that he could even make leaps of more than his own body length, then started scouting, climbing up the slopes of the crystalline hills that surrounded them.

The crystals were pale yellow, and their facets were often six feet across, stacked up in hexagonal columns that formed stepping-stones up the slope.

It was on one of these forays that he first caught a distant glimpse of the thing they pursued. Far off across the shimmering, heat-struck plains strode a manshape the size of a mountain. Wreathed in pink clouds, its head was lost in the haze, but the huge body was visible, legs like pillars, slab-sided trunk like cliffs. Then it moved into the clouds and disappeared. Relkin turned back to report.

Their opponent was enormous, far larger than they. Even Baz would only be two-thirds as tall as the golemoid Intruder.

The dragon's response was simple.

"Need to get close, make first strike without warning."

Now they stalked along through the valleys of soft rock, Bazil keeping his head below the level of the crystalline ridges. Every so often Relkin climbed to take a reading of the position of their foe.

The huge Intruder continued to stride relentlessly along, heading toward a range of much higher hills. These were cast with long, slab-sided faces that reflected the sunlight in blinding blasts. In places these huge crystals fell straight to the plain below from a high col, single enormous facets hundreds of feet long. When they caught the fierce blue light they coruscated in rainbow flashes.

On his next foray to the top of the nearest elevated point, Relkin saw a line of dark triangular shapes, huddled at the base of the distant hills. He studied them, knowing at once what they were—the pyramids of the Sinni. They moved slowly, almost imperceptibly it seemed at this distance, but were definitely crowding into a narrow canyon opening in the face of the crystal cliff.

But they were moving far too slowly to escape the Intruder, which was already in sight and bearing down on them. It would catch up long before they had all managed to float slowly into the canyon. And there was no real safety in the crystal canyon, for it could follow them in and smash them one by one from behind.

Then a new voice broke into his thoughts.

"So, Relkin of Quosh, you see our predicament. He will catch us here and smash us, one by one, and extinguish the Sinni, the keepers of the lamps of Los. And that will bring down the darkness on all the worlds."

"I see it. But I do not understand how I can see it, how I can be here? How can anything survive in this place?"

"It isn't easy, let us say that much. Nor is there time for me to begin to explain. Later, there may be an opportunity for all of that. For now, the question that we ask ourselves is simple. Can you stop that thing?"

"I don't know. It's enormous." Relkin hesitated, sensing a vast disappointment out there. "But, if we don't, he will destroy you, right?"

"Yes."

"Then we will."

A scene bathed in golden light filled his thoughts, a memory dredged from the past. The great Los was among them, filling them with his glory. An immortal, one of the children of Los, was giving up his life. The white-marble floor was bathed in the light. The sky was a purple masterpiece. There was a golden vessel standing on a tripod in the light.

It was gone leaving him grasping at straws. Where had it come from?

"You have heard of the Great One, Zizma Bos, who was prime among the children of Los?"

"His statue once stood over the city of Mirchaz. The Game Lords revered him. I think it's been pulled down since I was there."

"The withdrawal to Mirchaz was not the finest moment of Zizma Bos's life. Earlier he had predicted this would happen, that Waakzaam would come to destroy us here in our hiding place. We, who had thought ourselves immune because of the sheer difficulty of surviving here, would find ourselves trapped."

"You move too slowly."

"When we came here we grew these 'structs to protect ourselves. They were never intended to move very much. Our physical lives are restrained within their confines, but our real work is spread across the continuum, on all the worlds of the Sphereboard of Destiny. The 'structs might move a short distance, if the surrounding terrain shifted or became unsuitable, but that would only involve perhaps a mile or so at most. Now we have fled fifty leagues, crawling on the fingernails of our minds, bearing these 'structs. Nor do we have the time to grow new 'structs that might allow us greater speed."

"I understand. Why do I feel that I know you?" Relkin asked.

"You did. Your spirit came from one of us, child. You are mortal now, but once you were immortal."

Relkin was staggered. This was the answer to the question that had haunted him for years. He had always been sensitive to the magic, and at Mirchaz he had been a vessel for it on an awesome scale.

Awake! It had cried to him.

"And what then, is Bazil?" His question was automatic, spoken even as he thought it.

"The dragon is a great and noble wyvern, beasts that are the measure of men in the universe dictated by Waakzaam's treachery. The Broketail wyvern is simply the work of the Mother's Hand."

"You say the reverence for the Mother! Does that mean the witches are right? Are the Old Gods dead?"

"What is regarded as the Hand of the Mother can also be seen as the Hand of the Father. They are one and the same thing and an expression of the will of the All. But trouble yourself not with such concerns, for if we cannot stop the Intruder, then all will end in the triumph of Waakzaam and endless darkness and great evil."

Relkin floated for a moment as he tried to absorb this. Relkin of Quosh, another Bluestone orphan, left for the dragonhouse. And he came from these beings?

The memory! That golden vessel, standing on the tripod in

the brilliant sunlight. The marble was white. Death was pain-
less. Everything had been foretold long before.

He came to himself with a snap.

"Right. We're coming."

Chapter Forty-eight

⊚ ⊘

"There, at the end of ridge, we can catch it, if we hurry." The dragon pointed with a huge hand, and Relkin followed it to see the place where the ridgeline, a brown mass streaked with red from rusting iron deposits, snaked down to the plane. It petered out just a mile or so from the crystal cliffs. The two were crouched at the top of the low crystalline ridge. Shattered yellow crystals littered the plain below. The Intruder was tramping steadily toward the cliffs where the Sinni crowded together.

"He won't be able to see us until we go past that pinnacle near the end."

"This dragon move as fast as it can, we kill that thing."

"Kill!" screamed a tiny voice from somewhere.

Ecator glowed on the dragonform's shoulder. Relkin shivered at the determination he detected in the dragon's thought and the crazy hate in the sword.

"Let's go."

He pushed his tremendous body into increasing its speed. Relkin had to struggle at times with the scale of this new body, but a strange understanding of the pseudomusculature had grown up. The legs and arms took longer to respond; there was a moment's disconnect between his thought and the resulting action which had almost tripped him up a few times at the beginning, but now he was getting the hang of it. You thought something, and then it happened, just a moment later.

They scrambled down the long, slow incline, Relkin's jumps carrying his huge torso five hundred feet at a time. The dragon was bounding along, the ground shaking under his feet. Relkin wondered how anything could possibly not sense that something was coming.

But the Intruder was intent only on his prey.

Bazil reached the row of pinnacles. The crystal cliffs loomed quite closely now, and the glare from the enormous facets was overwhelming.

They passed the last pinnacle. Their quarry was clearly in view, striding across the plain, a man on the scale of a mountain. The huge steel hammer rested on its shoulder, carried in much the same way that dragons would carry their swords when they were out of their sheaths. And still the enormous thing had taken no notice of their presence.

They stepped into plain sight of it; still it marched on, intent only on the huddled pyramids clustered at the mouth of the narrow canyon.

"Now!" came a roar of exultation from the Intruder that broke into every mind attuned to those of the Sinni all across the universe. Everywhere the forces of the light quailed, their stride faltering. The forces of darkness, on the other hand, were heartened and took up their weapons with renewed ardor.

"Now I have you! At last you shall pay! You, who broke the ancient oath, shall feel the wrath of Waakzaam the Great, whom you have wronged most willfully."

After a long moment there came a calm and measured response.

"You have gone insane, great one."

"I shall smash your shells and let the cleansing blue light in to do its work. You will fry and broil at the same time."

There was another silence. Then the same calm voice.

"Can you not hear the madness in your own thought! Why do you talk always of killing and destroying? Why is it so hard for you to leave the creatures of the new worlds to develop their own cultures? Why must you arrange these things for them?"

"They cannot be trusted to do anything properly. They must be guided."

"But when you guide them they always end up being annihilated."

"It was necessary. Great work requires revisions!"

"What about the Gimmi, Great One?"

"They bred like flies, the Gimmi. They would have buried their world in their own flesh. Something had to be done."

"And what of the Eleem, or the Ixin, or any of the other peoples that you have destroyed in your long career of insanities, Great One?"

"The Eleem were actively rebellious! They raised their hands against me. But I brought them low, I showed them the power of the sword! I showed them that they were wrong not to pay me homage."

Bazil and Relkin had gained ground and were close behind now, and Bazil was contemplating just how he would lay the sword into the taller monster's legs from behind. Relkin took up position as he would have in combat under more normal conditions. It looked as if they might strike undetected.

And then Ecator gleamed, and hate blazed from the sword so strongly that the giant's awareness of them was tripped. The Intruder's head swiveled, and the eyes glowed with green fury.

"What is this? So, I see a dragon and a thing like a giant man. How? How could anything reach this spot, except myself?"

And then the Intruder tossed its huge head, understanding driving home.

"Oh, of course. How noble of you. You broke the great oath in more ways than I had imagined. The only way you could achieve sufficient physicality was by regaining corporeal life on a lower plane, and to do that one of you had to surrender immortality!

"I recognize these agents of yours; I have fought them before. This is exactly the kind of treachery I have come to expect of you. You swore to put aside all physical interference in the worlds, but break your oath again and again!

"First I will turn aside to crush this pair, then I shall return to deal with you. You will soon hear my hammer smashing your carapaces to flinders!"

The giant turned smoothly on pillarlike legs and deployed its hammer in both hands.

Relkin bounced out and behind the giant, which swiveled to

watch him. This was Bazil's opening. The great dragon suddenly dug huge feet into the hot ground and thrust forward, wielding Ecator in both huge hands, swinging for the giant legs.

The giant dropped its hammer into the path of the sword and shifted a step backward. The hammer was entirely made of magic steel, just as hardy as Ecator in its way. Ripples of opacity ran down the huge arms as hammer and sword forms struck huge sparks and set off a dull clangor in the hot, heavy air.

The vibrations from the clash shook the huge dragon. Bazil pulled back and went for the return stroke on the backhand. He was faster than the giant; the hammer only deflected the blow at the last moment, and the clash was more a skid than a solid contact. Still sparks flew.

The giant gave ground, moving very quickly for such a vast entity. Bazil returned with the forehand stroke and went through.

Ecator sank into the giant leg with a shriek of triumph. The sword went deep, but it was still no more than a minor wound to the enormous Intruder. The Intruder roared defiance and flailed back with the huge hammer. The stroke was ponderous, and Bazil ducked. As it whirled by, he thrust inside and came up with Ecator in front of him to drive home into the the giant's torso, above where the pillarlike legs joined.

Ecator shrilled his "kill!" cry once more as the blade sank home, deep into the vitals of the gigantic Intruder.

Red sparks erupted across vast areas of the giant. A long section turned black, losing the internal glow that infused the monstrous golemoid as huge areas of its steel tissues were destroyed.

Then a vast hand smashed into Bazil's head region. Bazil gave a squawk of dismay as he was unceremoniously toppled to the ground.

The Intruder let out a huge roar of pain, compounded with anger. The damage from this huge wound would interfere with its effectiveness in further combat. With another loud cry of rage, it tore out the sword and hurled it away. Then it swung up its hammer and took a step toward the fallen dragonform.

At this point Relkin bounced in at top speed and jumped as high as possible. His first jump took him to the level of the giant's face. He flew so quickly that the Intruder's raised arm missed him by a long way.

He crashed into the smooth front of the head and thrust into an eye with his sword, but it merely sank into the outer integument before he dropped free of the giant's face. Pushing off with both feet from the chest region, he did a backward somersault toward the ground.

His new body had amazingly athletic abilities, he thought to himself as he completed this trick and landed on his feet, which immediately sank deep into the hot surface.

Far above, the giant bellowed and clutched at its eye. Relkin struggled to free his feet from the semimolten rock. The giant looked down at him and raised its hammer. Relkin pulled one foot free.

Meanwhile Bazil had been able to crawl away and get back on his legs. Ecator was buried to the hilt in soft ground about a mile distant.

Relkin pushed free at last, moved sideways, and the Intruder's hammer missed him by a long way.

The Dominator had realized that he was pursuing the wrong target. Relkin saw the giant swing aside and accelerate toward Bazil. It was a race to the sword.

Relkin hurtled after them, caught up in two huge bounds, and leaped up onto the giant golemoid's back. Instantly a vast hand came around seeking to slap him away. Again he stabbed at the back of the monster's neck, but the sword penetrated no more than an inch or two before he was forced to leap away.

He wasn't quick enough to avoid all contact. The edge of the giant hand clipped him in passing and he felt himself spin, losing all control. He fell heavily on his backside and, to his horror, felt his huge, two-hundred-foot-long body blink, shudder, and turn off. He was left in darkness, with no sensation.

Was this death, he wondered to himself? Was it all over and he had lost? Was he going to wait here in this dark limbo until Gongo, God of the Dead, came to collect him?

Then something twitched in the darkness, as if it were on the other side of an invisible membrane and was trying to poke into his bubble of darkness.

And then a voice spoke loudly in the center of his thoughts. "Awake!"

The mind mass, it had to be! It called to him once more . . .

He knew what he must do—reach for those hidden powers, the things he had tried so hard to ignore.

And he struggled to awaken and reconnect with the giant new body. Nothing happened, and he tried again, concentrating with that fragile part of his mind that he could only just connect with. Still nothing, and despair began to well up in his heart. He concentrated once more with manic force, and was rewarded with the sense of fingers twitching. Then vision blurred back into life, and with it came sound and touch. He sat up.

There was no time to contemplate the meaning of life. The mountainous mass of Waakzaam's Intruder was just a step away and clearly intent on stamping him flat beneath its monstrous foot.

He rolled, then crawled, and finally staggered to his feet and pushed the great body into a stumbling run.

The ground shook behind him as the Intruder missed him by a few feet. He dodged aside, and the foot missed him as the Intruder tried to kick him. On slow and shaky legs Relkin danced into the giant's rear. He had to maneuver carefully now. One mistake and the Intruder would stamp him flat. He turned back to look and hurled himself aside as the giant hammer came down and buried itself in the soft ground where he'd been about to land.

Relkin sprang away despite the sudden stickiness of the surface, which had virtually liquefied around the hammerblow. His feet tore up long tacky threads of rock that fell away like glowing wires when they dislodged.

As he sprang Relkin noticed deadened sensation from the areas that had been rubbed hard across the rocks when he fell. His new body was getting old quickly.

There was still a degree of torpor about his huge body's movements, but he shook himself as he turned and began the pursuit of the Intruder. He couldn't leap nearly as far or as frequently as before. Still, Relkin had gained the dragon a second or two that he hoped would be enough.

The two huge forms were still driving hard for the sword.

First came the dragonform, then towering above and behind came the vast Intruder.

Bazil reached the sword in time to get hold of the handle and heave hard on it. It held fast, glued into the rock. He heaved again, hauling on the sword with all the strength he could find. At last it started to work loose. Bazil gathered his new body's strength and once more pulled with everything he could summon up. The sword started to rise slowly, then suddenly came free. He stumbled back a step and almost lost his balance.

The Intruder was almost in range, its hammer raised high. Bazil tried to get some purchase on the jellied surface and found himself sliding sideways and was then caught a glancing blow by the hammer as it zoomed past his head. Bazil lost all sensation for a few seconds. When he came to, he was down on one knee, head bent forward.

The Intruder came for him, braying in triumph.

And once again Relkin managed to get there in time to save the dragon. This time, though, he could only reach the monstrous golemoid's waist. But there he found rows of knobs projecting from the integument. He held on and found purchase for his feet on the damaged area caused by Ecator's first thrust.

There was now a cavity torn into the abdomen of the Intruder. It reached up past where Relkin clung, opening almost like a cave into the belly of the thing. The interior was a mad jumble of tubes and holes, a foam of passageways and wormholes, the whole thing flexing constantly to some great drumbeat while green energies zipped through the tubing. Relkin stabbed inside with his own sword and was rewarded with flashing green sparks and a cloud of black vapor.

Then he had to jump to avoid being seized and crushed.

As he fell to the ground he noticed that the dragon was slowly getting back to its feet. But too slowly, and once again the hammer clipped the dragonform. Bazil staggered backwards, slammed into the ridgeline of iron crystal, and sent one of the pinnacles crashing to the hot plain. An area of the metallic skin on Bazil's back was ripped up, and vapor and fragments were bleeding from below.

Bazil braced himself against the low crystal cliff, then pushed off and came back with a very quick riposte. The giant, off-balance, was still recovering from its clumsy swing of the hammer. The dragon's sword sank home deep into the waist region, and once again the spirit of the blade shrieked in triumph as it cut through the Intruder's integument and devoured its life energy.

The Intruder roared in disbelief as the dragon stabbed it through the middle, then pulled out and spun away. An ineffectual swing of a fist missed the dragon's head. Bazil had learned about that stinging counterpunch from hard experience and ducked as he retreated.

The Intruder's waist region was turning dark, and there was a definite slowing of its movements and a stiffening of its limbs. The huge construct gave off a wail that was part anger and part genuine fear as Waakzaam contemplated for the first time the thought that he might not be victorious.

Bazil came back a moment later, and Ecator cut deeply into one of the Intruder's arms. Then the dragon drove his great sword into that mountainous torso again, this time through the chest.

The Intruder dropped its hammer and seized him in a bear hug.

The dragon was swallowed up in the huge arms even while Ecator was buried in the Intruder's chest. While Ecator fairly howled with triumph, the Intruder started trying to tear Bazil's head off.

Desperate, Bazil wriggled hard in the huge grip and got his right shoulder free for a moment. He managed to get a leg up on the Intruder's thigh and pushed back, breaking free enough to punch the Intruder square in the face. The facial integument flattened into the head and the eyes went out, but a few moments later it revived. The Intruder held the dragonform with one hand and punched him in the head with the other.

Bazil staggered backwards, and toppled over the low crystal ridgeline, rolling down on the other side amongst shattered shards of crystal.

The Intruder snarled in frustration, Ecator still buried in its chest. It was too weak and clumsy to climb over the ridge. To get at the dragon it would have to go all the way to the end of the ridge and then come back up on the other side. It pulled the huge sword out of its body and hurled it to the ground. The hammer rose high and came down with full force upon the sword, but did not break the blade. Again and again the Intruder hammered the sword, trying to destroy it.

Suddenly a wave of darkness ran across the surface of the Intruder's integument. The huge thing came to a halt, unable to move. The Intruder was weakening fast and, as it did so, it opened the way for the Sinni to try and destroy it directly. If they could find the frequencies required, they might turn the great golemoid body to ash in a twinkling.

Waakzaam shivered at the thought that he might lose the capacity to exact revenge upon his hated foes. With a scream of hate he abandoned the sword and the dragon and set the Intruder to marching on the pyramids, which were still squeezing into the narrow canyon.

Bazil was left behind, to slowly pick up his body and get back on his feet. It took a minute or more just to stand up. Twice it almost toppled over and was only prevented by Bazil's putting a hand down on the ground. At last the dragonform stood upright.

Over the low ridgeline Bazil could see the Intruder's back. He tried to put his legs into motion. One huge foot lifted, moved forward, and set down again. Unfortunately the strain was too much. Suddenly everything blanked out and the dragonform went straight down to crash facefirst into the hot rock surface.

It didn't move.

Relkin came scrambling over the crystal ridgeline and halted beside the silent dragonform, still prone on the hot ground.

"Baz?"

There was no response.

"Baz!"

Relkin went to try and pull up the huge head, still buried in the soft rock. The head was too heavy for him to lift and the dragonform remained ominously silent.

Relkin contemplated the worst. Bazil was dead, extinguished along with the dragonform. And without Bazil they were done for. On his own Relkin knew he could never defeat that monstrous mountain-sized thing.

"Baz, you've got to wake up. We need you."

The dragonform remained inert.

Waakzaam would smash the Sinni and the light would go out across the Sphereboard of Destiny and the forces of evil would triumph. The very concept of justice would vanish forever.

"Baz?"

No response.

Chapter Forty-nine

"Baz! Wake up!" Relkin shook the fallen dragonform, causing it to rock back and forth slightly. There was no response.

Relkin stood back. The dragonform lay there, completely inert. Meanwhile the Intruder was closing in on the pyramids.

Helplessly, Relkin offered up a prayer to Old Caymo and all the other Old Gods. *If you can hear me, Old Ones, now is the time to help this worshiper of yours. . . .*

There was no response. He was crazy to think there could be. They'd said the gods were no more. The world was without direction. It was hard to break with the old thinking, however, especially in this place of crystal cliffs and blinding blue light.

Awake, whispered the thought in the back of his mind.

Awake!

But how? Relkin had no inkling of how he had connected to that magical power on the occasions it had manifested itself.

He willed himself to be calm.

There was lightning discharging from the pink clouds onto the Intruder's crown as it marched on.

He tried to reach out to the dragon with his mind, calling on him to awake.

"Bazil? Can you hear me?"

Still no response.

He glanced at the Intruder, who was in range of the laggards now.

Baz?

The dragonform remained motionless.

Relkin dug deep, reaching for that part of his mind that had produced magical effects more than once. It was in there somewhere. He might have left his body behind, but he had his own mind. He had all his memories, even those of Ferla, the goddess of love in Mot Pulk's grotto. He recalled Eilsa's dear face, her beauty of movement, the sound of her laugh. He recalled old Macumber and the dragonhouse in Quosh.

No question about it, he was still Relkin of Quosh. And he knew he could do these things, if he could only tap into the power.

He struggled, and he got nowhere. He still had no idea how to actually connect to that power.

The dragonform remained facedown in the soft rock surface. Nothing Relkin tried seemed to work, and while he strove to perform the unattainable, the Intruder caught up with the pyramids still creeping toward the narrow canyon in the great cliff wall.

At the back of the crowd was Yelgia Goldenhair, she of the pure voice, one of Puna's closest friends in ancient Gelderen. Seeing that escape was hopeless, she gave up the attempt and set her 'struct squarely in the path of the Intruder.

"Waakzaam! It is I, Yelgia, Puna's friend."

"You poisoned her against me."

"I did not have to. Puna never loved you. You were always too cruel, too cold. Puna saw through your pretense. She saw your deadly flaw."

"There is no flaw!" The hammer rose high with a gleam of doom. The clouds parted momentarily, and the light grew very bright.

Down came the hammer, striking only a glancing blow.

"Bah! Your tricks with the clouds will not stop me."

The hammer rose again.

Relkin felt a tug in his mind, but it didn't develop; no thought followed.

Down came the hammer once more. Yelgia's 'struct was hit hard, the crust shattered and fell away. Vapor clouds rose from the damaged zone where a crater was left.

For a moment Yelgia cried out in fear. Then her courage returned and her cry turned into song, and fair Yelgia began to sing of Puna and of her beauty and her untimely death, strangled by the dark, fell spirit of Waakzaam in Gelderen long ago.

"Shut up!" roared the Intruder, and smote her 'struct again with the great hammer. Fragments fell away as the crust broke up.

Yelgia's great voice, pure and golden, continued to rise above the scene of her murder. Waakzaam had gone berserk, and his hammer lashed the pyramidal 'struct again and again as fragments flew off and the crust crumpled.

Yelgia's singing stopped abruptly. Her catafalque bubble had been punctured, and the searing gas had entered.

Relkin turned back to his own struggle.

There, somewhere in the blank void, which was all he felt when he reached out, somewhere in there was Bazil. Relkin refused to think that his friend was dead. He was in there somewhere, and Relkin had to find him.

The tug at his mind came again and suddenly there was that other presence in his thoughts. The Sinni was back, Yeer, or Sweetwater.

"Hurry, Relkin, aid us in awakening the dragon."

"I am trying, but cannot find the way," Relkin answered despondently.

There was a strange moment of disconnection. Relkin felt a sudden blur of emotions and was left with a sense of nausea, which left him dizzy. The sensation passed quickly to be replaced by another feeling altogether.

He felt as if he were floating, his mind bobbing on a vast dark sea, like the ocean at night. Relkin recalled long, lazy nights in the doldrums on the equator, when their ship was sailing for Eigo. He felt as if he could slide effortlessly in any direction, penetrate any barrier.

He thought of Bazil, remembered his dragon from times long past.

By the gods, that time we were up on the hills and he ate those berries! He was such a sick dragon!

And at that moment he felt something in the darkness. A familiar mind surfaced and snapped back at him.

"Why do you have to bring that up? Boy never forgets that one."

"Baz!"

"Boy! This dragon lost in the dark."

"You're facedown in the ground, that's why. Pull up your head."

There was a long moment. Relkin glanced back to the distant cliff wall. The Intruder was pounding on another pyramid. Lightning blasts were discharging almost continuously as great shards of the 'struct were sent flying. The scene was starkly lit from the ferocious blue sun above, but Relkin saw the horror coolly, almost impassively. Somehow the destruction did not panic him. His thoughts were only for the dragon.

"Pull your head up, Bazil."

Slowly, Bazil lifted the huge head; hot rock clung to his face like threads of taffy.

"That better. This dragon can see again."

With pauses at each stage, the dragon pulled his enormous body upright and onto its feet.

"This dragon is weary. It hard to wake up."

"You can do it Baz. Think of Jumble; he killed Jumble. That's how he made this huge thing of his, he used Jumble's spirit. Dragon spirit is the strongest there is."

"Kill Jumble?"

Bazil came erect with a snap. The huge body was in motion. Bazil was finally back on his feet.

"Hurry!" came the cry from the Sinni.

Now the Intruder swung, and down came the huge hammerhead to smash into the shell of Empessi, the patron of weavers and tiers of knots. Empessi made no protest, only continued to lend all his strength to the effort to break the lock on the Intruder's integument. At this range, if they could unhook the magic, they would disintegrate the golemoid in a matter of moments. Alas, the spell holding it together was extremely powerful.

The hammer slammed into Empessi's pyramid. A great flash of light threw the scene into harsh relief, and left rocketing afterimages even on Relkin's and Bazil's adapted eyes. A heavy boom rocked through the dense gas. Shards of the pyramid fell away, then the bubble was smashed, the catafalque destroyed. Empessi ceased to exist.

Bazil wobbled a moment, then got a firm grip on his great body and set it to scrambling over the crystalline ridge.

It was a huge effort, but the dragon was still agile enough. Getting down was a little tricky, since the crystal outcrops tended to shatter under his enormous weight, but he reached the plain again on his feet, surrounded by a lot of shattered crystal.

He found the great sword lying on the floor of the plain. The eerie light had gone out. The blade was notched and bent, but still in one piece.

Bazil tore it free from the hot-taffy rock.

"Sword is battered. . . ."

Relkin bounced in, having recovered much of his energy.

"But still whole . . ."

Bazil swung the great weapon experimentally a time or two.

"Still a good sword."

Ecator's sparkle returned with a hesitant flicker.

"Ecator!" it said, faintly.

"There, that better! By the fiery breath, we finish this now!"

The dragon turned and set off after the Intruder as fast as Bazil could make it go.

The Intruder continued to hammer the pyramids into scrap. A line of broken pyramids now lay behind the huge golemoid, thin tendrils of smoke rising from the interiors of the smashed 'structs. Slabs of their shells littered the flat plain. Inside each 'struct, the fragile bubbles surrounding the catafalques of the Sinni had evaporated, along with their creators.

Gel-Marj Bos, he of the sparkling dawn light, patron of sailors and sailing ships, brother of great Zizma, was the next to expire as his 'struct was shattered and his catafalque broke asunder. The heat and pressure extinguished life in an instant.

"Now I bring you the justice of Waakzaam! How do you like it, oathbreakers?"

The Sinni made no response, except to redouble their efforts to disintegrate the integument of the Intruder. At last they found the right path. The Intruder was suddenly stuck fast, hammer high but immobile while the surface integument stiffened rapidly from the feet upward. A golden light sparkled over the surface as it did so. The Sinni had finally found the frequency. In another few seconds the integument of the Intruder would slough away and the whole thing would unravel, leaving Waakzaam helpless.

Alas, Waakzaam spotted a weakness in the Sinni's effort. He struck at the lacy, open structure of their spellsay and broke it asunder. The integument regained flexibility. The golden light blinked out, and the harsh green light within returned.

The Sinni strove to reweave their spell, but in the end his power was the greater. Was he not one of the Seven? And he resumed full control.

The Intruder came back to life, and the hammer descended to smash upon the pyramid of Narshoon, the King of Flowers. Narshoon continued to give all his strength to their joint effort to disintegrate the integument, but before long the bubble around his catafalque was breached.

Bazil had gained ground during that interval and was closing at a vigorous pace. The vapor had ceased to pour from the shoulder wounds, and both legs were working properly. He pushed the huge body to what felt like its maximum effort.

The Intruder took no notice of their approach, intent upon the destruction of the children of Los.

Relkin raced ahead to try and distract the vast Intruder. After running at top speed he bounced up toward its face. With a scream of rage it swatted at him with a huge hand, but missed, and he landed on the massive belly region. A huge area there was permanently blackened now, vapor and fluid escaping from several large tubes that had been severed. Relkin stabbed home within the wounded area and cut another conduit, which rewarded him with a blaze of green light from the damaged spot.

Again he had to leap free as a hand came up to crush him. He barely evaded capture and fell back to the ground. But the Intruder took no notice of him.

Doom rose with the giant hammer and fell upon Vuga the Mild. A huge flash of light broke across the scene accompanied by a great dull boom. From the crater came an immense puff of vapor.

Vuga's terror rose in their minds.

The hammer fell again and broke right through the crust, and Vuga the Mild was no more. The pyramid settled to the plain with dark vapor seeping up from the ruined area.

The Intruder went on, carrying the hammer with both hands, stepping up to the pyramid of Yeer, or Sweetwater, himself.

Yeer turned his mind to meet his doom as calmly as possible.

"I have served the worlds all my long life. I will surrender to the void."

"You will soon be void, fool!"

The hammer rose high. With Sweetwater's death would go the spirit that protected the waters of the worlds.

And then Bazil arrived. He came in with the sword deployed, his arms strong once more. The Intruder had ignored him for too long. He brought the sword down in a great overhand stroke into the back of the Intruder's neck.

Any lesser thing would have been decapitated. On the vast Intruder the sword merely stuck fast, while Bazil was carried forward by the sheer impetus of his charge and lost his grip on the sword.

The Intruder screamed and dropped its hammer, which sank partway into the soft ground. Reaching up with huge hands the great golemoid tore the blade free while it screamed again to the heavens. From the wound streamed a great cloud of dark vapor.

Bazil reached back, got a hand on Ecator's handle, and ripped the blade out of the Intruder's hand.

Taken by surprise, it was late in riposte, and its huge hand swung past him harmlessly as he ducked away. He came back with Ecator in another driving thrust, this time right into the midriff of the thing.

The sword went home. To pull it out Bazil had to put a foot up on the Intruder's clifflike chest and heave. There wasn't quite enough time for this maneuver, and the Intruder seized him by the neck and struck him with its fist.

Bazil went backwards—still holding the sword—then sat down with a crash. Hot rock flowed away from the impact point.

The Intruder, visibly slowed by its wounds, bent down to pick up the hammer.

Bazil suffered a momentary loss of his senses. He could see nothing, hear nothing. Panicked, he almost succumbed to fear; but then he forced himself to reconnect, as he had done before when boy reached him. It took a few anxious moments, but then he had it and recovered his faculties with a snap. Slowly he began to move, but the Intruder had pulled the hammer free of the surface rock and was moving toward Bazil, hammer raised high. Bazil would never make it in time.

The wound in the Intruder's head was a near-vertical slice, like a crack in a cliff wall. As the Intruder hefted the great hammer, the crack widened and flexed. The Integument was self-healing, but it would take time to recover from a blow like that, in particular from Ecator.

Relkin leaped once again and got a foot on the giant's leg somewhere and boosted himself to the shoulder. He heaved himself to his feet and caught hold of the upper edge of the wound.

As it stood over the fallen dragon, the Intruder was intent on raising the hammer. Relkin heaved back on the integument and the great gash widened. He raised his own sword and severed a cluster of thick tubes embedded in the dark material. Everything was shriveling and sending up black smoke as the hot air entered the wound. Relkin cut down even farther and was able to push himself into the wound, cutting deeper as he went.

He came up against a sheet of tough woven material which resisted the sword's first cut. Gas from the wound caught fire in blue flashes. He stabbed down again and broke through. He pulled the sword across the webbed material, and it parted for a hundred feet.

Inside was a circular chamber half-filled with translucent gel. On the gel floated a crystalline globe some twenty feet across, set in the center of the golemoid's huge head. Inside the globe was Waakzaam himself, staring back at him in horror. The gel blackened rapidly and began to shrink. As it collapsed, the crystal bubble sank down inside the empty space. The crystalline bubble was all that stood between Waakzaam himself and the harsh air of Xuban.

The perfect elven features of the Dominator of Twelve Worlds distended in sudden terror.

A purple bolt of energy spat forth from the bubble and knocked Relkin back for a moment.

The Intruder had missed his stroke, his hammer falling harmlessly past where the dragon crouched. Bazil rose up and drove the sword home once more. The golemoid staggered. One huge hand came up in a desperate, but clumsy slap that missed Relkin where he was dug into the monstrous neck. He heaved back and drove down with the sword, which skittered off the crystal bubble.

A mind-disabling blast leaped from Waakzaam's eyes, but Relkin felt the spell skitter away from his defenses. He had heard the voice of the gestalt being from Mirchaz; he had found the key to his own powers once again.

The bubble had settled into the bottom of the golemoid head. Relkin's hands were wrapped around the handle of the sword, and he brought it down just as the Intruder's huge hand finally caught hold of him from behind.

The force of the blow crushed Relkin's body and drove the sword home into the crystal bubble, which burst with a flash of green light and a howl that ran across the universe.

Waakzaam was slain. The Intruder's governing intelligence was gone. The hand fell away. A cloud of vapor lofted from the ruined head of the giant.

Relkin slid broken-backed down the clifflike shoulder of the Intruder, bounced off the lower leg, and slammed into the hot ground with punishing force.

His senses vanished, then returned, but weakly. He still lived, somehow, but his great body was broken. His legs did not respond.

His vision remained, though, and thus he witnessed the end.

Above him the Intruder's integument had darkened. The hammer slipped from nerveless fingers. The great body toppled, slowly at first, with a plume of dark vapor escaping from the head as it fell. It accelerated as it went and slammed into the ground with an impact to end an aeon.

The ground leaped beneath them, and there came a long, thrumming roar that went on for several seconds as the ground shook and rumbled. Walls of crystal slid down from the higher ground.

Bazil stumbled back and went down on one knee.

"Waakzaam has fallen. The worlds are saved from his wrath," said the voice of Sweetwater in their minds, while the world shook and shuddered and vast clouds of crystalline fragments flew up at the base of the cliffs and began to fall around them like snowflakes.

The Sinni immediately lifted their voices in song and in bitter-sweet beauty they incorporated the fall of Waakzaam and the deaths of Yelgia, Vuga, Gel-Marj Bos, and all the others into their great saga. Particularly they sang of Bazil of Quosh, and the dragonboy Relkin, whose strange tale was both a part of their own and entirely his.

While they sang, the dragon got back on his feet once more. He looked down at the small broken body on the surface.

"Boy dead?" he wondered. That last fall had been terribly hard.

The dragon bent down and poked the fallen body with a huge finger.

"Boy dead?" A huge sense of sorrow enveloped him.

Then Relkin spoke. "Not dead. But I don't think I can move."

"Boy live!" Bazil bent over and carefully picked up the broken body.

The Sinni continued their great song.

"This body is done for, Bazil. I have to leave this place."

"Dragon, too, must leave. This not a place for us."

Chapter Fifty

❦

Yeer spoke to them, his thoughts appearing magically among their own, exactly as if he spoke across a quiet room.

"Yes, you must both leave this place, and soon. Your forms are temporary and cannot function here for very much longer."

"Boy is hurt badly."

"We know."

Golden light suddenly suffused Relkin's broken body.

"He lives still," said Sweetwater. "But both of you must return to the Temple of Gold."

"This dragon not sure how to do that."

"We shall help. But first you must go back to the exact spot on which you entered this world."

"This dragon not sure he remembers how we came to this place."

"We will guide you. But you must hurry. Every moment is precious now."

And so the dragon turned and without a second look back at the prone form of the great Intruder, he headed for the crystal cliffs, carrying Relkin cradled in his arms, pushing the great body to its limits.

Behind him the Sinni were still singing, for to them there was a great deal more to the story. They were the recorders of the First Aeon, when fair Gelderen stood upon the hill and Waak-zaam was not yet the evil master of magic that he would become. They had many endings to relate and beginnings to recount, before the end would be fitted to the song.

Bazil pushed himself. Guided by the voice of Yeer in his mind, he made a quick passage across the hot surface of the giant world.

"Hurry," repeated Yeer now and then. "Your form cannot last much longer here."

At last it was done, and Bazil stood at the exact spot where they had entered this hellish place. Just another zone of rock and naked metal.

Then great Yeer called upon the other Sinni, and they turned away from the Great Song and focused all their energy upon Bazil and his plight.

Bazil sensed a rushing and darting around him, as if a hive of bees had been knocked over. But nothing stung him. The small zooming noises passed, and he felt the presence of the Sinni in his mind.

"Farewell, great dragon of Ryetelth, well have ye served us and the worlds. We shall sing of your great deeds until the last darkness falls across the worlds. May good fortune always smile upon you, friend of the children of Los."

An atmosphere of tension arose. Bazil's nerves jangled. An enormous spell was in the process of being laid. The dragon was sensitized to these things, something big was brewing. He cradled the boy's body carefully.

With a great boom in the superdense air, a Black Mirror twenty feet across snapped open in front of him. White-hot sparks flew from its surface; within whirled the vortices of gray chaos.

"Enter, Bazil, and return to the Temple of Gold. Your bodies will return to their normal selves during the transit of the maze. We shall sing your song for all eternity."

Bazil looked up to the hurrying clouds. "Farewell, dragon-friends."

Steeling himself, the dragon stepped through into the dark whirling gray of chaos and the Black Mirror closed behind him.

This journey proceeded more swiftly than the last, and in the space of a few moments within the ether of chaos they came into a realm filled with intense light.

Bazil felt a sudden warmth course through him. Coming after

the intense cold of chaos it made his skin tingle furiously. Then came a strange sensation, as if he were being turned inside out. For a moment a great gagging bout of nausea passed through him. He sensed that his body had changed. And Relkin had changed, too; boy was himself once more.

Bazil let out a bellow of joy and was rewarded with the echo of a wyvern roar scream booming back to him from the walls of the Golden Maze. He had his own senses, his own good arms, his own broken tail.

Because they were descending from the higher plane, the Sinni had been able to use their own great power to place them right back at the beginning of their fantastic trip across the heavens. It was a feat that could not have been attempted going the other way because the energies required were too great, even for the Sinni.

Bazil took a step and almost collapsed. Relkin had gone down on his hands and knees. Yeer had warned them that they would be exhausted. But not this exhausted! Bazil went down on all fours, feeling weaker than he had ever felt in his entire life. He had not the strength of a week-old sprat.

Relkin had rolled onto his back. "Baz! We made it back."

"But we cannot move. We die in here, lost in the maze."

"Can't die now, can't give up."

"Can't move, either."

Keeping those huge bodies going had completely worn them out. They were reduced to crawling, slowly, through the maze.

At each intersection Relkin would rest and study the way ahead. The walls were of gold, the floors and ceilings, too. They cast endless reflections.

And then in one direction there was a noticeable darkness. As they drew closer to it, the walls and ceilings changed from gold to marble, almost imperceptibly.

They were close to the exit now, which was a damned good thing since they were almost too exhausted now even to crawl. Bazil just could not haul his body any farther.

Relkin went on, then came back and tugged on the dragon's ear.

"Come on, Baz, it's not far now."

"This dragon too weak. Cannot move."

"We can do it; we got this far. Can't die here."

"By the fiery breath, feel like I'm going to die here."

"No, we have to go on. Can't stop. You can do it."

With a soft groan Bazil rolled over onto his belly again and got his legs under him. He heaved himself up, felt himself trembling in every limb. Relkin staggered ahead of him down the last passage and they turned and were out of the maze and standing in a room in the Temple of Gold.

It was night on the world Lygarth. A single lamp burned by the doorway. The temple was quiet. Outside in the forest somewhere an animal gave a long whistling cry, then fell silent.

The cat noticed their arrival. Servants came hurrying forward to assist them. Lessis was informed. Mirk woke up when the Lady stirred. He followed.

Outside the temple, lying on the steps in the light of two crescent moons, were the dragon and the dragonboy, exhausted, but still breathing.

They were carried to a large room in the temple forecourt. To carry the dragon required the combined strength of all the members of the order. They moved him on a stretcher made from long poles and many lengths of canvas. A great pile of hay had been set up. A cot was brought in for Relkin.

The greatwitch made powerful medicine for the boy. The dragon was more difficult in that regard, but a concoction of honey, beaten with eggs and lemons and diluted with hot water was poured into him and seemed to do some good.

She made sure that food was brought to them every hour. At first they had gruel, which was thickened meal by meal until they could manage solid nourishment. And with the food they were given water at first, but after a day or so, Lessis allowed a little beer.

As they lay there, drifting in and out of sleep, their wasted bodies slowly recovering strength, they were visited by the members of the order. Some of these beings merely meditated beside them, saying nothing. Others praised them for the selfless courage they had shown in defeating the Dominator. Still others sang the hymns of their kind.

Bazil's appetite came back within a few days, and after that they both seemed to eat their way back to health. After a full month of deep rest, they were able to begin the process of learning the spellsay for reopening the Black Mirror once again.

As before, it was arduous work, but eventually and with the assistance of the Order, they summoned up the baneful black opening into nothingness once again. And with the power of the order behind them, they returned across the simmering wastes of chaos with such speed no Thingweight could match them.

Abruptly they stepped out of the mirror again and found themselves standing on a hill under a gray sky, with clouds moving rapidly past. The wind soughed in the trees. Open meadows lay below.

"Ryetelth," said Lessis. "Home."

Chapter Fifty-one

They had emerged on a hillside in Kenor not far from Dalhousie. After getting directions from a farmhouse, they made their way on foot to the nearest town. From there they rode on a riverboat down to Dalhousie.

They discovered they had been gone from Ryetelth for three months and were given up for lost. The news of their return sent the whole camp into a frenzy of celebration. Horns, bells, and firecrackers rent the air for most of the night. The word was sent out immediately by birds carrying witch messages to the cities of the Argonath. Within a day the news was widespread. Within a day and a half even the emperor in far away Andiquant knew that the Broketail dragon and his boy were alive and back home, and that the great enemy had been brought down.

In Marneri horns blew from the tower and bells rang throughout the city. Great ships bore the word across the seas, and in passing mighty *Oat* and *Barley* exchanged horn blasts in the middle of the Cunfshon passage.

Bazil and Relkin were happy to accept a few casks of ale that came their way and distributed most of it among the dragons in the Dalhousie dragonhouse, mostly youngsters in a new unit, the 209th Marneri.

Both Bazil and Relkin noted that number.

"We've been in the Legions that long, my friend," said Relkin. "They've gone through a hundred numbers since we joined up."

"There been hard fighting during our time. Many battles. Many dragons die."

Sadly Relkin acknowledged the truth of this.

Orders came down the next morning, directing Bazil and Relkin to make their way to Marneri. The rest of the 109th Marneri were already in the city, and they were to rejoin the unit there.

While they were getting ready Lessis brought them another order, this one from the emperor himself. It was a special dispensation, mustering them out of the Legions early in recognition of the enormous service they had provided. They were to report to Marneri, where their papers would come through and they would be set free from their term of military service.

On top of that the emperor sent word that a special medal, the Imperial Star, was to be struck and presented to them. They would be the very first recipients of the honor given only for heroic service in the face of extreme danger.

Bazil accepted all this news calmly enough.

"We lucky to survive all these years. This dragon ready for retirement."

After a while the dragon went out to the plunge pool.

Relkin had had time to think during his recovery at the Temple of Gold. He had had to accept that behind the rational world there lay a fabulously complex other world that had dimensions which were frightening to behold. His memories of their strange, hallucinatory journey to that place they'd fought Waakzaam brought on a distinct sense of unease. The world seemed so solid, but with the Great Magic it could be pierced like a veil of fog to reveal other worlds, worlds upon worlds to infinity.

On top of that had come the huge shock of hearing of his own conception. He was literally a child of the Sinni, brought to life by one of their's death. From birth they had guided him, fashioning him into a weapon that was destined to aid their survival.

The Sinni had placed him as a newborn on the streets of Quosh, to be raised a dragonboy and paired with a fine leatherback dragon. And so, together, they had won through in the most desperate situations and finally brought down the greatest enemy of all the worlds.

Along the way Relkin had learned that he was not who he thought he was and that he possessed hidden powers that frightened him. There were things there that he absolutely did not want to confront. He was no wizard, no sorcerer. He was a man, no more and no less, and he would live the life of a man, with Eilsa Ranardaughter as his wife, Bazil as his friend, with land in the Bur valley and some good horses to help clear it.

Every time those powers rose up in him he felt a door opening to a hellish kind of omnipotence. He resolutely held shut that door, not wanting such temptations.

But seeing through to its other side, experiencing the awesome complexity of the universe, had challenged all his beliefs. As for the Old Gods?

He gave a sad inward shrug.

He had seen too much in too few years. There were no gods. The Sinni had told him that. The Lady Lessis always spoke of the Mother, but he also sensed that for Lessis the Mother was an abstract conception. It was a power that pervaded the universe, but not a living, breathing person, and that was what the Old Gods had been for him. They were personages, dreamed up by the shamans of the ancient tribes, back in the days before Veronath. They were invented by the shamans to explain the strange nature of the world. For thousands of years they had trod the stage of the people's imagination and heightened their lives with ritual and ceremony. And now Relkin no longer believed in them. It left him feeling a little sad, almost lonely.

Lessis asked him to walk with her down to the stable area where a fast coach was being readied for her. She was leaving for Marneri at once.

"There is another message for you, Relkin. One that I bear from the Office of Insight."

Relkin's heart sank. They were going to drag him off to Andiquant after all.

And yet, Lessis was smiling as she spoke.

"I am very pleased to be able to tell you that you will not have to endure any more questioning. The Office of Insight has terminated their investigations."

"No more Andiquant?"

"No more. Both of you deserve the chance to live a free life. You've given enough."

By dint of considerable effort, Relkin kept his immediate oath from breaking loose in Lessis's presence. But when she was gone he ran back into the dragonhouse and let out a wild whoop that ended with a dive headfirst into the big plunge pool. Now that he didn't believe in them anymore, the gods were finally showing a positive interest in his affairs. Old Caymo had rolled some winning dice at last.

Maybe the Old Gods did exist after all. Hiding somewhere behind the curtains, over the horizon, and beyond the dark side of the moon.

Relkin kicked up his heels until Bazil pinned him to the wall.

"What ails boy?"

"We're free, Baz, we're really going to be free."

The dragon understood instantly. Boy was not going to the place called Andiquant.

The dragon caught him up in huge arms with a happy roar that shook the rafters of the dragonhouse.

They left the next day on the upstream riverboat to the head of the waters at Blue Fork. From there they took the path over the watershed and started the walk down to the Razac road.

Four days later they strode into Marneri. It was late afternoon, and they'd covered many miles that day, but the sun was still shining, and there was even a small crowd gathered at the Tower Gate to welcome them. The sound of the horns and the cheering brought their spirits up remarkably well, and they marched into Marneri with heads high accompanied by loud huzzahs from folk along the way. As the word went out in the city, so the crowd grew with remarkable rapidity. Everyone wanted to be able to say that they saw the Broketail dragon and Relkin return to Marneri after the fall of Waakzaam.

At the gate of the dragonhouse they ran into a posse of jubilant monsters led by the Purple Green. Happy roars and screams echoed off the walls as Bazil moved among them exchanging grapples and hand slaps.

"You look as if you starved," said the Purple Green with genuine concern. "Look like you need some meat. Let us eat some bulls. We can eat a couple raw while we roast some more."

Bazil had to laugh. "You right, my friend. Food was boring. Nothing but mush, no akh."

"Why is it the first thing you say is about food?" said Alsebra elbowing the huge purplish bulk aside. "Bazil is back, and all you talk about is eating."

The Purple Green reared back with a snort and an angry blink.

"You ask him, then. What he really want to do?"

Bazil seized the opportunity.

"Well I'm all for roasting some bulls. But the first thing this dragon want is a pile of straw to lie down on. Need to rest the feet. Then a swim, then food, and then some ale."

A chorus of "This dragon agrees" arose from the scrum of great beasts jammed in the hall. The building shook as they moved in a mass down to the stalls. The Purple Green's huge voice could be heard over the thunder, bellowing something about bulls and fire.

Relkin was surrounded by all the dragonboys in the Marneri dragonhouse. There were two squadrons in residence at that moment, the 109th and the newly reinvigorated 145th, now with their new dragonboys.

"Hey, give him some room," said big Swane pushing the others back. "Welcome back, Relkin," said a voice, Jak. There was Manuel, and Mono, too, the only other survivor of the original 109th. Relkin reached out to grab hands, slap others.

"So glad to see your faces," said Relkin. "So damned glad. You'll never know."

There was a babble of questions, whoops, and young men jumping with sheer excitement.

"Hey, everybody, shut it. Let Relkin speak." Once again Swane was restoring order.

"The dragons are going to feast, I vote that we should, too. We set them up, get a big fire ready for the Purple Green so he can roast whole animals, and then we roll up some barrels for them. That will keep them happy for a good long while. So we can have a keg of our own and roast some meat and have a feed right here."

"And I'll pay for it," roared Swane. "I cashed out today."

"I'll help," shouted Jak, then others followed. The notoriously thrifty Manuel produced three gold pieces, and they all gave a whoop.

"We can order in a grand pie from the Tower Inn. Their ale, too, is worthy of the name."

More whoops followed this, a few more hands to clasp, slaps and hugs, and then, by common consent, it was over. After that young men were in motion with the peculiar speed and intensity that they can display when suitably motivated.

Relkin reached his stall unimpeded, deposited his kit, and sat down on the bench. He and Bazil had used this particular stall for years, and he knew every knot and cranny. There was a vertical crack up one wall and a protruding nailhead on the ceiling beam.

He relaxed into the moment. It was just damned wonderful to get off one's feet after so many miles on the road. They'd pushed pretty hard on the last day to get to the city before darkness. He kicked off his boots and lay back on the bench. The ache in his feet began to fade.

The familiar sounds of the dragonhouse came to him along with the smell of the swimming pools and the fainter, but pervasive scent of dragons. This was home, either here or in some other legion dragonhouse like Dalhousie or Dashwood.

These places were "home." They were all united by those sounds and smells, plunge pools and cooking, dragons and dragonboys.

And soon it would no longer be home. Relkin was about to move on from this world of the dragons and dragonboys. He would lose the fierce camaraderie of the 109th. He would lose the sight of the 109th on the march, the huge bodies swaying along, their swords on their shoulders. They were the heroes of Sprian's Ridge, they were unstoppable.

He would miss it, all of it, but he would not hesitate to leave it all behind. He'd sewed that joboquin, or the one before it, a thousand times too often. He'd made it to the end of his stretch, and ahead was another life, a quieter kind of life. He hoped he could get used to it.

Bazil rolled into the stall, set down the sword, and settled on the straw with a happy hiss. After a few minutes he rose up. Relkin unhooked the joboquin and helped pull it off. It needed work. It always did.

The dragon set off for the plunge pool, intent on a good long swim to get the dust of the march off.

Cuzo came by and congratulated Relkin on surviving to the end of his service period, one of the most brutal terms ever known. Relkin had been involved in a half dozen major campaigns and battles and had amassed a sheet of battle stars, campaign medals, and the very rare Legion Star, which he'd received for the fight at Tummuz Orgmeen. Indeed, he and Bazil had been involved in most of the fighting in the past half decade. Grim names surfaced—Tog Utbek, Salpalangum, Sprian's Ridge— places he didn't want to remember too often.

Cuzo felt awkward, as he so often had with Relkin. Both of them knew that Relkin should have been made Dragon Leader, but for the fact that he was left behind in Eigo after Tog Utbek and the volcano's eruption that ended the war.

"I've had good dragon leaders, sir," said Relkin at one point. "And I've had the other kind. You were among the best."

Cuzo's ears pinkened. "Thank you, Dragoneer," he said quickly. Then he grew formal.

"And, Dragoneer Relkin, we have to talk about this medal ceremony they want. The Imperial Star, no less, with half a legion on parade to see it. The kit will have to be spotless."

"Oh, of course, Dragon Leader, but please remember we just got in from a long march. The kit's a bust right now."

"Dragoneer Relkin, you will be given the assistance of twenty dragonboys. The kit will be immaculate."

Well in that case! "Oh, of course, sir."

"And please allow me to stand a round for your celebrations at the Tower Inn." Cuzo passed him a small purse filled with good silver coins.

About an hour later, as Relkin was getting ready to join the others for a dinner at the Tower Inn, he received word from Curf that there were visitors for him.

He went out to the hall and found Lagdalen and Hollein waiting.

Hollein wore the insignia of a full commander. Relkin saluted crisply. Hollein returned the salute and Lagdalen hugged him with all her might.

"I'm so glad to see you."

"If anyone could survive what you went through, it would be you."

"It is good to be back," said Relkin.

The other dragonboys were gathering in the hall, all visibly itching to be off to the Tower Inn. Swane and Jak exchanged greetings with Hollein and Lagdalen. Others noticed there was a full commander present and moved to salute.

Hollein returned the salutes, then dismissed them.

Relkin told them to go on to the inn without him. "I'll join you there."

When the nervous energy of hungry dragonboys had dissipated, Lagdalen spoke. "The Lady told me a few things about your mission. I think I understand what you did. The worlds themselves will always thank you, Relkin of Quosh."

"He's gone, our enemy. We settled him."

"It is as if a great shadow had been lifted from our hearts."

"And we're going to be mustered out, early retirements." His excitement showed.

"We heard that," said Hollein. "It was wonderful news. You two have served in enough battles for five lifetimes."

"Amen to that," said Lagdalen. "Now"—she pulled a scroll from her sleeve—"I have this message for you."

Eagerly he broke the seal and read the contents. It was from Eilsa, and she was on her way to Marneri to meet him. She had been at Widarf working with the chronically ill, mostly left over from the plagues of Waakzaam. Apart from needing more sleep, for they had been working long hours lately, she wanted for nothing except the need to see him.

Relkin kissed the scroll and rolled it up.

Lagdalen had further information. "Eilsa will arrive tomorrow in the late afternoon. It seems that your last message to

Widarf from Dalhousie was delayed or lost. She only received a message from Razac."

Relkin let out a restrained whoop. One more day to wait.

"I was going to suggest that you dine with us, the two of you, tomorrow. We'll find a way to leave you two alone. I know you have a lot to tell each other."

"Thank you, Lagdalen of the Tarcho. That would be wonderful."

"Come to our apartment at the sixth hour. And tell Bazil that the Tarcho family is ordering a pie up from the Fish Inn. It'll be the biggest pie they've ever baked. I know there's another squadron in the dragonhouse, and we wouldn't want to leave anyone out."

"Well that will be much appreciated. Where we've been, the food was really dull."

Before Lagdalen and Hollein left, she reminded Relkin that he should come by her office, there were messages for him from the bank in Kadein. His investments were safe, but there were matters for him to look into and papers to be signed.

Relkin read and reread the message and looked up to see the dragon, fresh from the dragon's dinner in the main hall.

"Message from Eilsa Dragonfriend?"

"Yes. She'll be here tomorrow."

"That is good, for boy need to fertilize her eggs."

"Ah." Trust the dragon to leap forward to that. "Well, actually not just yet. There has to be a wedding first."

"Why is this? You not need wedding before."

And trust the dragon to point out this embarrassing truth.

"Because, well it just has to be that way. I mean, in society that's the way people do it."

"Except when boy Relkin do it before? Like with girl Lumbee."

"No, those were exceptions. You know, we didn't know if we were ever going to be coming home."

"What about the princess in Ourdh?"

Relkin shrugged. "That was different, I don't exactly know why. It was her decision. I mean she couldn't marry me, I was an outlander, and I was a dragonboy in the Legion. Besides I was too young."

"You were too young for wedding. But not too young to fertilize the eggs."

"Yes."

"But now you have to have wedding and then you can fertilize the eggs?"

"Well, yes."

"Humans make the fertilizing of the eggs a very complex process."

"And dragons don't?"

"No."

"What about fighting for the females? Don't you have to do that first?"

Bazil softly clacked his jaw. "Sometimes."

"Well, we don't have to do that, though some of us do anyway."

"Fight is pretty simple. Weddings, this is complicated."

"Yeah, you're right about that."

Bazil seemed to mull this over for a few moments.

"Still, this dragon look forward to seeing Eilsa Dragonfriend."

The next day it took a good swim and a pint of cold water to clear his head, but Relkin rose early, made sure the dragon was set with a bucket of hot kalut and some half dozen loaves of fresh bread and hurried out to the narrow streets of the Elf Quarter. His first stop was at the smithy of Lukula Perry, an elf smith who had made the current scabbard for Ecator. Relkin had written to Lukula with another kind of request. Relkin was very satisfied with the smith's work, paid him in Marneri gold, and left. From Lukula's smithy he went on down Half Moon Row to a small shop on Hat Street. The door was very stout, but it opened to a rap from the knocker, and he went into the dark interior.

Twenty minutes later he emerged once more and made his way quickly back up Tower Street to the top of the hill. He did not go into the dragonhouse, however, but crossed over the hill and went on down Water Street to Lagdalen's office.

There he signed the bank papers, examined the statements of his assets, and drew up a will.

When all that was done he had just enough time to show her

what he'd bought in the shop on Hat Street. He pulled out a small velvet pouch and from it withdrew a great square-cut sapphire mounted on a simple gold necklace. The stone was awesome, the kind that a wealthy banker might bestow on his bride, and unable to stop herself Lagdalen asked, "Relkin, how did you come by this? This isn't loot, is it?"

"I bought it from the jeweler on Half Moon Street, Fipps is the name. He's had this stone for a while and I saw it in his shop a long time back. No one had wanted to pay his price, until today."

Relkin had haggled hard for the stone, but still paid more than fifty gold pieces.

The blue gem was gorgeous and sent flashes and gleams of blue light all around the room. Deep down, Lagdalen thought the stone was a little excessive. She imagined that Eilsa would, too, but she recognized that this was not how Relkin saw it. He had grown up in a military camp; he hadn't been exposed to the finer aesthetic of the higher culture.

And, she reflected, if anyone had the gold to buy such a bauble, it was Relkin. Lagdalen had seen those accounts sent up from Kadein. Relkin and Bazil were well set for their new lives. She congratulated him on the purchase and even expressed a little envy of Eilsa to make him laugh.

He left soon after and returned to the dragonhouse. There was a lot to take care of. The joboquin needed new straps, the armor-plate inventory had taken some hits, and the tail sword was notched. Getting the leather he needed took him a while. Not even the famous Relkin of the 109th could get the clerks in the commissary to work any faster than they had to.

His own kit was pretty torn up, too. There was just time to put in a request for new shoes and jacket to replace those worn beyond repair. Then he brushed down the dragon and worked on the dragon's feet, which had the usual blisters from a long march.

The lunch bell rang, and soon huge portions of stirabout laced with akh were rolled out to the waiting wyverns.

His leather requests came in after lunch. He went down at

once to collect them—a mound of thick leather straps, all ready to be sewn into the joboquin to replace the worn-out ones.

Bazil was in the exercise yard, working with the sword on the butts. Relkin took up needle and thread and starting repairing the joboquin. Cuzo had offered the help of twenty dragonboys, but Relkin knew better than to accept that one. He'd be cleaned out of thread, needles, glue, and who knows what else in no time. Then they'd be into his stock of liniment.

Time flew as his needle flickered and the strong thread was worked through the joboquin, replacing the stretched and sagging belts and straps.

When she entered the doorway he didn't look up at once and when he did their eyes met and time seemed to come to a stop.

She flew across the intervening space. Aunt Kiri's cry of "No!" could be heard out in the main passage, but he and Eilsa were too busy kissing to care.

Chapter Fifty-two

The wedding was held on a fine day in the third month of the year. It was warm for the season, and the folk of Marneri came out in great numbers to bid farewell to their heroes.

Eilsa's wedding dress was in the classic Wattel pattern, with white satin and lace plus the pale green sash of the clan over her shoulder. Relkin wore full Legion uniform, with his new blue coat bearing a raft of medals, including the new Imperial Star.

At his appearance, the pack of dragonboys in the audience let out a storm of whistles and whoops and had to be hushed by a curt bark from Cuzo.

A dozen of Eilsa's relatives were in the city for the ceremony. They formed a group to one side and displayed a coolness toward the proceedings that was painful for Eilsa, but fully expected. As she was wed, they removed the clan sash. She was now out-clan, and no longer the titular head of Clan Wattel.

At her throat she wore the enormous blue stone that Relkin had given her. She knew her relatives would not approve such an open display of ostentation, but she wanted them to know that while she had married a dragonboy, an orphan with no family and no estate to inherit, she hadn't married a poor one. He'd have an estate someday, and she would share it.

The ceremony went off very well. At the appropriate moment Relkin produced a pair of gold wedding bands, crafted by Lukula in the elven manner. The gold was braided with pale yellow electrum, three strands of each. Now Eilsa took one band and placed it on his finger and he took the other and put it on hers.

The priestesses sang the wedding hymn in the sweetest way and afterward the happy couple paused on the steps of the temple for the traditional first public kiss.

At the bottom of the steps the well-wishers whistled and whooped and once again the boys of the 109th had to be barked at by Cuzo to curb their excesses. Hollein and Lagdalen were there; so were several senior officers of the Legion, plus all of the Tarcho clan.

Absent were the representatives of Eilsa's family. They had withdrawn early, taking the clan sash with them. There was no secret about the fact that Eilsa's family had taken this marriage badly. Her heartbroken mother had not even come. Eilsa had expected all this, had known it would be like this from the moment her heart had been given to Relkin of Quosh. Hard as it was, she had grown to accept it. And yet she felt a lingering sorrow at her mother's absence.

From the temple they rode in a carriage up to the tower. There they went up to a small suite of rooms that had been set aside for them in the grand Tarcho apartment, and they didn't come out again until late in the afternoon when the cornet sounded for the evening meal in the dragonhouse.

There, they joined the dragons and boys of the house for a feast in the dragonhall. Sides of beef were roasted over a huge mound of hot coals and served with buckets of roasted potatoes, noodles, and hot akh. Even while this was being devoured a series of grand pies was rolled in with accompanying horns and explanations. A gift pie from the merchants of Marneri and Bea was brought in, another one was from the Tarcho family, and each of these was broken open and the insides dished out. Ale from the Tower Inn was rolled in and sent round to wash it all down.

"Does it feel different?" said the Purple Green, who had finally eaten his fill and was reclining against the wall of the huge space given over to dragon dining.

"Does what feel different?" said Bazil.

"Being out of Legion."

"Doesn't feel much different. Later, I expect this dragon will be lonely."

Both huge beasts made the dire sounds of dragons when they laugh.

"Hah! You will miss us."

"Hard to imagine, but true."

"We all retire soon. Maybe this dragon come and settle near you. Boy Manuel say he want to be farmer, so he tells this dragon all the time. I am to be a farm dragon, too."

Bazil was silenced for a moment by this thought. His impulse to sarcasm faded away. Even the ferocious spirit of the Purple Green would grow calmer as it grew older. Maybe he would even be a good farm dragon. Certainly he had strength to spare.

"That would be good. You can grow all the food you like."

"Yessss." The big eyes gleamed at this thought. "Like you we have gold that men value so much. We will have horses to do the heavy work. This dragon like that idea."

"Still be plenty of work. Boy Relkin explain to me what we are going to do. It is much more than just cutting down trees and sawing them up. We build house and barns. Have to build a mill. Boy insist we build near a mill stream. Have to cut millstones. That be hard work. Also have to build bridges. It is complicated."

"As long as boy understand how to build it, this dragon can help with strength."

"That is true," said Bazil, once more considering the awesome bulk of the Purple Green.

"Whatever it takes, we get the job done, that I learn from boy Manuel."

"See? You did learn things in Legion."

The wild one blinked dangerously, then softened. Why evade the truth any longer? He'd been fighting this idea for years. It was time to give it up.

"Yes, you right about this."

"And soon you be retired, too. By the breath, you've been in enough fights. They should retire you now."

The Purple Green made an approving grunt. "This dragon kill many, many brasska."

He had taken ample revenge. Around the enemy's campfires the Purple Green of Hook Mountain was a figure of dreadful legend.

Vlok and Alsebra came over and took up positions beside them. Vlok set down a fresh keg of beer. The Purple Green took a lengthy swig, downing a couple of gallons. Vlok was in an excited state.

"By the breath, boy Swane tell me how much gold we have. This dragon cannot think in such numbers. Numbers too big. They hurt this dragon's head."

Bazil winked at the Purple Green, who kept his retort to himself.

The members of the 109th who'd fought in Eigo had been given gold by the King of Og Bogon. Despite the plagues their investments had done famously well, and now they were well set for retirement.

"This dragon have to thank you, Bazil," said Vlok. Vlok had had his fill of ale, Bazil could tell.

"Thanks to King Choulaput. He give us enough gold for all dragons in this squadron to retire and have horses."

"Can we buy land near you?"

"Of course, Vlok. I'd hope you would. Boy Relkin would miss boy Swane."

Bazil and Alsebra exchanged raised eyebrows.

"To think that we will end up as neighbors of Vlok. . . ." said Alsebra in wonder.

The Purple Green started to say something unkind, but Bazil hushed him and said, "This dragon like that idea. A village of old friends."

Alsebra clacked her jaws quietly.

"Jak want to live in home village. This dragon not sure boy Jak would want to go to Kenor."

"Kenor is a long way, but land there much cheaper than in Blue Stone or Seant."

Alsebra could see the logic of that. But she could not overrule the dragonboy, who had planned his retirement carefully.

"Chektor be retiring very soon," said Vlok, spotting a huge brasshide dragon coming toward them. "What will you do when you retire, Chek?"

Chektor was a big, heavyset brass, who had been in the 109th from the beginning and seen fighting all over the world and survived it all. He and Bazil were the only survivors from the original squadron. He would be the next dragon to reach retirement.

"This dragon like the idea of living close to old friends. Boy Mono wants to do this, too."

"How does boy Swane think?" said the Purple Green to Vlok.

"Boy want to live in Seant. Where we grow up."

"It is crowded in Seant. Land is expensive."

"That is good point. This dragon will bring that up."

They passed around the keg and drained it dry. Chektor set it down behind him.

"This dragon has a question," rumbled the Purple Green.

"Yes?"

"Why does boy Relkin need wedding to help fertilize the eggs? Is it because of magic?"

The Purple Green was still trying to fathom that place where magic ended and civilization supposedly began. To his wild ways, simple bookkeeping was magic. The enormous web of social controls that kept the city of Marneri operating also seemed like magic.

In fact, Bazil had been thinking about this for weeks. He had watched Relkin consumed by innumerable anxieties during the preparation process, and Bazil had learned just how complex and expensive a wedding could be.

"No," he said. "It is ceremony they need because they live together afterward. See, dragons mate and then separate. Female not want us around when she raise young."

They all nodded thoughtfully. Wild female dragons were scarcely approachable when they had young. This applied to wyverns as much as to winged dragons.

"Humans live together. They need big ceremony. This dragon thinks it makes their new life special. They make big fuss and then remember this fuss and that helps them when they disagree."

"Ah," said several listeners.

"That explain much to this dragon," said the Purple Green. Humans were obviously quite mad.

As for Relkin, he could not escape the attentions of the 109th dragonboys forever. They surrounded him, and he had to drink

a pint of ale and sing a verse of the Kenor song atop the keg before they'd let him go.

"Good-bye, Quoshite!" said Swane, pounding him on the back.

"By the Hand, Swane, you take care of yourself. How you're
going to survive without me to take care of you I cannot imagine."

Swane roared. "Listen to that Quoshite!"

"Farewell, Relkin," said Jak with a long handclasp.

"Good-bye, Jak. Are you sure you don't want to take land in
Kenor?"

"Well, I think I'd like to go back to my own village. Try it
there first. Then, if I don't take to it, we'll come up to Kenor."

"Don't want to wait too long; you might miss all the best land.

"And this holds for all of you," Relkin faced them. A dozen
faces turned to him.

"What does?" roared Rakama.

"Come up and settle in the Kalens valley. There's good land
up there, and there's going to be an Imperial chute built to cut
out the big rapids on the Bur."

"So it'll be easy to move grain downstream, you mean," said
Swane.

"Hey, you got it, big man."

"Sounds good to me," said big Swane, whose plans for going
back to Seant had just been jettisoned by some process that he
never would understand.

Others agreed loudly that it was a fine idea. The more of them
there were, with dragons, the bigger the projects they could under-
take for their mutual good.

"Start our own village," said Mono.

"First I have to get a wife," said Endi, always the practical one.

"We'd better wish Endi a lot of luck then!" said Rakama.

"Hey," said Swane, "Endi's no uglier than me."

"By the Hand, that's not saying much."

Swane and Rakama started tussling and spraying ale on each
other until they were separated and subdued by the others.

"Farewell, Relkin, 'til we meet again," said Manuel, coming
up a little later to bid Relkin good-bye.

"You're coming up to the Kalens right?"

"That's the plan. Thanks to you two we have enough money to make a really strong start."

"I heard that the Purple Green is looking forward to being a farm dragon."

"Well, I wouldn't put it quite that way. Let's say he understands better what it will mean. I finally got him to listen, and I explained about using horses for the heavy hauling. He really wasn't keen on the idea of hauling and pulling a plow."

"Oh, you might as well pull that plow yourself as try to get a dragon to do it." Relkin paused a moment, having caught sight of his bride for a moment. A flash of white silk amongst a throng of girls in blue and pink. She was laughing, eyes flashing and so wonderfully alive that Relkin felt his heart soar. Then they were gone, a pack of Tarcho girls and his wife, off about some mission of their own.

"The Purple Green could be great for building up a farm. He's stronger than a dozen oxen."

"And over the years he's learned how to wield an ax."

"Hey, Relkin," said Endi, breaking in, "what do you think of this new plow they're talking about?"

"Oh, the Imperial?" It was the sensation of the moment, a wonderful new design from Andiquant that worked out to about half the cost of the older plows.

"Right. I saw one being used up at Dashwood. Looked strange."

"Supposed to be strong but light. Takes less metal."

He dropped back into the conversation about farm equipment and the merits of oxen and horses and the disadvantages of both animals. This was all part of a long list of things that they were all becoming familiar with as retirement loomed closer.

They talked long into the night and the kegs went around and around, even after the dragons themselves had tired and gone to their stalls for sleep.

Relkin, too, had long since gone. After a brief stop in the stall to be sure the dragon was sleeping comfortably, he headed up to the tower and the apartment where Eilsa was waiting.

At first light they rose and went down to the dragonhouse to wake Bazil and see to getting an early breakfast for all three of them. Bazil and Relkin were no longer in the Legion, and they could leave whenever they wanted.

While the rest of the dragonhouse slumbered on they ate quickly and made a quiet departure. Relkin had bought a brand-new wagon and a team of four horses to pull it. The wagon was stuffed with everything from tools to cloth, thread to leather. All the materials that would be essential in starting their new life on the frontier.

Bazil had put the sword on the wagon at first, but then when pulling on his pack, he had felt oddly bereft without the harness, scabbard, and the great sword, Ecator, on his shoulders. It didn't feel right.

He'd demanded that Relkin help him reequip right away. After seeing the look in the dragon's eyes, Relkin did so without a word. The dragon was uneasy. A huge change was coming, and there were uncertainties in the future. Bazil looked to have the sword close to hand. It had always been a good policy in the past.

Eilsa smiled quizzically when he jumped back up to his seat at the front of the wagon.

"Dragons don't like change. He missed the weight of the sword."

Eilsa understood after a moment. "It's reassuring to him."

"Well, it's certainly reassuring to me. Anyone foolish enough to try and rob this wagon will have to deal with Bazil and that sword."

And so they exited the North Gate, with a shout to Osver, the spirit of the gate. The sun was well up now, and the white city was lit up in golden light. The guards waved farewell to the Broketail dragon, and then they were gone, marching into history.

PENGUIN PUTNAM

online

Your Internet gateway to a virtual environment with hundreds of entertaining and enlightening books from Penguin Putnam Inc.

While you're there, get the latest buzz on the best authors and books around—

Tom Clancy, Patricia Cornwell, W.E.B. Griffin, Nora Roberts, William Gibson, Robin Cook, Brian Jacques, Catherine Coulter, Stephen King, Jacquelyn Mitchard, and many more!

Penguin Putnam Online is located at
http://www.penguinputnam.com

PENGUIN PUTNAM NEWS

Every month you'll get an inside look at our upcoming books and new features on our site. This is an ongoing effort to provide you with the most interesting and up-to-date information about our books and authors.

Subscribe to Penguin Putnam News at
http://www.penguinputnam.com/ClubPPI